Slice of Heaven

Lane Bristow

authorHOUSE™

1663 LIBERTY DRIVE, SUITE 200
BLOOMINGTON, INDIANA 47403
(800) 839-8640
WWW.AUTHORHOUSE.COM

AuthorHouse™
1663 Liberty Drive, Suite 200
Bloomington, IN 47403
www.authorhouse.com
Phone: 1-800-839-8640

First published by AuthorHouse 4/30/2007

ISBN: 1-4208-6932-9 (sc)

Printed in the United States of America
Bloomington, Indiana

This book is printed on acid-free paper.

This book is lovingly dedicated to everyone who does not tip their pizza delivery guy, i.e., those who do not appreciate that the pizza guy has to personally pay for the delivery vehicle, gas, general maintenance, and delivery insurance, all from what is generally a minimum wage check.

I forgive you.

"I'm your pizza guy; I know everything."

–Boris Joseph Morris

CHAPTER ONE

Any story worth telling should mention a girl in the first sentence. My story is no exception.

I fired an angel.

Her name was Angel Bates, and she was one of the best employees that I ever had at my restaurant. Good help was hard enough to find, let alone keep, and Angel was fantastic. When I worked with her, it made me smile. The woman exuded life. Actually, that does not even come close to an accurate description of her. She was so much more than that. I guess that the best words I can find to sum up Angel is to say that her life celebrated life.

She grinned all the time. It was a big, wide grin, too, and it was infectious. She loved coming in to work, and everyone loved working with her. Of all the people I have ever known, she is the only one whom I would call a true joy to be around, always.

She was cheery. She was generous. Her brutal honesty was legendary. You could not know her without loving her. And I fired her.

I had never asked to be a boss. I always felt that I was blue collar enough to spend my entire life working for others. "A servant's heart," my dad used to call it. I was content to serve. Giving the orders, leading the way, breaking the trail, calling the shots, that was not me. As far as work was concerned, I just followed. At least, that was how it used to be. My leadership was thrust upon me in the form of an inheritance. My name is Sidney Karl Myers. My inheritance was a pizza shop in the small logging village of Chetwynd, British Columbia, Canada.

Have you ever thought about your pizza guy? For most of you, the answer is probably "No." You just find a number in your phone book. You call it, and you tell the voice on the other end what kind of pizza you want. What size, which toppings, how many, your phone number, and your home address. The voice tells you that your order will be at your door within thirty minutes. Thirty-five to forty minutes later, your doorbell rings. You open the door. Your pizza guy says, "Hey, sorry about the wait." If you say, "That's fine. How much?" a cash transaction will follow. However, if you complain about the delay, the pizza guy will look sheepish, and deftly blame everything on a faceless organization only ever referred to as "the kitchen guys." Convinced that the delivery driver is the victim of circumstances beyond his or her control, you then pay, tip, thank, and shut the door. Your pizza guy is now out of sight and mind.

Well, I do not blame any of you for feeling that way. Pizza guys, both the male and female variety, are sort of low on the totem pole of modern status. They do not discover, or advance, or program, or engineer. They just take a bunch of foodstuffs, make them taste good, and take them to your table or place of residence. It is a humble job, and it will rarely make anyone rich. Yet, if there is one thing that my life has taught me, it is to take a closer look at everyone, no matter how wealthy or poor, overlooked or prestigious, whether a friend or a total stranger. Every face that you look into holds much more than it reveals at the first glance. The life of everyone you meet could be a book, or even a series of books, with laughter, tears, suspense, betrayal, fear, love, romance, and a hopeful ending. You need to really get to know someone before you can even begin to read the first chapters, but everyone should be appreciated for that which is chronicled within them. Every life can tell you a tale, if you will only take the time to read what is right before you. Even your pizza guy has a story, and this is mine.

It was early in May, and it was a Wednesday. The day could scarcely have had a more perfect beginning. My father, Karl Myers, and his army sergeant brother, Uncle Reggie, were with me at a beachfront resort in Hawaii. Dad told me that he had someone that he wanted me to meet. Someone turned out to be Canadian actress Elisha Cuthbert, who immediately fell in love with me. As I was flagging down my limo to take us to dinner, I overheard my younger sister, Cindy, giving the "We can still be friends" speech to her boyfriend, my employee, Boris J. Morris. As she left him crying on the shore, hostile cannibals captured Boris and began carrying him toward a vat of boiling liquid, possibly oil, or maybe soup stock. I actually liked Boris, but I had always suspected him of cheating on Cindy, at least once. Anyway, I knew that he would be fine as soon as I woke up.

I had a hard enough time falling asleep, and, once I did, I liked to hang onto my sleep for as long as possible. I woke up a lot sooner than I would have liked, and at the hand of someone whom I would just as soon never be woken up by.

Actually, I was not awoken by Boris's hand. I was awoken by his elbow.

"Wake up, Sidney!" The voice was Boris's, and the words were in a low, sing-song tone. My mattress was moving. Boris was in my room, bouncing on my bed like a little kid. Elisha Cuthbert was slipping out of my arms, being pulled away into the darkness.

"I'd better still be dreaming," I snarled through clenched teeth, my eyelids clamped shut as I pulled the red comforter over my head.

"Nope," Boris assured me. *"Elbow drop!"*

The full weight of Boris's skinny frame slammed into my chest, nearly blowing the wind out of me. My throat wanted to scream and gulp for air at the same time, but my mouth was still too tired to open, so the only sound that escaped through my nose was a high-pitched *"Eeeeeeee!"*

"Hey, Sid. You awake?"

I let my nostrils take a very long and deep inhalation, allowing my mind to count to ten. Boris's sense of humor takes a few months, maybe years, to get used to. He was a member of the genus *pizza delivery guys*. As a general rule, they were one weird bunch.

Don't kill him. He's probably going to marry your sister.

"Boris?" I said, my voice muffled by the blanket over my face.

"Oh, did I wake you up?" he replied innocently.

Following the sound of his voice, my left hand shot out from under the blankets and seized his thin neck. It felt good to shake Boris, applying just enough pressure to make him reconsider the wisdom of waking me up before seven o'clock on a Wednesday, the only day of the week that my restaurant was closed.

"I think I woke you up," Boris gurgled.

I pulled the blankets off my face with my free hand, and groggily sat up in my pajamas. My eyes were open. I was awake. Elisha Cuthbert was gone, Hawaii was gone, Cindy was still dating Boris, and my father had been dead more than four years.

"Good morning, Boris," I yawned, still shaking him half-heartedly. "How are you?"

"Need air, Sid," he croaked. "Anytime."

"I had a date with Elisha Cuthbert, Boris. *Elisha ... Cuthbert!*"

"Oh shoot, sorry. If you kill me, I'll understand."

I gave him one more good shake and then released him. My head sank back into my pillow, as he took a deep lung full of air. Wednesdays should not have had to be like that.

"Good grip, Sid," he said, rubbing his throat.

"Boris?"

"Yeah?"

"You're on my bed."

"Sorry." He was scrambling off, then pulling up a chair beside the bed. "Listen, Sid ..."

"Boris?"

"Yeah?"

"You're in my house."

"Yeah, you should really lock that front door."

"I *did!*"

"Oh …. Well, you should lock the laundry room window."

"You crawled in through *the window?*"

"You just said the door was locked."

"Ever hear of a doorbell?"

"I didn't want to bother you."

"Very considerate of you."

"Thank you."

"Don't mention it," I groaned, looking over at the clock radio on my bedside table. Six thirty-seven in the morning.

Does this man ever sleep?

Boris never looked tired, although I do not know how many nights a week he actually went to bed before four a.m. Sitting by my bed, he looked as alert, and semi-crazed, as ever. His shaggy head of black hair was tussled, and his slightly bulging eyes were blinking a lot. That was not a good sign. Boris only got blinky as a nervous mannerism, usually when he had to tell me something that he knew I would not take well.

"Okay, what is it? Did you burn down By The Slice after I left last night?"

"No, it's fine. But, uh … we have to go in today."

"What? Why?"

"Just before midnight, someone from Hidden Valley Elementary called. They want fifty large pizzas delivered to the school at 11:30, Thursday morning."

"Thursday? They always order for Fridays!"

"Stinks, doesn't it? Now, they want it tomorrow."

"And we only open at ten," I sighed, shaking cobwebs out of my brain.

"So, our options are either go in and get them ready today, or show up three hours early tomorrow."

"I'm working right from ten until midnight tomorrow," I snapped. "No way I'm turning my fourteen-hour day into seventeen."

"So, we go in today?"

"Yeah, we'll go in around eleven. Is Clancy coming?"

"I told him to. What about Kat?"

"No, Kat's worked six days straight, kitchen and dining room. We'll let her have her day off."

"We need another server, Sid. Kat hates being a substitute waitress."

"I know. She's only happy when she's running the kitchen. I'm looking at resumes."

"You know … Clancy said he could bring that new girl of his in today. It would be good practice for her."

I cringed. "I don't know, Boris. I'm not too crazy about the idea of hiring one of Clancy's girlfriend's. It's hard enough to get that boy to focus on his work without his love of the week working beside him. Love is distracting."

"Well, be fair, Sid. With Clancy's track record, this girl will probably be an ex-girlfriend inside of a week. Anyway, I've met her. I think she'd be good as a waitress."

"Has she done it before?"

"I don't know, but you know as well as I do that all you need to wait tables is basic hand-eye coordination and good people skills. She's got that. Really friendly, you know?"

"All right, all right, fine. Tell him to bring her in. It'll just be the four of us. We'll let Kat and Cindy have the day. No sense in all of us losing the weekend."

"Does it ever strike you as odd that we are probably the only people in town who consider Wednesday 'the weekend?'"

"No, actually it strikes me as scary."

"Yeah, I know. The last time I had a Saturday and Sunday off, I had a 104 temperature."

"I remember that. Go away."

"Sorry," he said, standing and straightening his blue sweatshirt. "See you at eleven. I'll go in at ten and get the dough started. Try to find Elisha again."

"She's gone, Boris. Gone...."

"I'm gone." He ducked out into the darkened hallway.

"Boris!"

Boris peeked back into my room, agitated.

"Yes, Sid?" he said cautiously.

"If you have any interest in marrying my sister," I said dryly, "I would recommend *not* waking her up before you leave. She's not the morning type. Waking her up before *noon* on a Wednesday can be dangerous. Just FYI."

"I wasn't going to. She's mad at me."

"Yeah, I figured that. What now?"

Boris sighed heavily. "She saw me talking with Mandy before work yesterday. She thinks we're getting back together."

"Mandy?"

"Yeah, don't you remember? Mandy Walker?"

"The day care teacher with the black belt? You broke up with her two years ago."

"We're still friends, that's all. Cindy's just being...."

"Reactional?" I guessed.

"I wasn't going to say it until a blood relative did."

"Well, straighten her out soon. I can't stand the way she cleans the house all night every time you guys argue. She sings *Solitaire* the whole time."

"Eek." Boris shuddered. "I'll talk to her later."

My eyelids were already sliding shut again as he turned from the doorway. I wondered vaguely if he would exit the house through the same window he had entered from. It would not surprise me. For a twenty-three-year-old man with an uncanny grasp of the human condition, Boris could still be surprisingly infantile.

Sure enough, the last sound that I heard before dozing off again was the reverberating footsteps of Boris clambering over the washing machine. A lot of employers would probably fire any employee who broke into their homes and jumped on their beds, but that was what made me different. I guess I was a bit of a lousy boss. Like I said, I never asked for this.

CHAPTER TWO

If this is the first time that you have ever heard of Chetwynd, do not worry. No one had ever heard of Chetwynd. Located in the foothills of the BC Peace Region, the village, population less than ten thousand, was all but invisible until you drove into the forested valley. Its primary purpose for being was the log and gas industries. Two lumber mills kept the town alive, and two video stores kept the citizens alive. A standing joke around there was that, in Chetwynd, you either drove a logging truck, or you served fast food to those who did.

What else did we have? Well, we were awarded the '1993 Logging Capital of Canada.' I am not sure what the actual significance of that was, but I do remember that Prime Minister Mulroney actually stopped by, presumably to commemorate the occasion. I was sixteen at the time, but I never got to see him. Stupid flu.

More recently we were awarded the title of 'Chainsaw Sculpture Capital.' I sometimes wondered who actually set out with the intention of making chainsaw sculpting their vocational goal, but, apparently, it must have worked out for some people. Many of the businesses in town, and even private residences, were guarded by wood-sculpted bears, rams, eagles, and deer. My own restaurant, By The Slice Steak and Pizza, was watched over by a wooden coyote and beaver in the reception lobby. I always thought that the coyote looked cross-eyed, but my dad ordered them when he still owned the shop, so I kept them to greet everyone who came through the front door, in the mood for the best pizza in town.

Okay, so we had wood, wood awards, and wood sculptures. Aside from that, there was the recreation center/ice arena, a wave pool, grocery stores, convenience stores, tire shops, metal shops, body shops, gear shops, four schools, one college, a movie theater, and only one set of traffic lights. We really needed a bowling alley.

When living in a town that seemed to have just sprouted up in the midst of the evergreens, you took what you could get, as far as "location, location, location," was concerned. Given the choice, I would have established my restaurant in an upscale, uptown neighborhood. The problem was that Chetwynd was too small to even have neighborhoods. Chetwynd *was* the neighborhood. So, regrettably, my restaurant could be found between the Little Prairie Bakery and Morton's Muffler Shop on the North Access Road, along main street. My establishment was opened from 10:00 a.m. until 12:00 a.m., Thursday through Tuesday, closed Wednesdays. I know that made an unusual weekend. We used to be open seven days a week, but no one ever came in on Wednesdays, and no amount of special offers, one day coupons, or catchy slogans could lure them in. Perhaps the problem was that it is impossible to make a slogan with the word Wednesday in it sound catchy. In any case, my father began closing one day a week in the spring of 1991. Twelve years later, people still came in and said, "Hey, I thought you were open seven days a week." You had to love a small town. Otherwise, it could drive you absolutely bonkers.

I was only twenty-two years old, and Cindy was twenty when our father died in 1999. He left Cindy his red F-350 crew cab, and a collection of rare coins. He left me his house in the Rodeo Sub-Division, and the pizza business. Presto, I went from friend and co-worker to boss in the blink of an eye. I suppose that is why I was a lousy boss. Throughout high school, I was one of the prep cooks, then graduated to full time delivery driver after graduation. Dad made me assistant manager as a twentieth birthday present, evidently considering the promotion to be more fiscally responsible than the hunting rifle I had asked for. However, my new position really taught me the ropes of the pizza business, knowledge that would be sorely needed when Dad died two years later.

I divided my employees into two categories, students and staples. Students were, of course, those who are working part time through high school, or needed a summer job to help with tuition fees. Staples were also jokingly referred to as lifers. Counting myself, there were six staples that year, all of whom had worked a full year for my father, and felt a strong tie of loyalty to the restaurant as a result.

Twenty-six-year-old Katherine MacDonnell was a close friend of mine ever since childhood, and hired onto the restaurant at the same time I did, when we were both still in the ninth grade. She was now the head prep cook, and the undisputed queen of the kitchen. Even as the owner, I never argued with her when she said, "Don't touch that!" Her right-hand man was the twenty-one-year-old smooth talker known as Clancy Grover. Together, they would put together the best pizzas in town, no exaggeration. They were a great team, in spite of the continuing drama of Clancy hitting on Kat, and Kat shooting him out of the saddle. It kept the kitchen entertaining.

When the pizzas came out of the oven, they became the responsibility of the dining room servers or the delivery driver. Boris J. Morris knew the streets of Chetwynd like the back of the school bus he always got stuck behind, so he was a natural delivery guy. He remembered names, addresses, and phone numbers with such ease that we rarely had to write complex directions on the delivery receipts. Usually, we just wrote "Bob's," or "Burrito Kevin," or "The Meatlover and Artichoke Guys," or "The People With the Angry Dogs," and Boris found them every time. However, I did eventually have to tell him that his custom-made "Relax; I know where you live." bumper sticker was not really helping his customers to relax. So, he had a new bumper sticker made, proudly bearing his personal motto: "I'm your pizza guy; I know everything." Customers absolutely adored him. On average, they paid him more than I did, and I was shelling out twelve bucks an hour.

The dining room used to be attended by my two remaining staples, Cindy Myers, my sister, and Spring Stevens, my high school girlfriend, but Spring had finally put in her two weeks notice just before Christmas, 2002, to pursue her dream career in journalism. After so many years of working side-by-side with her, along with a long-running personal relationship, it just seemed wrong to hire someone else to fill her shoes. Cindy had tried to make do with students, but with little success. Why, I am not certain. As Boris had pointed out, almost any biped with opposable thumbs and a basic mastery of vocal communication could be trained to wait tables. I do not know if the high school students that year were exceptionally stupid or what, but I had already fired three of them since New Years. Much as it pained me to agree with Boris, about *anything*, he was right. We needed a new waitress.

And Clancy wanted me to hire his new girlfriend.

I do not deny that I completely lacked optimism as I eased my old blue Chevy extended cab truck, "Sid's Rig," into the restaurant parking lot that morning. The majority of Clancy's girlfriends (satirically referred to as "Grover Girls") whom I had previously met were in no way notable for anything, with the possible exception of their hairstyles. To be quite frank, if Clancy had ever published his top ten dating prerequisites, I doubt that intelligence would have even made the list. The only time that I ever had to remind Kat of her good host training was near the end of a very long three week trial period with one of Clancy's high school flames. Her name was Monica Presby, a former cheerleader who could have written the definitive thesis on stereotypes.

If I recall correctly, Kat's exact words were, "Clancy, do you deliberately seek out the dumbest chicks in this town?!" I actually had to lecture Kat in my office about that one, not the easiest thing to do when every fibre of my being was trying to burst into hysterical laughter. It is a basic rule of comedy that cruel honesty is hilarious.

Boris's glossy black 2002 Pontiac Trans Am GT was already parked by the front door when I arrived, living proof of how much his customers spoiled him. Boris, sipping a cola, was lounging at one of the outdoor patio tables, which were quite popular in the summer months. Boris was looking relaxed in his white tee-shirt, khaki shorts, and sneakers, his fish-belly white legs serving as a pleasant reminder that winter was over. The only nice thing about coming in to work on our day off was that it was an automatic casual day. My black sweat shirt, blue jeans and black cowboy boots were a nice change from the formal shirts, vests and ties that we usually wore. I liked giving my establishment and employees an upscale look, but formality was the last thing that any of us wanted on a Wednesday.

"Hello again, Sid," he greeted me, as I bashed open the sticky door of my truck.

"Hey, Boris," I nodded, sitting across from him, sipping from my plastic travel mug of coffee. "Beautiful morning."

"You slept through the best part of it," he chided me. "I've been up since.... Actually, I've never been down." He held up his pop as a toast. "Long live caffeine."

"Caffeine," I agreed, clinking my mug against the aluminum. "You do realize that your driving career is destined for a fiery demise if you don't start getting more sleep. Death is not good, okay?"

Boris shrugged. "When I die, another will spring up from the ashes to take my place. This is Chetwynd. Pizza guys are as much of an essential service as the grocery store, the cops, and the drug dealers."

"You're sick. You know that, right?"

"Hey, how many kids have you had to fire for smoking weed on their cigarette breaks?"

"One. And that was three years ago."

"Which is probably why we have such a hard time getting help around here. The word on the street is that Sidney Myers is *partius pooperus*."

"Yeah, I guess I won't be able to attract all the stoners and crack-heads to my shop. I'll get over it."

"You'll never get used to living in this town, will you?"

"It's part of being a Baptist."

"Try being Catholic," Boris grinned, then belched. "See? I feel guilty about that."

"Should I call Father Makkie for you?"

"Nah. I can take care of it at home now. They've got this great new confessional system. Just log onto *www.onlineabsolution.com.*"

"Are you jerking me around?"

"I jerk you not," he snorted. "You can download an entire Sunday mass, and buy communion goblets on E-Bay."

I shuddered. "I feel like I could be struck by lightning just for hearing that. Did you get that dough started?"

"It's all ready to ball and sheet," he confirmed. "I took some more pepperoni out of the freezer, too."

"Cheese?"

"Me and Kat filled the bins last night. We're good to go. Oh yeah, and they said to make sure that all the slices are the same size. Otherwise, the kids get mad."

"Dang kids," I growled. "Speaking of which, where's Clancy?"

"Oh, right, he's inside, showing his lady how to mix pizza sauce."

"Really? Where's his truck?"

"Down again. I gave them a ride."

"What's wrong now, the alternator or the drive shaft? They've both been making noise."

"I believe the term he used was 'torque converter.'"

I raised an eyebrow. "And I believe the bottom line for that is in the neighborhood of seven hundred dollars."

"I know. He's paying more for maintenance on that rig than he would for payments on a new one."

"Sentimental fool that he is."

"If he cared for any of his girlfriends like he does for that truck, he'd be on his second honeymoon by now," Boris chuckled.

"I heard that!" snapped Clancy, who had just swung the front door open, and was towering over us. At an inch over six feet, Clancy Grover was a hair taller than Boris, with dark brown hair, and a lean, muscled build, though not as wiry as Boris. I had more of a stocky build than either of them, but at five feet, ten inches, they still made me feel short. For the record, I have brown hair and eyes, and a beard, always neatly trimmed. I admit it. I am fussy about grooming.

"Oh, hi Clancy, we were just talking about you," I said mildly, still sipping my coffee.

"Good morning, Sid." Clancy joined us at the table and took a swig of Boris's pop, sporting a comfortable pair of old corduroys and a Vancouver Canucks jersey. "It's such a relief to know that your sarcasm is still intact."

"We're pizza guys," I explained calmly. "We spend our lives placating some of the stupidest people ever to be placed on God's green earth. Sarcasm is the only weapon we have. Where's your girlfriend?"

"No worries, dude. I put her right to work. She's balling up the pizza dough."

"Are you out of your mind? You left an inexperienced, unemployed wannabe waitress alone in my kitchen? Kat's going to kill you."

"Sid, the place is not exactly a minefield."

"Beside the point. She's unsupervised. Now I have to go in there before I finish my coffee. Have you ever worked with me before I finish my coffee?"

"Uh … I don't think so," Clancy reluctantly admitted.

"Sid, you never finish drinking coffee," Boris commented.

"This is mug number one," I grumbled, standing. "You usually see me on mug three or four. Move it, Casanova. You just called down the wrath."

"Ah, Sid!" Clancy complained, following me across the red brick veranda surrounding the brown sided building. "You're overreacting. She's not hurting anything. She *can't* hurt anything."

I pulled the white door open, and stormed into the varnished oak-paneled reception lobby, pausing just long enough to set my sunglasses on the cross-eyed coyote which stood guard over the two white *'please wait to be seated'* sofas.

"Clancy, I've had three employees who nearly severed their own fingers while chopping vegetables. Another guy burned his face by tripping on his shoelaces while putting a pizza in the oven, and you needed six stitches for getting your fingers sucked into the dough press. Don't tell me she can't hurt anything. Can't is a very big word."

A voice drifted into the lobby from the kitchen to our left.

"Clancy, I'm done!" The female voice was somewhat low, but cheery and full of life.

"Done?" Clancy was puzzled. "Done what?"

"Well, like *duh!* The pizza dough."

"But you just started!" Clancy blurted.

I stared at him, suspiciously. He held up his hands and laughed weakly.

"She's good, Sid, what can I say?"

"'Well, like *duh?*'" I muttered, eyes narrowing. "Yeah, she sounds good." I pushed past him and hit the black batwing doors into the white-walled kitchen. "Ma'am, please step away from the pizza dough."

Her back was turned away from me, toward the mechanical dough press against the opposite wall. The counter in front of her was lined with rows of neatly rolled balls of dough, all of them nearly identical. It only took a moment to realize that she had indeed finished all fifty.

"Wow." Clancy was right behind me. "You did all of them."

"Well, duh." She turned to face us, a cute, fairly short girl with big brown eyes and thick reddish brown hair, pulled back into a somewhat tussled ponytail. She had to be almost a foot shorter than Clancy, probably only an inch or two over five feet. It had been quite a while since I had seen anyone wear khaki bib overalls, but she actually looked quite nice in them, with a black tee-shirt and white sneakers.

"Angel Bates?" I said slowly, still a bit shocked as I held out my hand. "I'm Sidney Myers."

The girl was already laughing as she grabbed my hand. She had a wide open, full voiced laugh that revealed somewhat large, but very even white teeth.

"Sidney! That is too cool! I had a dog named Sidney once. He's dead." She was furiously pumping my hand with both of hers. "It's great to meet you, Boss."

Boss?

No one had ever actually called me that. I was not sure that I liked the sound of it. I glanced back at the dough on the counter.

"Nice job with the dough, Miss Bates," I said with an approving raised eyebrow, after I had gotten my hand back. "How old are you?"

You know, Myers, a good boss would never ask that.

"Twenty-two, Boss." She obviously liked having an authority figure to refer to as that.

"Clancy," I said, "you're twenty-one. You have one year to be as fast as she is, or else I'm firing you again."

"Uh, you've never fired me, Sid."

"Haven't I?" I said, thinking back.

"I think you mean Boris."

"Oh, right. Sorry."

"Did I miss something?" Angel asked, curiously.

"Sidney fires Boris at least twice a month," Clancy explained. "It never lasts more than a couple of minutes. It's kind of a tradition."

"Someday, it will be for real," I assured them, grinning evilly.

"Hey, I'm standing right here!" Boris snapped as he entered the kitchen, tying on a white apron.

"Shut up and start sheeting," I said absently. "Show Angel how to do it."

"Cool, I'm making pizzas," Angel chuckled. "Me likey."

"You realize, of course, that if I do hire you, you'll mostly be working in the dining room," I reminded her. "But, I like everyone here to have a basic grasp of … everything. Just in case."

"Sounds reasonable," she nodded. "This is too cool! Fire 'er up, Boris!" I had never seen anyone so enthusiastic about having a job that she did not even officially have yet. In the words of Clancy, it was "kind of weirding me out."

Boris switched on the dough press, a raised metal table on the counter with two large lever-adjustable rollers. Once the rollers were activated, a floured ball of dough was fed between them, squishing and stretching it into a pancake. The process was repeated until the dough was flat and round enough to sheet onto greased pizza pans. The press also featured an emergency trip-bar, which automatically shut down the whole machine when raised. This was mostly to ensure that no ball of dough that was too large could fit under it, but was also quite convenient for occasions when fingers or clothing somehow ended up between the rollers. Yes, it had happened, and it was not pretty.

"Cool," Angel remarked as Boris ran the first ball through the press. "Big shiny rolling pin."

"Essentially," Boris nodded. "And it can turn your fingers into big, bloody spatulas if you put them too close. Clancy can tell you all about it."

"Six stitches!" Clancy said defensively. "That is not all that bad."

"Poor baby," Angel grinned.

Clancy kissed her cheek as he walked past them to a shelf of large size pizza pans, sixteen inches in diameter, and began oiling them for sheeting.

"Heck, I can do *that*," Angel was saying to Boris, as I began opening the fridges and pulling out large bins of sliced sausage meat and grated cheese, setting them on the central prep table. "Gimmie a ball. Actually, give me three."

My back was turned to them, but I could hear the sound of Angel's palms catching the dough, followed by rapid pattering of dough against skin.

"Hey, nice." Boris was impressed.

"Miss Bates," I said, without turning around, "please do not juggle the pizza dough."

"She's really good, Sid," Clancy stated, admiringly. "That takes skill."

"Sorry, Boss." Angel was laughing again. "It's one of my unwinders. Therapeutic, you know?"

"Unwinders," I mused. "Good word use. And my name is Sidney. You can call me Sidney. No one calls me 'Boss.'"

"Well, maybe they should. Respect for authority figures is something we don't see enough of, lately."

"Are you a revolutionary, Miss Bates?" I asked with half a smile.

"Nah. I'm just me. Just a little different."

"Well, different can be good." I shrugged. "Boris is living proof."

"Hey!"

"I only find it somewhat disconcerting, Miss Bates, that you require therapeutic 'unwinders' after the better part of ten minutes in the kitchen."

"Sorry," she giggled. "I guess it's just the high-stress environment."

"And she hasn't even met the customers yet," Boris said, smirking.

"Why?" she asked. "What's wrong with them?"

"I'll put it to you this way, hon," Clancy chuckled. "You know how most businesses say 'The customer is always right?' A better motto for here would be 'The customer is never right, just don't let them know that.'"

"Catchy," Angel said slowly, a bit unconvinced.

"You work here for a week and it'll make sense," Boris assured her, as he began twirling the first pizza crust over his head.

"Okay, *that* I have to learn," Angel asserted, pointing at the spinning dough.

"It's pretty simple," Boris explained, keeping the dough floating over his head like a white UFO. "All in the wrist. Catch it on your fist, not with your fingers, that tears the dough. Just keep it one smooth motion. Let the law of centrifugal force work through you."

"Whatever you say, Yoda," Angel said wryly.

I liked this cheery girl. Within fifteen minutes, she had begun casually insulting Boris. She was going to fit in just fine.

CHAPTER THREE

Sitting in a folding chair across the desk from me, Angel glanced skeptically around my small office, as I perused her resume. I could not blame her. I am sure that most employers do not keep their office walls lined with stacks of pizza boxes and flour sacks, or racks of canned goods, not to mention a humming deep freeze unit. My wooden desk was not very big, crammed in between the freezer and my dad's old filing cabinet. The office was my sanctuary, but it did look more like an engulfing tidal wave of groceries.

"Your office is your dry goods storage." Angel was a person not bothered by stating the obvious.

"Secrets of a successful business, Miss Bates," I said. "Keep your overheads low."

"Yeah, I feel like I'm bumping my head already."

She had a bit of a sharp tongue, too. I wondered if that would be a problem.

"Okay, your resume is very, um, descriptive, Miss Bates...."

"You keep calling me Miss Bates."

"Do you prefer 'Ms.?'"

"*Angel,*" she said, emphasizing every syllable. "Angel!"

I looked over the top of the resume at her, taking off my reading glasses.

"*Angel,* I've been making pizzas with you for an hour and a half, and you haven't called me anything but 'Boss.'"

"What, you don't like it?" She almost looked hurt, her puppy eyes widening slightly, and her lips getting just a little bit pouty.

"No, but, just as a general rule, you only call someone that *after* they hire you."

"So, I'm jumping the gun a bit." She shrugged off the specifics of title address. "Can it hurt?"

"I guess not," I sighed. "Okay, resume…. You've put here that you are *'hard working, courteous, cheerful, a team player, a source of encouragement ….'*"

"I'm the first one to give the ol' pat on the back," she interjected brightly.

"Well, that's … positive, I guess. Um … *'brutally honest, amiable,'* good word use, by the way. Uh, ' … *extroverted, introspective, and convoluted.'*" I let the sheet slip from my fingers and waft onto the desk. "I'm at a loss for words, Angel."

"You don't like it?" There was that same, irritatingly cute, hurt look.

"Just help me out here, Miss … Angel. *'Introspective?'*"

"Psychology 101, Boss. One who contemplates contemplation. Or something like that."

"Right…. Convoluted?"

"I'm one complex cat."

"Yeah, I'll believe that. Have you ever worked at a restaurant before?"

"Nope. Never."

"Well, I had to ask, since you seem to have entirely left out previous work experience on this resume."

"Oh, that," she said with a dismissive wave of her hand. "I didn't leave it out. This is my first job."

"Excuse me?" I could not believe this entire situation.

"This. Here. Now. First job." Angel used a lot of twitchy hand gestures to support her incomplete sentences.

"You're twenty-two years old, and you've never had a job?"

"Better late...."

"Very late, don't you think?"

"Not really." She was smiling, almost condescendingly.

"Have you been in school, or what?"

"Nah." She shook her head. "Post-secondary education is for people who want to change the world. I just want to serve coffee."

"You'd be happy doing that?" I did not hear that very often.

"You'll have to hire me to find out," she teased. "I'm good with people. Heck, I've already got Clancy and Boris wrapped around my finger. How bad can paying customers be?"

"How long have you been in Chetwynd?" I asked suddenly.

"About three weeks. Why?"

"Because you look familiar. Have you been around here before?"

"I'd barely even seen the town until I moved here," she replied, but I noticed that she looked down at the floor when she said it. For some reason, she did not want to talk about that.

"How'd you meet Clancy?" I asked, changing the subject.

"I just ran into him at the grocery store a couple weeks ago," she said. "I mean, I literally ran into him. He was coming into the canned soup aisle just as I was coming out, and I slammed the cart right into him."

"That sounds like a good icebreaker," I observed, smiling at the mental image I had just received.

"Well, it was almost a knee-breaker, but I guess he didn't mind too much. He asked me out about five minutes later."

"Yeah, that's Clancy," I nodded grimly.

Looking curious, Angel leaned forward and reached across the desk to pick up my white, personalized coffee mug.

"'Sidney's Cup of Wrath,'" she read the dark, bold print aloud. "You have wrath?"

"That's a Christmas present from my younger sister, Cindy," I explained. "She works here, too. I guess she thinks I'm turning into a grouch, or something. I keep firing her boyfriend."

"Boris?"

"Yeah."

"Oh…. Is this a sore spot, Boss?"

"No. It's just older brother prerogative. Do you have a brother?"

"I'm an only child. I guess I was enough."

No kidding. I tried not to smile.

"Do you have a car?"

"'03 Cavalier, Boss. Red. I like red. Why?"

"I might need you to do some back-up delivery work, just when Boris gets swamped. I usually do it, but the more drivers, the better."

"No *pro-blemo.*"

Angel set my mug back on the desk, then leaned back in her seat and crossed her arms.

"So, what's the scoop on the job, Boss?"

"You have to wear a tie."

"Neck, or bow?"

"Your choice, actually. We've got both. The basic uniform is a long-sleeved white shirt, black tie, a vest, black pants or a skirt, again your choice, and black shoes, closed-toe, closed-heel."

"No sandals?"

"No."

"Sounds snazzy. What colour is the vest?"

"We have a few to choose from. Sewing is one of Kat's hobbies, so she keeps us stocked with vests and shirts, and we also supply your tie. Bring your own pants."

"Kat?"

"Katherine MacDonnell, head prep cook. Don't ever touch the big pizza knife in the kitchen, because Kat *will* find out. She's, uh … a bit possessive."

"What colour is *your* vest?"

"I wear a black one."

"Neck or bow?"

"Necktie."

"You're telling me that you only wear black and white here? Where's the life in *that?*"

"Life?"

"Colour, vibrance, pizzaz ... ambience."

"I call it formal. I'm not looking for ambience."

"You poor man," Angel sighed. "Can I have a red vest? I like red."

"We have a couple. Rose or cherry?"

"Cherry. I want a bow-tie."

"You do know that I haven't hired you yet, right?" I clarified.

"I know. I want a bow-tie."

"Okay, fine. If I hire you, you get the cherry vest and a bow-tie."

"Perfect," she said contentedly. "Bow-ties are sexy."

"You know ... I've honestly never thought of them that way before."

"Hey. I had a pizza delivered on Friday, and Boris wasn't wearing a tie. He just had a vest and a white tee-shirt."

"Yeah, well, with Boris, I'm surprised I even got him to wear the vest. He's not big on formality."

"So ... was the bright orange vest his own choice?"

"He got Kat to make it, just for him."

Angel cringed. "You're kidding."

"I guess it protects him from drunk deer hunters, or something. He's a delivery guy. He's weird."

"Okay, let's talk money."

My mouth took a few moments to recover from its slack-jawed state, and then began forming words again.

Where did this girl come from?

"You're a very to-the-point person, Angel."

"Money is one of those happy things, Boss."

"Then I assume you want full-time?"

"Oh yeah."

"Good, because that's what I need right now. You'll be part of my staple crew, which is me, Clancy, Boris, Kat and Cindy. You'll get at least forty hours a week, and I pay ten bucks an hour, plus tips. If you last a year, I bump you up to twelve bucks."

"Sounds good." She nodded approvingly. "Do you pay everyone that much, right off the bat?"

"I get a lot of part-time students coming through here. They get minimum wage, mostly washing dishes and clean up. Also, you should know that Clancy is presently the newest guy on the staple crew. He's only been here five years."

"Holy …! You guys must be an oiled machine by now!"

"We stay in business," I smiled. "I'm only mentioning this because I need you to understand what the job is. The waitress you're replacing worked here for seven years. We survive that long by learning to ignore pet-peeves. You understand?"

"I'm a people person."

"Yeah, that was the impression I was starting to get," I said drolly. "A few more ground rules: No fighting, no swearing, and in this town I really need to emphasize that last one. If you smoke, please smoke outside the back door on your breaks, not out front, and only smoke cigarettes, cigars, or a pipe. If I catch you smoking weed or anything that involves a cigarette lighter and a spoon, you're gone. And it would not be the first time."

"Yeah, gotcha," she said, rolling her eyes. "I'll try not to be that imbecilic."

"Good word use. Imbecilic…. I like that. But, like I said. It has happened. The drugs per capita rate in this town is disgusting, so I have to spell it out for you. Don't let me down."

"Relax, Boss; This is *me.*"

Clancy swung my door open and leaned through the doorway. The man never knocked.

"Hello?" I said, glancing up at him.

"They're all boxed up, Sid, in the cooler. Who opens tomorrow?"

"Me, Kat, and that new Becky kid. I'll come in early and start cooking. Thanks. Sorry about your weekend."

"Hey, the day's not over yet," he consoled me. "Are you coming to the movie tonight?"

"What's playing?" I asked.

"Some big Donald Sutherland flick that came to other movie theatres four months ago."

"The joys of small town life," I groaned. "Sure, I'll see you there."

"I'm coming!" Angel cheered. "He's my favourite actor."

"He is?" Clancy said skeptically. "Sid, are you done with my girlfriend?"

"Yeah, pretty much. You're hired, Miss Bates. Welcome to By The Slice. I'm scheduling you in for 3:30 tomorrow afternoon."

"Don't call me Miss Bates," she said, smiling patiently.

"Don't call me Boss."

Angel followed Clancy out the door as I got up to put her resume in my files. I am sure that she believed herself to be out of hearing range when she asked Clancy, "Is he always like that?"

"You know, I had a dog named Angel once," I called out, loud enough for them to hear.

Angel was laughing again.

"Yeah right, Boss!"

CHAPTER FOUR

It was nearly two o'clock in the afternoon when Boris drove Clancy and Angel home, leaving me alone in the restaurant with only a chainsaw sculpted beaver and a cross-eyed coyote for company. I did not know why, but once I was at my restaurant, even on a Wednesday, I did not want to go home again. Perhaps it was because my dad always used to be there that I felt I had a responsibility to keep a constant vigil, even when the place was closed. I locked the front door again after Boris closed it behind him, then lay down on one of the white reception sofas, and dialled my home number on my cell phone. Cindy answered on the second ring.

"Hello?" Cindy's low voice still sounded sleepy.

"Hey, sis, it's me."

"Hey, Sid, where are you? I got up this morning and you were gone."

"You did *not* get up 'this morning,' Cindy."

"Okay, at one-thirty. What's up?"

"I'm at the shop. We got a fifty large order for tomorrow morning."

"Crap. Who ordered that?"

"Elementary school."

"You want me to come down there?"

"No, Boris and Clancy were here, we're done. What are you doing?"

"Eating junk food, watching cartoons. Why didn't you call me in?"

"You and Kat needed the day off. We handled it."

"Just the three of you?"

"No, the new girl was there, too."

"Becky?"

"No. Clancy's girlfriend."

"Oh brother. How was that?"

"Actually, pretty good. I hired her."

"A girl who's dumb enough to date Clancy?"

I smiled. "No one's perfect."

"You remember Monica Presby?"

"Yes, no matter how hard I try to forget."

"It could be the same thing all over again, Sid."

"I don't think Angel's going to break any dishes while rehearsing cheerleader choreography."

"Her name is *Angel?*"

"She's different from his other girls, Cindy. I saw definite signs of brain activity from this one."

"Well, that's a first...."

"We're going to the movie later. You wanna come?"

"Yeah, sure. Are you coming home?"

"I'm gonna hang out here, for a while. I'll call Kat and see if she wants to come tonight."

"It's about time you asked her out. Neither one of you dates enough."

"Are you still mad at Boris? He's coming, too."

"He told you, huh? I guess I was being a bit...."

"Reactional," I interrupted. "Just make up, okay? The house is clean enough, already."

"Sorry," Cindy laughed. "Did I keep you up?"

"No, not really."

God should smite you for that lie....

"Okay, yes, you kept me up."

"You should take a nap if you're going to stay at the shop."

Yeah, right.

"I might. I'll be home in a bit."

"Okay. Bye."

"Bye." I folded the phone, knowing that I would not be able to catch anymore sleep on that sofa than I would in my own living room, amidst all the exploding dynamite and falling anvils reverberating out of the television.

I stretched out on the sofa anyway, letting my boots hang over the cushioned armrests. I loved naps. I just hated the time they took up. Cindy used to tell me that I had a psychological condition which left me in a perpetual fear that I was about to miss out on something. As she once snapped at me for insisting that I was not tired, "This is Chetwynd, Sid! You could *hibernate* and never miss anything!" She was probably right, but the fact remained that I had not taken a nap since the age of five. I had other methods of killing time, most often just drinking more coffee. However, I also jogged, read, did crossword puzzles, and listened to music.

I had one other hobby, but no one else was allowed to know about it.

I could only lay and stare at the ceiling for about half an hour. By then, I needed more coffee. None had been made that morning, but I knew Boris well enough to be certain that he and Clancy had not emptied out the coffeepot the night before when they closed the shop, so it was a safe bet that Tuesday's coffee was still in the kitchen.

I rolled off the couch and trudged into the dark kitchen with my travel mug. Sure enough, the coffeepot was nearly full, but turned off, thank goodness. I pried the plastic lid off the mug with my teeth and filled it up with the cold, black liquid, unable to get the word 'treacle' out of my head. A lot of people are repulsed by stone cold, stale coffee with a consistency reminiscent of pancake syrup, and, I will admit, it was an acquired taste. I loved it. Black, two sugars.

The first sip sent a jolt of caffeine through my body, causing my teeth to grit and my eyes to water. Boris never drank the coffee he made, but I had seen his perking procedure. He liked to see how many grounds he could heap into the filter without overflowing it. Fortunately, not many people come to By The Slice for coffee. I swallowed that first mouthful, and then carried the mug into the dining room.

I left the lights off as I crossed the deep red carpet of the darkened room. The dining area had only two tinted windows in it, to maintain an elegant, dimly lit atmosphere. Five hanging light fixtures gave just the right amount of low, yellow ambience to the dozen round dining tables, some with four chairs, some with only two. The place settings were all prepared for the next day's customer, forest green tablecloths arranged with pale blue paper placemats, folded napkins, and cream-coloured coffee mugs inverted on saucers. I liked the room best at times like these; dark, ready, and waiting. It reminded me of me.

There was a baby grand piano in the far corner of my dining room, on an elevated, carpeted platform. It had been my father's prized possession, acquired by his parents and brought over from Ireland when they immigrated to Canada in 1942. Dad used to play it almost every day, and he was a wonder to listen to, having taken lessons from his sixth birthday onward. I had never taken lessons, having grown up in a decade which considered such skills to be "uncool." We were more concerned with our tragic sense of fashion, hairstyles and pop music. I really did not miss the eighties.

I slid onto the polished bench, and carefully uncovered the genuine ivory keys. I set my mug on top of the instrument, something which I constantly warned others to never do. I had no sheet music in front of me. I never did.

My patrons occasionally asked me if I played the piano, usually after they nostalgically reminisced about the way that my father used to play. My standard reply was, "Nah. I just plink on it once in a while." Cindy was now the real pianist in the family, having followed in our father's footsteps, also from a young age. Frequently, she would serenade our dining patrons, many of whom would attend the restaurant simply for the sake of the dinner music. Cindy read music like she could read a book, and had even written songs, a couple of which had been true masterpieces, in my proud, older brother opinion. I could not read music. I just closed my eyes, and "plinked." I only did so when I was alone.

But, the fact was that I plinked better than most people could play.

That was my hidden hobby, my secret gift. It was a blessing that even I was unaware of for many years. The first time that I ever touched that piano was on the evening of my father's funeral. I left my sister, friends and relatives to grieve at my house, while I went to the restaurant that was suddenly mine, and locked myself inside. All that I could think about was Dad, sitting every day at that piano, filling the dining room with music. He would not want his beloved instrument to sit in silence. I sat down and played a song, one that lasted for nearly two hours, and I never stopped until I knew that it was complete. It was a work of musical beauty, one that I had unsuccessfully attempted to replicate ever since. Every piece that I played was beautiful, but I had never managed to recapture the magic which I had created on the night that my father was buried. In spite of the beauty, there was also fear almost every time that I began to play. I could rarely stroke those keys without revisiting my final moments with Karl Myers, and the images still frightened me.

My father was killed in a vehicle collision. I was in the vehicle with him.

I took another sip of the potent coffee and closed my eyes before I began to play. I played a spring rainstorm, using short, high notes to create a light pattering of rain trickling down a dark window, and holding low notes until they became the distant thunder, drawing ever nearer. The music grew darker and louder as the melodic storm clouds advanced, settling in like a black fire overhead. The musical lightning lit up the dining room, and thunder beat down on the rooftop.

* * *

"*I think we're gonna get wet,*" *I commented, glancing up at the stormy, midnight sky as I locked the front door and pocketed my key.*

Dad held up a quarter and tapped his knuckles on the hood of his old blue Chevy Blazer.

"*Call it, Sidney.*"

"*Tails,*" *I replied. The first raindrops were beginning to pelt down on us. I was not even wearing a jacket, and wondered if my vest would need washing after getting rained on.*

The quarter spun high into the air, briefly reflecting a bolt of lightning off the caribou head, then dropped with a dull clap into Karl Myers' beefy palm. He closed his fist over the coin, and slapped it onto the back of his other hand.

"*Heads,*" *he chuckled.* "*I drive.*"

"*I don't think it's possible for the coin to put you in the driver's seat every single time,*" *I said, giving him a sceptical raised eyebrow as I crawled in the passenger side.*

"*The theory of probability is crap, Sidney.*"

* * *

I took a very long swig of coffee, letting the thunder fade for a moment as I made the torrential rain fall with one hand.

* * *

I could barely see through the sheets of rain as we pulled off the North Access Road onto main street. I loved this kind of rain more than any other, but preferred to watch it from the back patio door in our home.

"Well, this hit fast," Dad remarked, trying to make out the dividing lines on the dark road ahead of us. He could only safely drive about twenty kilometres per hour, but our house was still only about five minutes away.

"I looked at some apartments today," I informed him, watching the rain wash down my door window. "There's one open in Summit Crest Manor. It looked pretty good."

"You know I'm not trying to kick you out of the house, Sidney," he reminded me.

"I know, but it would be nice to get my own place, for once. Don't worry, Dad. I'm not a big partier."

"That's the British side of you talking. The Irish know how to have good times, boy." He laughed.

I could see the lights of the convenience store ahead, on the corner of the 48th Street intersection.

* * *

I let the rainfall lighten, but held one long, deep thunder note. I could feel it rumble through the entire building.

* * *

"It's easing up a bit," I commented, realizing that I could almost see the fast food restaurant on the other side of the intersection.

The green digital clock on the dashboard read 12:27. A green truck with monster tires appeared in my father's driver-side window, driving so fast. There were no headlights. There were no red brake lights at the stop sign.

"DAD!!"

* * *

The YMCA jingle of my cell phone made me start, all of my fingers instinctively jumping back from the keys. I slammed the cover down over the ivories, and bolted up off the bench. I strode quickly into the lobby before I pulled out the phone and flipped it open. I hated telephones.

"Hello?" I made myself sound upbeat.

"Sid, what's up?" The female voice was clear and well enunciated, but obviously suspicious.

"Hey, Kat. Nothing much."

"Cindy told me you were working today."

"You needed the day off, Kat. We took care of it. Relax."

"Is my kitchen wrecked?"

"We cleaned up good. I was here the whole time. No one touched the pizza knife."

"Good. No heads will roll today."

"Thank you." I rolled my eyes. "You got plans for tonight?"

"Easy there, big boy."

"I love you, too. We're going to the movie later. Are you coming or not?"

"Which one?"

"All I've heard is Donald Sutherland."

"The 24 guy?"

"No, that's Kiefer. Donald's the one with the beard."

"Kiefer had a beard in *The Three Musketeers.*"

"Donald's the one with the *white* beard."

"He's still alive?"

"Yes, Kat," I sighed. "He's still alive."

42

"What time?"

"Eight, I think. There's only one show on Wednesdays."

"And no crowds, because every normal person goes to the movies on the weekend."

"This *is* our weekend, Kat. What are you doing right now?"

"I was just talking to Evelyn for the last two hours. How come you never talk to me that long?"

"I hate phones. And you know that. How's Evelyn doing?"

"Pretty good. She just got her first nursing job in Saskatoon. She seems happy."

"Glad to hear it. When did she get back to school?"

"Last year, she finally went back and finished. Heck, she dropped out for almost six months after Roger died."

"Wow. You only took two weeks."

"I'm like you, Sid. It's easier to work yourself to death than to actually deal with loss. It's probably not healthy, but it's easy."

I paused for a moment, and then asked, "How are you doing, Kat?"

"You know the answer to that, Sid. It's the same answer you always give."

"'Fine?'"

"Exactly. And you wouldn't believe me, either."

"Probably not. Feeling up to a game of chess?"

"Bring it on, cowboy. Are you wearing those boots?"

"It's Wednesday, casual day. I'll be over in a few minutes."

"The board's set up. You're going down."

"We'll see."

I hung up, snatched my shades off the cross-eyed face of Wood E. Coyote, Cindy's choice for his name, and headed for the front door, still sipping Boris's coffee of death, chewing through the grounds that had been flooded out of the basket into the pot.

If I tried to stir this stuff, the spoon would either bounce off the surface, or just dissolve....

CHAPTER FIVE

Even after two years, I still had a hard time thinking of Kat MacDonnell as a widow. She was less than a month older than me, and had been one of my best friends for as long as I could remember. To me, she would always be Kat Kelly, the little girl three doors down from the acreage that Cindy and I grew up on, just on the outskirts of town. Times and locations had changed. Dad had sold the acreage and our three beloved horses, and moved us into town when his back began troubling him years before, and Kat had moved into her own apartment after high school, when her parents retired to Red Deer, Alberta. She was no longer the girl sitting across from me on the second grade teeter-totter. She had married her high school boyfriend, Roger MacDonnell, shortly after graduation, and the two had made a decent living. Kat was working at the restaurant, and Roger drove logging trucks for three years, but it all ended far too soon as Roger was diagnosed with liver cancer, and died within a few months. I had already lost my father, so her loss drew us even closer, but Kat showed a lot more strength than I ever had. I never saw her cry once, not even at Roger's funeral. I am sure that she did, but only in private. Kat was strong. She was the support that helped Roger's parents and younger sister, Evelyn, to carry on with their lives. I wished that I had her strength.

"Check," Kat was smiling sweetly as she slid the white bishop into firing position.

I also wished that I had her mastery of the chessboard which sat on the coffee table before us.

"Uncheck," I replied, capturing the bishop with my remaining knight.

"Checkmate," Kat laughed, her rook sweeping in for the kill, capturing a pawn, and leaving my king hedged in by her knight. Smiling triumphantly, she leaned back into the beige couch we were sharing with a contented sigh.

"Ug," I gurgled, flicking my black king over with a forefinger. "I don't love you anymore."

"Sid, that hurts," she grinned, slamming back the last drops from a can of root beer, her self-proclaimed single addiction.

I usually picture a widow as a grey-haired lady who has a lot of grandchildren to make the pain of loss easier to bear. Kat was a striking twenty-six-year-old, with shoulder length, jet black hair, hazel eyes, and a really cute line of freckles over the bridge of her nose. She was as tall as me, and athletically built. Her favourite toy was the treadmill in the corner of her second storey apartment living room, where she ran at least six miles a day, six days a week. That is, every day except Wednesday.

"So, you hired Clancy's *girl du jour*," she mused, placing the chess pieces back to their starting positions. "She can compete with the ghost of Spring Stevens?"

"No. She can't," I said plainly. "But, she can work full evenings, and she can pour coffee."

"Speaking of competing, Sid, you might have to be ready for some pretty stiff competition in the next while."

"Why?"

"Nothing's in stone, but a little bird told me that we might be getting a Redmond's Ribs in town."

"Are you kidding?" I winced at the thought.

"Never. The world's best chain of steakhouses could be moving in next door."

"Well, crap! How reliable is the little bird?"

"Okay, it was Boris. He knows everything."

"Boris is a supermarket tabloid," I muttered. "He knows everything, and he knows it before anyone else does."

"Yeah, it's kind of creepy."

"Have you ever tried Redmond's Ribs?" I asked.

"'Mmm, maple roasted ribs are the *nummiest ...!*' Do you remember those commercials?"

"Of course. The little girl peeking out from behind a platter of ribs that's bigger than she is? They're classics. She was the Mazda 'zoom-zoom' kid of the mid eighties."

"What'd they call her?" Kat wondered, trying hard to remember.

"Little Maple," I replied. "How could you forget Little Maple?"

"I don't like their new ads," Kat remarked. "Restaurant mascots can be cool, but Rib Rack Ricky is just bloody irritating."

"Yeah, he sounds like Daffy Duck on helium," I agreed. "I can't believe Boris never told me about this, the little worm. He's supposed to be our information hotline. When did he tell you?"

"Just before I left last night, around eleven. You were already gone."

"How did he find out?" I demanded.

Kat gave me a disgusted look, such as I have never seen since that time when I forgot which toppings went on the house special.

"You still even bother asking that question? Boris knows all, and never reveals how. Journalists could take confidentiality lessons from him."

Kat suddenly fell silent, as though deep in thought.

"What?" I asked.

"I just remembered," she answered. "Journalists. Have you ever heard of *30 Days Up North?*"

"It's a trade magazine, right?"

"Yeah, it's a monthly publication, highlighting people and businesses in the Peace Region. They're based in Dawson Creek."

"What about it?"

"They called the shop last night, looking for you."

"Don't tell me they want to do a profile on By The Slice."

"Kind of…. Sid, I think they want to do a profile on you."

"*What?!*"

"I was talking to a Linda Matthews, one of their writers. She said that you're a hero who never got properly recognized."

"Is she out of her *mind?*"

"Come on, Sid. You pulled your dad out of that Blazer, and you tried to save the driver of the other truck, the whole time with a big gash on your forehead. That's heroic."

The very memory caused the faint scar on my right temple to itch slightly.

"My dad's dead. Everyone in that truck is dead. I didn't save anyone."

"But you tried. Don't beat yourself up for that. It's not every day that you get a shot at being called a hero, Sid. Don't walk away from this too fast."

"Kat, I barely remember what happened. I can't exactly give anyone a detailed account. The last thing I remember is pulling Dad out of the Blazer. It took me weeks to even remember that much."

"You got knocked out, Sid. Some memory loss is common. These guys know that. They said they're talking to that girl from the convenience store, too. She saw the whole thing, and remembers it better."

"Well, tell them to make her the hero, then. She called the ambulance, and she pulled me away from the pool of flaming gasoline. *She* saved someone."

"You tried, Sid. You passed out trying."

"I shouldn't have even wasted my time. I should have let him burn, and stayed with Dad."

"Karl was already dead!"

"Says the doctors.... Okay, fine. I waste my time trying to help everyone, I help no one, and *now* they want to call me a hero. Did the cops ever tell you how I got knocked out?"

"The other truck blew up."

"Yeah, it did. And a side view mirror blew off and slammed into the side of my head. Cartoon characters get knocked out like that, Kat. Not heroes."

"Sid, I hate to make this about money, but this is going to be an article about the shop, too. Having the reluctant owner painted as a hero cannot hurt business. We could use the publicity. Especially if someone really wants to open a Redmond's Ribs here."

I sighed heavily, leaning back into the couch and looking up at the ceiling.

"I don't think I could do it, Kat. It's just not right."

"Just think about it, Sid, please? I know it's painful, but I know Karl would want you to have this. He would have called you a hero."

I closed my eyes and sat in silence. Kat slowly leaned into my shoulder, and I put my arm around her. I did not deserve a friend like her.

"Just think about it," she said again, giving me a squeeze.

I kissed her forehead and turned to look out the second storey window. There was no traffic at all, and the neighbourhood was still and silent.

"Fine," I said. "You know I'd only do this for you."

"I know," she grinned. "Or for money."

"That too."

"You did everything that you could, Sid. I say you were a hero." Kat held her hands up, envisioning a headline. "'Sidney the hero....'"

"And I say you ought to sell used cars," I quipped, with a hint of a smile. "But please don't leave if you do."

"Nah. This town is too much of who I am, drug dealers and all. I could never leave."

"Can I have that in writing?"

"Come on! You'd starve to death if I ever left, and so would half of Chetwynd. This town needs a woman who can make pizzas."

"Okay, I love you again."

"That's a relief," she chuckled. "Can I be assistant manager now?"

"Kat, if you really wanted it, I would *give* you a full partnership, but I've already told you. I don't need an assistant manager."

"You do so! You need someone there, running the place when you're gone."

"I'm never gone."

"That's my point." Kat was getting into her mothering tone. "I want you to start taking two days off a week, just like the rest of us. No more being there every day, even Wednesdays, for crying out loud. Don't give me that look, Sid! I want you to start taking off days when the shop is actually open. We can handle it, okay? You're in there every single day, and for how long? At least ten hours per shift? You're working yourself into a ... a ... Well, something bad, anyway."

"Okay, okay, I'll think about it," I muttered.

"You're just saying that to shut me up, aren't you?"

"Well, I understand that kissing you to shut you up only works in the movies."

51

"Actually, it does work," she admitted. "Just not when a *guy* does it to a *girl*. Your kind is easier to manipulate."

"Hmmmm," I intoned, smiling mischievously. "Are you speaking from experience, here?"

Kat laughed. "Roger used to go off on these rants about the scale operators. I did what I had to. Jeepers, Sid, you don't know any of this. I need to get you a girlfriend."

"I'm looking into mail-order brides," I groaned.

"Seriously, when was the last time you had a date? Two years?"

"More like three. And the purpose of that one was to tell Spring that it was over. Yeah, yeah, I know. I'm one of those cads who breaks up in nice restaurants."

"Three years." Kat shook her head. "You aren't pining for Spring, are you?"

"That's the strange part," I sighed. "I'm not. I couldn't date her because she was suddenly an employee, but then I couldn't bring myself to date anyone else while she was working for me. It's like I was comforted by the fact that I was with my ex-girlfriend every day, like there was some hope for the two of us because we still worked together. And now she's gone, and the scary part is…. Heck, I don't even miss her."

"So, at the very least, now you feel like you're ready to try dating again?"

"I don't know. Are you?"

Very smooth, Myers. Would you like to stick a knife in her, too?

I closed my eyes and gritted my teeth, as though bracing for a hit.

"Sorry, Kat."

"It's okay, Sid," she chuckled. "You're right. We both need to move on."

"Kat," I said firmly. "I lost a high school romance. You lost the man you pledged the rest of your life to. Don't act like it's something you can just shrug off, especially just to make a dork like me feel better for sticking my foot in my mouth."

"I wasn't. I just meant—"

"And don't give me any crap about the ticking biological clock, either," I interrupted. "You are young and beautiful. No arguments."

"Sid, let's get married." She said it so matter-of-factly, I almost wondered if she meant it.

"Hey, if you want to try that pact where we get hitched if we're both still single when we turn thirty, I'm all for it, but we've still got about four years to go."

"We could never get married, could we?"

"Probably not. Married couples argue, we don't. We have absolutely no...."

"...sexual tension?" Kat guessed.

"Exactly. I guess I'll just have to be satisfied with a friend that I always get along with."

"As hard as that is," Kat grinned.

I could only look at her and smile. She was my employee, but it never seemed like that. Maybe that is another reason why I was such a lousy boss. I loved most of my employees too much. My staples were as much like my family as Cindy was. They were a real blessing to me and my sister. It was Kat, Clancy, and even Boris who helped us get through the loss of our father. One of my bigger fears was that I would someday be a boss who lost touch with his workers, caring only about the business. However, as long as I had my staples, there was not much risk of that. I wondered if Angel would understand that. Perhaps it was actually a good thing that she had never had a job before. My working environment might have seemed a little bizarre to anyone who had preconceived notions of what a job, or a boss for that matter, should be like.

"Sidney the hero," I mused. "I suppose I could get used to that."

"Okay, it's not *that* big of a deal!"

"Well, here's something even you can't argue with. Heroes exude wisdom, whereas I just hired a twenty-two-year-old Grover Girl who's never had a job."

"You're kidding."

"Nope."

"Sid, even Monica Presby had had a job before."

"Monica Presby had three different jobs in the month before she showed up on our doorstep."

Kat could not help shaking her head at the memory.

"That chick was unbelievable, Sid. I mean, *dumb....*"

"Well, this one's not like her. She's a bit of a smart-aleck oddball, but.... I don't know. 'Infectious' is the only word I can think of. She really grew on me, just in the couple hours she was there."

"Infectious and grows on you," Kat said snidely. "In some cultures, they call that gangrene. Is she hot?"

"Jeepers, Kat!"

"She's never had a job, she's twenty-two, she's dating Clancy, and you hired her because she 'grew on you?' Yeah right! I'm betting she looks like an adult film star."

"Actually, no she doesn't. If you must know, she's kind of cute, but she's tiny. 5-2, maybe."

"And you like tall blondes."

"And I like tall blondes," I agreed.

"5-2 is not 'tiny!'"

"Whatever. She's short. I hired her because I think the patrons will love her."

"That's what you said about Monica."

"And the male segment of our customers did love her."

"Because she looked like an adult film star," Kat stated insistently.

"Exactly. Monica had the looks, this girl actually has a personality. You'll like her, Kat. I already warned her about the pizza knife."

"Thank you." Kat was clearly relieved. "Well, I hope she works out for you, Sid. I know it's hard for you to replace Spring, no matter what you say about not missing her."

"Oh, Angel will be fine," I said confidently, then frowned slightly. "She keeps calling me 'Boss.'"

"*Angel?* She's actually called that?"

"Yeah."

"With a straight face?"

"A lot of people are named Angel."

"I can think of one Hollywood actress and a vampire. Maybe it's more common with adult film stars."

"Would you please drop it? Are you hungry? We should go grab something before the show."

"Hey, if you're buying. What do you want? Chinese? Seafood?"

"Something besides pizza. How come you never call me Boss?"

CHAPTER SIX

If nothing else, our night at the movie proved that my new staple crew was off to a good start. Angel had no trouble making new friends. We all met at my house around seven o'clock, and Angel was the one who insisted that we go to the theatre early so that we could play the arcade games in the lobby. I have never seen my sister get so involved in a game as she did with the *Blaster Buck* console she shared with Angel. Perhaps it was because Angel got so wrapped up in the game herself, frequently yelling at the digitized characters, "You call that *combat?!* My *gramma* could kick your butts! Boom, baby!" Cindy never got quite as vocal, but her blue eyes were filled with an unusual icy intensity as the onscreen aliens beat the blue blazes out of each other. She even let out a victory whoop as her purple muscleman stomped his opponent until the red health bar disappeared from the top of the screen.

"Oh yeah!" she cheered, her straight blonde hair hanging in her eyes. "Who's the champ? Me!"

If you ever want to quickly determine which pet peeves your friends or co-workers possess, just take them to the movies. Boris chewed bubble gum with his mouth open. Cindy went to the bathroom every twenty minutes. Kat told the actors what to do for the first half hour, and then fell asleep on my shoulder, paralysing my right arm for the next hour and a half. Sitting to my left, Clancy and Angel never stopped whispering and giggling, and I am fairly certain that the popcorn they were sharing was not the sole source of all the slurping and smacking I was listening to.

Hey, Myers! Now you know what it feels like to be a ghost, doomed to spend all of eternity trapped in the backseat of a honeymoon limo.

The movie was pretty standard action fare, something about Alec Baldwin and Donald Sutherland being veteran FBI agents, trying to stop Billy Bob Thornton from assassinating some high-ranking government official who was not even the President, which kind of took the fun out of the whole show. Apparently, *not* targeting the President was the film-makers' idea of originality, which was more than could be said for Jennifer Love Hewitt playing the rookie "FB Eye Candy," as Clancy described her. Angel seemed to love every second of the film, in spite of Clancy's best efforts to make the most of their two hours of darkness. The man never changed.

I grew up with my old staple crew. Kat and I used to do homework together at my house, while Cindy, Boris, and Clancy were still playing House in the basement. Cindy and Boris were always Mommy and Daddy, and Clancy was the dog. In retrospect, that explained a lot.

Then there was Spring Stevens. We used to play House with some other friends when we were younger, and I always wished that she would ask me to be Daddy, but I was too stressed out in love to wait for the impossible offer. I always cracked and volunteered to be the dog. We were both sixteen when she finally told me that she had always been waiting for me to ask her to be Mommy. I asked her out later that day.

Ten years later, I was a single man in a movie theatre, surrounded by employees. My right arm was as fast asleep as the woman leaning on it, and my left arm was just itching to reach behind Angel's seat and smack Clancy on the back of the head to get him to focus on the movie screen. In spite of all her giggling, I could tell that Angel really wanted to watch the show, but such subtleties were often lost on Clancy. In a slightly reversed way, the two of them were reminiscent of myself and Spring. She always wanted to get cuddly at the best part of the movie, and it drove me nuts. I had to watch *The Usual Suspects* three times before I could figure out that Kevin Spacey was the bad guy. Even so, one thought still came to my mind as I glanced over at Clancy and Angel.

It must be nice....

I had not missed Spring very much since she left, but I found myself suddenly wishing that she was there to spoil the surprise ending, which was a little lousy, anyway. An impromptu kissing session would have beat the heck out of realizing that Billy Bob was just a smokescreen for Baldwin's evil secret plan to assassinate the President. I hated betrayal endings, but the climax sort of made up for it. In a nutshell,

Sutherland shoots Thornton, Baldwin tries to shoot the President, Sutherland takes a bullet for the President, and Baldwin takes about fifteen bullets from Jennifer Love. As Sutherland lies dying, he tells Jennifer, "I'll be fine. I don't feel a thing." If my right arm could have talked, it would have told Kat the same thing.

Angel was actually crying when the house lights came on, quite possibly the only person in history to cry at a Jerry Bruckheimer flick, but, like she said, she was a Donald Sutherland fan. I wondered if she was one of those types who fell in love with grandfather figures, a Hollywood notion that always seemed a bit nauseating to me, but who was I to argue with Hollywood?

"Kat, wake up," I said loudly, tapping on the top of her head with a forefinger.

"Who's dead?" she croaked at the same instant that she jolted awake.

"All three male leads … and my arm," I replied, innocently.

"Oh. Crap. Sorry," she mumbled sleepily, rubbing some drool into my sleeve with her fist. "Was it any good?"

"Ah, they didn't even get the President," Boris snorted. "Any intrigue movie that doesn't end in complete political chaos…. It doesn't make the grade in my book."

"Why is Angel crying?" Something about the sleepy confusion in Kat's voice made the others laugh. Even Angel cracked a teary smile.

"It's just such a great ending!" she replied, wiping tears and grinning.

"I hate those kinds," I remarked. "You spend the whole movie watching a guy being noble and heroic, and then suddenly ... he's not. It's depressing, that's what it is."

"But I love it when the hero dies," Angel pointed out. "It's so sad, I just *love it!*"

"You love being sad?" I asked skeptically.

"I love heroism!"

Kat smiled evilly. "You should talk to Sidney.... Ow!"

"Boss, did you just kick her?" Angel seemed shocked.

"Maybe," I admitted. "We only have to be nice in the shop."

"Here, let me see that." Cindy grabbed the cuff of Kat's jeans, pulled the injured shin into her lap, and began massaging it.

"That's it. I don't love you anymore!" Kat said with mock ferocity, cuffing the back of my light brown hair.

"Don't mess with my hair," I said, dead serious. "It's my best feature."

Kat guffawed. "Sid, hydrochloric acid couldn't hurt your hair. How much gel is in there?"

"It's spray," I snapped. "Gel is for the fancy occasions."

"Just so you know, Angel," Cindy explained, "your boss is obsessed with his hair. He loves it like Clancy loves...." By the way that she abruptly cut herself off, I could only assume that she had been about to say something like "dumb chicks."

"... his mirror?" I said dryly, helping her find less offensive words.

"Hey!" Clancy exclaimed. "That is *not* ... uh ... okay, it is kinda true." Modesty never was one of Clancy's strong points.

"Well, it should be," Angel smiled, kissing Clancy quickly as she stood up and pulled on her red jacket. There were no crowds to fight to get to the exits. Besides my crew, there might have been a dozen other people in the theatre. The curse of the Chetwynd Wednesday apparently did not restrict itself to my restaurant alone. Late night entertainment in my town was somewhat limited, particularly if you did not drink or use drugs. In my case, I was pretty much restricted to watching movies and hanging out with friends. Randall Harrigan, another high school friend of mine who had just returned from studying business in Grande Prairie, was in the process of opening his own gym. He had promised me that it would be open until one o'clock in the morning, Monday through Saturday, but, until the red tape was cleared, all we had were the movies.

As we walked out into the dark street, Clancy lit a cigarette, his first one in six hours. He had been "trying to quit," ever since junior high, but could never do so for more than a week. Kat called herself a recreational smoker, and prided herself on never smoking more than a single pack in a year. I cannot stand the smell of tobacco in any form, but that was not the reason that I grabbed Boris and hauled him away from the group, over to my truck. I had something more pressing than second hand smoke on my mind.

"What?" Boris demanded, rubbing the left ear that I had been towing him by.

"*Why didn't you tell me that we were getting a Redmond's Ribs?*" I hissed through gritted teeth.

"Why would you need to know?" he replied in that maddening apathetic tone which he liked to use when I was obviously dying for want of information.

"Because I would not be the first restaurant to go out of business within two months of Little Maple moving in next door!"

"Little who?"

"You have absolutely no culture, you know that?"

"Sid, you told me that Cindy was the reactional one. Cool down, man. This cannot be that bad. We've survived the opening of every other big chain that's hit the town. We can handle anything."

"Boris, no one can compete with Redmond. They're the best. And, as their competition, it's bloody hard for me to say that. All the class of a five star, all the fun of a drive thru, and the prices of a freaking dollar store! Their ingredients are so fresh they must grow their own produce in the basement, the staff wears tuxedo shirts and cummerbunds, and, to top it all off, they have those mouth-wateringly delicious maple roasted ribs which absolutely no one else can figure out how to make! They're *unstoppable!*"

"Wow." Boris looked impressed. "Have you ever thought of doing a commercial for them?"

"Have you ever considered being in the '*Don't Let This Happen To You*' ads?" I growled.

"Sorry. But, we deliver to your door."

"So do they!"

"Oh … well, their delivery drivers aren't as good as me. I know the people in this town, and they love me."

"No kidding…. But, Redmond's drivers drive fancy company cars with logos on the doors."

"And I can make *lawyers* consider it a privilege to give me a 30% tip. I'd like to see one of those Redmond hacks do that."

"Redmond's drivers have insulated oven bags that actually time release heat to keep the food warm."

"Chetwynd is too small for the food to get cold anyway."

"And they carry portable interac machines."

"Those *scum-suckers!*" Boris gasped, appalled. "Crap, we're toast! I don't even know how to write a resume."

"What are *you* worried about?" I said, disgusted. "Your gratuity account could tide you over for about three years, and you'd never have to work a single day of them. The rest of us little people are the ones who can panic about this."

"I don't want to use my life savings just because I don't have a portable interac! That account is what's going to let me retire at 35."

"You honestly believe that?"

"Just watch me, Sid."

"Look, man, who told you Redmond was coming? I need to know if this is for real."

"Sid, you should know better than to even ask."

"I know. And maybe Cindy should know that when you two broke up last year, you were reported to be spending a lot of time with one Roxanne Ardent … aka 'Foxy Roxy.'"

"Sid, you're *evil!*" Boris's voice was a panicky whisper, his hands frantically gesturing for me to keep my voice lowered.

"Actually, she probably already knows. Hey, Cindy!"

"Jeffrey Morrow!" Boris snapped.

"Who?"

"You know, Councilman Morrow? Town council, works with the mayor, handles zoning issues, does a great Tim McGraw at karioke night? That guy?"

"You're telling me ... that a member of the zoning board just happened to *tell you* ... about a major real estate development?"

Boris rolled his eyes. "Sid, pay attention. Jeffrey Morrow, 5243 Centurion Crescent, off 47th Avenue in the Crown Sub-Division. Orders two large pepperoni and mushrooms with extra cheese and olives on the side, easy done, not too much sauce, every Friday around seven p.m. He tips five bucks, unless his kids get the door, in which case I get two. He always asks if I caught the game, then tells me about the boring board meeting that made him miss it. People trust me, Sid. I have an inquisitive yet secretive face."

"Who told you that?"

"My mom. Anyway, there's nothing for certain yet. It's like that Super 8 Motel we're always supposed to be getting."

"We're getting a Super 8?"

"My point exactly. Now, if you're finished grilling me, I was going to take Cindy for a drive. You can take everyone else home, right?"

"I'll take Kat," I replied. "I don't think Clancy will want to miss out on this moonlit walk opportunity."

"How long do you give them?" Boris inquired, grinning. "A couple more weeks?"

"I don't know. She really seems to like him. I'll give them a month."

"Twenty bucks?"

"You're on."

"Silver, gold, diamond…." Boris mused, glancing over at Clancy and Angel, who were hugging under the glowing neon marquee over the theatres main entrance. "What do you call a one month anniversary? Clay? Peat?"

"Lignite," I guessed. "In any case, I don't think Clancy's ever reached that landmark occasion yet. Maybe she's the one. Did you know she's never had a job?"

"Really?" Boris obviously was unaware of that.

"Really. This is vocation number one."

"She must have rich parents," Boris said presumptively. "Just our luck, we're getting a spoiled rich brat."

"I don't think so." I shook my head. "She's got too much of a cutesy, sweetie-pie thing going for her to be living off Daddy's plastic."

"Yeah, she's pretty cool that way," Boris admitted. "So, what do you think's the deal with her?"

I raised my hands resignedly. "It's her story, not ours. I just hope she can serve coffee. Unless you want to give up deliveries and let her drive. You'd be a good waitress."

"Don't even joke about that." Boris's eyes were narrowed and hard.

"Sorry," I cackled. "But I do want to train her as your back-up, just for Fridays and Saturdays, in case you get swamped. Teach her, okay?"

"*My young apprentice,*" Boris gargled his great impression of the *Star Wars* Emperor. "You don't want to be back-up anymore?"

"I'll still drive on your day off, but, if possible, I like to stay in the kitchen when it gets busy."

"Get her to take a few tomorrow," Boris suggested. "The dining room's usually empty after eight, anyway, ever since you took the Non-Stop Shrimp Thursdays off the menu. It's all just pick-ups and deliveries until twelve. You know, I still miss that shrimp. We should bring it back."

"Boris, the way food prices are going up, I'm not even sure how long we can keep the All You Can Eat Hot Wings."

"You're cutting the hot wings, too?! Are you insane? Big Ronnie would kill us." He had a point. Sixty-eight-year-old Big Ronnie Alders took advantage of our hot wing special at least three nights per week, and four hundred pound customers were the ones whom I really did not want to offend.

"Look, I hate to say this," I groaned. "We put the 'Limited' in 'Limited Company.' Big Ronnie may have to find his non-stop cholesterol somewhere else."

"Like Redmond's Ribs?" Boris said mildly. "I hear their wings come in seven different flavours."

"Shut up, Boris."

"Reactional…."

"Go away."

"Already gone, man." He was turning back to the others as he spoke, and strode briskly away.

Your sister could one day bear that man's children.... *Heaven help us all.*

I needed a coffee.

"Kat, let's get some caffeine," I said loudly, unlocking the Chevy truck and climbing inside, the old door creaking on sticky hinges as I slammed it shut and rolled down the window. The evening was warm, and, with no hint of wind, the night air was a little muggy and humid. Even so, it was my favourite time of year. The last grey drifts of snow had melted from the curbs, and the trees were finally becoming more green than pale brown. May in Chetwynd always felt like a clean slate, the late spring flurries and thaw mud wiped away, and not yet marred by the smears of stifling valley heat or mosquitos. It was a time for barbecues, girls in tank tops, and sitting on the front lawn in white plastic reclining chairs, looking up at the stars without a jacket on. On May evenings, Chetwynd was at peace. I liked to think that we needed to have May twice a year. I certainly would not have complained if March was replaced with another May. I *really* hated March.

"See you guys tomorrow," Kat called over her shoulder as she clambered into the passenger seat. A small puff of dust rose from the tattered, blue dashboard as she banged her door shut. My truck was in better condition than Clancy's, but it was still eleven years old. I dreaded the day when I would have to trade Sid's Rig for a newer model. My truck was a defining aspect of my life, almost as much as my staple crew and my coffee mug.

Boris and Cindy waved as they drove by behind us in the black Trans Am, and Clancy stopped kissing Angel long enough to toss us a quick thumbs up as we backed out into the empty street.

"Bye, Boss! Bye, Kat!" Angel quipped, taking advantage of the three seconds when she had her lips to herself.

"I wish them all the best," Kat said with a smile, leaning back on her headrest as I eased the truck forward, the bouncing headlights illuminating the drug store, bank and grocery store along the same street. "It'll never last."

"It never does," I shrugged. "How's she doing in the first impression department?"

"Well, she doesn't look like a porn star."

"Okay…. That's not always a bad thing."

"Honestly, Sid? She's a bit of a spaz."

"So is Boris," I replied, turning past the grocery store to the solitary set of traffic lights, the all-night coffee shop appearing just on the far side of them. The light above my truck was green, but I stopped to allow old Rob Gorman to continue his drunken stagger across the intersection. The man never bothered to look both ways or check for a green light. It was a miracle that he was still alive. I sometimes wondered if he was even the slightest bit aware of anything except the direction of the bar that he was resolutely shuffling toward.

Does this guy have a life? Did he ever?

"Let's move, Robbie," I called out the window, firmly but without sounding rude. "You're holding up traffic, bud."

Rob made a concerted effort to veer from his path, turning his grizzled face to Kat's passenger window. His foul breath seemed to fill every inch of the cab. I had never seen such wide, bleary eyes.

"You have to watch the traffic lights, Rob," Kat reminded him kindly. "You don't want to get hit by a bus, right?"

Rob stuttered out a few slurred syllables, each one seeming to drain what strength was left in his slouching form. It sounded like some form of apology.

"You have to be careful," Kat answered. "It's dark. Hard to see. Someone in a bus might not have seen you, okay?"

Rob began spewing out his unintelligible mumbling, motioning in the direction of the bar down the street to our right.

"The bar's only a hundred yards away," I said, more bored than annoyed. "You don't need a ride there."

"I think you should get a ride home, Rob," Kat suggested gently. "Can you call a cab?"

Rob shook his head defiantly, and made a few demanding grumbles, scratching his stubbly beard.

"We're not going to the lake," I replied. "You need to find another ride or call a cab. Okay?"

Rob kept muttering as he looked back at the bar, just to make sure that it was still there. I did not even want to know when his denim jacket and grungy sweat pants had been washed last, most likely around the same time that he had last taken a bath.

"There's a phone over at the coffee shop, see?" Kat was pointing across the street. "You can call a cab from there. Then you can get some sleep in your own bed. Wouldn't that feel good?"

The old man was pleading now, gripping the window base with both hands to make standing easier.

"No, I'm not coming with you," Kat laughed. "You need to get some sleep. You go call a cab, okay?"

His tired eyes eventually found the pay phone, and he actually fell silent as he stared at it for a long time. Then, shaking his head as though he had just recovered his senses, he turned away and scuffed his grungy shoes onwards toward the bar. He was still mumbling, whether to us or to himself, I could not tell. We watched him go.

"You know what's really sad?" Kat said, sounding depressed.

"Besides the obvious?"

"He started out like every partying teenager in this town. He just wanted to forget some troubles, or have a good time. Now, it's his whole life."

"He doesn't have a life," I muttered. "He's just a shell. Half the kids in this town will end up just like him." I turned my attention back to the road, but the light was just turning red.

"He's more than a shell, Sid," Kat scolded me tacitly.

"Are you telling me you can still see a man in there?" I said disgustedly. "He's a zombie who's been uncorking his own grave for fifty years. All those kids who think they won't end up like him are just deluding themselves. Hey, it's all just fun, right? 'Take a hit, pass it on. Chug! Chug!' Bunch of idiots…."

"I like to think there's still hope for everyone," Kat commented. "Sometimes a good hangover is all it takes to put a kid back on the right path."

"Are you serious, Kat?" I said, turning in my seat to face her. "Have you ever listened to a so-called teenage battle of wits in this town, lately? 'You're a loser.' 'You're so stupid.' 'You're a bleeping-bleep-bleep.' That's the best retorts they can come up with. And they're not just naturally stupid. They've fried themselves right out of the realm of intelligent dialogue."

"You spend half of your time at the shop saying 'Shut up, Boris,'" Kat reminded me.

"I'm just using words he understands," I said defensively.

"Green light," Kat said.

I drove through the intersection and parked by the row of pay phones beside the coffee shop entrance. The parking lot was all but empty, except for one man at the pumps, fuelling up his tan suburban.

"Coffee at 10:30," Kat murmured. "And then you tell Boris that he doesn't get enough sleep. You mind if I just get a doughnut?"

"You never drink coffee, do you?"

"Yuck."

"Bite your tongue. It's *life*."

"It's bad for you."

"And doughnuts aren't?"

"I run six miles a day. I can afford the odd doughnut."

"I compromise," I smiled. "I only use the low-cal sweetener."

Kat snorted derisively as she undid her seatbelt and began fighting with her sticky door handle.

"Kat?"

"Yeah?"

"That Linda Matthews lady you were talking to.... Did she say when she would call back?"

"Actually, she asked if you could call her sometime tomorrow. I wrote her office number in the kitchen log for you. Are you actually going to call?"

"She wants to talk. We'll talk."

"Well, don't sound so enthusiastic...."

"Believe me, Kat, I sound more enthusiastic than I am."

"Just do it, okay? For your dad."

"Yeah," I sighed, kicking my own door open. "For Dad."

CHAPTER SEVEN

I was always amazed by the way that a lot of people talked when they called my shop to order pizza. People who could chat for hours with friends, thanks to their great monthly plans, seemed to be at an utter loss of coherence when ordering take-out.

As I walked back into the kitchen after delivering the fifty pizzas to the elementary school on Thursday morning, the phone by the coffee mug cupboard began ringing. Kat and Becky Lowell, our newest student recruit, were busy sheeting dough, both wearing white, sleeved aprons over their uniforms. I picked up the phone on the second ring, grabbing for a bill book and pen, both of which were supposed to sit right beside the phone at all times, but had a tendency to drift over the course of a work shift.

"By The Slice," I said brightly, neatly disguising my misery after a truly lousy night's sleep, followed by a foggy drive with fifty steaming pizzas turning my extended cab truck into a sauna.

"Uh ... hello?" the puzzled, dull voice on the other end replied. "You guys got pizza?"

No, you idiot, we just keep the words 'Slice' and 'Pizza' on the sign over the door because of their sentimental value.

"We sure do, sir," I said, scribbling the date on the top of the bill.

"Oh…. Can I make an order?"

No. You can't.

"Ah sure, why not?" I said it as though I was doing him a special favour. "What can we get you?"

"Uuuummm…. Uh, do you … um, do you got the…. What is it? Uh, I think it's…. Hey, guys! What do we want?"

Does it ever occur to you to decide that before you call?

Other muffled voices began carrying over the phone line.

"Large!"

"Something with ham!"

"Get pineapple on it, too!"

"Yeah! Pineapple!"

"A Hawaiian!"

"Ask if they have a Hawaiian!"

"Uh … do you guys got Hawaiian?"

"We do, sir," I quipped briskly, tapping my pen impatiently against the pad.

"Oh … okay…. Can we get one large Meatlover?"

"One large Meatlover. You got it." I spend more time rolling my eyes on the phone than I do while training students to use the cash register.

"But, can we get that with no onions, and no olives? No feta, either."

Which part of the word 'Meatlover' confuses you?

"I think we can do that for you, sir. Pick-up or delivery?"

"Uh…. Do you deliver?"

No. We don't.

"We sure do. Where to?"

"Uh…. Dude! Where are we?"

"Spruce Lane Apartments, 208!" a background voice shouted back at him.

Hi, Devon.

"Uh…. We're at Spruce Lane Apartments, number 103."

"103?" I said skeptically. "Are you sure?"

"Oh, sorry…. Guys! What number did you say?"

"You're at Devon Finn's apartment," I informed him, simply writing 'Devon's' at the top of the bill. "Spruce Lane, 208. You were only off by a hundred and five numbers." Speed at math is an asset in the world of veiled sarcasm.

"How'd you know that?"

It seemed like a good time to steal from Boris.

"I'm the pizza guy. I know everything. It'll be there in about thirty minutes."

"Thanks, dude."

"You're very welcome, sir," I said dashingly, hanging up the phone. "Idiot."

I lived in a cycle of unfulfilled dreams, and one of them was to be the owner of an elitist, five star dining establishment that catered chiefly to the triple-A grade of society. I lived in the wrong town. Chetwynd was still classified as a village, so any business that wished to pander to high society only would be patronized by approximately six customers, and would go out of business in about as many days. Still, I refused to acknowledge my hometown as a redneck nesting ground, although I certainly would not be the first to do so. Suffice to say, we did not have a Rolls Royce dealership there. In fact, the only cars for sale in Chetwynd were parked on the front yards of private residences, with a phone number on the windshield, and one or more flat tires.

I did try to keep my establishment upscale. The formal dress code for employees definitely helped, and I did not tolerate unkempt appearance or dirty fingernails. I admit it; I was a *bona fide* "square," but it had kept my business in the black ever since I took over management. The hardest part was finding employees who were willing to give up their quasi-rebellious grunge looks, or at least get a haircut. Of the three students whom I had fired that year, two were terminated partly as a result of poor grooming, along with tardiness, absences, and coming to work while stoned. The third one was fired because he was, to put it honestly, a slack-jawed dork. Either I was a lousy character judge, or these teenagers knew how to mask their unbridled stupidity just long enough to pass a job interview. My biggest worry in regards to hiring Angel was that she seemed like the perfect server type to me, and thus was certain to end up being an overdue volcano nearing the end of its dormancy period. So far, I had had the most success with the people whom I had been most certain would not work out, i.e., Boris.

"Kat, I need a large Meatlover, no onions, olives, or feta," I called across the kitchen, as I finished scribbling the price on the bottom line and hung the bill on the sliding steel rack over the main prep table.

"Is that those morons in Spruce Lane?" Kat demanded, her back still turned to me.

"Yep," I said, looking in the mirror which hangs over the telephone as I straightened my tie. When I turned around, Becky was already making the pizza. She was a short, chubby Native girl with glasses, eighteen years old, who rarely spoke, but obviously listened well. Kat said that Becky was the best help I had hired all year, which I assumed was a compliment, but could not be sure. Kat was also a master of veiled sarcasm.

Becky was fast. She was sprinkling the final shreds of grated cheese over the sausage slices within thirty seconds of setting the pan on the stainless steel prep counter, then slid it into the oven and set the egg timer for fifteen minutes. Without a word, she walked back to the sheeting counter and resumed spreading tomato sauce on the fresh pizza crusts. The crusts would then be refrigerated until needed. Business was usually slow until noon, which was why the opening crew was referred to as the prep shift. The basic idea was to get as much preparation done as possible before the dinner and supper rushes began. The restaurant was void of customers at that moment, so there was no worry of falling behind, especially as we were about to get some extra help.

"Hi, Boss."

We all turned to the kitchen entrance. Angel was standing politely in the doorway, hands folded in front of her black skirt, head cocked to one side as though waiting to be invited in. Her tight navy blue turtleneck sweater looked expensive, as did her glossy black shoes. She was early.

"Angel," I said. "Very decent of you to be here in good time."

"Aw shucks, don't mention it, Boss. No way I'm going to be late for my first day of work!"

"Angel, you're four hours early."

"Do I get a gold star?" She smiled sweetly.

"No. You get a uniform. Kat?"

"I'm all over it," Kat replied, towelling flour from her hands as she walked briskly to the back storage/laundry room, where extra uniforms were stored in a closet. "Small vest and shirt should be about right."

"Cherry red vest!" Angel called after her.

"And a sexy bow-tie," I said loudly.

"Boss, you remembered!"

"It's hard to forget."

"Well, you look snazzy. I guess black and white is a good look for you. You hate those shoes you're wearing, don't you?"

I looked sharply at her, startled.

"How'd you know that?"

"I always know," she shrugged. "My high school majors were fashion design and marketing. Why don't you just wear those cowboy boots? They'd match the outfit if you switched to black Wrangler jeans. 'Urban cowboy' is a style that would really work for you."

"Thanks for the input," I sighed. "I'll bring that up at the next staff meeting."

"Hey, I'm great if you ever need fashion advice."

"I don't doubt it. Angel, Becky. Becky, Angel."

"Hi, Becky!"

Becky smiled, nodded, and kept on working.

"Cool. We have *staff meetings?*" Angel was in awe of her apparently amazing good fortune.

"Don't get too excited," I cautioned her. "We usually only have staff meetings to chew everybody out for repeated screw ups."

"But, still, it just sounds so *official!* Staff … meeting…." She seemed to relish the taste of every word as she followed Kat to the back room.

Okay, I wasn't totally convinced before, but I am now. This girl has never had a job….

I glanced down at my own black shoes. I did hate them. They did not have the cushioning of running shoes, and could never be broken in like my Ropers. I did not own a pair of black Wranglers. Suddenly, those cowboy jeans seemed like a top priority.

I wished that I was a cowboy. A cowboy would have had the "gumption" to make the phone call which I was so loathe to make, and yet wanted so badly to get over with. I reluctantly picked up the kitchen log, a two hundred page spiral notebook, and shut myself in my office. Setting the book open on my desk, I flipped through to the latest entry, dated Tuesday. Kat had filled it in with her near perfect handwriting.

"Pretty busy night," she had written. *"Note to self: We'll need another lasagna cooked on Thursday, used most of it tonight. Sid, do we have any more salad dressing coming in? Might have to pick some up at the store if you didn't order it, almost out. Herb Bolant from Evergreen Trailer Court #15 called again, said that he found a hair in the pizza he ordered two months ago, wanted a free one. You have to admire his perseverance, the drunken bum…. One complaint from some old guy who claimed to have found a human tooth*

in his sirloin, but we figured it out: Guys with dentures should not eat rare steak. We're almost out of romaine lettuce, too. Hey Sid, a lady from 30 Days Up North wants you to call her about a business profile or something. Kat "The Chief" MacDonnell.

Under the phone number, Boris had scrawled, *"Those freaking elementary kids want fifty large pizzas for Thursday at 11:30. There goes the weekend...."*

I snatched the receiver off the black phone on my desk and punched in Linda Matthews' Dawson Creek phone number. The phone only rang once.

"Linda Matthews," a rather eloquent female voice introduced herself. She sounded to be in her forties.

"Ms. Matthews, this is Sidney Myers. I understand you wished to speak with me?"

"Ah yes, Mr. Myers, thank you for calling back. As I believe you know, *30 Days Up North* is a regional publication, focussing on Peace Region businesses. We are particularly interested in small, independent businesses which have achieved long term success. As I understand it, your restaurant has been open and thriving for.... Is it twenty-five years?"

"Twenty-seven, actually," I replied. "Karl Myers, my father, founded it in 1976, about a year before I was born."

"And he ran the business right up until his passing?"

"That's correct."

"And, how long have you been the owner?"

"Four years, ma'am. But, I've worked here steady for eleven years. Heck, I was making pizzas ever since I was five."

"That is great. I would definitely mention that in the article. I was wondering when would be an opportune time for me to have a full interview? I can be in Chetwynd just about any day of the week."

I cringed, and grabbed a pen off my desk, twirling it between my fingers to calm myself.

"You mean we can't do it over the phone?"

"Well … we could, but it would be better if I could visit the restaurant, take some photos, interview the staff and patrons, maybe try some of your pizza, hmm? Unless that would be an imposition. I would understand that completely."

"No, it's no impossession, ma'am…"

Impossession? Myers, you idiot....

"… but, it's just that … uh…. Heck, when's a good time for you?"

She just said any day is fine!

"Oh…." Linda Matthews was somewhat taken aback. "Well, this month's issue is already being prepared for distribution, and our deadline is mid month, so … would sometime early next month be convenient?"

"Sure! No problem. Early June…. How about June first? That's early. Right?"

"Uh, certainly. Sunday, June first. What time should I schedule?"

"June first is fine."

"Yes, but what *time?*"

"Oh, uh … anytime. We're open from ten until midnight, and I'm always here. Brown hair, 5-10, black vest, and cowboy boots."

"Okay, I … guess I'll know how to spot you."

"That's 10 *a.m.*, to midnight, not p.m."

"Yes, I had figured that you would be open for more than two hours a day, but thank you. I look forward to meeting you, Mr. Myers."

"You can bring your husband!" I blurted.

"Excuse me, what was that?" The woman clearly could not believe her ears.

"I mean ... unless you don't have one. That's fine too. Bring a friend."

"Okay...."

"Sorry, I gotta go, Miss Myers.... Matthews! Ms.! Sorry. Bye."

"Thank you very much. Goodbye."

Actually, I was often more amazed at how *I* talked on the phone. I hung up and emptied Sidney's Cup of Wrath in one long, cold swig.

"*KAT!*"

Kat cautiously cracked the door open and peeked into my office.

"Are you going to throw something?" she asked suspiciously.

"I hate telephones!"

"So, you called her?" Kat looked relieved as she pulled up the folding chair across from me.

"You know I hate telephones. Why can't you make those kind of calls?"

"Because ... she wanted to talk to you...." Kat's slow voice clearly implied that I was an idiot, an implication which I could not have argued with, anyway. "It's the owner's job to make the important calls ... or, the assistant manager's," she added innocently.

"Can't I just make you my secretary, instead?"

"You're funny, Sid, but you're not hilarious."

"That woman probably thinks I'm on crack. I asked her if June first was 'early next month.'"

"Hey, you got the month right."

"Crap! How's Angel doing?"

"She's trying to figure out the bow-ties."

"They're clip-ons. What's to figure?"

"They're *clasp-ons*. Those clasps can be tricky. Anyway, what do I do with her? You can't pay her for four extra hours. There's not much to do, right now."

"Scrubbing the dish cupboards?" I suggested.

Kat shook her head. "I made Clancy and that Sammy kid do them on Monday. The place is spotless."

"Well, we can find something for her. I mean, she wants to work…."

"Can't you take her on the delivery with you? You wanted her to be a back-up, right?"

"Yeah, I could, but…."

"Take her, Sid! Her … bubbliness is already getting on my nerves. At least Becky let's me work in peace."

"You're jealous, aren't you?" This was a delightfully unexpected twist.

"Jealous?" Kat was confused. "Of what?"

"Angel," I chortled. "She's dating Clancy. I bet you actually miss all his pick-up lines when he gets a new girlfriend."

"I'm not jealous!"

"Yeah. Cain said that to Abel, once."

"Just take her, okay? See how well she can handle those slacker stoners at Spruce Lane."

"Good point," I agreed. "208. That's Devon Finn's place. If she can handle him, she can handle anyone."

"What, is he a dealer?"

"Yes. Don't you remember Devon? A couple grades below us in high school? A chemistry whiz with no ambitions except being a wannabe dope pusher? He'll probably try to sell her a dime-bag instead of paying for the pizza."

"One of the really subtle ones, huh?"

"Yeah, it's amazing that he's never been busted yet. But, that just makes him cocky. They'll get him someday."

"But, until our tax dollars start paying for his three squares a day, we have to feed him," Kat sighed. "Wait a sec.... I think I remember. Devon Finn.... Doesn't he have kids?"

"Yeah, two kids. Heck, he had his first one when he was like fifteen or sixteen. That kid's gotta be … nine or ten, now, I guess."

"Yeah, I remember. Debbie Browning was the mother, right? Is she still with that loser?"

"I think so. It's sad."

"Does he tip?"

"Most drug dealers do. I always feel weird taking it, though. It's not like our dealers go around whacking people, but still...."

"It's the world we live in, Sid," Kat said acceptantly. "Love it, just don't be a part of it."

"No offense, Kat, but that kind of sounds like a dumb philosophy."

"It's not a philosophy. It's the rule that's kept me from getting into drugs."

"Have you ever wanted to?" I was curious.

"Not really." Kat shook her head. "I'll have a beer with friends, but anything hallucinogenic is too left of centre for me. How about you?"

"I almost got into it, once," I intoned. "When I was sixteen, I smoked a joint at a party. I guess I have Boris's Catholic guilt, because I could barely look anyone in the eye for a week. A few years later, some friends started offering it again, and this time I thought, 'Hey, everyone's doing it. They ain't dead.' But, then…." I sighed and let the sentence hang in the air.

"But, then your dad died," Kat guessed.

"And, presto, Sidney Myers only drinks coffee."

"And I respect that," Kat nodded. "But, I can never forget those nights when Roger and I would stay at home, and light candles in the dark, and he would open a bottle of wine. Those were the best nights of my life."

"You kept it at home. You never got behind the wheel."

Becky appeared at the door, knocking lightly on the doorframe.

"The pizza's ready," she said quietly, and was gone again before I could even open my mouth to say, "Thanks, Becky."

"She's a bit of a ghost, isn't she?" I observed.

"Yeah, but she's worth her weight in gold in the kitchen." Kat sounded like a proud mentor.

I stood up and grabbed my burgundy windbreaker from the back of my chair.

"Angel!" I barked, sliding my arms into the rustling sleeves.

Angel staggered into the office, looking both attractive and comical in her new, snug red vest and long sleeved white blouse, as she furiously fumbled with the bow-tie. Her long, thick hair hung loose on her shoulders, but was getting messy from the strain of the battle.

"This does not work!" she said, frustrated as the elastic neck strap slipped from her grasp and snapped back out of sight under her collar.

"Here, let me see," Kat sighed, standing and flipping Angel's collar up. With one flick of her wrists, she had the elastic clasped onto the bow. "There. It's not hard."

"It's slippery!" Angel complained, as Kat walked around her to straighten the creases out of the collar.

"But, it's sexy," I said dryly, zipping up my jacket. "Angel, you're riding with me. Welcome to Pizza Delivery 101."

"Sweet!" Angel cheered, instantly gleeful again. "Can I drive?"

"No." I strode out of the office, Angel right on my heels. "So, how well do you know the town, so far?"

"My house and the grocery store," she admitted.

I pointed to a large map of Chetwynd, posted on the wall over the pizza warmer.

"This is Chetwynd, deconstructed into a bunch of tiny squares with numbers on them. Get to know this map. The main subdivisions are colour coded. We're going to Spruce Lane Apartments, right on the eastern outskirts of town, past the RV park, right here." I tapped the spot on the bottom right corner of the map.

"Got it," Angel said solemnly. "That's those three townhouses just off to the right on the way out to Dawson Creek, right?"

"Very good," I congratulated her, turning and pointing to the white pizza box sitting on the steel rack in the large, glass warmer, lit up pink by the red heat lamps. "That is the pizza warmer. The white box in it is called a *pizza box*. There is a *pizza* in it. Remove the pizza and pizza box from the pizza warmer, and place them inside one of the canvas pizza bags on the bottom shelf."

Angel obeyed, seeming to take the mundane chore very seriously.

"Sid, some people do get offended by condescension," Kat whispered, standing just behind me.

After Angel had bagged the pizza, I led her to the front desk of the reception area, and popped open the change drawer on the cash register.

"This is the cash register," I said in my bored tour guide voice. "Do not touch it." I quickly counted out several bills and a handful of coins. "This is fifty dollars in various denominations of Canadian currency. Do not lose it. It is called your float, and you will use it to make change on your deliveries. At the end of the shift, put it back."

"I thought I didn't touch the till."

"Put it back indirectly. Give it to myself, Cindy, Clancy, or Kat, and we'll put it back."

"Got it."

"Now, most people will not want all of their change, which leaves you with a surplus, which counts as your tips. Also, you will notice that there is a bill stuck to the lid of the pizza box, with the customer's name, number, home address, and total price. Add one dollar to the bottom line of any delivery. That is the delivery fee, and it is also yours. Any questions?"

"Yeah. Do we have a portable interac machine?"

"No."

"Do you have boxes for everything here? You know, steak boxes, baked potato boxes, soup of the day boxes?"

"We have a 'pizzas only' delivery policy. We tried delivering everything before, but no one really ordered anything except the pizzas, with a few really irritating exceptions. Have you ever tried delivering a dozen banana splits? It ain't pretty. Let's go."

"Cool. We have banana splits?" Angel still sounded awed as she followed me outside.

We both attacked the rusty-hinged doors of Sid's Rig, managed to wrench them open, and climbed inside. Angel held the pizza on her lap as I gunned the engine into a roaring, rattly life and pulled out of the parking lot. We took a right turn off the access road onto main street, and rumbled down the highway. Noon traffic was not very heavy as we headed out of town, the May sky overcast, but not rainy.

"One thing you'll notice right away on night deliveries," I explained. "The street lighting in Chetwynd stinks. Also, a lot of people seem to enjoy hiding their house numbers with shrubbery, burnt out porch lights, or just by painting them the same colour as the rest of the house. In those cases, use process of elimination, figure out the spacing between the numbers and just count down. If that doesn't work, call the house and get a description of it and any vehicles in the driveway. And, if all else fails, just look for a house with the living room light on, and a bunch of slack-jawed kids staring out the window. They always look a bit like E.T. '*Waaaahhh ...!*'" I always prided myself on my E.T. impression. Angel laughed.

"Do you have a cell phone?" I asked. "They're lifesavers on this job."

"Actually, that's all I have. I haven't hooked up a phone at my house yet."

"Where are you living?"

"Long Road Place," she answered. "The duplexes past the ball diamond in the Rodeo Sub."

"I've seen those," I noted. "They're pretty nice places. What's the rent?"

"Oh, not too much." She was looking at her shoes again, just like she had when I asked about her moving here. She obviously did not like talking about her home life.

She's running from something....

"Do you have family around here?" That question seemed safe enough.

"Nah, my parents live outside of Edmonton. It's just me here."

So, what in the world are you doing here?

Very few people would just move to Chetwynd and look for a job. People were either born there, or came in response to a job offer. Furthermore, it seemed as though most girls Angel's age were desperate to get *out* of Chetwynd, not move in and settle down.

I took another right onto the gravel driveway leading to Spruce Lane Apartments, three long, green townhouses, set up in a horseshoe pattern with the driveway making a complete circle around them. I followed the curved, bumpy road around to the second building and eased to a stop in front of the rickety wooden steps of door 208, in the narrow space between Devon Finn's white Ford Mustang and blue 3500 Dodge Ram.

Spruce Lane Apartments had once been among the finest in town, but had long since become dilapidated under shoddy management. Some of Chetwynd's more cynical citizens had taken to referring to the townhouses as "Welfare Way."

"This is Devon Finn's place," I said blandly. "He's one of our many resident dope pushers. You can tell by the low income housing and the high income cars. Smile, and remember to thank him if he tips you, which he will, because you're female."

"You don't mince words, do you, Boss?"

"I give it to you straight."

"Wow," Angel said, ramming the door with her shoulder to bash it open. "I get to meet a real, live drug dealer."

"Get used to it, Miss Bates."

I watched Angel carefully navigate the front steps, each one wobbling dangerously under her foot as she settled her weight onto it.

What a dump.... I could build three cars from all the parts leaning against this building alone. Is that the hood from a Volkswagen? Who keeps this stuff?

Devon Finn was a man who would have been handsome if he had smiled once in a while. I had seen him leer at girls occasionally, but he usually just looked tired and bored. I doubt that he was full Indian, but I knew that his mother was. I had no idea who his father was, or even if he was alive. Devon had dark skin and long black hair, which made his emerald green eyes seem out of place. I could see them light up a bit when he saw who was bringing his pizza, but he still had that same vacant expression on his face. I had heard that the smart drug dealers never touched their own product, but I did not believe that Devon was one of the smart ones. He certainly was not careful about hiding his profits. Aside from the expensive vehicles, his house was filled with big screen televisions, surround sound systems, and his shelves were lined with CDs and DVDs. He had a lot of weights and workout equipment as well, and his sleeveless shirt was proof enough that he used all of them regularly.

Devon could be pleasant, though. He was never rude to me or Boris when we delivered to him, and he was being downright chatty with Angel, although that was most likely just him trying to make a good first impression on a cute girl, and he definitely was not getting any help in that area by his company. I could see several teenage boys wandering around inside the apartment, shouting curses and laughing.

The friends who will stick by you until you get busted or run out of marijuana.... Welcome to Chetwynd, Angel.

I often wondered how Devon had started down this road. In high school, he had been an absolute genius in science, chemistry, and biology. The teachers virtually sang his praises to the skies, and spoke of how he would go on to UBC, or the U of A, or medical school. Yet, somehow, the man destined for a doctorate had ended up on Welfare Way, and seemed quite content.

Devon even shook Angel's hand after paying for his pizza. He was smooth about it, too. First, he shook her hand twice, and then just held it still for a moment, letting his hand linger on hers, while appearing to be enraptured by her face. Pretending to start back to his senses, he gave a little nervous laugh, and fidgeted sheepishly as he backed through the doorway, waving at her. Angel cheerily waved back as she clambered down the stairs. She was trying not to laugh, an effort that was immediately abandoned once she was back in the truck.

"Boss, did you see that? He actually tried the reluctant release handshake on me! Girls stop falling for that after the age of thirteen! Ha!"

"Yeah," I grinned. "*No one* falls for that anymore."

Oh.... So, I was wasting my time when I introduced myself to that hot little bank teller last week....

CHAPTER EIGHT

Angel got a three-dollar tip from Devon Finn, which was pretty good, although Boris could usually snooker at least five bucks out of anyone, regardless of the size of their order. I just wished that Boris was also possessed with Angel's sense of punctuality. I had worked with him for six years, and had never seen him come into work less than five minutes late. I believe that his record was three years earlier, when he had walked into the restaurant at nine minutes before midnight, and asked, "Hey, do I work tonight?" His punishment of working the next three weeks straight, including maintenance work on Wednesdays, was probably illegal, but very satisfying as well.

The bottom line was that I could not fire Boris, for more than an hour, anyway. His customers loved him. The whole business would have suffered if I had ever put the boot in his butt. The fact that my sister was madly in love with him raised some serious job security issues as well, and I did not need the headaches. I had a hard enough time sleeping as it was.

Clancy and Cindy arrived for work almost on the stroke of 3:30, and Boris was only about seven minutes behind them, which was actually good time for him. His average was sixteen minutes late, and I knew this because Kat and I had once kept track of his arrival time, every day, for two months. When I had confronted him with this exhaustive scientific assessment of his tardiness, his response was, if I recall correctly, "Huh, whattaya know…. Do I have any deliveries up?"

I was in the back laundry room, folding the load of forest green tablecloths which had just come out of the dryer when Boris arrived. He shuffled in apologetically, head low, hands in his pockets, trying to look meek. The old washing machine was roaring through a load of aprons.

"Hey, sorry I'm late," Boris said, as he did every day.

"No problem," I growled, as I did every day.

"Look, Sid, I gotta talk to you. You got a second?"

"Folding laundry doesn't affect my hearing."

"I need to marry Cindy."

I froze in mid fold.

"Excuse me?"

"Cindy. I need to marry her. Is that okay?"

"Boris … where did this come from?"

"Last night. I guess I finally realized how much I love her."

"*How* did you realize that?"

"I had a dream about her."

I silenced him with a finger pointed threateningly at his face.

"Boris, you are speaking to big brother here. Proceed … *very* … carefully!"

"No! It wasn't like that! Okay, it was kind of like that, but it wasn't *really* like that, you know what I'm saying?"

"No. Do I want to know?"

"I was her hero."

"You had a damsel in distress dream about Cindy?"

"I kicked some serious bad guy butt."

"Which is about as accurate of a true love test as … goose bumps."

"Think about it, Sid!" he implored me. "Dreams are more often than not just the thoughts that we don't let our minds consider in the daylight. They're based in the deepest of truths."

"Boris, I once dreamed that I turned into a duck and had a light saber battle with Britney Spears. I'm not sure what that was 'based in the deepest' of, but I'm pretty sure that it was not truth."

"Britney Spears?" Boris seemed confused. "I thought you told me that you had a fight dream with Eliza Dushku."

"That was another time. She was chasing me with a shotgun."

"Double-barrelled?"

"Slide. So, tell me. Where's the truth in that?"

Boris had to consider that for a moment.

"Beautiful, famous, rich women are destined to hate you?" he guessed.

"Get back to work!"

"Sid, this is important! I want to marry your sister!"

"Have you talked to *her* about this?"

"Uh ... no. I wanted to ask you first."

"For what? Permission? It's not my call. It's Cindy's."

"Yeah, but Cindy can't fire me if she doesn't like the idea." Every once in a while, Boris could demonstrate real strategic savvy.

"Boris, to use an overly theatrical cliche, I always knew this day would come. Now, I can at least stop dreading it."

"You are a cruel man, Sidney Myers.... But, that almost sounded like the go ahead."

"Go ahead," I sighed. "You're already annoying enough to be a full brother. You might as well be my brother-in-law."

"Sid, you are the *best!* Cool! Now, I *never* have to ring your doorbell again!"

"That's the important thing," I groaned. "Are you sure you're ready for marriage? Because, I should warn you that if you end up being in the fifty percent of marriages that end in divorce ... I will hunt you *down!*"

"Sid, I love Cindy. She's my reason for getting up in the morning. You know that."

"Yeah, I know," I admitted. "Tell me something. How long have you known?"

"A few months. But, it only really hit me the other day when she saw me talking to Mandy. I knew she was mad, and my first instinct was to tell Mandy that her momma wore army boots."

"You didn't...."

"Of course not. Mandy could break every bone in my body and never break a sweat. But, it did tell me

97

how much I wanted Cindy to know … she's my only one, I guess."

"You're not proposing to her right now, are you?"

"I was thinking about it. Why not?"

"A proposal in the kitchen, during work hours?" I was disgusted. "What kind of a lousy, life changing moment is *that?*"

"Not in the *kitchen*," Boris said indignantly. "I was going to hit my knees in the dining room, so all the supper patrons would be like '*Aaaaaawwwww....*' and then they'll all start chanting '*Yes! Yes! Yes!*' and it'll be harder for her to say no."

"Isn't that … swaying the vote a bit?"

"What, you think she'll say no?"

"Boris, I have no idea. Do you even have the ring?"

"Not yet," he admitted.

"Get back to me when you do. Just wait until then, okay? Get to work. Please."

"Okay fine." He hopped down from the table and grabbed his freshly laundered orange vest out of the closet, pulling it on over his white tee-shirt, which was as formal as I had ever seen him. "Are you going to let Angel take some deliveries tonight?"

"She already took a few," I said, placing the stack of linens on a shelf in the closet and closing the doors. "And she wore the tie, too. You could learn from her."

"When did she have time for that? I'm not that late." He looked down at his watch, the battery of which had died several weeks earlier. "Am I?"

"Oh, didn't you hear? She showed up four hours early. Pressed, dressed, and ready to work. She's already making you look bad."

"Eek," Boris grimaced, buttoning his vest. "She's making us all look bad. Kind of hot though, huh?"

"If you like short."

"Yeah, yeah, I know, tall blondes. Hey, I thought Harrigan was setting you up with someone. What's up with that?"

"Ah, yes, Randall. He keeps telling me about his cousin. She's moving in from Grande Prairie to run the gym with him, or something. He says she's perfect for me. You know how Randall is, always playing the cupid."

"So? Are you going to ask her out when she gets here?"

"Well, I was thinking about waiting until I actually *meet her*. You know, get a first impression, maybe find out what her name is, that sort of thing?"

"Hey, how bad can she be? That is, assuming she looks absolutely nothing like Randall."

"No, he showed me her picture. No hair lip, no scar through the eyebrow."

"How did he get that, anyway?"

"He was the best boxer on our high school team. One guy that he KO'D took it personally and hit him with a beer bottle a few days later."

"*Ouch.* That doesn't sound very nice…. But, his cousin is hot, right?"

"Seemed to be. Hey! You're trying to marry my sister. Quit talking about how hot other women are!"

"I was just curious," he protested. "Anyway, you should let me help. Me and Randall could set it all up, like a blind date."

"The offer's appreciated. No!"

Cindy walked in from the kitchen just then, having exchanged her usual black skirt for slacks that evening. She loved blue, and her jewel toned deep blue vest always made her look even prettier than usual, although she preferred the necktie over the "sexy" bow. Her long, blonde hair was tied up in one thick braid down her back, her bangs curling down over her forehead. Boris's breath caught in his throat with a barely audible "Ulp!" as he saw her approaching.

"Boris, you've got two deliveries up," she said. "Kat says to get your butt in gear."

"*Vroom-vroom!*" Boris grinned, as he followed her into the kitchen. I wondered if he had intended that to be some form of innuendo. Boris never was good at hidden meaning.

Cindy Morris.... That just sounds wrong.

I walked back into the kitchen as the washing machine began its spin cycle, the sodden, spinning aprons getting louder and louder. The vibrations could be felt throughout the building. I kept expecting my patrons to run into the streets, yelling "Godzilla! Godzilla!" every time the washing machine entered its final stages.

Kat and Clancy were the only ones in the kitchen. Kat had seniority, which meant that Clancy automatically got the short straw.

"Clancy, your turn," I said absently, snatching the whisk out of his hand and taking over mixing the pot of spaghetti sauce he had been cooking on the stove-top. "Hurry, before it gets away."

"Ah, Sid!" Clancy grumbled. "It must be nice being the boss...."

He was still muttering as he stormed out of the room, yanking off his apron in preparation for hand to hand combat with the large appliance.

"You are evil," Kat commented, turning two sizzling New York cut steaks on the grill, while simultaneously grilling two sides of garlic toast. A basket of French fries was sputtering and hissing in the deep fryer.

"I sat on the last two loads," I said, defensively. "I'm still vibrating here."

"We need to get a new washing machine."

"I could get you a bucket and washboard," I suggested, smirking. "We can just wring the laundry out with the pizza press."

"Sounds really hygienic."

"Any other orders up?"

"No, we just got the Reynolds and three tree planters in the dining room. We're going to have to vacuum the carpet after they leave. Do those guys ever clean their boots?"

"Tree planters already? I thought they didn't show up until June."

"Nope, we got some early birds. Grab some plates."

You're the boss....

"How many?" I said, crossing to the dish cupboard.

"Three. The third guy said all he wants is fries and some tomato juice."

"Do we even have that?" I wondered, setting the plates on a serving tray.

"I found a bottle in the fridge. I don't know how long it's been in there, but that stuff never goes bad. At least, I don't think it does…. I never drink it."

The health inspector is going to love hearing that….

"I hate you, Sid!" Clancy's voice yelled from the store room. The shaking washer made him sound like he was yelling through a fan.

"Just another thirty seconds!" I called back, neatly arranging a garnish of lettuce and shaved carrot on each plate, as Kat finished up the steaks. "Twenty-nine, twenty-eight…."

"Is there no way to nail that thing down?" Kat asked, loading up the plates and handing the tray back to me.

"No. There isn't," I replied simply. "Cindy! Order up! Table six!"

Cindy and Angel both entered from the dining room. Angel proudly held up a five-dollar bill between two fingers, still holding the coffeepot in her other hand.

"First dining room tip, Boss!" she proudly announced. "I told that nice couple that they were the first people I had ever served coffee to, and they gave me five smackers!"

"The Reynolds," Cindy muttered, shaking her head in disbelief. "They tipped her, and they haven't even ordered yet. She's a keeper, bro."

"Nice work, Angel," I said with apathetic blandness, passing the loaded tray to Cindy. "You're an inspiration to us all. Table six."

"Do you ever get excited about *anything,* Boss?" Angel seemed concerned.

"I am right now," I said in my usual dry monotone. "This is me when I'm hyper."

"You should see him when he's bored," Kat quipped. "It's scary."

She was probably right.

Cindy took the tray out to the dining room, sidestepping Becky, who was just coming in, pulling on her coat.

"I'm gone," she said, tossing her time card across the prep table at me. "Four and a half hours."

"Thanks, Becky," I said to her retreating back. The girl did not believe in wasting daylight.

"See ya, Beck!" Angel managed to call out before the front door slammed again.

I shook my head. "That girl's vocal cords have gotta be in mint condition. Speaking of which…. Hey, Clancy! Is your truck fixed yet?"

"I hate you, Sid!"

With one final bang, the washing machine slammed to an abrupt silence. Clancy emerged from the back room, trying to shake off the vibrations.

"Man, I hate that thing! No, they had to order the part in. I'm probably on foot all week."

"Poor baby," Angel cooed, setting the coffeepot back on the hot element. "Hey, guess what? I got to deliver pizza to a drug dealer today!"

"Isn't life a hoot?" I commented.

"A dealer?" said Clancy. "Which one?"

"Beats me. Boss said he would try to tip me with a roach."

"Devon Finn," I clarified. "You'd better keep an eye on that one, Clancy. He really liked your girlfriend."

"That charmer," Clancy grumbled, pulling a box of green peppers out of the vegetable cooler and slamming it down on a cutting board. "Knife."

I pulled a serrated knife from the butcher block, and twirled it through my fingers, presenting it to him handle first. Clancy pulled up a stool to the cutting table as he began coring out the green vegetables.

"By the way," I remarked, "I want those thin sliced. *Slices*, not *wedges*. Who's been cutting those?"

"Boris cut the last batch," Kat replied. "I think he cuts one pepper into about six pieces. You could use one of his slices as a spoon to eat soup."

"Exactly how long has Boris been here?" Angel asked quizzically.

"Oh, it's only been six years," I sighed. "Can't expect the boy to have it all figured out just yet."

"Does he really know every dealer in town?" Angel was curious to know.

"Most of them," I nodded, pouring myself a coffee. "Unless some of them are more subtle than usual. If the cops ever really wanted to clean up this town, all they'd have to do is get an undercover narc running deliveries here for a month or two."

"That almost sounds … scary," Angel said cautiously.

"There's not a bunch of cartels here," Kat pointed out. "Mostly it's a bunch of slackers, selling out of their parent's basements."

"So, that makes it okay?" Angel was clearly disturbed by her own inference.

"They're a fact of life in this town," I said with a dismissive shrug.

"Whatever happened to small town values?" Angel asked. "Heck, that's one of the reasons I came here in the first place."

"I think Andy and Barney skipped town," I drawled. "We've got one of the highest drug rates in the province."

"Huh," Angel grunted. "I always thought drugs were just a big city problem."

"I wish," I chuckled humourlessly. "But, if you really need something to cry about, we're out of chopped onion."

Angel had no trouble mastering the kitchen chores, but it was her resounding success in the dining room that had us all stunned by the end of the night. The patrons absolutely fell in love with her. She fell easily into conversation with even the most reclusive of them, and on the rare occasions when her big, toothy grin could not win their hearts, her infectious laughter would. I am quite certain that her gratuities well exceeded her hourly wage that night, something that was almost unheard of on a medium busy Thursday. Even Jean-Paul Remy, an old logger and one of my most notoriously surly customers, was joking and laughing with her as though she were a dear friend. It was about time that someone cheered up that old crab cake. Jean-Paul's small pizza and coffee cost just under fifteen dollars. He gave Angel a twenty and a ten, and left without his change. A one hundred percent tip is the kind of thing that even Boris only dreams of, and

Angel had managed it on her first night of work, and from Jean-Paul Remy, of all people.

Not many of my workers could deny that there was a constant, unspoken status struggle in the serving business, and it was determined by who got the most tips or rapport with the patrons. Angel won in both areas that night, and in most of the nights that followed. However, I only truly realized this around eight o'clock, when Angel briefly forgot which table she was supposed to be serving. She did not get flustered. She got honest. This remains one of my fondest memories of Angel.

I was clearing a vacated table during our busiest hour of the evening, when Angel strode in from the kitchen with her coffeepot, stopped in the middle of the room, and looked around curiously. Then, she simply raised her left hand like a student seeking the teacher's attention, and announced to the entire room, "Ladies and gentlemen, I will require your attention for just a moment." Every head in the room turned toward her, including mine.

What are you doing ...?

"I'm new here," she admitted, her voice mixing pride and sheepishness as she scuffed the carpet with the toe of a black shoe. "I'm new at this job. And, as an honest recognition of my imperfection ... I cannot remember who ordered this coffee."

She hung her head in dramatized shame, but she had a sly smile at the edge of her lips.

As one body, the entire congregation of diners erupted into delighted laughter, cheers, and even applause. Several of them even rose from their seats and gave her a standing ovation, clapping and whistling gleefully.

The truth will set you free....

Angel's face was flushed, but in a satisfied way, and her chin was held high once more as she jogged over to the loudest cheering family at table eight. They were all laughing as they waved her over, holding their empty coffee mugs aloft. A star had officially been born in my dining room.

Boris liked to say, "This job is not exactly rocket surgery," but I think Angel always considered it to be much more than even that. To her, waiting tables was a privilege, a rare honour. She was like my father. She had a servant's heart.

She also had an acute fear of snakes, but I only found out about that later.

CHAPTER NINE

As a general rule, I did not laugh. Yes, I did have a sense of humour. I thought a lot of things were funny, like those election year ads about one federal party, sponsored by the registered agent of another federal party, and *The Red Green Show.* They made me grin, snort derisively, or occasionally just roll my eyes. I did not laugh out loud. Certainly, there had been exceptions, such as when I fired a nineteen-year-old boy, only to have him inform me that "This place will never last without me." That was probably the only time in my post-pubescent life that I had laughed, uncontrollably, for the better part of forty seconds. Aside from that, my laughs had been short, stifled, or repressed.

Angel made me want to laugh.

Perhaps it was because her own laugh was so contagious, and was such a common occurrence. She could find humour in things that most other people found simply commonplace. Things like fat people, for instance.

I realize that I just made Angel sound like the cruelest, most derogatory woman alive. All that I can say in her defence is that Angel almost instinctively loved everyone that she met. Sometimes, she just thought that they were funny, too. She thought Boris's eyebrows were funny. According to her, my earlobes were funny.

She had been with us for a little over a week. April and May were generally the slowest months at my restaurant, but Angel had no trouble even handling the busy, weekend supper rushes. It was in the middle of one such busy Friday that she rushed up to me at the front desk, still clutching her ever-present coffeepot. She looked as if she was about to explode from holding back a laugh, her face positively glowing with repressed mirth.

"Boss, did you see him?"

"See who?"

"That guy!"

"I see a lot of 'guys,' Angel."

"I know, but did you see *that* guy?"

"*Which* guy?"

"Well, like *duh!* In the dining room!"

"Angel, I've fired people for less than this."

"Boss, he's *huge!*"

"Huge?"

"*Ginormous!* I asked what he wanted to eat, and I half-expected him to say, 'You.'"

"Please drop a couple of decibels when you're making fun of paying customers," I groaned, resting my face in my palm as I leaned against the cash register. In a lot of ways, Angel reminded me of a little girl with a quiet, more successful than usual resistence to growing up.

"Sorry, Boss, but you have to see this!" she whispered eagerly. "I know a lot of people are sensitive about their weight, but … dang! If I put a paper bag over his head, I wouldn't know which way he was facing!"

Cruel honesty…. Don't laugh, Myers. Don't you even smile!

I had to move my hand in front of my mouth and force my eyelids to droop a bit, creating an impression of bored indifference.

"You came out here to tell me that we have a fat man in the dining room? What kind of preppy club do you think this is? Fat people flock to us, like … lemmings to a cliff."

"Boss, lemmings would flock to this guy, thinking that he *was* a cliff! He's sitting on both sides of the table."

"Okay. Which table?" Even I got curious.

"Seven, wearing a striped western shirt and a Blue Jays cap … just in case you can't spot him."

"Blue Jays…. Wait a sec. Handlebar moustache? White hair?"

"Yep. You know him?"

"Angel, that's Ronnie Alders. He's a retired firefighter. You know, one of those guys who saves people's lives for a living?"

"That guy used to fight fires?" Angel could not believe that. "How? By sitting on them?"

DON'T LAUGH!

"You should have seen him twenty years ago," I managed to cough out with a straight face. "He was the most beefed up guy in town. He was Lou Ferrigno with a better tan."

"Lou who?"

"Never mind."

"Well," Angel said, shaking her head, "suffice to say, the moon has waxed. The beef has turned to tallow, you know?"

"You can be a very cruel woman. Has anybody told you that before?"

"My dad did," she replied solemnly. "He always said things like that. And Mom…. She never said a thing…." She let the sentence hang glumly in the air for a moment, then burst out laughing again, socking me on the arm. "Just kidding ya, Boss!"

Boris looked a little unnerved just then, as he returned to the lobby from his latest delivery. For a second, I thought that he might be smarting from Angel's last crack about his eyebrows, but Boris was self-deprecating enough to be able to take a joke, and Angel's put-downs were too jovial to be taken seriously.

"Boris, you look antagonized," I commented. "Need a coffee?"

"I need an exterminator," he said. "There's a snake in my car."

"Come again, please?" I cringed.

"*Wha-ha-hat?!*" Angel gasped, every drop of blood draining from her cheeks.

"A … *snake*," Boris elocuted. "Elongated, limbless reptile, tongue like a licorice whip. My guess would be the garter variety, two and a half to three feet long."

"It's in your *car*?" I demanded.

"You put a *snake* in your *car?!*" Angel squawked. "Are you *insane?!*"

Boris stared at her curiously.

"No," he said slowly. "It must have crawled up the tires and into the engine. It was climbing up the windshield from under the hood while I was driving. Kind of freaked me out."

"*There's a snake in your car?!*" Angel hissed.

"Keep it down!" I admonished her. "The last thing that any of the patrons want to know is that the pizza guy has a snake in the same car he delivers their pizzas in."

"But, I hate snakes!" Angel whined. "*Hate 'em*, you get me?"

"Yes, that was the implication that I was inferring," I growled. "Boris, you don't have any more deliveries up, so get your car out of sight around back and give it a cavity search. Find … the snake!"

"Gross, Boss!" Angel chirped.

"I don't care! Strip search it, and get the dang thing out of there. Believe me, snakes are a public relations nightmare. *Get rid of it!*"

"Okay, whatever," Boris said defensively, hands raised. "Do we have any gloves?"

"Make sure it's dead!" Angel insisted.

"He's not going to kill it!" I said, disgusted. "Just dig it out and toss it in the bushes."

"So it can come back?" she said, accusingly.

"It's not coming back," Boris assured her. "Most likely, it'll wander in here, looking for fresh blood." He turned and exited so quickly that he never did get to see the expression on Angel's face, which is a pity, since it was priceless.

"I hate snakes!"

"Yeah, you mentioned that. If it slithers in here, you can kill it with the coffeepot. Just make sure you wash your hands after."

"I didn't know snakes lived this far north!"

That deserved an eye rolling.

"Yes, Angel, snakes live this far north. We're not exactly into the tundra yet. Were you … constricted as a child, or something?"

"No," she sighed. "Snakes are just … icky."

"Icky?" I said. "I've been commending you on your good word use, and the best term you can come up with for the sum of all your fears is 'icky?'"

"Sorry." She shrugged. "Grammar never was my most unbad subject."

I think that was intended as a joke.

Between deliveries, Boris probably spent over an hour digging through the mechanical labyrinth that lay beneath the hood of his Trans Am that night. The snake was nowhere to be seen. Several times, Boris decided that the reptile had slunk out on its own, but then reported that his windshield wipers seemed to be slithering as he drove. He would stomp on his brakes and bound out with a flashlight, and the snake would disappear. In the kitchen, shortly before midnight, I asked Boris if he had caught the snake yet. He shook his head.

"I'm telling you. He's onto me, Sid. He knows I'm looking for him."

"Boris, snakes don't know anything except 'flick tongue, flick tongue, eat rodent, eat rodent,'" Cindy remarked.

"Yeah right!" Boris exclaimed. "Salami is dang *smart!* He only shows up after my speedometer passes fifty."

"*Salami?!*" I gurgled, unbelievingly.

"Okay, so I gave him a name. I think that's a good name for a snake."

"Boris, he is not a pet," I explained carefully. "He is a vile, disease-ridden monster who will kill your delivery service *and tips* if the general populace ever finds out about him. Got it?" The situation was inherently amusing, but I was attempting to run a reputable and icky-free establishment.

"All right," Boris said sourly. "I'll keep hunting." He slouched out the back door in dogged pursuit of his adversary.

"*Kill it!*" Angel rasped after him.

I certainly hoped that Boris would not allow himself to form an attachment to the snake, although that would certainly be just like him. As a child, he had spent many of his summer days catching frogs, and was always reluctant to set them free again afterwards, no matter how crispy they became after several hours in his pocket. Now, he had been in quasi-possession of a snake for three hours, and he already had a name for it. He would probably be leaving live mice on his dashboard soon, if I did not put my foot down.

I suddenly had this disturbing image of Boris capturing the snake, but then deciding to keep it for his own diabolical purposes, most likely as payback for customers who did not tip.

BORIS: *You're absolutely right, sir. Taking an extra three minutes to get your pizza to your door is certainly reason* enough to withhold my tip, cuss me out, and complain to my boss. So, just hold out your paw, while I reach into this special, securely zippered pocket, and place your exact change right in the palm of your hand.

WHINY CUSTOMER: *SNAAAAAAAAAKE!!*

Leave it to Boris to find a practical use for a snake.

It seems odd to think back over the chain of events that followed the snake's arrival, and realize the role that this humble, icky creature played in altering the courses of several human lives. Without even doing anything so drastic as, say, eating someone, the snake would soon facilitate both the end of a romance, and the beginning of a friendship. Boris had said that the snake was smart, but who can truly fathom the snake mind?

Why the snake would take up residence in Boris's car remains a mystery, and an even bigger puzzle is why he steadfastly refused to come back out. Over the next few days, he would make frequent appearances while Boris was on deliveries, but never remained in the open long enough to be captured and evicted. His slithering apparently knew no bounds, particularly after he noticed that Boris usually kept the windows rolled down. Driving around with a snake under your hood is one thing. Driving around with a snake under your feet is quite another. Boris was getting depressed, and understandably so. His regular, late-night drives with Cindy had been indefinitely postponed.

"I'm not driving anywhere with that dang viper!" Cindy had snapped one evening, when Boris arrived at our house to pick her up. He who drove with a snake, drove alone.

Angel's behaviour was even more erratic. She gave the Trans Am a wide berth anytime that she had to walk past it in the restaurant parking lot, watching it as if she expected the hood to pop open and the whole vehicle to pounce on her. To be perfectly honest, I did not like snakes, but Angel was getting ridiculous.

"Did you get the snake out?" she would ask Boris, immediately upon his arrival at work.

"No, I didn't get it out," he would sigh.

"Well, get it out!"

At the time, I only had three students working for me, Becky, Sammy, and Mark. All of them had been sworn to secrecy in regards to Salami. Almost one-third of the restaurant's income came from delivery orders, and I was not going to jeopardize that. The health inspector would probably have flayed me alive if she had ever found out about the snake, but, fortunately, her standard inspection only involved checking the fridge temperatures and the soap dispensers in the washrooms. She never asked if I had a reptilian invader, and I never volunteered the information.

Sometimes, Salami would not make an appearance for a day or two, leading Boris to believe that the snake had finally left. Then, he would reach into the glove box for his sunglasses, and a forked tongue would tickle his fingertips. One day, Boris even returned to the shop with a bruise on his forehead, which he claimed was the result of a high speed impact with the steering wheel. Apparently, Salami's summit attempt on Mt. Headrest had been a successful one, and he had proudly informed

Boris of his conquest by licking the back of his neck. I
hated to think that Boris was becoming like Angel, but
the man was getting wan and jumpy.

Then, in the middle of the month, the snake
abruptly disappeared. It took Boris almost another
week to accept that Salami had either slithered out, or
was making revolutions in the fan belt, but after that,
things actually seemed to be getting back to normal.
Cindy resumed her night drives with Boris, and, on
one Wednesday, she even convinced Angel and Clancy
to go on a double date with them in the Trans Am.
The four of them went to dinner and a movie in
Dawson Creek, the small city about an hour's drive
from Chetwynd, near the Alberta border. It was not
exactly a sprawling metropolis, but it did have malls
and a bowling alley, and the theatre there showed new
movies about a month before Chetwynd did. One of
the quasi-nice things about Chetwynd was that you
could watch a movie at the theatre, and, if you liked it,
you could walk down the street to the video store and
buy it on the same day.

One of the other nice things about Chetwynd was
that "rush hour" lasted for about ten minutes. The only
time that traffic ever backed up was when the train
routinely cut the town in half, or when an eighteen-
wheeler ran out of gas under the traffic lights. As a
result, even though it was five o'clock when I drove
to Kat's apartment for our weekly chess match, the
drive still only took the usual six minutes. We had been
invited to join the others for a triple date, but I had
long ago realized that the only times that Kat and I had
absolutely nothing to say to each other was when we

were on anything remotely similar to a date. Suddenly, I would have this feeling that everyone was waiting with bated breath for me to hit my knees and pull out a ring. Kat and I had never dated, but everyone we knew wanted to believe that we had.

We played four games that evening, all of which adhered to the time-honoured tradition of Kat winning in eight moves or less. Chess was all about the mathematics of the board, but my math was not *quite* that good. It struck me as odd that I could still remember the smell of the perfume that the unbelievably gorgeous Grace Landre wore when she sat next to me in grade ten math class, but that was all that I remembered. I was very fast at adding, subtracting, multiplying, and dividing, but if advanced math truly was a universal language, I knew that I would be in deep trouble if aliens ever landed. While all of the chess masters, or at least those who could remember the basics of algebra, had their applications for the enlightening cranial upload accepted by the extraterrestrial visitors, I would probably be sent to the dancing bear troupe.

"Sid?" Kat's voice abruptly bounced me out of my paranoid delusions. "You've got that scary, thoughtful look on your face again. It's the same look you had when you came up with the creamed spinach and artichoke pizza."

"I liked it."

"It was cattle fodder!"

"With three cheeses."

"So? What were you thinking about?"

"Math." Not many people really wanted the whole truth when they asked me questions like that.

"You hate math," she pointed out, sitting cross-legged on the sofa in her matching white shorts and tank top.

"Which is why I lose at chess. Math is everything. If Revenue Canada gets any fussier, the shop is going to be in trouble."

"And that would not look good in our profile. Unsung heroes and audits…. Bad mix."

"What are you talking about?" I asked.

"Our profile," she said, as though it should have been obvious. "Have you planned anything out yet?"

My blank expression and darting eyeballs must have finally tipped her off.

"You forgot, didn't you?" Kat's accusing tone was one of the most intimidating sounds I had ever heard.

"Forgot what?" I said weakly.

"Sid, you've got an interview with *30 Days Up North* in four days!"

"Oh," I said. "That. I guess I've been preoccupied with trying to get Sammy to figure out right from left, and trying to keep Angel from attacking Boris's car with an axe. Have you ever seen someone that afraid of snakes?"

"I don't think so." She shook her head. "By the way, I've been meaning to tell you. Uh … Sammy's an idiot."

"I know," I sighed. "Remind me to fire him tomorrow. I watched him make one pizza in the time that it took Clancy to make four."

"I think he's a perma-fry. You know that open-mouthed 'huh?' thing he does whenever you ask him … anything? I'm getting tired of saying everything twice."

"Look," I said, exasperated. "I run a small restaurant with a minimal staff. Is it too much to ask for nine workers, none of whom require weed to subsist? Believe it or not, I don't like constantly firing people."

"What about Monica?"

I chuckled. "Okay, I liked firing Monica."

"Well, it's almost June," Kat commented. "Summer rushes are going to be starting. Now we need another student."

"We might need two. The hotels are going to be packed with crews, and they have no mama, no papa. All they've got is us."

"Do you think Angel can handle it?"

"Angel is doing great," I admitted. "Sometimes, I think she has the mentality of a five-year-old, but a well-disciplined one."

"The bubbliness still gets on my nerves," Kat said, "but she can pull off some good shots…. Boris's eyebrows…." The sentence was cut short by a choked back laugh.

"Yeah, she's getting a lot of mileage out of that," I grinned. "Yesterday she told him 'Frida called. She wants her eyebrow back.'"

Kat almost snorted her root beer up her nose.

"Sid!" she blurted. "Wait til I'm done drinking!"

"Sorry."

"Anyway, what the heck is her story?" Kat asked, curious. "She's new in town. Why'd she come here?"

"Honestly? I have absolutely no idea," I confessed. "I've tried to bring it up a couple of times, and she never wants to talk about it. Her story belongs to her."

"Interesting," Kat mused. "I just can't believe that she's dated Clancy for nearly a month. That's gotta be a new record. Do you think they'll last?"

"They seem happy at work. Actually, I don't know how much time they spend together after work. Have you noticed how they kiss at the beginning and end of every shift? It's almost like their hello and goodbye. It's weird. I don't think they spend much time at each other's homes."

"Well, they definitely aren't shacked up," Kat remarked. "Maybe Angel's private, but Clancy isn't. He would have mentioned it. Hey, where's he living, anyway? He did move out of his gramma's basement, right?"

"Yeah, I helped him move out. He's living in Evergreen Trailer Court with that buddy of his, Marty Collings. Angel's on the other side of town, Long Road Place. I see them driving around together quite a bit, but I've never seen his truck at her place, or her car at his."

"Do you think Angel's got religion?" One of the few things about Kat that annoyed me was her habit of grouping anyone who attended church or held biblical values under the "got religion" heading.

"Possibly," I said. "Either that, or she's realized that Marty Collings is a bigger idiot than Sammy. He's really loud."

"Do you like her?"

That question was unexpected.

"What?"

"Angel. Do you like her?"

"She's … fine, I guess," I answered slowly. "Why?"

"Because I'm going to get you another girlfriend if it's the last thing that I ever do," she replied simply. "Why not her?"

"You want all the reasons?" I asked skeptically.

"Sure."

"One, I'm her boss. *Duuuhhhhh....* Two, she's dating a friend. Three, bubbly people don't date deadpan people. Four, she's short and not blonde. And five, Randall has vowed that I'm going to fall in love with his tall, blonde cousin.... And, Boris owes me twenty bucks if Angel and Clancy make it for a full month. It's fiscally advantageous to *not* date her."

"Do you sit at home and just come up with terms that no normal person would ever use? 'Fiscally advantageous?'"

"It gives me the satisfying illusion that I know what I'm doing in life."

"So what does holding onto the hope of a tall blonde give you? You're one of the most mature guys that I know, except when it comes to your perfect doll standards of female compatibility."

"Now who's using big terms? And, for your information, it's not a *standard*, it's a *preference*. As I recall, you always had a thing for curly hair and chin clefts. For a Scotsman, Roger seemed to fit the French stereotype."

"Okay, fine, when is Miss Blonde-and-Tall coming here?"

"I'm not sure. I was going to stop by Randall's gym later and talk to him."

"Mind if I tag along?" Kat asked. "Shoot, I haven't seen him in like a year."

"Sure. Your chessboard doesn't like me, anyway."

The horizon was a deep red when we drove away from the apartment, turning the bordering western mountains into a pale rose colour. It was my favourite time of the day, just before twilight. I wished that I could spend more of my evenings watching the sunset, but I ran a business that got busiest after darkness had settled over the town.

CHAPTER TEN

I had seen a lot of businesses come and go in the nearly three decades that I had lived in Chetwynd. Some were establishments that had closed their doors after years of family management, while others had been new ventures that simply could not find a market. There were restaurants, pet stores, tack and western shops, and, yes, even a bowling alley. I wondered often how long my own pizza shop would last. Nothing lasts forever, even in a small town. I hoped that my friend Randall's gym would be more of a success than the catering business and buffet that had previously occupied the spacious, beige-sided building across from the post office. It had lasted about two months. The baron of beef was too dry, and one of the chefs was constantly coughing, like a cat hacking up a hairball. It was not a favourable sound in a place that was supposed to conjure up healthy appetites.

Randall Harrigan obviously used every piece of workout equipment in his gym, regularly. A proud Cree man with short buzzed black hair and a build like a barrel, he was a head shorter than me, but almost fifty pounds heavier, all of it muscle. He had been a good friend ever since junior high, and we had all missed him in the time that he had been away, studying business management in Alberta. I had enough "hands on" experience to keep my own restaurant operating, but often wished that I had the time to take some of the same courses that Randall had. If nothing else, it might have kept me from having to fire people all the time.

When Kat and I arrived at the nearly completed gymnasium, Randall was busy assembling the elevated boxing ring, with the help of a few local labourers. Kat actually ran up behind him and jumped on his back, covering his eyes with one hand.

"Hey, Randy. Guess who?" she quipped.

"Kat!" he whooped, using a judo-like toss to sling her over his shoulder, right into a bear hug, still holding a greasy crescent wrench in his right hand.

"Why haven't you come to see me?" Kat demanded. "And don't say you've been busy."

"I've been busy," he said in a humourously defiant tone, a broad grin across his equally broad face. "You shouldn't come in here looking so beautiful, Kat. You're giving me ideas."

"Oh, shut up!" she laughed, playfully elbowing his hard stomach. Randall pretended to double over in pain, but he, too, was laughing.

"So, Sid, how do you like my gym?" he boomed, good-naturedly. He never was the subtle type when it came to fishing for compliments.

"It's awesome, man," I replied without lying. The place was impressive. Half a dozen treadmills lined the western wall, facing the final red rays of light shining through large picture windows. Various weight benches, stair simulators, rowing machines, and stationary bicycles were grouped neatly along the south side, along with the doors to the showers. To the east, four punching bags dangled from the low ceiling, flanked by the reception desk on one side, and the soda and snack dispensers on the other. The boxing ring was central, surrounded by cardboard boxes filled with gloves and padded helmets, and thick coils of rope.

"Looks like you're ready for business," I commented. "Congrats, big time. It's what you've always wanted."

"All my life," he agreed. "And this is just the frame work. Once the business takes off, I'm going to install TVs above the treadmills. Give people more to look at than sunsets while they jog. And, over here, check this out."

He led us past the front desk to the north wall, which was only occupied by a couple of benches, and a huge blocky mass covered with an old green tarp. The block was about six feet high, and the same width across the front. With a sharp tug on the left corner, Randall yanked the tarp loose, and it rustled to the concrete floor.

"No way," I said.

"Oh, *yes!*" he grinned, patting the consoles of the two arcade games. "I think people should be able to come here and unwind, whether or not they're working out. Pretty sweet, huh?"

"*Moto Cross 9000* and *Dinosaur Slayer*," Kat read aloud. "So you can jog, watch TV, pump iron, beat someone's face off, and blast dinosaurs, all in the same room. I'm impressed, Randy."

"So, when's the big day?" I asked.

"Grand opening, a week from Monday. I'm helping Karen move up here this weekend."

"Who?" Kat asked.

"My cousin, the one Sid's going to marry," Randall chuckled. "Karen Malloy, my business partner."

"I haven't even met her yet!" I protested.

"She said she really wants to meet you," he remarked casually. "Oh yeah, and if she seems overly interested in your past ... I told her that you were Canadian Special Forces until you had to take over the restaurant."

"*What?!*"

"Come on, Sid. She likes army guys. You fit the part. Stocky build, nice hair, rugged beard, cowboy boots, no sense of humour. She'll buy it."

"You're insane," I said, incredulous.

Randall curiously poked my biceps under the short sleeve of my black golf shirt.

"You're getting pretty toned there, Sid. You been working out much lately?"

"As much as I can in the garage," I answered. "I've just got some dumbbells, and Dad's old punching bag. I knock it around a few nights a week."

"Well, you're not allowed to, anymore!" Randall said sternly. "You have to come here from now on!"

"You really told her I was Special Forces?"

"Relax, Sid," Kat said soothingly. "If she knows Randy at all, she'll know that he's just a cupid who's full of baloney."

"But, just in case she doesn't know...." Randall advised, "how's your unarmed combat training? Karen likes demos."

"It's rusty, at best," I said sourly. "But, I sort of feel like snapping someone's neck right about now."

My dad's only sibling, Reggie Myers, had instructed Canadian soldiers in hand to hand and close combat for over a decade at the Edmonton army base. He tried to visit Cindy and I once or twice a year, and he always had some new move to show us, just in case we ever needed to control, incapacitate, or terminate some type of life-threatening adversary in our small town restaurant. Thus far, such a situation had never arisen, but the information was, at the least, empowering.

Canadian Special Forces.... Randall, you idiot.

"Here, Sid!" he called out, tossing a pair of brown boxing gloves at me. "Wanna have a round? Old times sake?"

"Thanks, anyway." I shook my head as I caught the gloves. "I haven't boxed anything but the bag since high school. I kind of miss it, but I'd miss my brain cells and powers of coherent speech more."

"Oh, come on, Sid!" he scoffed. "How are you ever going to survive in this vicious world if you aren't conditioned to taking your licks?"

"Conditioned?" I said. "That's false advertising, Randy. Faces get smashed in. They don't get conditioned."

"Hey, my face is conditioned!"

"Your nose is thrice broken, your eyebrow's scarred, and your lip is... well, I guess you've always had that, huh?"

"You're the only guy I know who can use the word 'thrice,' and make it sound natural," Kat interjected. "Are you British?"

"About one quarter, on my mother's side."

"Let's go, Sid!" Randy implored me. "It'll be fun."

I did not say anything. I could only stare down at the boxing gloves for a long moment. They were heavy in my hands, and felt heavier by the second.

"Fun," I said. "It always is, isn't it?"

So many things are fun....

"Yeah, so let's go."

I was silent again. Few things in my life have ever held my unflinching gaze longer than that worn pair of padded leather gloves. They were not just gloves.

"Sid?"

They were weapons.

"Sid?" Kat was clearly puzzled about what I was staring at.

It's all so fun.... Parties, drinking....

Such small objects I held in my hand, soft and cushioned, and yet so potentially deadly. Handled the wrong way, even boxing gloves could kill. Just like alcohol. Just like drugs.

Just like a truck.

* * *

"DAD!!" There was no screaming of brakes. Dad never had time to react, and I doubt the driver of the other truck was ever aware that he had hit something. He simply drove into Dad's door at around eighty kilometres per hour.

I did not remember the moment of impact. All that I remembered was the fear. In my memory, there was no crash. There was only terror. Then, there was silence.

I was still in my seat, but rain was hitting my face. Hot blood was running down my face from a gash on my forehead.

I had smashed the passenger window with my right temple, and rain was pelting into the cab. The Blazer had been slammed straight sideways into the wide ditch separating main street from the South Access Road, and the Ford truck was still wedged into Dad's door. Dad was slumped over his steering wheel. He was so still.

"Dad?" I said, my voice quavering beyond my control. "Dad, talk to me." I was fighting with the seatbelt. It was stuck.

Someone else was slumped over a steering wheel. All that I could see of the green F-150's driver was that he was a young man, wearing a backwards, red baseball cap. I recognized the hat before I recognized the driver.

* * *

I handed the gloves back to Randall.

"Sorry, man. I can't box right now."

"Are you okay, Sid?" Randall looked concerned.

"I'm actually not feeling too good," I admitted. "I'm gonna head home. Sorry."

"Well, take it easy," he admonished me. "Kat. Great to see you again."

They hugged once more, and Kat followed me out to the slowly darkening parking lot. Randall waved as we pushed through the glass doors. My stomach felt tight and cramped, and I had to take a few long, deep breaths.

"What's wrong?" Kat asked.

"I just feel a bit sick," I answered quietly. "I just need to go home."

When I dropped Kat off at her apartment, she gave me a kiss on the cheek, and took on her mothering tone when she said, "You go straight home, and straight to bed."

"Yes, Mom," I said, grinning weakly. I had no intention of going to bed.

I did not need to go to bed. I had experienced this sickness before, a burning knot in my stomach, a dry lump in my throat. It only happened when memories of my father's death were triggered. One thing that surprised me was how such simple things could cause the pain to resurface. A pair of boxing gloves, the smell of rain, the flipping of a coin, and a hundred other minor events, objects, or senses could instantly drag me back to the last time that I ever rode in that old Chevy Blazer. Sleep and Tylenol would not help. Only two things seemed to help. One was to play my piano. The other was suspended from the rafters of my garage.

Some people had told me that a punching bag was therapeutic, a safe way to burn off rage. I had heard others say that such things were dangerous tools, used to cultivate violent fantasies. I did not know which, if either, was true. What I did know was that punching the living daylights out of that bag diverted my attention from the pain in my gut, even if just for a few minutes. I knew that diversions from pain were nothing more than band-aids. Everybody who had ever lived with pain knew that, yet most of them were still like me. They did not care.

My house was split level, four bedrooms, two bathrooms, kitchen, living room, dining room, den/ office, laundry room in the basement, and an attached two car garage with a punching bag in it. Well over half of my life had been lived in that house, ever since we had moved from the acreage. I still missed the horseback riding. It was definitely more therapeutic than the punching bag.

I often wondered if I was a weak person for always needing a hiding place. I preferred the term 'sanctuary,' but knew that it meant exactly the same thing. At work, I had my office. At home, I had my garage. I would lock myself inside, and start punching.

That evening, I boxed the punching bag for nearly thirty minutes, nonstop. Every blow came straight from my pounding heart. Every punch was personal. I could not stop until I was too tired to swing anymore. Wheezing harshly through clenched teeth, with icy sweat pouring down my brow and cheeks, I could only keep on swinging, hating that freezing cold bag. When I looked at it, all that I could see was a red, backwards ball cap.

My legs were shaking from the adrenaline pumping through them, making it hard to stand any longer. That was not a problem. I just dropped to the floor on my knuckles and began doing pushups, counting them out in a breathless whisper.

"*One! Two! Three ...!*" I had to keep going, as fast as I could possibly go, up and down again. The concrete floor was cold on my hands, but my stomach still hurt. I could not stop.

"*Twenty-eight! Twenty-nine ...!*"

Now, my knuckles were on fire from the friction, rubbing against the floor. I could barely gasp for breath.

"*Seventy! Seventy-one! Seventy-two!*"

I collapsed to the floor. I could almost hear my heart pounding against the concrete. My skin quivered with racing blood and perspiration. I had not bothered to change into workout clothes, or even trade my cowboy boots for running shoes, so I was an exhausted, dishevelled, sweaty mess. And I did not feel sick anymore.

Four years you've been doing this, Myers. Do you really think it's helping you?

"Yes!" I choked. I hated it when I would begin vocalizing my responses to my own inner dialogue, but it was a habit that I tended to slip into when safely locked in my garage.

Sweat was dripping in my eyes and beard. I finally gave up on blinking, and just pressed my eyelids together. Slowly, my body temperature dropped back to the point where the concrete floor did not feel so cold anymore. Now that I no longer felt sick, I just felt dead tired.

Okay, go take a shower and go to bed, before you fall asleep on the floor....

The next thing that I remembered was Cindy's toe nudging me awake.

"How was the movie?" I mumbled, my cheek pressed into the concrete.

"Sid, you're on the floor."

"Yeah. My Feng Shui master said the furniture arrangement was perfect, unless I was standing up."

"You know, it does kind of freak me out when I come home and find my beloved older brother lying face-down in the locked garage."

"It's not like it's the first time," I yawned, pushing myself up onto my elbows.

"Do you think that some people might consider exercising until you pass out on concrete to be a sign of…. I don't know, say … some type of imbalance?"

"An imbalance? Are we talking chemical, hormonal, or emotional?"

"You tell me, Sid," she sighed. "How about gravitational?"

I sat up groggily, my jaw feeling as though it had been hit with a hammer. I shook my head to clear the fog.

"It's dark," I observed sleepily, glancing out the small windows on the bay doors. "What time is it?"

"A little after two."

"You just got in?"

"Yeah. The only light on was here. Tough day?"

"No, it was great, it was Wednesday," I said flatly. "Man, I slept for five hours. Is the side of my face as flat as it feels?"

"Sid," she said quietly, "you have to stop doing this to yourself."

I could only stare blankly at her.

"Why?" I said. "Why should my life be easy?"

"Because it could be."

"I don't want it to be," I said simply. "Did you go out after the show?"

"Yeah, we went to a pub, had a few games of pool."

I stood up and turned to face her.

"What was the name of the movie?"

"Why?"

"I knew it. You're drunk."

"Hey, I didn't drive!"

"Who did?"

"Boris."

"Was he drunk?"

"He only had one beer."

"Not good enough, baby sister. Did everyone drink?"

"I don't think Angel did. Clancy's hammered."

"So, why didn't Angel drive?"

"Goodnight, Sid." She turned to the side door on the west wall, leading into the porch.

"Josh Kelton only had one beer," I called after her.

"Goodnight, Sid." She closed the door behind her, and shut off the garage light.

I leaned back against the front fender of Sid's Rig for a long, silent minute, and then pulled out my cell phone.

It only rang twice.

"Hello?" The voice was sleepy.

"Boris, did I wake you up?"

"Hey, Sid. No, I just got in bed."

"Sorry to bother. I just needed to tell you … the next time you drive my sister, you have zero blood alcohol. You got that?"

"Oh … sorry. I wasn't drunk, you know."

"I know. It's okay. Just next time …. Zero. Goodnight."

I closed the phone, and went to bed.

CHAPTER ELEVEN

Recently, I wondered if I had ever undergone any type of interview prior to June first of that year, aside from a few grilling sessions with the high school guidance counsellor. I had not exactly needed an interview to work for my dad, and that was the only job that I had ever had. I hated the looming prospect of my interview with Linda Matthews even more than I had hated scheduling it by phone.

I liked to go to church on Sundays, so I usually did not get into the shop until one in the afternoon. However, as I had stupidly told Linda Matthews to come anytime, I had absolutely no clue as to when she would arrive. Thus, when Kat arrived at ten to open the restaurant, I was already there, mixing a batch of pizza dough, and I knew that I would likely be there right until midnight. Well, Kat needed the help anyway. Sammy had been on the schedule for that morning, but he had recently lost employment status. The guy was an idiot.

Sunday mornings were usually slow. Most people in Chetwynd would spend the morning in church, enjoying the day off at home, or just sleeping off the Saturday hangover. This gave me and my crew plenty of time to prepare for the busy evening.

"Sid, are we out of oregano?" Kat asked, digging through the spice rack.

"Why do I have to do this?! I didn't *ask* for this!"

Kat raised an eyebrow. "Chill, Sid. It's an interview. It's publicity. It's good, okay? Are we out of oregano?"

"It's on order. Kat, work with me, will you? I'm trying to freak out here."

She laughed. "You need to work on it. You're too used to being unflappable."

"I don't like talking about myself to strangers. I don't even like talking about myself to friends."

"Well, this will be good practice for you. Teach you to open up a bit, hmmmm? Anyway, they're probably going to be asking mostly about the shop. They'll just get some staff information for the sake of human interest. Haven't you ever read *30 Days Up North?*"

"No," I admitted. "I just like the crosswords."

"Sid, you're on the shady side of thirty. Don't be a baby on me now. Make yourself a coffee."

Boris had left the coffeepot full again. I filled my Cup of Wrath with the thirty-six-hour old brew, the opaque black liquid somewhat sludgy from the overflowed grounds. I could almost smell the clutch burning out of my digestive tract as I took the first noxious swig.

"*Eeee ...!*" I squeaked through clenched teeth, my eyes watering. "Now, *that's* coffee!"

"Sugar?"

"Please. Lots."

The day was still, hot, and excruciatingly slow. Kat and I had a grand total of three eat-in orders and one delivery by the time Angel arrived at two o'clock. She was in her usual high spirits, bubbling over with the joy of her *Hakuna Matata* existence.

"Hey Kat, hey Boss!" she jabbered excitedly. "You've got to hear this. Clancy is, like, so ... *sweet!* Know what he did? Can you guess? Never mind, I'll tell you. He picked me up at like four this morning, and we drove out to his aunt and uncle's farm, down near the Pine Pass, and we sat by the duck pond and watched the sun come up over the mountains, and it turned all the ducks red, and it was *so cool!* Couldn't you just *die?*" Angel had this cute habit of bouncing up and down on her toes whenever she related fond memories. I wondered if she ate the sugary cereal with marshmallow bits every morning.

"That's romantic?" I said, uncertainly.

"Totally!"

"Getting hauled out of bed in the middle of the night to sit in the dark on dew soaked grass, and look at a swamp?" I clarified. "Did you get an engagement out of it, at least?"

"No, nothing that good," she assured me, adding confidently, "Any day now...."

Girl, the harsh realities of life are going to eat you alive 'any day now.'

"May you be blessed with many happy years together," I said dryly. "We need a bin of mozzarella grated up."

"You don't have a girlfriend, do you, Boss?"

It was more of a statement than a question. Kat choked a laugh back down into her stomach, and I shot her a quick glare.

"You're almost toeing the 'point of no return' line, Angel," I growled, sipping my coffee.

"Look, all I'm saying is that you've got a thriving business, your employees are your best friends, and you're still so uptight all the time," she explained, condescendingly. "Take it from me. When a guy like you is always uptight, it means one of two things. Either he needs a girlfriend, or he already has one."

The down side of working with Angel was that I kept finding myself at a loss for words every five minutes or so.

"Your powers of deduction are absolutely mind-boggling," I eventually remarked, shaking my head, a very common mannerism when having discussions with Angel. You had to love her.

Angel disappeared into the walk-in fridge, but kept right on talking.

"And you won't believe what else Clancy's got planned." She had to speak loudly to be heard over the whirring fans in the cooler. "Next Wednesday, we're going down south to Prince George. We get to spend the day shopping, and then we're going to a concert."

Kat and I exchanged sharp glances.

"Clancy's going *shopping?*" Kat whispered, incredulous. "Jeepers, he *is* in love!"

Angel emerged from the cooler with an armload of plastic packaged blocks of white cheese, kicking the door shut with her heel.

"You know, Boss, I hear that a lot of restaurants order in pre-grated cheese."

"Yeah, I'll bring that up at the next staff meeting," I croaked. "Which concert are you going to?"

"That's the best part," Angel said smugly, dumping the cheese onto the cutting board next to the round, motorized cheese grater. "Only the greatest rap duo in the Canadian music industry. I'm talking about the one, the *only ... Bacon N Da Egg!*"

"Ah, yes," I said knowingly. "Canada's latest *thang* in the Great White Rapper genre. Their trademark concert opening line alone is destined to make them epic: 'Pass da salt, *yo!*'"

"Shut up, they're awesome!" Angel snapped, ripping the wrappers from the cheese blocks. "You're just jealous that you didn't get tickets."

"And yet, somehow, I'll survive," I said mildly.

"Are you telling me you don't like rap, Boss?"

"That is exactly what I'm telling you," I replied, weighing out lumps of dough for the press.

"What *do* you like, then?" Her tone indicated that there was no other type of music.

"I'm a child of the seventies," I said. "I like classic discotheque."

"*Classic* disco? Who's your favourite?"

"ABBA."

"*ABBA?!*"

"Hey, any band that used to be Sweden's largest independent source of foreign income has to have something going for them. They were the best."

"I like country," Kat remarked.

"Boris likes classic rock, and Cindy likes pop and the masterworks," Angel rattled off. "How do we all manage to *survive* in this place?"

"It's called being eclectic," I said. "Straighten your bow-tie. We've got to look extra snazzy today."

"Ooooh, is someone getting the jitters?" Angel cooed. "Oh, by the way, Boss, I meant to tell you. We're out of oregano."

"Thank you, Angel," I sighed, as she switched on the grater and began running the first block through it into a large, clear plastic bin.

"Pass da salt, *yo!*" Angel murmured, before humming the title track of *Bacon N Da Egg's* debut *Crack N Fry* album. There was not enough coffee in the world to get me through that day.

Three-thirty brought Cindy and Mark into the shop, along with a handful of customers, but Linda Matthews seemed determined to give me an ulcer simply by not showing up. Boris had the day off, and Clancy was only scheduled in at eight, but I could not leave until I got that dang interview over with.

It was just after seven-thirty, and I was at the reception desk, when the front door opened, and a heavyset, fortyish woman with short grey hair entered, accompanied by a tall, bald black man in his early twenties, both well dressed. She carried a clipboard, and he wore an expensive looking camera around his neck. I downed my fourth cup of coffee, and stood as they approached the desk.

"Well," the woman chuckled amiably. "5-10, black vest, brown hair, and…." She leaned across the desk and glanced down at my feet. "Cowboy boots. You must be Sidney Myers."

I actually gave a short laugh. I figured that was a good start. "You remembered, Ms. Matthews," I smiled.

"Call me Linda," she scolded, shaking my hand firmly. "Sidney, this is Trent Calloway, who takes photographs for *30 Days Up North.*"

"Trent," I nodded, shaking his hand.

"Howdy, Mr. Myers," he grinned. "This is a fine restaurant."

"We do our best," I said modestly. "Welcome to By The Slice. Let me show you around." I started the tour in the kitchen, introducing each of my staff members, and explaining the role that each played in the running of the pizza shop. Already, I was surprised by how easily I could fall into conversation with these strangers. They asked a lot of questions, and Trent even cracked jokes to ensure that everybody was smiling as he took a group photo of the staff, Linda, and myself in front of the cross-eyed coyote. Linda had a funny sounding, giggly laugh, and I heard it often as I gave her an apron and helped her make her own house special.

"Excellent, Linda," I said as she slid the pizza into the oven. We all applauded her first pizza, and Linda bowed jokingly, while Trent captured every moment for posterity.

I joined my guests of honour at a central table in the now crowded dining room, and Cindy serenaded us on the piano. Angel was promptly in attendance to serve our drinks, and then proudly presented us with the pizza that Linda had made, cooked to perfection. I could not believe this. I was *enjoying* myself.

"This is absolutely wonderful!" Linda exclaimed. "Your sister plays beautifully. Not many restaurants have dinner music anymore. I love it."

"Yeah, she started taking lessons when she was nine," I said proudly. "My father also played. Every single day."

"Do you also carry on the family tradition?" Linda asked, sipping her tall glass of iced tea.

I smiled. "I just plink on it once in a while. Cindy actually wrote the piece that she's playing now, as a birthday present for our grandmother. She worked on it for seven— Holy *crap!*"

My charming host eloquence was instantly replaced by a look of frozen horror. I could not believe my eyes.

"Excuse me?" Trent said, confused.

Boris had just walked into the dining room. He was wearing a tuxedo.

He's going to do it right now....

Linda, Trent, and Cindy all had their backs turned away form Boris, and had not yet noticed him. Boris took a long breath and strode determinedly in Cindy's direction. I grabbed his elbow as he tried to rush past my table.

"Linda, Trent," I said loudly, standing. "This is Boris J. Morris, prep cook and main delivery driver ... and he's wearing a tuxedo. A two button, single-breasted shawl with a red cummerbund ... and that's kind of unusual."

"I got the rock, Sid!" he whispered nervously, his bulging eyes getting blinky. "Now, or never."

I groaned as I slumped back into my seat. Cindy had stopped playing and was staring, open-mouthed, at Boris, as was every other person in the room.

This is going to be a very interesting article. More ... coffee!

"Cynthia Adele Myers," Boris proclaimed, the high volume apparently preventing his voice from shaking. "You know I love you. You're my reason for getting up in the morning. If you'll have me, I'm asking you to be my wife."

Cindy was already getting teary eyed, and covering her mouth with her hand. The enraptured patrons let out a collective "*Aaaaaww ...!*" just as Boris had planned. My Cup of Wrath was empty. Angel was only a few feet away with the coffeepot, but the tears in her eyes assured me that it would be a few minutes before she would be able to serve again.

Boris was on one knee, as Cindy slowly stood from the piano bench.

"Marry me, Cindy," he said, smiling weakly. "We can split the rent on my apartment and save a bundle. It's economically sound reasoning."

Cindy let out a tearful laugh as Boris took her left hand in both of his.

"Please say yes, Cindy. I think I'm kneeling on someone's wad of bubble gum."

Boris's predictions had been right. The patrons had begun chanting.

"*Yes! Yes! Yes ...!*"

"Oh, just shut up, Boris," Cindy smiled, pulling him to his feet and kissing him for a long time, the crowd giving them a standingovation. Linda and Trent cheered the loudest of all as Boris slid the glittering diamond onto her finger.

Wow. I'm an in-law.

CHAPTER TWELVE

The most wonderful moments in life can end up being real nuisances if they are not timed properly. I was trying to get an interview over with, and my sister was simultaneously getting engaged. Now, I had to crassly ignore the joyous occasion and try to continue with the official business at hand. On the other hand, I have never had the world's greatest success with joyous occasions. The worst case of hiccups that I had ever had struck me just as I was attempting to toast the bride and groom at a wedding for two old high school friends.

Myers, does it ever occur to you that your life is a bit like a worse than average reality TV show?

Up until the point when Boris hit his knees in the dining room, wearing a tuxedo that I had not even known that he owned, my interview with Linda had been more of an informal chat in a relaxing environment. However, from the moment that Cindy accepted the ring, civilized conversation became an impossibility in that dining room. Kat and Clancy both rushed in from the kitchen to join in the hug-fest, Cindy and Angel were weeping uncontrollably, and Boris had to shake hands with every single patron in the room. Meanwhile, Big Ronnie Alders was trying to order a round of milkshakes for everyone, and I still needed a coffee. It was time to relocate the interview.

I excused myself from my guests and gave Cindy a long hug, her joyful tears making the side of my own face damp as she clung to me.

"Congrats, baby sister," I whispered, kissing her forehead. "I'm proud of you. Dad always liked Boris, even that time when he almost ignited the deep fryer."

She laughed, stepping back and wiping tears with the back of her hand.

"Well, we can laugh about it now. I love you, Sid."

"I love you, too," I smiled. "I have to finish this interview. I'm sure no more work is going to get done tonight." I gave her one more squeeze, then turned to give Boris a good natured, one-handed shake of the collar, twisting his bow-tie just enough to momentarily inhibit his air flow. If timing was everything, Boris had nothing.

Trent was busy taking pictures of the happy couple when I invited Linda to step into my office for the duration of our talks. Once we had settled into the relative silence beside my humming deep freezer, and I finally had my coffee refill, the journalist began chuckling again.

"You didn't warn me about *that*," she said.

"They didn't warn *me*," I sighed.

"But, you don't seem surprised."

"Boris and my sister have been an item, on and off, ever since the first grade. This day was inevitable."

"Do you disapprove?" she asked, surprised.

Your connotation needs work, Myers....

"No," I assured her quickly. "She's found a good guy who knows how to save money. You know, Boris saves almost every tip that he has ever made in a separate bank account. He's got like sixty thousand dollars in there. The man is *fleecing* this town. It's sickening, actually."

"You must be very happy, then."

"I am," I nodded. "I just wish they could have waited another forty-five minutes."

"Relax, it gives the article a lot more humanity. Our readers will love it."

"Mind if I ask you something?" I ventured, after Linda managed to stop giggling.

"Fire away."

"How did you even hear about this place? Or me, for that matter?"

"We get all kinds of letters, recommending businesses and people for profiles. Several months ago, I received a letter from a Pamela Millerton."

"Who?" I had never heard the name before.

"That's right," Linda remembered, shaking her head. "She's married now. You may remember her as Pamela ... Gregson? Does that sound right?"

I froze for a moment, with my mug halfway to my lips. I slowly set the coffee back on the desk.

"The girl who saved me."

"Well, the girl who saw you and called for help, yes."

"Ms. Matthews, I outweighed her by about forty pounds. She dragged me, deadweight, away from a spreading pool of gasoline. She saved me. She was the only hero that night."

"I am inclined to disagree," Linda said quietly. "I spoke with her personally, and she told me everything. I know what you did."

"You know what I tried to do, and failed to do. Three people died, and I lived."

"I do not judge heroism by success or failure," she explained patiently. "A hero is judged by what he strives for, and what he risks to achieve it. The outcome is simply the part that goes into the history books. Sidney, our readers need to know that businesses are about more than buying and selling and time-clocks. I want to show them the human faces behind the financial machine. People like you, who have suffered the sting of loss, and yet still carry on the family tradition. You know about purpose in life, Sidney. This town lost three beloved citizens in one night, yet one more survived, and decided to pick up the plough that his parents left sitting in the field."

This woman is either a poet or a farm girl.

"I don't have parents," I said calmly. "I never did. I had a father."

"Oh...." She was somewhat taken aback. "Sorry. I did not mean to offend."

"You didn't. I was just ... letting you know."

Silence hung uneasily over the room for a short while, until I inquired in a low voice, "How is she?"

"I'm sorry?"

"Pamela Gregson. Is she okay?"

"Oh, she seemed fine. I don't know if you've kept in touch at all, but she's married and works as a photographer and photo developer in Dawson Creek. Actually, she's a friend of Trent's. I guess that's how she heard about me, and the magazine."

"Good to hear." I nodded. "If you see her again, please tell her I said hi."

"Certainly," Linda agreed. "I'll let her know."

"I'd appreciate that, Linda."

"Mr. Myers, I hope that we can make one thing very clear to you. I want this article to be respectful of you, your business, and your personal feelings. If you would prefer that I not go into the details of that night, I will respect that."

"All of my friends here want me to be revered as a hero," I said. "But, I cannot accept that title, or any kind of praise. I can't tell you what to write or not to write. You wouldn't be a real journalist if I did that. But, all that I am going to tell you is that I was involved in a tragic car crash. My father and two other people were killed. I survived. I survived, and decided to keep my dad's dream alive. That's all."

"Well, I can only write the account you give me," she sighed acceptantly, clipping her pen back onto the top of the clipboard. "I fully understand. It must be hard for you to talk about the accident at all."

I looked up at her.

"Accident...." I mused, sipping my mug. "A car ... *accident*. Is that what the papers called it?"

"Yes, I believe so," she said, puzzled. "I read through the archives of Chetwynd papers. Why?"

"It's just an interesting term, that's all," I shrugged.

"Interesting, how?"

"Well, the word itself implies that there were no culpable or contributing factors, that the entire event was perfectly random, yet inevitable. It *had* to happen, but nobody caused it."

"And you don't believe that?"

"I don't believe in accidents. The basic theory of cause and effect doesn't allow for it."

"Well, I'm not sure that the word accident implies that there was no cause. I have always considered it to mean that there was no intent, just circumstances beyond our control."

"Yeah, that's probably it," I admitted. "Sorry, I was just … thinking out loud."

"Do you believe that your father's death was in any way intentional?"

"No," I said. "It was circumstances beyond our control. It was raining, hard to see. I've never seen another storm like that one. No one should have been on the roads that night. There was no intent."

"Well," she smiled, "you survived. And you've kept this restaurant as a place you should truly be proud of. Also, if she's single, you should give some serious thought to marrying that cook of yours, Kathy."

"Kat," I corrected her. "She hates being called Kathy. You know, it's strange. This makes three people who have tried to marry me off to three different girls in the past week. I'm starting to feel old."

"Get used to it," Linda grinned. "Are you thirty yet?"

"A few more years."

"Well, enjoy them. Once you hit thirty, you'll never stop feeling old."

151

"Too late," I groaned. "I started feeling old about the same time that I started shaving."

"Fifteen?"

"Thirteen. Luck of the Irish, I guess."

"I just had one more question, Sidney. What do you see for the future of your restaurant?"

"Well, if the rumours of a Redmond's Ribs turn out to be true, maybe nothing. Otherwise, I have no big changes planned. Just keep on living, keep making pizzas."

"You're happy doing that?"

"It's a job, Ms. Matthews. I keep my life simple."

CHAPTER THIRTEEN

I thought that my *30 Days Up North* interview would be a relief to have finished, but in the days that followed, I found myself somewhat depressed and constantly uneasy. It was as though something essential had been left out. I had no idea why I even cared. In spite of the easy-going manner of Linda Matthews, I had not wanted to be profiled in the first place, yet now I was being eaten alive by a sense of incompletion. I made the decision to never talk to journalists, ever again. The potential publicity of news coverage was not worth this bizarre form of post-traumatic stress. The next time that someone called about an interview, I was going to say, "Here, I'll let you talk to my assistant manager," and hand the phone to Kat. I hated the telephone. I was finished with it. I was not going to talk to reporters, investment corporations, telemarketers, charitable organizations, or anyone else who was not interested in ordering a pizza. If the phone rang and the voice on the other end said, "Stand by for the President," I was going to hand the phone to Kat.

I must have been in a bad mood on the following Tuesday evening, because Angel's bubbly nature, which I usually found to be strangely soothing, was running my nerves through a psychological cheese grater. I did not want to be at work, but I still had not found a replacement for Sammy, so I was stuck with another fourteen-hour shift. Actually, that was the only comforting reminder that kept me from freaking out that night. Sammy was gone. Callous as it may sound, the colours were brighter and the birds sang sweeter since his expulsion. True, he was no Monica Presby, but at least she had a personality. Sammy struck me as being little more than a blank stare and a severe case of jaw muscle atrophy.

Statistically, Tuesdays were the slowest nights of the week at By The Slice. Angel, Boris and I were the only ones on duty after nine o'clock, and we had not had a customer in over an hour. We already had everything cleaned and prepped up for the next day by ten o'clock, and, although I had decided to close an hour early, that last hour still seemed like a very long time. Boris and I had probably uttered six words apiece in the preceding thirty minutes, whereas Angel had not been able to shut up all night. She could not get over the fact that she and Clancy would actually be at a *Bacon N Da Egg* concert the following night. She was a giddy child, about to come face to face with the inventor of the Lite-Brite. Yes, I realize that sounds like a bad metaphor, but you would have needed to be there to appreciate the honesty of it.

"Boss, if you're ever going to be excited about anything, it should be now," Angel insisted, as she

154

slid the last rack of dishes into the automatic washer. "These guys are like the greatest rappers to come along in … in…."

"… the last fifteen minutes," I growled, wiping down counters with a damp cloth. "You want me to tell you what part of *da hood* your *gangsta* heroes came from? 'Bacon' was a burger-flipper, and 'Da Egg' worked for Canada Post. 'Pass da stamps, *yo!*'"

"Say what you like, Dr. Mood Swing," Angel remarked. "It's going to be great."

"When are you leaving?" a glazed over Boris asked, leaning wearily against the prep table.

"Right after work. Clancy's got a friend in Prince George who said that we can crash at her place until morning."

"You're leaving at *eleven?*" Boris was appalled. "It's a three-hour drive through the Pine Pass, and there's avalanche zones all the way through. It's nasty enough in the daylight."

"It's June, Boris," Angel commented. "Even in the Peace Region, I doubt there's going to be any slides this late."

"Hey, do you know what avalanches are like?" Boris said, ominously. "You hear a rumbling, you turn in time to see a white wall coming at you at over a hundred miles per hour, and, when that thing hits you, your teeth come out the back of your skull. Have you seen that? I've seen it. You don't wanna see it."

Boris, you've never seen an avalanche in your life….

The man's sense of humour was always too bizarre for me to even figure out, but he could usually get a laugh out of Angel. On the other hand, Angel once cracked up while reading the ingredients in Kat's homemade pizza sauce. Apparently, 'parsley' is one of those words that sounds funny when you say it three times, really fast. I had never seen anyone who could laugh so much. Sometimes, I had to wonder if Angel was a recovering drug addict, or something like that, with hyperactivity being one of her lingering side effects. She seemed to share my own disapproval of drug use, but maybe that was just her defence against cravings. Honestly, I had no idea. No one else did, either.

I found myself staring at Angel, as she quickly towelled off the inverted bases of the steaming white coffee mugs which she had just pulled out of the washer. I could not figure her out. She was so happy, bubbly, and open-hearted, and yet extremely private as well. Clancy had admitted to me that he had never once been invited into her home, and they had been dating for over a month. I had the twenty dollars from Boris to prove it. Angel was the most extroverted recluse that I had ever met, and that contradiction of terms was really starting to bother me.

Good grief, she was in jail....

"Boss?"

"Huh?" I said, startled by the realization that she was staring back at me.

"Are you checking me out?" She almost seemed to like the idea.

"No!"

"Are you sure? Because you really looked like you were checking me out."

Boris was suddenly watching both of us, with an irksome amount of interest on his face.

"Sorry, Angel," I said, embarrassed. "You walked into the middle of my staring off into space."

Angel smirked. "Boss, if I had a nickel...."

"Yeah, I hate it when people do that," Boris said casually, with a quiet smile that I was really tempted to wipe off with a baseball bat.

Don't kill him. He's officially going to marry your sister. And, Angel, don't flatter yourself. You're cute, but not that cute.

When we finally did close up the restaurant, Clancy was waiting outside in his newly repaired silver Dodge truck, that had to date back to the late eighties, at least. Angel blurted out a quick goodbye, bounded into the passenger seat, and the two of them roared off into the dark night.

"Ah, there's nothing like a late night drive through a Rocky Mountain pass," Boris said nostalgically. "Clancy and Angel, see you in the obituaries."

"Have you ever actually driven the pass at night?" I asked him, locking the front door.

"Just once, that time when my grandpa was really sick down in Invermere. Remember that? Mid January, and it snowed all the way. Very, very nasty. That was the longest night of my life."

"Well, they shouldn't have trouble tonight. It's been warm enough. I just hope they brought coffee."

"Yeah, a drive without caffeine is chaos," Boris agreed.

"Preach it," I chuckled, crawling into my truck. "Are you coming over? Cindy was renting some movies. I think Kat's already there."

157

"Sure, I'll be right there," Boris replied, then laughed. "Does it seem weird to you that we all spend every working hour together, and then we hang out together on our days off? Does that make us communists, or a hippie farm?"

"We're By The Slice Steak and Pizza," I said simply. "We're one of a kind."

Cindy had assured me that, in celebration of her engagement, there would not be a trace of healthy food in the house when Boris and I arrived. She kept her promise. There were bowls of potato chips, ice cream floats, and Kat had brought a batch of her famous peanut butter cookies. Dieting was not a pressing matter that evening. As we all settled into the sofas in front of the TV, Kat toasted the engagement of Boris and Cindy with her root beer float, and we all clinked our frothy glasses together.

Tuesday nights marked the beginning of the weekend, so movie marathons at my house were common. Cindy had decided that it was "Killer Gorilla Night," so the movie rentals included the original *King Kong*, *Congo*, and *The Planet of the Apes*. By the end of *Kong*, we were all feeling sick from too much junk food, and the following goriness of *Congo* did not help matters.

When Spring Stevens and I were dating, she always waited for the best part of the movie before deciding that she needed a cuddle, or a conversation, and it nearly drove me crazy. That is probably why my first thought was that Spring must have been the one calling when my cell phone unexpectedly rang, just as Laura Linney was charging the mutant gorillas with a laser gun. Cindy must have been more frightened than she wanted to admit, because the disco jingle made her scream and grab Boris, nearly squeezing the air from his lungs.

"Relax, Cindy," I said. "It's Barry White, not the … boogiemonkey." I pulled out the phone and flipped it open, glancing at the clock over the fireplace. "Sheesh, it's two-thirty."

"*Ssshhhh!*" Boris hissed, his bulging eyes still rivetted to the carnage on the flat screen.

I sighed, and heaved myself off the sofa, letting Kat's sleeping form slide down sideways, until she was lying with her head on Cindy's lap. I carried the phone into the kitchen, trying to shake some life into my sleeping left arm. I loved Kat, but I knew that someday I would watch one too many movies with her, and my arm would fall off, right onto the carpet.

"Hello?" I said, punching the glowing 'talk' button.

"*BOSS!*"

Oh, no….

"Angel?"

"Help!"

"Angel, is that you?"

"Boss, I'm not kidding! We need help!"

"Are you okay?" I asked, still surprised, and beginning to get alarmed.

"Yeah, we're fine," she scoffed. "I just called you at two in the morning and said 'Boss, help,' for the fun of it."

"Well, if you can still afford to be sarcastic, then obviously your life is not in too great a danger. I'm hanging up now."

159

"No! Don't! Sorry, but you've gotta help us here."

"Fine. What's wrong?"

"We're stranded," she gurgled. "Did I wake you up?"

"What?!"

"Clancy's truck. It blew up. Again."

"What's wrong with it?"

"Boss, I'm no mechanic," she wheezed. "If I had to guess, I'd say that the transmission dropped right out. Ka-*poot!*"

"Wait a second. Are you telling me that you're still in the Pine Pass?"

"Right in the middle of it," she croaked miserably. "Boss, you've gotta come get us. The mountains are closing in on us, and they look angry. Not that I'm getting paranoid, or anything," she added with a cough.

"You're sounding hoarse, Angel," I noted.

"You be hoarse too," she snapped, "if you had to climb a mountain to get your cell phone to work! 'Course I'm hoarse. But, I think Clancy's going to be worse by the time you get here."

"Uh-oh. Did he go off on one of his screaming fits? That's how he does home repairs on his lawn mower. Lots of kicking and screaming."

"No," Angel replied coldly. "But, when I hang up this phone, I'm going to wrap my vice-grip fingers around his windpipe, and, by the time you get here and pry them off, he's going to be pretty croaky himself."

Feel the love.... I think they had a fight.

"Climb down to the truck," I groaned. "I'll be there in about an hour. Are you sure you can't get a ride with someone passing by?"

"Hitch-hiking's illegal in BC," she scolded me. "You should know that. And, besides ... *not one bloody car has gone by in the last two and a half hours!*"

She was still shouting into the phone when her battery began dying, so all that I heard after that was garbled roaring, which is probably a good thing. Burdened by the stress of the past hours, I seriously doubt that Angel was very concerned with maintaining a ladylike vocabulary. I hung up.

The night was cool, so I pulled on my heavy brown leather jacket as I walked back into the living room.

"Who was that?" Cindy asked, playing with Kat's dark hair in her lap.

"Clancy's truck blew up in the pass, and I've got to go save his life before Angel kills him," I said, matter-of-factly. "Where's my cowboy boots? I can't go on a rescue mission without my cowboy boots."

"Are you serious?" Boris said incredulously.

"No joke. Cindy? Boots?"

"I just cleaned them, they were all dusty. They're in the hall closet. You're seriously going out there at this time of night?"

"Yup," I said, pulling the boots out of the closet and tugging them on. "Boris, did you turn off the coffeepot at the shop before we left?"

"Of course."

"Did you empty it out and wash it, as the health regulations demand?"

"Uh ... no."

161

"Good," I said, snatching my travel mug off the fireplace mantle, nearly knocking Cindy's tenth grade musical achievement award to the floor. "I'm going to need a lot of cold coffee." Without another word, I was gone.

"Do you want us to come?" I heard Boris call out, just before the door slammed shut behind me.

I have said it before. I was a lousy boss. The boss was supposed to be a great and terrible vessel of wrath, one to be revered and respected by employees. My employees crawled in laundry room windows to wake me up with professional wrestling moves, or called me at two a.m. because they were afraid of the dark. Who would have thought that having close friends work for you could be such a subtle curse? Obviously, I did not.

Main street in Chetwynd was actually the BC Highway 97 running through the middle of the village, and was also one of the few routes from southern BC to the Yukon and Alaska. During the summer months, the highway filled with tourists, domestic and American, making the great trek "North to Alaska." However, to even get as far north as Chetwynd, they first had to funnel through the Pine Pass, just north of Prince George. Known as the Gateway to the Peace Region, the Pine Pass was one long stretch of highway, seemingly hewn straight out of the stone base of the snow capped Rocky Mountains, but interspersed with strips of farmland in broad valleys. It was one of the most scenic mountain drives that I knew of, which had not been classified as a national or provincial park. The flow of tourists had not gone unnoticed by the governing authorities, and such attractions as the famous Powder King ski hill could also be found along that occasionally treacherous road. As Boris had forewarned, the pass was filled with such unnerving warning signs as "Watch for Moose," and, "Avalanche Zone: Do not stop!" I was not certain how long it had been since anyone was actually caught in an avalanche, if ever, but the possibility did add a certain degree of tension to the otherwise wonderful sight-seeing experience. I suppose if my truck had conked out in the pass in the middle of the night, I might have called for help too, even in the early days of summer. I did not even want to know how much the bill for a tow truck would be, which was probably why Clancy and Angel had called me. I worked cheap.

I stopped at my darkened restaurant long enough to fill up my mug with Boris's special brew, and then pulled out onto the 97 South, heading for the Pine Pass, and my cast away co-workers.

Other bosses would just fire people for asking inconvenient favours. I agree without question.

The drive was long and boring, the enveloping darkness preventing me from even enjoying the craggy mountain scenery. I tried hard to keep my mind focussed on the road, but it was beginning to wander into the realm of deep thoughts, even as it subconsciously told my hands to swerve around the occasional kamikaze moose.

Are killer gorillas real?

I was driving too fast, but it was still over an hour before I spotted Clancy's silver Dodge parked on the right side of the road ahead of me, the hazard lights blinking their rather pointless warning to other drivers.

I had not seen another moving vehicle since I pulled out of Chetwynd.

I didn't know hitch-hiking was illegal ....

I was still casually sipping from my mug as I sauntered into the beam of my headlights, my advancing shadow looming over Clancy's tailgate. As I approached the driver side door, I could see Clancy and Angel asleep inside, each one's head resting against a fogged up window. That was odd, especially knowing Clancy as I did.

Oh boy.... Sitting on opposite sides of the cab, not huddled together for warmth.... Somebody's angry.

The night air was even colder in the pass. I could see my breath and even shivered a little as I tapped an index finger against Clancy's window. He started awake, and groggily sat up. I could see his lips mouth the words "Hey, Sid" as he swung his door open and staggered out to the pavement, stretching and rolling his cramped arms and shoulders. I could smell alcohol.

"Well, the weekend's off to a good start," I commented. "Coffee?"

"I just wanna go home, man," he mumbled, seeming a bit unsteady on his feet. "It's too cold."

"My truck's nice and warm," I assured him. "Sheesh, guy, are you drunk, or do you just need to change that air freshener? I've never smelled evergreens like that before."

"I was bringing a six of beer to my friend's house in Prince," he explained dully. "I figured I might as well drink it now. We ain't getting there."

"No, you're not," I agreed, glancing at the truck. "Think it's the tranny?"

"Beats me. You wanna pop the hood?"

"You know dang well that I don't know a thing about engines," I snorted. "We'll call a tow truck in the morning."

"Good enough," he yawned, limping toward Sid's Rig. "I call shotgun. Angel's mad."

"Yeah, I figured that much," I said blandly, leaning across the steering wheel to give the slumbering girl a gentle shake. "Angel, wake up. I'm getting cold."

"Serves you right," she muttered, turning away from me towards the window without opening her eyes. "Go 'way."

"Angel, it's … Boss, not Clancy. Wake up."

"I wanna coffee!" she whined, still half asleep.

"This is Boris coffee," I said loudly. "You don't want it, believe me. Wake up."

Angel moaned and slowly uncurled her body from its fetal position. Her reddish hair had come loose from the ponytail, and was mussed up comically. She sat up straight, blinking a lot.

"Boss?" she inquired with sleep-induced stupidity. "How'd you get here?"

"Don't tell me you're drunk, too."

"I don't drink," she yawned, stretching. "It's dumb. Kind of like Clancy."

"Hey, that's just cruel."

"Sorry, Boss," she muttered, crawling across the seat, and sliding her sneakers out onto the road. "We just…."

"You had a fight."

"We had a fight."

"Great. Tell me all about it on the drive home."

165

"Hey, you came to get us." She said it as though the obvious had just occurred to her. "Thanks. You the man."

"Don't mention it," I said, slamming Clancy's door shut behind her. "Let's just go."

Angel slid my front seat ahead and crawled in behind it, stretching out across the back seat. Clancy was already asleep in the passenger seat when I got in.

"How many did he have?" I could not help asking, waving a hand in front of his snoring face.

"The whole six," Angel mumbled from behind me. "He's a grouch."

"Go to sleep, Angel," I said dryly, turning the truck around and heading it back toward home.

"Nope. I can't," Angel decided. "I'm the one who has to talk to you, so you don't drift off at the wheel."

She sat up again and stretched, then folded her arms across the seatback between Clancy and I, as though waiting for me to start the conversation.

"Relax, Angel. I don't drift very easily. Get some rest. It's almost four."

"Hey, I know this really nice dead man who used to say that he'd never drift at the wheel. You know what happened to him? I'll give you a hint. He died."

"Okay, fine, talk," I said. "Tell me your life story."

She chuckled. "How about you tell me yours?"

I just knew you were going to duck that one. You were in jail, weren't you?

"My life story," I mused. "Do you want me to just go back as far as I can remember, or do you want what I've been able to piece together from my baby photos?"

"Which would be less boring?"

166

"Believe it or not, I actually look excited in the baby photos."

"Start there, then. I don't want you to put yourself to sleep."

"Hey, my life is not *that* ...! Uh …. Okay, it's pretty boring, but I've seen worse."

"It's okay, Boss," she grinned, socking me on the shoulder. "We've got the same job, and I don't mind it a bit. It's invigorating."

"Invigorating? How?"

"Some would say that being a servant to others is the noblest job of all. It's totally selfless. That's invigorating to me."

"Well, some would also say that the noblest jobs have a lot more spiritual than monetary rewards."

"Like I said, it's selfless. So, tell me your story."

"Well, I was born and raised in Chetwynd, and I'm still in Chetwynd, and the most exciting thing that's ever happened to me involved a chili eating contest at a community bake sale. I own my own business, I'm debt free, I'm making money, and, although I'm not a certified chef, I can cook *anything*. You were right, I don't have a girlfriend. One of the weirdest men that I know is marrying my sister, and I approved the match. The end. Your turn."

"For what?"

"Well, you aren't going to tell me your story, so you might as well tell me what you and Clancy were fighting about."

"He's a dork!"

"Be more specific, please."

167

"Okay, so we leave town, and everything's cool, and the radio's blaring, and I'm like 'This rocks,' and he's like 'Yeah, baby,' and then we almost hit a moose, so that gets me thinking, like, where are we going? So, I ask him where exactly are we going to be staying, and he says 'With Callie Freemantle,' and I'm like 'Who's that?' and he's like 'I used to date her,' and so I'm like 'Like, *what?!*' So, then he tries to tell me that they're still just friends, and I didn't believe him, and he blew up a bit, and I start crying, and then *he* wants to start playing penitent, and it didn't work, so we're both giving each other the silent treatment, and I am like *so choked!* Then we're driving and no one's talking, and I'm thinking, like 'No one's talking here,' because we're both mad, and then we're just driving and driving and driving, and I say, 'This is stupid, I'm sorry,' and he says he's even sorrier, and I start crying again, and *BAM!!*"

Angel slammed a palm down on the seat back to emphasize her mimicked explosion. It made me jump, and even the drunkenly slumbering Clancy gave a short twitch in his sleep.

"'Bam,' what?" I cautiously asked. Even Boris's coffee never gave me jolts like that, anymore.

"The truck blew up."

"Like ... exploded? Are we talking about a fireball and a charred blast radius here, or what?"

"Um ... no, not really," she answered thoughtfully. "It just kind of went '*Kaaaaaaa*-CHUNK! Whump whump whump! *BAM!!*' And then it stopped."

"And, I take it that you didn't use the down time to make up?"

"No," she sighed. "We started fighting again. He said that I should just call you, but I didn't want to wake you up. He said you were never asleep anyway, especially on a Tuesday night, so I try to call, and the phone doesn't work."

"And Jack and Jill went up the hill," I said absently. Even with the coffee, the late hour was beginning to tire me.

"Yeah, we did, and let me tell you, *not fun!* Look at these fingernails, Boss. Just look at them. Actually, don't look, watch the road. But, they're bad."

"So, you fought with Clancy all the way up the side of a mountain, trying to get a decent carrier signal?"

"Jack just about got his crown broke," she growled. "I said it was his truck's fault, that he should scrap the piece of junk, and, uh, that really set him off. He said the truck was worth more to him than anything ... or anyone." For the briefest moment, I thought I heard a sob catch in the back of her throat.

Some relationships just can't handle the give and take aspect....

"Hey, you're both worked up and tired," I soothed her. "You said things you didn't mean. Just stay out of his face for a while, until you're both ready to run crying into each others arms, and then you'll be done with it."

"I know," she admitted. "Just, right now, I'm still mad enough to throttle him in his sleep."

"Don't," I said. "He's scheduled to open the shop on Thursday morning ... if he's sober by then."

"Yeah, yeah, business before vengeance. Is that your personal credo?"

"It's kept me from killing Boris many times. Did you know that he once delivered twenty pizzas to the wrong hotel? An oil crew actually paid him and ate them, knowing that they hadn't ordered them, and left me to deal with an angry hockey team down the street."

"How angry?"

"A dozen teenagers with sticks. Even a little bit of anger is potentially fatal."

"Did they get violent?" Angel seemed eager to hear some gory details.

"Sorry to disappoint, but I just had to listen to their coach rant on the phone for half an hour. I never even said a word. I'm not kidding, I actually handed the phone to Cindy while I went for a coffee. He never even knew that I had left."

"No violence?"

"Only verbal."

"Have you ever been in a fight?"

"High school boxing team."

"Yeah, and I know judo and kick-boxing, but that's not real. Ever been in a real fight?"

"No. I'm pretty benevolent."

"Do you know how?"

Does knowing how to snap someone's arm off count? Oh wait, that's combat, not fighting....

"Not really."

"Come on, Boss, everyone needs to know some kind of self-defence, especially a business owner. You know, in case of a robbery or something."

"Well, that would definitely be useful knowledge, if the guy was holding up the place with a pair of boxing gloves or a moderately sharp pencil. For most robberies, some famil-training with sidearms would be more appropriate."

"Famil-training," Angel parroted. "I've only ever heard two other people use that term, and both of them were military."

"I've got an uncle in the army. I must have picked it up from him."

"So, you've never been in a fight. Have you ever wanted to?"

I did not answer her for a moment, as I stared at the dark road ahead.

Don't start. Do not start.

"Only once," I replied, very quietly.

"Who was it?" Angel grinned. "School bully?"

"No. Just some guy who made me mad."

"What'd he do?"

I shrugged. "He made me mad."

"But, you didn't fight him."

"No."

"Boss, you cannot tell me that no one else has ever made you mad, and yet, out of all of them, you only ever wanted to fight this one guy?"

"That's right."

"So, why didn't you?" The curiosity was obviously killing her.

Do not tell her.

"Suffice to say, cruel irony kicked in. He learned his lesson."

"Boss, you're being evasive."

"Like you never are?"

"Hey, I'm just keeping you from driving into the ditch. Come on, Boss, you can't just leave me hanging, here! How'd he learn his lesson? Did someone beat you to it?"

I nodded. "Yeah."

Yeah ... he died before I could kill him.

"Look, Boss," Angel said softly, after a silent moment. "I already said thank you, but I just want you to know that I think it's awesome that you would drive all the way out here, this late, to rescue us. You're the best, you know that?"

"I know," I said honestly. I was too tired to be modest. "Don't worry about it. I'm something of a night owl, anyway."

"Really?" Angel was skeptical. "You strike me as the type who likes his sleep."

"I do," I answered. "It's just ... I can't."

"What?"

"I can't sleep."

"You do drink a lot of coffee, Boss. At night, not smart."

I smiled half-heartedly. "I started drinking coffee when I realized that I was going to be awake anyway."

"Why?" Angel was reverting back to her five-year-old alter-ego. This was the one topic that I did not want to discuss with her, or anyone else, but if I did not tell her now, she would ask later.

"My dad was killed in a car crash four years ago," I replied platonically. "I've had trouble sleeping ever since."

"Oh ...." she said in a low voice. "I'm sorry."

"It's okay," I said. "It's just something that I need to deal with."

Angel rested her right cheek against her folded forearms, and looked sideways at me.

"What about your mom?" she murmured.

"She's gone," I said simply. "I never knew her."

"I don't know what I'd do if I lost my parents," Angel admitted. "How do you deal with it?"

"It depends. Time does heal, if you let it. Sometimes, I just go for a walk in the middle of the night. Or a jog. I do push-ups until I collapse, or beat the stuffing out of my punching bag. Go to the shop, play the piano, drink more coffee. I guess I just try to exhaust myself so that I can go back to bed and pass out." In the moment of quiet that followed, it occurred to me that I had just confided to someone that I actually touched the piano. I never did that.

Wow.... Did you mean to tell her that much?

"That doesn't sound really healthy, Boss...." Angel said, concerned.

"It's not."

"Actually, it sounds awful."

"That's not even the worst part," I sighed.

"What is?"

Why are you even telling her this? It's none of her business! Oh well, it's too late now....

"When I do fall asleep," I said slowly, "I never want to wake up again."

"Oh." Angel sounded surprised. "I guess ... that would be worse. You want some advice?"

"Sure."

Enlighten me....

"Warm milk. Mom swears by it. I didn't believe it until I tried it, but it works."

173

"I'm not really good with milk," I replied. "Putting a creamer in my coffee gives me cramps."

"Well, it was a thought. Hey, I didn't know you could play."

"What?" I knew exactly what she was talking about.

"The piano."

Lady, I'm the best ....

"I just plink on it once in a while. It's therapeutic."

Angel was yawning again. After having her previous slumber interrupted, even an emotionally edged conversation could only keep her awake for so long.

"Get some sleep, Angel. I'm not going off the road. Like I said, this is Boris coffee."

"All right," she yawned, lying down across the back seat again. "Don't die on me, Boss. Got that?"

"Got it," I chuckled.

The road ahead was winding, and I wished that I could listen to the radio, but wanted to let my passengers sleep. From then on, it was going to be a silent ride.

"Angel?"

"Yo, Boss?" she mumbled sleepily.

"You *did* say that you almost hit a moose, and *that* was what got you wondering about Clancy's ex-girlfriend, right?"

"Yeah. Why?"

"No reason," I said, rolling my eyes. "Go to sleep."

Human thought patterns.... Who can account for them?

It was almost four in the morning. The black sky was fading slowly to a dark grey, but the density of the cloud cover was not about to let any light of dawn peek through just yet. We were still over a half hour's drive from Chetwynd, and I must have been dreaming with my eyes open, because I thought that my windshield wipers were moving. The movement was vague, almost as thought the wipers were vibrating at the base of the glass.

Don't doze off, Myers. Don't die.

Clancy stirred fitfully, belched, and sat up, embarrassed. I knew how Clancy's body operated when he was drunk. Only one need could rouse him from an inebriated snooze.

"Go ahead," I said. "Just roll the window down."

"Thanks, man," he said tiredly, shaking a cigarette out of his pack, while cranking the window open. The cool breeze was refreshing, but then I thought that I must truly have been hallucinating. The windshield wipers were still moving in the darkness.

Oh, good heavens.... They're not moving. They're slithering.

Salami the garter snake had indeed moved out of Boris's vehicle. He had moved into mine.

Angel.... Don't say a word!

Clancy took a long drag from his cigarette, and blew the smoke out the window. He had not seen the snake yet. I wondered if I should tell him, but, for some odd reason, I thought that it would be funnier not to tell him. At four in the morning, strange things start to seem funny.

"Whazzat?" Clancy yawned, stretching. "I thought I saw something move up there."

"Ah, probably that loose windshield viper," I said dismissively. Clancy missed the pun, and seemed satisfied with the explanation as he relaxed with his smoke.

From the glow of the cigarette, I caught a glimpse of something on Clancy's side view mirror. Something long and thin.

Salami was trying to crawl in the window! Unfortunately, this was a feat that the snake had never before attempted at speeds in excess of one hundred kilometres per hour, and he had failed to factor in the wind variable. His tiny green and yellow head had just touched the base of the open window when a gust scooped him up and deposited him right onto Clancy's lap.

Oh, this cannot be good....

"Oh, *sick!*" Clancy said disgustedly, groping around in the dark for the overhead light button. "Sid, I think a bird just flew in and hit me. The poor thing's probably dead, and got blood and feathers all over my—"

"*Don't!*" I yelped, too late. The overhead light clicked on to reveal Clancy and Salami, nose to nose.

A little bit late, I realized that Clancy, too, was afraid of snakes.

"SNAAAAAAAAAAAKE!!"

The next few seconds were something of a blur in my memory, but I will relate them as best as I can remember. Clancy's terrified exclamation seemed to lift both Salami and the previously dozing Angel about a foot into the air. Clancy filled the air with karate chops, in an effort to knock Salami back out the window, but it was futile. The snake landed right back on his lap. The air was then filled with Clancy, who ricocheted madly about the cab, his movements only slightly countered by his seatbelt. The snake was flung from his trouser legs, and whiplashed straight at my face.

"Is that a *snaaaaaaa* ...?" Angel squawked, her brown eyes even larger than usual.

I caught Salami with one hand, and, in what is arguably the stupidest and most ill-conceived action of my life, I tossed him back to Angel. Angel wasted little time in passing the snake back to me. Salami probably passed back and forth between us about five times in the next couple of seconds, while the truck swerved erratically across the highway, and Clancy dug frantically into the front of his tee-shirt in an effort to fish out the cigarette which had fallen down his collar. Never before had I heard human vocal cords produce sounds even remotely similar to those coming from the throats of Clancy and Angel.

Finally, I missed my catch, and Salami landed under my feet. As panicked as he undoubtedly was, I cannot really blame him for scooting up my right pant leg in search of shelter, yet sympathy somehow managed to evade me at that moment. My efforts to dislodge the serpent resulted in the brake and accelerator pedals being alternately slammed through the floorboards, and I probably damaged my own hearing even more than Clancy and Angel combined.

By then, the truck had ground to a full halt, so I was able to use my right hand to seize the snake's tail which still protruded from my pant leg, and unravel Salami from my boot. I tried to fling him out of the open passenger window, but I had not factored in the wind variable, so the writhing reptile went right down the collar of Clancy's shirt. I had never seen anyone else manage to exit that vehicle without opening a door, or even undoing a seatbelt, but having a lit cigarette in your shorts and a snake burning doughnuts around your abdomen tends to give one unusual powers of flexibility.

Clancy was in the headlights by the time Angel and I rushed to his aid, and the dance which he was performing would have earned him an immediate disqualification from any family-oriented talent competition.

"He's in my shirt!" he howled. "Get him! Get him!"

I could only watch in pained silence as a crazed Angel charged to the rescue, clenching my tire iron in both of her quaking fists. At times like those, I was always surprised by how quickly and eloquently I could pray.

God, if I interfere right now, I'll die too. Please deflect that iron from anything too vital.

God spared Clancy's life, but the next seconds were still the most brutal that I had ever witnessed. Angel gave Clancy's ribcage a flurry of short blows with the four-spoked wrench before I could grab her elbows and pin them behind her back. Clancy was doubled over and gasping, winded, but miraculously did not seem to be shattered or punctured anywhere.

Uh ... thanks, God.

"Angel, my dear," I sighed, trying to hold the frenzied girl still. "Communication is extremely important. As a case in point, when Clancy said 'Get him!' just now, I believe that his literal meaning was 'Get him out of my shirt.' But, I could be wrong."

"I hate snakes!" Angel rasped, no longer struggling, but still shaking.

"I hate *you!*" Clancy roared, hugging himself.

"Hey, calm down," I snapped. "Where's the snake?"

"Where's the snake?!" Angel hissed.

I grabbed a flashlight out of my glove compartment and shone it around the dark highway. It took several moments before I had my final glimpse of the snake, unscathed, as he slithered into the grassy ditch.

And that was the last time that any of us saw Salami, that two foot long garter snake who liked to crawl into cars. The limbless reptile had evaded tires, fanbelts, alternator blades and capture by his human hosts for nearly a month, but he had truly left his mark on all of us, most visibly on Clancy's torso. But the snake had done much more than that. He had ensured that Angel and Clancy would never again go on a date.

CHAPTER FOURTEEN

The longest night of my life, up to that point, was not over yet. By the time the three of us had calmed down and finished the drive home, it was five o'clock in the morning, the clouds had lifted, and the sun was just beginning to rise in the red sky. I took Clancy to his home in the Evergreen Trailer Court first, and it was a silent drive. I do not think that any of us said a single word until he got out of the truck in front of his small, unmowed lawn. Then I said "Goodnight, man," and he said "Thanks, Sid." He did not kiss Angel goodnight, and she did not look disappointed. I watched him as he gingerly made his way up the dirt walkway. I wondered if he would even get out of bed before he had to get up to open the shop on Thursday morning.

Angel was sitting in the middle of the backseat, arms crossed, wearing an expression that could have turned a weaker man into stone. Fortunately, after dealing with old Janet Haggerty's complaints about "too chewy" pizzas for the past eight years, I was fairly immunized to dirty looks. Angel was too cute to ever look really scary, anyway, unless she was packing a tire iron.

"Be perfectly honest," I said carefully, watching Clancy limp up the front steps into his mobile home. "Who were you trying to kill, the snake or your boyfriend?"

"I hate snakes, Boss. I panicked, and I guess I got a little carried away."

"Does the term 'downplay' mean anything to you?"

"Isn't that some type of mud wrestling?"

"Nope."

Angel's duplex was only a couple of blocks from my own house, on a street that was an offshoot from the edge of town, a long gravel stretch that tended to get a lot of pot-holes every spring. Even so, it was one of the nicer areas of town. The estates were mainly upscale, with large yards, and the duplexes where Angel lived, Long Road Place, were generally considered to be the finest in Chetwynd. This was the first time that I had ever driven her home, and I was impressed by the size of the place.

"Well, we're back, safe and sound, and with no snake," I said drolly, parking behind Angel's red Cavalier. "Goodnight, Angel."

About then, I heard the first sob from behind me.

"Oh, come on, Angel!" I groaned. "It's been a very long night, and you guys are angry, but it'll blow over. Clancy never stays mad for very long. Call him tomorrow, and you'll be fine. Couples have fights. It's a growing experience."

"*Growing experience?!*" Angel choked through her tears. "Boss, I just attacked him with a crowbar!"

"Actually, it was a tire iron," I reminded her. "If it had been a crowbar, he'd have a sheet over his face right now."

"It's over! He'll never forgive me for that!"

"Well…. Okay, it might take longer than tomorrow, but he'll figure out that you were just having an … automated self-preservation episode."

"Did you just make that up?" she sniffled.

"Yes, I did. But use it when you talk to Clancy. Big words are convincing to him."

Angel rolled wearily over the backrest, and slumped into the front seat alongside me, tears still rolling down her face.

"What if he charges me for assault?" she sobbed, looking up at the overhead light.

"He won't."

"My life is over. You know that, right?"

"Hitting a snag, and hitting a brick wall are two different things, Angel. Come on, you're a survivor. I doubt that you've ever died in your whole life."

That actually prompted a tearful laugh from Angel.

"I know you're trying to help, Boss, but it's not working. I'm miserable, and I'm staying that way."

"Hey, just console yourself with the knowledge that more of the world is on your side than you'd like to admit." I smiled wryly. "That is, aside from millions of religious extremists who want to kill you simply because of your nationality. Life is good."

That really made her laugh, and she was hugging me before I knew it.

"Thanks, Boss," she whispered, giving me a quick kiss on the cheek. "You're the best. We don't deserve you."

Whoa, Nelly, ease up there. I'm your boss.

"Yeah, that's great," I said quickly, sitting up straight. "And it'll all work out fine. Just get some rest, and you'll feel better in the ... mid to late afternoon, most likely."

"Yes, and thanks again for the rescue," she smiled, climbing out of the cab and swinging the door shut.

"Goodnight," I yawned through the open window. "Enjoy the sunrise."

"Sidney...."

I almost gave myself a whiplash as my head spun around to look at Angel, shocked. I was not used to hearing my name come from her mouth. She was looking at me, curiously, through the rolled down window.

"Yeah?" I replied.

"You can't sleep. What do you need?"

"I don't know," I admitted. "Answers.... Maybe, I just need a reason to wake up."

"Well," she said with a sympathetic smile, folding her arms across the window base. "I hope you find it."

"Relax," I assured her. "I will. Goodnight, Angel."

"Goodnight, Boss."

I watched her walk away until she was at her front door. She turned and waved at me as I backed down the brick driveway.

I think I just made a friend....

I loved watching the sun rise, but I was not the type who romantically stayed up all night just to witness the grand event. When I finally got back into my own house, the sun was shining light into the living room, the orange beams illuminating the sleeping forms of Cindy, Boris and Kat, all slumbering on the couch in front of a snow-filled TV screen. They looked so peaceful and rested that I could not bring myself to wake them up. Instead, I simply stole Cindy's enormous plush gorilla from her bedroom, and set it up on the coffee table in front of them. Then I walked down the hall to my own room, realizing that my sister's screams would probably be my alarm clock.

I actually slept right through the alarm, but was awoken shortly afterwards, when Cindy kicked open my door and hurled the gorilla at my head.

"Good morning to you, too," I mumbled, my face buried in my pillow. "What time is it?"

"It's noon!" she snapped. "You scared me to death with that thing!"

"Good. Next week we'll rent *The Birds*, and I'll cover your bed with rubber duckies while you sleep." Actually, I was surprised that Cindy was awake already. She usually slept a couple hours past noon on Wednesdays.

"So?" she inquired. "Is Clancy still alive?"

"He was last I saw," I yawned, sitting up and rubbing my eyes. I realized that I had collapsed onto the bed and slept through the morning without even getting under the covers. "Man, that was a lousy sleep."

"Sid, you're still dressed. You're wearing your jacket and boots!"

"Oh," I said, looking down at my rumpled clothing. "I knew I was forgetting something…."

"Long night, huh?"

"Long day, night, and early morning," I groaned, cramming the gorilla under my head in lieu of a pillow. It was comfortable, in a fuzzy, plushy sort of way. "You won't believe this. You remember Boris's snake? It showed up in Sid's Rig last night."

"You're kidding." Cindy was incredulous.

"No kidding. Four in the morning, it shows up, goes bananas, and Angel killed Clancy with a tire iron."

"*What?!*"

"She was trying to kill the snake. It was in his shirt."

"But, *how* did it …? Uh…. You know what? I don't want to know. For as long as I live, I never want to know." She turned and walked out. Several minutes went by, and I had almost drifted back to sleep when the cell phone rang from inside my jacket pocket. I was a little surprised that I had not smashed it in my sleep. The caller ID read *Clancy Grover*.

"By The Slice," I said groggily, answering the phone without even thinking about what I was saying, or where I was.

"Hey, Sid. Did I wake you up?"

"No. I'm already up and dressed."

"Good. I just wanted to let you know that I'm still alive. And I don't think I ever really said thanks for coming to get us."

"No problem," I said. "I'm just glad you're okay. Bet you're stiff as a board, huh?"

"I was. I'm feeling better now." "Uh…. Has Angel talked to you?"

"She tried. I haven't been answering the phone when her name comes up."

"Get over it, Clanc! She was in a blind panic. She didn't mean to hurt you."

"It's not about that. It's about the fight we had before. I mean, that's what really made me mad. I've been nothing but good to her, and she starts freaking out about nothing."

"Yeah, maybe you should have told her that Callie was an old flame a bit sooner."

"Well, what am I supposed to do? Read her mind, figure out what's going to tick her off? It's not like she ever tells *me* anything. How long have we been together? A month? And I still haven't even seen the inside of her house! Aren't I at least entitled to *that?*"

"Hey, so she's private about her home life. Don't take it as an insult. Maybe it's messy and embarrassing for her. Or maybe her parents were strict about gentlemen callers, who knows. It doesn't mean that she's not in love with you."

"Well, not only that, but then she starts ragging on me for drinking that six. She says I shouldn't drink, ever!"

Heaven forbid….

"She's just looking out for your liver, man. Calm down."

"Well, it wouldn't be so bad if that's all she was looking out for, but she wants me to give it all up. No beer, cigarettes, weed, coke, *nothing!*"

He stopped ranting and just breathed angrily into the phone for a few moments. It took him awhile to notice that I had settled into a shocked silence. Then he realized the mistake he had just made. Our entire friendship began to change, starting at that very moment.

"Whoa," I said, expressionlessly. "Clancy, you got mad just now, and you started venting. But … you didn't mean to tell me that, did you?"

"Ah, crap…." Clancy sighed helplessly.

"She wants you to give up weed *and* coke? Oh, she's a monster, that one. Is that why you're 'feeling better?' Got a little buzz on?"

"Sid…."

"You know, I *had* wondered if you were a bit of a stoner, Clancy. I wouldn't say that I suspected it, but I did wonder. But, cocaine…." I could only shake my head in disbelief. "I never would have guessed that you were running the rails. Am I that hard to trust?"

"Sid, listen. I never told you, because I knew how you felt, and I didn't want you to get the wrong idea. It's recreational, okay? I'm not an addict, and even you can't say that it's affecting my job performance."

"No, it isn't," I said flatly. "Don't let it start. I'm not kidding. You're my friend, but if drugs start holding you up … you're looking for a new job."

"I promise, Sid. I value steady income, okay?"

"Is it worth it?" I could not help asking.

"Sidney, I just got worked over with a tire iron. Right now, it's worth it, believe me."

"So, who's your dealer?"

Silence.

187

"I'm not gonna rat him out, Clanc. I'm just curious."

"Finn."

"Devon Finn?"

"Yeah. He's actually a pretty good friend."

"Wait a second. Devon's just a slacker with a few surplus dime bags. He doesn't sell coke."

"Hey, businesses expand. He's moving up in the world."

"Businesses get glutted by competition, too. How many dealers do we have in this town now?"

"General narcotics, or are we still talking about coke?"

"Coke, for starters."

"Just off the top of my head…. Six, that I know of, anyway."

"That, plus the dozen or so that I know who sell weed, 'shrooms, and X. That makes about eighteen dealers, and about six thousand people in the town and surrounding region, so that's … uh…." My sleepy mind was still able to do the math swiftly in my head. "We've got a drug dealer for every three hundred thirty three point three three three people. I love this town…. Do you think New York has a ratio anywhere near that?"

"Well, that's assuming that we know them all."

"If we don't, Boris does. He knows everything."

"Do you ever wonder if Boris is actually one of those agents who spends his entire life undercover, and then suddenly whacks all the dealers in town, all on the same day?"

Clancy watched a lot more movies than I did.

"Actually, I don't think that there are that many narc units out there who are so committed to their cause that they'd resort to planting sleepers in small towns," I remarked. "But, hey, I've been wrong before. I was wrong about you."

"Hey! What's that supposed to mean?"

"I wondered if you were a stoner, but I never would let myself believe it. I thought you were ... you know...."

"What?" Clancy demanded. "Smarter? Is that you wanna say, Sid, that you thought I was smarter? Go ahead. Say it. I want to hear you say it."

"I thought you were smarter."

"Dang, Sid! I was being theatrical! I didn't *really* want you to say it!"

"I don't like bluffs. As a matter of fact, I hate bluffs. Look, Clancy, you know I don't like drugs, but I'm your friend. I'm not going to lecture you. Do you want me to come over? Have a game of cards or something?"

"No, thanks anyway. I just broke up with my girlfriend, and I think she crippled me in the process. I'll probably just sleep most of the day."

"Hey, don't give up on her so quick. This is Angel we're talking about. She's a sweetheart. She's like.... I don't know.... She's like Kat on a sugar buzz."

"Well, maybe I'm tired of Kat with a sugar buzz. I need a level-headed girl."

"Clancy, are you telling me that you're going to start pursuing steady, intelligent women?" That was a new one.

"Yeah. Why? What's your point?"

189

"Nothing. I'll let you get some rest. If you don't think you'll be feeling up to opening the shop tomorrow, give me a call in the morning. I can cover for you."

"Sid, you were going to take the morning off."

"Stuff happens. Call me if you can't handle it."

Clancy sighed tiredly. "Thanks, Sid. And thanks again for coming for us."

I shrugged. "Hey, what are employers for? See ya."

The curse of Boris's coffee was that it could wake me up even the morning after I drank it. As tired as I was, my eyeballs were wide awake, so sleep was no longer an option. The only way to deal with life at that stage was to get up and drink more coffee. I rolled out of bed and tucked the gorilla under my arm as I headed for the kitchen, stopping in the bathroom long enough to grab my toothbrush.

Cindy was at the stove, frying bacon and eggs for Kat and Boris when I entered the kitchen, still scrubbing my molars. All of us had slept in our clothes, and I am certain that they felt as rumpled and dishevelled as I did. Kat was seated at the dining table, sipping a mug of herbal tea, while Boris leaned against the dishwasher, reading the comics in the local paper.

"Morning," I slurred, through a mouthful of Aquafresh. "Coffee." I spat in the dish sink, and turned on the hot water to rinse off the toothbrush. Cindy hated it when I did that, but I was too tired to care. I had to force myself not to leave the toothbrush on the edge of the sink, something which Cindy hated even more. After rinsing, I stuck the brush behind my ear, grabbed a mug of coffee, and sat across the table from Kat, setting the gorilla on the chair next to me.

"How are you feeling, Sid?" Boris asked.

"Coffee," I replied, taking a long swig.

"That bad, huh?" he remarked.

"Coffee."

Kat leaned forward and clasped her hands around her own mug, looking curiously at me.

"Let's hear some deep thoughts, *mon ami.*"

"Excuse me?"

Kat was grinning. "You were out on a daring, all night rescue mission, featuring a crazy woman and a killer snake. You've got to have some pretty profound insights into the human condition after that."

"Angel hates snakes," I said dryly.

Cindy laughed. "That's the only thing you figured out, big brother?"

"No," I said, icicles forming on every word. "I figured out that I hate snakes, too. They are reptilian vermin. May they all rot in their sleeveless, scaly hides!"

"Eggs?" Cindy inquired, dishing them out onto plates.

"Three. I want cholesterol to kill me before a snake does."

Boris cringed slightly. "Do you want salt on that bacon? Anyway, what did you do to my poor Salami?"

"He left," I said sourly. "He wreaked havoc, and then he left. He's evil, but he's fine."

"Okay, Sid, come clean here," Cindy ordered, setting out the breakfast plates. "What's wrong?

191

You've been up that late before, and you are insanely grumpy right now. Why?" She and Boris took seats next to Kat, and the three of them sat very still and stared at me. I was starving. I loved bacon and eggs, and I felt like I was not even allowed to touch my fork while people were staring at me like that.

I just got off the phone with a close friend who only admitted that he is a habitual drug user by accident, because he obviously didn't trust me enough to be up front about it. Can I eat now?

"Because I'm tired," I replied, and began eating. I had munched my way through the first forkful of slightly burnt egg white, and they were still staring at me.

"What?" I said lazily, trying to maintain an air of boredom.

"That wasn't an answer," Cindy pointed out, making a vaguely threatening gesture at me with a butter knife.

"Your eggs are getting cold, baby sister," I said, nibbling on a strip of bacon.

"You're dodging, Sid," Boris said. He probably did not intend to sound as snide as he did, but I could only take so much antagonism on a Wednesday.

"Okay, that's it," I snapped, standing and taking my plate to the counter by the sink. "I do not need to answer to a dang review board every time that I have a bad mood. I put up with bad moods every bloody day of my life, and maybe I'm entitled to one of my own, just a couple times a year, okay?" The review board stared at me, appalled, as I scraped my breakfast into my plastic travel mug, and jammed a fork into it.

"Sid, what are you *doing?*" Kat asked, gaping.

"I am making a nice, transportable cup of breakfast puree," I growled, vigorously chopping the food into scrambled eggs with my fork. "And I'm taking them for a walk."

"Hey, we didn't mean to grill you, man," Boris defended them. "It's curiosity. Nothing more."

"Well, I still need to walk it out," I sighed. "If I hang around here, I'll just pass on a bad mood to you guys. Cindy, where's my cowboy boots?"

"You're still wearing them," she said weakly, obviously anticipating that the truth would annoy me even more than complex directions.

"Oh," I said, looking at my feet. "I guess ... uh.... I'm leaving now. Sorry."

"Uh, Sid?" Kat called as I headed for the garage.

"Yes?" I stopped, and forced myself to sound patient.

"You've still got your toothbrush behind your ear."

The walk in the warm summer sun did help to calm me down, but the churning feeling of betrayal was not going to go away anytime soon.

Clancy Grover. My friend ever since grade school. Why didn't you just tell me? Did you think I'd hate you? Fire you? I'm not like that. I don't fire people for using. I'd never keep a staff in this town if I did that.

In twenty-seven years of business, over forty people had worked in my restaurant. As I walked, I realized that I had fired more people in the past four years than Karl Myers had in the twenty-three years prior. I wondered if that made me a worse employer, or a more efficient one.

Forget it. You're a lousy boss, Myers.

I walked all the way across town that afternoon. I did get a few odd looks from other pedestrians, but not enough to concern me. I guess some people had never before seen a man eating eggs from a plastic mug while walking down the side of the road. They were good eggs.

I was still feeling cranky as I finished my breakfast/ lunch and walked into a downtown convenience store to refill the mug with coffee. The manager knew me, and waved as I entered. Almost everyone who served coffee in Chetwynd knew me.

"Afternoon, Sid," the tall, beefy man nodded, his elbows propped on the counter by the cash register as he flipped through a hunting magazine.

"Morning, George," I said dully.

"Coffee?"

"Yeah. Mind if I rinse some bacon grease out of this first?"

"Go ahead," George said, motioning for me to come around the counter. "I'm not even going to ask."

"Late breakfast," I explained, running hot water from the sink behind him into my mug. "How's business?"

"No complaints."

"Fire many people lately?"

"No, they've been pretty good. You?"

"Not as many as last year."

"Good to hear," George chuckled.

I walked to the other end of the store, and was pouring my coffee when an unfamiliar voice spoke my name.

"Sidney Myers?"

I turned around, and found myself facing one of the most beautiful women that I have ever seen.

Oh good heavens.... Tall, blonde, and she's wearing cowboy boots.

"Yes?" I cracked.

"I thought that was you! I've seen photos of you with my cousin, Randall." She smiled brilliantly and held out her hand. "Karen Malloy. I am so absolutely thrilled to meet a former Canadian Special Forces! Randall told me all about you, and I would just *love* to hear about your experiences in Bosnia."

CHAPTER FIFTEEN

Clancy insisted that he was feeling well enough to open the shop on Thursday morning, and I still told him to go ahead and take the day off. Kat often told me that I deliberately went out of my way to make my own life harder. She was probably right. I was taking on another fourteen-hour shift that I did not have to, but the fact was that I did not care. I was suddenly in a good and re-energized mood.

I had spent most of Wednesday afternoon making the acquaintance of Karen Malloy. We had walked together from the convenience store, and then around town, as I showed her the essential locations of Chetwynd, i.e., grocery stores, banks, and hairdressers. We ended up at the new gym, and later had supper with Randall at his house. He could not have been more thrilled to know that the two of us had already met, and his behaviour was even more embarrassing than my grandmother's attempts to get me to marry Kat. Even so, it was one of the most enjoyable evenings I had spent in months. Asking Karen for a date suddenly did not seem like such a foreign concept. I did not make friends very easily, but she naturally put me at ease, and I could not shake the feeling that she was attracted to me, as well. She had even laughed when I quickly assured her that I had absolutely no military background, aside from my uncle.

Being smitten by someone is a fairly decent band-aid for inner turmoil. I kept humming at work all day Thursday, and the thought of Clancy's drug use, or his fight with Angel, barely crossed my mind. I had decided to stay away from those issues entirely, and just try to focus on my own life for a while. They could figure out their own problems by themselves for once.

Well, it started out as a good idea, sort of like the American isolationist policy prior to the Second World War, but it was a lot shorter lived. In fact, minding my own business, and avoiding everyone else's, was a concept that did not live out the night. I did not know why. I must have had an aura, only detectable to those plagued by petty troubles, which identified me as a wiseman sitting cross-legged on a mountaintop. Never let your employees be your friends.

Everything was going fine until around five o'clock. I was working with Cindy, Boris, Becky, and Mark, and business had been pleasantly steady all day. Everyone was asking questions about Karen, and even the usually silent Becky had joined in some good-natured ribbing at my expense.

Then Angel called, looking for me.

She wanted to know what was the best course of action to get Clancy to forgive her. I did not want to be a crying shoulder anymore, so I told her to buy him a get well card and the latest *Bacon N Da Egg* album, and then I hung up. In retrospect, advising her to console Clancy with his favourite rap duo, whom he had only recently been prevented from seeing live, on account of costly car repairs, was probably very bad advice. However, desperate as she was, she only heeded my words, not my flippant voice tone. I never did hear the specifics of their meeting, but the impression I got later that night was that it had not gone smoothly.

I had already sent everyone else home, and finished closing up the restaurant alone, just after midnight. I was still feeling upbeat, and realized that I had not played my piano since the day that Angel was hired. I missed my own music.

I usually tried to play a person, place, or event, whether that be a childhood friend, a memory, or even a weather pattern. I would simply let my mind ramblingly ponder whatever I had pre-selected, and my fingers would act it out on the ivories. The result often seemed more like manifestation than music. I could see the smile and hear the laugh of a friend. I could feel the rain, or sunshine, or wind that my fingers had created. No matter what I played, I could see the face of Karl Myers. Usually, he was smiling.

There was only one person to play that night. Sitting in the dark, as my fingertips pressed rhythmically and fluidly over the keys, I could see that one loose lock of blonde hair that hung so alluringly over her left, emerald green eye. The sharp clip of her cowboy boots on the sidewalk was a clear sound in my ears. At least, it was until a harsh banging on the locked front door very rudely interrupted it.

"We're closed," I mused, my eyes still shut, knowing that whoever it was could not hear me anyway.

There was silence for almost a minute, and then the knocking resumed.

"We're closed!" Whoever was out there was not leaving. The banging did not stop.

It's after midnight, the 'Open' light is off, all the other lights are off, the parking lot is empty, and the front door is locked. The obvious conclusion should be that—

"WE'RE CLOSED!" I did not even like raising my voice to be better heard in a conversation at a crowded party. My good mood was officially over.

BAM! BAM! BAM!

"WE'RE CLOSED!!"

Who is that? Emeril?

"Open the door, Boss!"

Well, that narrows the field....

"Coming," I sighed, walking away from my piano in the darkened dining room, and unlocking the front door in the lobby. Angel literally fell inside when I swung the door open, only stopping herself from face planting by snagging the lapels of my black vest. Her oversized purple sweatshirt and yellow leggings seemed a bit mismatched, and her normally minty breath was soured considerably. It seemed to take every ounce of strength in her body for Angel to pull herself, hand over hand, up the front of my vest, until her glazed eyes could glare right into mine.

"Angel, what are you doing here?"

She blinked twice, each one nearly exhausting her reserves of energy.

"He dumped me," she slurred, "and it's *all ... your ... fault!*"

"Have you been drinking?" I inquired, cringing as I received a full blast of Angel's milk-curdling breath.

"It's *your fault!*" she repeated emphatically. "And I'm not *drunked!*"

"Clancy dumped you?" I had known that he was angry, but I had not expected that.

"Oh-ho, *yeah!*" she gurgled. "It's over! It's gone! Kapoot! *Budda-boom, budda-bing!* Through no choice of my own, I'm *celibate!*"

"Let go ... of my vest!" I said with slow malice. "You're going to crease it."

Angel momentarily disregarded the warning as she craned her neck forward, raising her face to within an inch of mine.

"I need ... *pizza!*" She somehow managed to keep her footing as she released my uniform and serpentined her way to the unlit kitchen.

"You're making pizza, *now?*"

"You bet, right now!" she grumbled. "Complacency is bad."

"I think you mean procrastination."

"Whatever. It's your fault!"

It was one of those situations where all that I could do was sink into one of the front sofas and stare vacantly at the cross-eyed coyote in front of me, listening to Angel banging around in the kitchen, apparently still trying to find the light switch.

Don't fire her. She could probably take you to the Labour Board with a diminished capacity defence.

After the kitchen light finally came on, I listened to her clamour for a few minutes, a din that was soon made even more cacophonous by Angel's less than melodious rendition of Ronnie Millsap's *Smoky Mountain Rain*.

"Sidneeeee!" she eventually whined, quite pitifully.

I heaved myself off the couch with a weary moan, and followed the sound of her whimpering into the kitchen. She was standing by the open pizza oven, holding the long-handled pizza paddle, and pouting.

"Yes, Angel?" I said, patiently.

"My pizza's not cooking," she griped.

In spite of her best efforts to retain, I managed to pry the stainless steel paddle out of her hands, and place it on a high shelf that she could not reach without the aid of a chair. Then I reached into the oven with my bare hand and pulled out the pizza pan.

"Well, for one thing," I said, "the oven's been turned off for over an hour. And, aside from that...." I handed her the empty pan. "... you're missing a few key ingredients."

Angel cautiously took the pan, utterly dumbfounded as she flipped it upside down and gave it a few good shakes, as though expecting a pizza to fall out.

"That is so *totally* freaking me out, Boss!"

"Yeah, it's empty," I assured her, tossing the pan onto a nearby counter top. "Now, I'm going to go way out on a limb here, and guess that you're not used to drinking."

"Hey, I only ate one worm! That's all!"

"Your first bender, and you go straight for *Tequila?* Are you out of your mind? Never eat the worm!"

"Do I ever tell you not to drink coffee? *Huh? Do I?!*"

"Okay, I'm also going to further assume that you've never been dumped before."

That assumption was all that was required to start the waterworks. Angel was bawling into my vest, while venting her frustration by tugging angrily on my tie.

Great. Water stains.

"Yes!" she wailed. "No one's ever dumped me! I dump guys! They do *not* dump me!" She wiped her nose on her purple sleeve, and snorkled noisily. "And I need to throw up."

Those are possibly the most terrifying words that a woman can utter while her face is pressed into your shirt. I gingerly took her by the shoulders and steered her over to the large dish sink.

"Puke in here, not on the floor, not on my boots. And, when you're done, disinfect the sink. Hot water and bleach."

"Gotcha," she croaked, hanging her head over the silver rim. Not exactly wanting to participate in what was to follow, I trudged back out to the lobby and lay down on my couch, humming loud enough to drown out any unpleasantness. I must have dozed off for a few minutes, because Angel seemed fully composed when she reappeared over me, slapping my shoulder with rapid, cartoonish strokes of her palm.

"Wake up, Boss!" she said, more brightly than I would have expected. "I think you need to go home."

"I am home," I muttered.

"What? Speak up!"

"Nothing."

"Come on. I'm not drunk, but I'm too drunk to drive." She giggled, obviously finding herself to be witty.

"You're seeming suddenly cheerier," I yawned, sitting up.

"I feel ... just *groovy*, Boss," she sighed contentedly, smiling. "You know that really exhilarating rush you get right after you put your face over the toilet bowl and just let it all—"

"Yeah, I know," I grimaced, standing. "Let's go." I pointed her in the direction of the door, and gave her a light shove to ensure that she actually got there. After I locked up, Angel grabbed my arm and attempted to lead me into the street.

"Come on, Boss, let's walk. It's only a couple miles. And I think a truck ride would make me sick again."

"It's one-thirty!" I said sharply. "I am not walking anywhere. Get in the truck. Where's your car, anyway?"

"Ah, I told the last bartender that he could keep it. Piece of junk.... Do we have to drive?"

"We do," I growled. "I'm *really* not in the mood for this right now."

"You know what would be just *so great*, Boss? I haven't done it in years. Can I sit on your lap and hold the steering wheel?"

"You can sit in the back," I said, sliding the driver side seat ahead, and pushing her in, none too gently. "And if you barf in my truck, I'm bumping you down to minimum wage."

"Somebody's grumpy...." I heard her sing-song from behind me, as I fired up Sid's Rig. "Hey Boss, do you have my pizza? I think I forgot it."

"Angel.... Remember the empty pan? The cold oven?"

"Ohhhhh...." Angel seemed to be having a revelation as I pulled onto the dark road. "There is no pizza.... Kind of a Nirvana thing, huh?"

"That must have been quite the meeting with Clancy," I remarked. "Is he out getting drunk, too?"

"He's stoned," she said absently. "He's a dummy. And I'm not drunk."

"Right, I forgot. Did you clean the sink?"

"Yep," she said proudly. "Hot water, and a whole gallon jug of bleach."

"*You used the whole–!*" I had to force myself to stop and take a few deep breaths.

She's drunk. She's drunk. She's drunk.

"Tell me something," I ventured. "Did you know Clancy used drugs?"

"Oh yeah," she acknowledged. "I didn't like it, but he asked me not to tell you, or the others. Oh, wait ... I just did, didn't I?"

"Relax, I already knew." I shook my head, still trying to figure out Clancy's accidental admission. "I wonder how he kept it a secret. Not many people can. Most kids in this town have loud, public discussions about their drugs."

"Maybe he's ashamed of himself," Angel guessed. "Or, maybe, he was afraid that you wouldn't be his friend anymore." Those were the first intelligent words that I had heard her utter all evening.

"Maybe," I nodded, flipping my cell phone open and hitting the speed dial to my house. Cindy would still be up.

"Hello?" she answered on the second ring.

"Hey, Cindy, you're opening tomorrow, right?"

"Yeah, me and Mark."

"Good. I need you to pick up a jug of bleach before you go in."

"What? I thought we had enough for the week!"

"Had a little accident. It spilled."

"Okay, whatever. Are you coming home, or what?"

"Yeah, I'm just driving Angel home first."

"Angel? What's she doing there?"

"Well, right now she's singing," I said loudly, trying to make myself heard over Angel's drunken *Straight Tequila Night*.

By the time I pulled into Angel's driveway, she was halfway through George Thurgood's *One Bourbon, One Scotch, and One Beer*, and she was surprisingly good at it.

"'*I look down the bar*,'" she jived. "'*I see my bartender.... I said 'Look mon! Come on down hya!' He gets down there.... I says "Whattaya want?"*'"

"He says," I interrupted, shifting into park under the pale glow of her porch light.

"What?"

"It's 'He says.' Not 'I says.'"

"Who?"

"The bartender."

"What are you talking about?"

"In the song. The bartender says 'Whattaya want?'"

"The bartender …?"

"… says 'Whattaya want?'" I finished her sentence, addressing her reflection in the rearview mirror.

Angel slammed an angry palm onto the seat back, sending up a puff of swirling dust.

"How would you know?!" she demanded. "Were you *there?!*"

"No!" I said defensively. "I'm just saying…."

"Just saying what?" she challenged.

I booted my sticky door open.

"I'm just saying 'Get out of my rig, I'm sick of your inebriated mood swings.' Come on, move it."

Angel's mood had done another abrupt 180 degree turn by the time she had stumbled out of the truck. She was giggling, even as she swayed unsteadily on the interlocking bricks under her feet.

"You're so cute when you're mad, Boss. Thanks for the ride."

"So, you're happy now?" I said carefully, wanting to be sure.

"Just peachy," she said, smiling sweetly. "Just kiss me goodnight, and we're all hunky-dory."

I froze, already halfway back into the truck. When I put my foot down from the running board and turned back to face her, she was standing calmly with her hands behind her back, wearing a quiet and inscrutable smile. The *Mona Lisa* was easier to comprehend than Angel.

"Excuse me?" I said skeptically.

"You heard me."

"I'm not kissing you."

"Yes, you are," she assured me. "It's *entirely* your fault that my ego got smashed tonight. Now, you're going to do something about it."

"Let me be more specific," I explained coldly. "A few minutes ago, you woofed your cookies into my kitchen sink, and I have not detected mouthwash since then. I'm not kissing you."

"Whattsa matter?" she chided me, poking my chest with one of her small index fingers. "You afraid to lock lips with a drunken, rebounding employee? Pucker 'em up, Sid!"

I groaned. "You know, I would pay a lot of money to see your hangover tomorrow."

"I'm waiting."

Her voice was patient as she tilted her head back and closed her eyes, lips puckered expectantly. I could only stand and stare at her, but it soon became clear that she was not budging until she got her kiss.

"Okay, fine," I said with mock resignedness. "You wanna swap spit, you got it."

Taking advantage of her closed eyes, I made a fist puppet with my right hand, gave the thumb and forefinger a good, wet lick, and pressed it firmly against her mouth, twisting my wrist enough to convince Angel that this was the most passionate kiss she had ever shared.

Angel dreamily smooched my hand for nearly twenty seconds. As drunk as she was, she probably would have continued for an indefinite amount of time, but I finally had to withdraw my hand after her tongue kept trying to get involved. This was the closest that I had come to kissing a woman since I had said goodbye to Spring, nearly six months earlier, but even I could tell when something was getting just plain gross.

Angel's eyes slowly drifted open, and her lips parted in absolute awe. "Wow," she breathed. "*That* ... was unbelievable. Now I know why I've put up with you for so long."

I was already back in the truck, wiping my hand on my pants.

"Yeah, wonderful," I said, before slamming the door. "We'll always have the moment. Get some sleep."

The absurdity of the situation would have been enough to restore my good humour on the drive back to finish Karen's song on the piano, and I likely would even have had a good chuckle. Unfortunately, before the laughs could kick in, I drove past a vacant lot on the right side of main street, formerly the location of a used book store. The white sign must have been new. I did not remember seeing it before.

It read, in large black capitals *FUTURE HOME OF REDMOND'S RIBS.*

CHAPTER SIXTEEN

In spite of his innumerable shortcomings, I had to credit Boris with being an optimist. He was the only one who held out hope that Clancy and Angel would reconcile. Kat laughed hysterically when I told her about the breakup, and Cindy would only say, "Figures."

Admittedly, the whole situation had taken me by surprise. Regardless of all the fireworks which I had witnessed between them on "Snake Night," my assumption was that they might give each other the cold shoulder for a few days. I had never before seen Clancy date anyone for more than nine days, so I guess I had actually started to see the two of them as a couple. Somehow, I had managed to forget that Clancy's fear of commitment rivalled Angel's fear of snakes. No amount of optimism would ever bring about reconciliation. Personally, I blamed the snake.

Now, my greatest concern had been realized. The inevitability of a split between Clancy and Angel, which had been so obvious to me when I first hired her, had managed to slip below my notice over the past month, leaving me with a dangerous degree of complacent self-assurance. Then, the other shoe had dropped, leaving me with the task of trying to keep the peace in a cuisinary battlefield. Clancy and Angel deplored one another. Within the next two days, they had both approached me in private, each requesting that I fire the other, just as a personal favour. I did not feel that I particularly owed either of them any special consideration, and I certainly was not going to fire anyone over a lover's quarrel. This situation had added various new dimensions to my already too multidimensional role as an employer. Thus far, I had been primary revenue source, friend, set director, disciplinarian, good cop/bad cop, public relations supervisor, constructive critic, pep-talking coach, and crying shoulder. Now, I had to be a referee, a hostage negotiator, and a dang goodwill ambassador. My life was getting too complex. I never had time to just be Sidney Karl Myers anymore.

The first step was rescheduling. The last thing that I wanted was Clancy and Angel having a blow up in front of the patrons, so I had to set up their work schedules in such a way that they could each work their full forty hours a week with as little overlap as possible. I suppose I could have done what most employers would have, that is, tell them to get along whenever they were in the workplace. Yeah, that might have worked, sort of like appointing Jamaica as host to the world championship ice-fishing tourney. I was enough of a literalist to know that my instructions were not going to be viewed as having any divine authority behind them.

"Okay, talk to me," I growled.

I was sitting behind the desk in my office, glaring at Clancy and Angel who sat across from me, having slid their chairs apart in an effort to maintain the invisible, three-foot barrier which had been a constant between them ever since their fight. They did not say a word.

It was Saturday evening, and it was the first time that I had been forced to order them into the office, after a dispute about which tray of food was supposed to go to table nine had bordered on becoming a screaming match. It was clearly going to be one of those weeks when I started longing for the monotony of an assembly line job. I was already having some serious simplicity cravings.

"I'm not kidding here," I said. "I don't care if you take your breaks together so that you can throw rocks at each other in the back parking lot. When you're in here, don't ... even ... *talk to each other!*"

They were both surprised by my warning, so much so that they even acknowledged their shared confusion by briefly looking at one another.

"I'm ... I'm sorry," Clancy clarified, puzzled. "Did you just tell us to go ahead and keep fighting?"

"You're going to anyway!" I snapped. "It's human nature. You've only got a few hours of overlap every week, so, during that time, you're not even in the same room unless the world starts coming to an end."

"That's your advice?" Angel was disgusted. "Fight, but don't let you see it?"

"Exactly," I smiled. "Or the customers. You guys have been turning this place into the soap opera that time forgot."

"Boss, you're *the boss*. Get it? You're supposed to force us to work together, and order us to get along in the process."

"But, then I would be a stupid boss," I pointed out. "And I don't feel like being stupid, seeing as you two are already doing such a…. Okay, I'm not even going to go there. The bottom line is that you two are only human, and, as such, you will continue to hate each other until you eventually realize that enemies are a lot more high maintenance than friends are. *Then* you'll try to reconcile, *then* you'll be able to work together, and *then* you'll wish back every bitter and nasty word you've said, but it's already too late for that! You may get back on friendly terms, but you will remember the sting of every insult for as long as you live. Whenever you look at each other, when you look in each other's eyes, you'll remember the anger you saw there, once. You won't remember what the fight was about, but you'll never forget that look. It's in the eyes. You'll always be amazed by how quickly and irrevocably your relationship was ended, and the thing that will haunt you the most is knowing that no matter what you do, or how sorry you feel, or how many times you apologize, you can never again be what you were. After a while, maybe a few weeks, forgiveness may come, quite easily even. But, the trust …. That's gone forever. You can only lose trust once. You may find a shard of it, but never the whole thing. Nostalgia won't bring it back. Even the return of romantic feelings won't bring it back. It's gone. You'll only be able to think back, and wonder what it was that you once had that you'll never have again. Sorry, kids. Not many people realize how precious trust is, until they say, or do, that one little thing that destroys it."

212

I leaned forward in my chair and folded my hands on the desk.

"It's kind of sad, isn't it?" I remarked. "You two let your tempers get the better of you, just once, and it set your lives on such opposite courses. Beyond your control, too. It felt so viscerally satisfying to shout those insults, fan the rage. Now, the most that you will ever have a hope of being is two suspicious friends. Sound like fun?"

Clancy shifted awkwardly in his seat, looking both disturbed and uncomfortable. Angel stared at me with her mouth wide open, as silence hung over the room for what seemed like a very long time. My face was expressionless, but inside I was just as shocked as they were. I could barely believe that the preceding speech had come out of my own mouth. I prided myself on my eloquence, but also on my brevity.

"Well," I sighed, eventually, "that's the longest I've talked in years. Get out of my office, go outside, and keep fighting. Clancy, straighten that tie."

Angel was at an utter loss for words, a situation that was a definite precedent. She slowly stood up and walked out to the kitchen, absolutely numb. Clancy was looking at me, as though trying to figure out some great riddle as he stood and followed her out.

Within five seconds, he had rushed back into the office, and was back in his seat, agitated.

"Okay, where did that come from?"

"A combination of vocal cords, lips, tongue, lungs and diaphragm. Why?"

213

"Sid, you did not just have a revelation and share it with us. What you just said…. I mean, whatever it was…. That was personal experience."

"Life experience, not personal."

"Were you talking about Spring?"

"Get back to work."

He actually chuckled at my bluntness, reluctantly getting out of his chair.

"You are in a bad mood, aren't you?"

"Did you spark up before work today?" I asked innocently.

He stopped on his way through the door, and turned back to give me a wry smile.

"Whether you're asking as my friend or my boss, I still don't have to answer that."

"Well, tell me this. Did I lose your trust, or did I just never have it?"

"You seem to place a lot of emphasis on trust," he commented, resting a forearm on the doorframe.

"And you don't. Which could be why your relationships end this way."

"You're going to lecture me about relationships?" Clancy snapped. "You've had one steady girlfriend in your entire life. A life-long friendship, and six years of dating that went absolutely nowhere. Where is she now, Sid? Do you even know what city she's in? What province?"

"She said she'd call once she gets settled," I said coolly.

"Six months, Sid. She could have set up a moon colony by now."

"She hasn't unpacked yet."

"Six months."

"It was a big suitcase. And those zippers are nasty when they jam up."

After he was gone, I leaned back in my swivel chair and gnawed on a pen. I hated to admit it, even to myself, but Clancy was right. I did not even miss Spring, but I still felt a bizarre loyalty to her that was keeping me from even looking for anyone else. After losing a lifelong crush, I honestly had no idea what to do with my life, besides work.

Spring and I had told our friends that we had stopped seeing each other because it would have been inappropriate, but we both knew that was not the whole truth. We had stopped seeing each other, unofficially, on the day that my dad died. Sure, we still dated for the next few months, but it was never the same. It was my fault. When Karl Myers died, I stopped. I shut down. I closed. From that time on, I could not stand to get close to anyone, or let them get near my heart.

A year after Dad died, Cindy wrote a song about a sea shell, polished but hollow, with only the lingering sound of the ocean that had once filled and surrounded it. To this day, I am sure that she was writing about me. I did not know if that was an accurate description, but it was a reasonable assumption on her part, given my change in emotional expression. Cindy thought that I had become almost void of emotion. In that, she was wrong. My emotions were a constant, raging cesspool, trapped like a genie in a bottle. I hated that closure within myself. There were so many times that I just wanted to express or weep or scream my frustrations to a sympathetic ear, and there were plenty of those around, but I simply could not do it. I had to be strong. I told myself that Cindy needed me to be strong. My employees needed a strong boss. Strength was a state of mind, a thought pattern and mood set that kept weakness at bay. If I could just shut out the feelings of weakness, I would never be weak. The only problem was that, deep down, I wanted to be weak. Even if it was just for a short while, hours, even minutes, I wanted to let someone else be strong for me.

That was probably a really bad reason to decide that I needed to have a date being at least in the planning stages within the hour, but it was the only reason that I had. I needed to ask Karen out.

I had started to reach for the phone, when I suddenly realized that I had no clue how to ask a girl out. My first date had been over ten years earlier, and it had come about through a clumsy admission of mutual attraction, complete with all of the usual teenage awkwardness: shuffling, coughing, fidgeting, and embarrassed laughs that sounded painfully like birds chirping. Now, I was attempting to ask out a girl whom I had only met twice, once at the convenience store, and then two days later when she had dined at my restaurant with Randall and his girlfriend, Bess Nolan. What did dating etiquette demand? A phone call seemed somehow presumptive, but, if she actually liked me, perhaps she would not mind. Would it be better to stop by her apartment and just come right out and ask her, or would a better approach be to wait until I bumped into her on the street, and then make small talk?

Get off the details, Myers. Get on the dang phone.

Pondering menial details was never my strong point. I picked up the phone.

"Hello?"

"Karen, it's Sidney Myers."

"Hey! Sidney, how are you?"

"Oh, fine. I just had to give a motivational chew-out to some bickering workers."

"Really? Which ones?"

"Uh, Angel, the girl who served your tea last night, and Clancy, the cook who came out of the kitchen and asked for your sign."

"Oh yeah, he's hard to forget. What was the fight about?"

"They broke up. Big time."

"And you have to keep the peace. Poor baby."

Okay, it's been a long time since anyone called me that....

"Yeah, poor me," I chuckled. "Would you like to do something with me, later?" I could tell by the silence on the other end that she had probably expected the question, just not so early in the conversation, or so directly.

Get used to it, baby. This is the new Sidney Myers.

"Oh...." She sounded taken aback. "You want to go out with me?"

"Did I phrase it wrong?" I asked casually.

"Well, no, I'm just a little off guard. Usually, the only guys who come right out and ask me are creepy guys in bars."

"I hope I don't fit into that category," I remarked.

She laughed. "No, you don't. That's what's so neat. Not many guys will just ask a girl out."

Well, directness seems to be working. Go for it!

"I like you," I said plainly. "I would like to take you for a walk, or a drive, dinner and a movie. Your choice, as long as there's a you and me involved."

"Are you busy tonight?" She actually sounded eager.

It's Saturday, Myers. Statistically, the second busiest night of the week. Chaos will reign if you leave.

"No, tonight's fine," I said, compliantly. "Have you ever been to The Bavarian?"

"No, actually I've only been to your place since I moved in."

"It's European cuisine," I explained. "Very good food, great spatzli."

"Spatzli? What is that, wine?"

"It's the central European equivalent of French fries. It's good."

"I'll take your word for it," she giggled. "Sounds great. What time?"

I glanced up at my wall clock. "Uh, it's just after eight. Pick you up around nine?"

"Perfect. Bye!" Karen had this really cute way of saying "Bye!" in an excited whisper.

Heaven! I'm in ... Heaven!

Actually, that was the only line of the song that I knew.

I grabbed my burgundy windbreaker off the back of my chair, and pulled it on as I walked into the kitchen. Kat and Clancy were both dishing up plates of entrees, and Cindy was drinking a soda as she waited for them to finish. It had been a steady shift, but not too busy. Saturdays, however, were notoriously treacherous.

They lulled you into a false sense of ease, and then the shop would suddenly be flooded with calls from drunken partiers, wanting pizzas delivered to all ends of town. There were roughly three thousand people in Chetwynd, and I had one pizza delivery guy. You do the math. Fortunately, our unofficial motto was "If it's not at your door in thirty minutes … it'll probably be there in forty." Time guarantees just stressed everybody out, and they also made customers really snobby from the overblown expectation of perfection.

"I'm taking off for awhile," I announced, zipping up my jacket. "Call my cell if it gets busy. I can be back here in two minutes."

It was happening again, just like on the day that I first met Karen. They were all staring at me.

"Why?" Kat and Cindy asked the burning question at the same instant.

"I'm taking off for awhile," I repeated dryly. "Call my cell if it gets busy. I can be back here in two minutes."

"Sid, it's Saturday," Clancy said. "You don't leave on Saturdays."

My eyes narrowed.

"I'm sorry, Clancy. Was that an *order?*"

"No, no," he replied hastily. "That was an observation. I've never seen you leave on a Saturday. Not since … ever."

"Well, I'm leaving! Call if it gets busy."

"Why?" This time, all three of them asked.

"Because I just won a multimillion dollar lotto, and I'm going to my new mansion just over the hilltop to celebrate with eight beautiful blondes, a dozen movie stars, a retired British rock star, and my own pet rhinoceros, and *none of you* are invited! I do *not* answer to you! Cindy, that's table three's order, and I specifically heard them say they wanted a caesar, not garden. Change it. Croutons, people, croutons!"

"Oh, my goodness gracious." Kat looked just a bit pale, her mouth in the shape of the letter 'O.' "He's evasive, and he's cranky. Guys ... he's got a *date!*"

The laugh that Clancy tried to cough back into his throat was the harshest blow to his job security that I could remember.

"Yes, I have a date," I sighed. "So, when I say 'Call if it gets busy...' Don't call unless you see The Conqueror, The Killer, Famine, and Death riding ghostly horses through the night sky, looking very, very hungry."

"You asked Karen out?" Cindy's voice was a strange mixture of delight and startled horror. "How could you? You're destined to marry Kat."

"My broken heart will mend, eventually," Kat snickered. "Isn't the second rider of the Apocalypse called 'War?'"

"Whatever," I groaned. "Ask him if you see him. Or, ask Boris when he gets back. He knows everything. I have no idea. I'm leaving now, goodbye, see you, goodbye." I walked out, feeling about as prepared for a romantic conquest as a general setting forth to conquer an enemy country, armed with a finely sharpened thumbnail.

As I passed the dining room, I caught a glimpse of a strangely sombre Angel, serving drinks. Usually, she never stopped smiling and chatting, but tonight her lips were sealed, and her brow was furrowed. I could not tell if her expression was angry or simply disturbed, but I was about to have my first date in three years, so I was not about to let a sullen employee spoil it.

"Hey, Boss!"

I tried to pretend that I had not heard her as I ducked out the front door, but she caught up with me before I could make a dash for my truck. She still held a serving tray under her left arm as she ran through the door.

"Boss, wait!"

"I'm kind of busy, Angel."

I had thought that she was angry, but, as she walked up to me, I could see the glitter of surfacing tears.

"Please, Boss...." Her voice was cracking.

"Angel, what's wrong?" I was annoyed, but made my voice sound quietly empathetic.

"Please tell me you just made that up!" she cried. "All that talk about how me and Clancy can never trust each other again, that we'll always be suspicious. You were just spouting out a theory, right?"

"As a rule, I try not to spout. But, as for what I said.... If there are exceptions, I've never seen them. You and Clancy hurt each other, and, as long as you have memories of that pain, you'll be afraid to trust. Sorry to ruin your secret reconciliation hopes, but the only people who completely restore trust are those with poor memories."

"Boss, what do I *do?!*" she wailed. "I still love him!"

Okay, this is the third time this woman has come crying to you this week.

"Do you?" I asked. "I mean, really? Or is he just a teddy-bear for you to squeeze when you're sad?"

"I know what love is, Boss. Me and Clancy…. It was real, okay?"

"So, why did you just use past tense? Love is forever. You've done nothing but fight with him all week."

"Lover's quarrels!"

"Earlier today, you told him to go bite something with an alternating current! You remember *that?*"

"I was trying to get an apology! The man does not know how to apologize."

"And you do?"

"I bought him a CD and a card. It didn't work."

"Well, maybe you just need to…. Hey, you know what? I'm on a date. Goodnight."

Even after I got in the truck, she tried to get me to talk more by banging on the window, but I backed up and drove away without saying another word.

Oh boy, is she going to be mad at you now….

CHAPTER SEVENTEEN

Not long after I took over the position of restaurant manager, my friends began telling me that I was a workaholic, even before my dad died. I shrugged it off for years, but it was not until I tried to go on a date on a Saturday that I realized how right they were. I drove home, took a shower, and redressed in a black turtleneck, khaki slacks, and semi-casual brown suede jacket, and, the whole time, all that I could think of were disaster scenarios, which seemed certain to be realized in my absence.

Boris could finally succeed at igniting the deep fryer. Heaven knows he's tried hard enough....

Clancy and Angel are trying to figure out whether to love or hate each other. That alone could send the place up in a mushroom cloud.

When was the last time you recharged the fire extinguishers? It's Saturday! Are you insane, Myers? You don't leave on Saturdays!

What's better for a date? The leather casuals, or the cowboy boots?

I went with the lucky boots. I did not even believe in the existence of luck, but, after three years, I was not about to take anything for granted.

Karen had rented a downtown apartment. When she answered her door, she was wearing a little blue dress that positively transformed her from beautiful to drop-dead gorgeous.

"Hi." Her smile was dazzling. She could have done toothpaste ads. "Thank you so much for asking me out. It's sweet."

"My pleasure," I said, holding out my hand.

Attraction test, number one....

Thankfully, she smiled even wider, and we held hands as I walked her to my truck.

"You look beautiful," I said. "That dress is perfect."

"Thank you," she said appreciatively. "Hey, you clean up good, too." She rubbed my sleeve slowly with the palm of her hand. "You didn't get this off the rack."

I chuckled. "Don't think you've snared yourself a rich businessman, Karen. This jacket is the only piece of custom clothing that I own. My *suits* are off the rack."

"Relax, I'm not a gold-digger," Karen laughed. "If I was, I would have invested in something besides a gym."

The Bavarian was arguably the classiest restaurant that Chetwynd could offer. It occurred to me, as I pulled into the hedge surrounded parking lot, that a reservation might have been a good idea, as the large restaurant tended to be a full house on weekends. Such were the hazards of spontaneous date appointments.

I only had to take one look into the lavish dining room to realize that we were not getting a table for at least an hour. People who had reservations were still waiting in the reception lounge.

"Oooh boy," I sighed, glancing over at Karen. "How hungry are you?"

"Not very," she admitted with a grin. "I can wait, Sidney."

I managed to motion over the white-tuxedo clad maitre' d, who quickly assured me that no one would be getting a table without a reservation until eleven o'clock, at the very earliest.

"You close at eleven," I pointed out.

"Exactly, sir," he said glibly. "And that's when our earliest opening is. And no amount of bribery will help you, either. Not on a Saturday." He turned on his heel and strode off. He had to be French.

"You know that you're ruining my date," I called after him.

"Call next time, sir."

I would have fired anyone who tried to be that snooty.

"What a creep," I muttered, as we walked back outside. The sun was low, preparing to slip behind the encircling mountains to the west. The waiter had blighted my favourite time of day.

"What, your restaurant wouldn't do the same thing?" Karen chided me, leaning on my arm as we approached my truck again.

"No, we'd do exactly the same thing," I said mildly. "His attitude is just all wrong. You want to know the secret to getting angry customers to come back? Blame the kitchen staff. Or the owner. Or some other sinister, faceless, unreachable group. No matter how much the patrons hate the situation, they have to love the person that they're talking to."

"How do you do that?" she asked, leaning against the blue tailgate and looking out at the pink clouds on the horizon.

"By mastering the art of being sheepishly apologetic, and mixing it with a sort of wry, dogged sense of humour. Make them laugh at their predicament, and feel sorry for you."

"And that actually works?"

I smiled. "When you're as good as me, yes."

She laughed. "So, your whole job is the performance of a lifetime?"

"Do you ever wonder why unemployed actors always end up as politicians, animal rights activists, or waiters?" I commented.

"Why?"

"Because, those are the jobs that demand natural born actors. It lets them hone their craft, it just doesn't pay as well. Shoot, I am so sorry about dinner. Do you want to go somewhere else?"

"I'm not even hungry, Sidney," she remarked. "We can just hang out here for awhile. Watch the sunset. How often do you watch the sunset?"

"Not as much as I'd like," I confided, lowering the tailgate for us to sit on.

"Nobody does, anymore," she said softly, the last red beams of sunlight turning her straw-coloured hair to pure gold. "It's one of the curses of our busy, technological lives. People like you work all evening in a hot kitchen, making money. People like me actually have most of our evenings off, but we spend them by turning on a TV, or sitting in front of a computer. We turn our backs on sunsets. We even close the blinds so that we can't see the reflection of that beautiful red sky on our screens. I don't know why. Lately, every TV show and chat-line looks exactly the same, but I have never seen two sunsets that were alike. It's almost like they're alive, independent of every other one. So much can change them. Whether you're in the country or in the city, the time of year, the wind, the temperature, clouds, even sounds and scents. I am amazed every time I watch the sun disappear.

"I don't call myself an alarmist, but it does bother me, sometimes, that we seem to spend so much time trying to make a better life, to make our lives beautiful, and then we refuse to appreciate the beauty right outside the window."

"Be careful, Karen," I cautioned her with a grin. "We're too young to think wistfully of simpler times."

"Well, it is a good lesson, don't you think?"

"Which lesson, specifically?"

Her smile was delightfully mischievous as she replied, "Learn to appreciate what's right in front of you."

"Oh, you're good," I said with sly admiration, putting an arm around her waist.

"I'm good," she agreed, resting her lovely blonde head on my shoulder.

Heaven! I'm in ... Heaven!

Thus far, the date was going perfectly, in spite of our being given the boot by a snotty waiter. I was sitting on my tailgate, with a beautiful girl on my shoulder, watching the sun go down. This was living, and I had almost forgotten what that was. True living was the company of a young woman, and damaging my retinas with direct sunlight, all on an empty stomach. This was the best Saturday evening that I had experienced in years, and I was not even doing anything. The irony of that hung as heavily in the air as the romance.

And, just my luck, my moral conflict had to choose that exact moment to kick in.

Who is this woman?

That was how it started. In a single moment, with a single question, my date was ruined. Suddenly, all that I could think of was how foreign Karen was to me. I did not know her.

I could kiss her right now, and she's not even my friend.

This was wrong. Everything felt wrong.

I don't even know this girl. I shouldn't be touching her. I don't have the right.

Dad had once told me to never marry a woman who was not my best friend. Spring had not been that, but at least I had known her. I had known her all of my life.

Who was Karen Malloy? I had no idea who she was. Randall's cousin. Blonde and tall. Liked sunsets. That was the extent of my knowledge.

What are you doing, Myers? Why are you cuddling with a borderline stranger, aside from the fact that she's insanely hot?

Mystery. That had to be it. There was something inherently seductive about the unknown, a drawing force that made us wonder what lay on the other side of the closed door. Entire relationships could be forged on nothing more than mystery, and they were generally doomed from the start. In a mystery relationship, the fascination was not so much with what lay behind the closed door. The fascination lay in the fact that there *was* a closed door. Eventually, the fascination is was replaced by curiosity as to who the person behind the mystery really was. Sometimes, after finding out the truth, we wished that we had not. Mystery relationships did not last. The people in them were forced to constantly wear masks. No one knew who anyone else really was.

I was surprising myself as I thought about all of this, but it did make me realize what I really wanted. I wanted to date a friend, not a stranger, no matter how perfect she seemed.

She's beautiful, and you're lonely. That carries a lot of weight. But, you're about to take this relationship straight into romance. Do you really think that'll work? It won't.

She was not watching the sun, anymore. Her cheek was resting against my jacket, and her green eyes were searching deep into mine. Almost imperceptibly, she was moving her mouth closer to mine.

Suddenly, I was terrified. My perfect date was about to lead to a perfect kiss, and that was absolutely scaring the crap out of me.

"Do you want to go for a walk?" I suggested.

She seemed slightly disappointed, probably wondering if I was a bit dense, but replied, "Oh … sure, let's walk around. Show me the town."

"Such as it is," I smirked. "What haven't you seen yet?"

"The railroad tracks," she giggled. "I want to walk down them. I love the tracks."

"Then let's do it," I said, stepping down from the tailgate, and offering my hand to steady her as she slid off. With the sun gone, cool night air was filling the valley. I slipped out of my jacket, and hung it on her shoulders. If nothing else, my father raised a gentleman.

I locked the truck and we left it in The Bavarian's parking lot, walking, hand in hand, away from the turmoil in the building. Darkness was settling in, and the streetlights were coming on over us as we headed westward on the South Access Road. For some reason, Angel's words seemed like the best choice.

"So, tell me your life story."

Great, Myers. Now that you're already on a date, try to find out something about her.

We were about half a mile from the tracks, so Karen had time to give me a brief history of her life, while I kept asking questions to keep her going. Her mother was Cree, her father was a combination of almost every Western European nationality, so her blonde hair had been a bit unexpected. She had grown up in Grande Prairie, had considered a career in law, and was possibly the most devoted Bob Seger fan on the planet. Her greatest fears were tainted drinking water and the possibility of leprechaun existence.

"How about you?" she asked suddenly. "What are you afraid of?"

I knew what my greatest fear was. I had known for years, and yet it was still such an odd fear that I was frequently bothered by it. No one else knew what it was, and I did not feel ready to tell it to this beautiful stranger. I did not have very many secrets in my life, but this was one that I wanted to keep. I decided to throw some poetry at her, instead.

"I'm not afraid of nuclear war.
I'm not repulsed by snakes.
I get unnerved by vampire bats,
And people with limp handshakes."

"What's that from?" Karen laughed. "That's great!"

"My sister writes songs and poetry," I said. "That's one line that I've always remembered." We started walking down the train tracks, which ran through the forest surrounding the village. I knew what Karen liked about them. There was always something adventurous about following the rails. Even on the open prairies, they always seemed more secluded than any highway, or even dirt roads. There was also the vague threat of danger, an almost repressed concern that you might encounter the next train on a narrow overpass, spanning a river or gorge.

Karen was feeling playful, walking on one rail, one foot in front of the other, with her arms held out for balance. Every few feet, her sandals would slip, and she would windmill her arms and laugh, trying to stay on course. Finally, she would start to topple over, and I would catch her under her arms as she fell. Somehow, every catch seemed to end up a lot more like an embrace.

Now, just for those of you who have lived your entire life in a sealed envelope, I am going to share a bit of information regarding human nature. When a pretty girl falls, and a guy catches her, the first instinct of both is to laugh together, then fall silent, look into each other's eyes, and immediately begin smooching. *Not* kissing Karen every time that she collapsed into my arms in a fit of giggles was the hardest thing that I never did. I wanted to, and she wanted me to, but, in the back of my mind, I could not shake the feeling that giving in to the urge would be something that I would come to regret. It was not a pleasant contest when moral conviction was matched up against the heat of the moment. In the end, it was only my father's advice that made me decide to not kiss Karen. Dad had not married his best friend, and, although he never said as much, I believe that he always regretted the decision. It was a regret that I did not intend to share. I did not want to waste Karen's time, or my own, by instigating a relationship that neither one of us was prepared for.

Good grief, you are a square, Myers. You know what your problem is? You hate enjoying anything. You're too afraid that something will blow up in your face.

I abruptly stopped walking. My turtlenecked sweatshirt was warm, but I suddenly felt a chill. A faint breeze stirred the branches of the trees around us, exposing the pale underside of every leaf. It was getting darker by the minute, and I could smell rain on the wind.

Oh, come on. Don't do this to yourself. Not now....

"Sidney?" Karen had walked about twenty feet farther down the tracks before she noticed that I had stopped. Now, she was looking back at me, curiously.

Something will blow up in your face....

In my mind, rain was the foulest smell on earth. It smelled like death.

A robin launched into the air from the branches over my head. As I watched it fly off, I could see the first rain drops coming down from a grey sky. There was a long silence, only slightly broken by the scratchy creaking of gravel under my boots.

* * *

My seatbelt had locked, and wouldn't come loose. My fingers had blood on them, which made the jammed buckle slippery as I tried to undo it.

"Dad, it's going to be all right," I said shakily, punching the glove box open. My hand was trembling beyond my control, making it extremely hard to locate and open the Swiss Army knife. "I'm getting you out."

Karl Myers gave no response. Blood was seeping through his white shirt and rust coloured vest. In a panic, I sawed through my seatbelt, and began hacking at the straps which had my father tied to his crumpled seat.

I could see and smell flames, but, in my chaotic state of mind, I could not tell if they were coming from the Blazer, or the F-150 that had hit us. My right temple was throbbing, the gash on it pouring warm blood down the side of my face and into my collar.

"I'm getting you out! Come on! Talk to me!" I severed his seatbelt, kicked my door open, and wrapped my arms around his torso. As I hauled his limp form out of the vehicle, I saw that the tinted canopy window had been shattered on the driver side. For the briefest moment, I thought I caught a glimpse of a shoe on the base of the smashed-in frame.

233

My head was swimming from the blow it had taken against the window, and I felt like I could barely stand, but I had to get him away from that fire. Dad was an inch taller than I, and almost forty pounds heavier, but I managed to clasp my wrists around his chest and drag him away from the burning vehicles.

"Dad?" I said anxiously, laying him gently on the wet pavement. "Can you hear me? That's Josh. I've got to get him out of the truck before it blows. I'm coming right back, you hear me? Dad?" He did not move or open his eyes. The left side of his face had been completely lacerated by glass shards.

"Dad?" I quavered, a lump in my throat nearly choking me. I could not breathe. A single tear mixed with the blood on my face. I placed a hesitant hand on the side of his neck, trying to find a pulse.

"Dad?!"

There was no pulse. There was nothing. Nothing but the smell of rain.

"DAD!!" I screamed.

He never moved.

* * *

"Sidney?"

I was looking at the sky. The robin had flown out of sight. Karen must have been wondering what was wrong with me. All that I could think to say were my exact words from that rainy night four years ago.

"I think we're gonna get wet."

"Oh." She looked up at the black clouds rolling in across the dark sky. "Do you wanna head back?"

"I don't like rain," I said quietly. The first drops were already leaving dark spots on my sweatshirt.

"Is that your greatest fear?" she asked. "You never did answer that one."

"Do I have to?"

"This is a first date," she reminded me, walking slowly back in my direction. "No holds barred. Trust has to be established."

By then, my shirt was damp and clingy. My gaze was drawn to the large runoff drops of rain collecting and then trickling down the green leaves all around us. Thunder was beginning to roll into the valley, very faintly, from many miles away.

"Trust has to be earned, not just set up," I replied evenly. "I realize that's probably the worst possible thing to say to a first date, but it is the truth."

"You're an honest man, Sidney Myers," she noted, solemnly. "You say it like it is. I trust you."

"Trust is also extremely fragile," I warned her. "I have found that it does not pay to give it lightly."

"Then prove that I can trust you," she said, standing close in front of me. "Answer me honestly, or don't answer at all."

"Very well," I smiled. "Fire away."

"What's your greatest fear?"

"I'm not prepared to tell you that, yet," I answered. "I will tell you one of my bigger fears. I'm afraid of burning to death. That's probably my second fear."

"Okay," she nodded. "That's fair."

Judging from the way that she was biting her lower lip, I could only assume that her next question was almost burning her tongue off.

"When we were sitting on the tailgate...."

Uh-oh....

"… you didn't kiss me. Most guys would have. Why didn't you?"

The rain was now slapping noisily against the trees, and matting our hair. Karen's one stray, blonde lock which always hung over one eye, now looked more like a wet, golden rope.

"I wanted to be your friend," I said.

She was disappointed again, folding her arms across her midriff.

"You ask me out on a date, and then go straight for the 'Let's just be friends?' Is that it?"

"No. But a kiss would have just been a cliched ending to a romantic moment. After that, we would officially be starting a relationship based on nothing but attraction. That would never last."

"Are you afraid of me?" she inquired, looking skeptical.

"I'm highly attracted to you," I stated. "But, if I kissed you, then or right now, I would never be your friend."

"You're attracted, but you won't prove it," she clarified. "Is there something wrong with me?"

"To the naked eye, absolutely nothing," I assured her. "But … I was dating a girl named Spring for six years before I met you. I'd known her my entire life. I haven't seen her in months, and I don't even care. Because I was never her friend. I look back and think … those six years were a mistake. They never should have happened. I cannot make a mistake like that again. Can you understand that?" I wondered if I had said too much, too soon. Karen looked uncomfortable, hugging herself to keep warm in my jacket, which was too large for her. I hoped I had not offended her, but I could not tell what she was feeling. She took one more long look up at the sky, her wet lock of hair dripping rain down the side of her face.

"It's not going to let up anytime soon," she sighed. "We should head back. You're going to get sick."

Great. I'm the next apostle Paul, the great celibate.

The walk back to The Bavarian was quiet and, in the rain, seemed to take about four times longer than before. It would have to rain on my first date in years, but, after what I had just said to her, I was certain that her spirits were already dampened. I decided to simply learn to be content as the most miserable man in Chetwynd.

Everybody's right. Just go home and marry Kat.

Karen surprised me by saying more than "Thanks, goodnight," when I finally drove her back to the apartment. I parked in front of her door, and she slipped out of my jacket, folding it over the seat between us.

"Sorry for being so quiet," she said softly. "I was ... just thinking a lot about what you said, and it really surprised me. I guess I'd never thought about dating and friendship in the way that you talked about them. You had a good point. That girl you were dating wasn't your friend, she was just your girlfriend. I can see why you wouldn't want to do that again."

"I wasn't trying to preach, or anything," I sighed. "I just wanted to know you better."

"No, it's okay," she grinned. "I totally understand what you meant. It's cool. But, still.... Do you think it's wrong to have feelings for someone you barely know?"

I smiled, relieved. "No. I liked you from the moment that I met you. We had fun walking those rails, and, if I may say, I do not believe for a second that your balance was half as bad as you made it out to be."

She laughed at that, causing her wet hair to flick droplets on my face. "Busted," she admitted. "But I liked it when you caught me, and you liked catching me. So, I guess we'll call this date a success … in a wet, philosophical kind of way."

"Yeah, next time we'll walk down a subway track. We're more likely to get taken off the face of the earth by a train, but at least we'd have a roof over our heads." I walked her to her door, and she gave me a long hug. Just like in all the movies, my cell phone rang right in the middle of it.

"Is that YMCA?" Karen asked with a raised eyebrow, slowly releasing me.

"*In the Navy,*" I said, pulling the phone off my belt clip and flipping it open. "Fifty-one downloadable disco ring tones. You should check it out."

"You like disco?" she ventured, running a hand through her wet locks.

"Disco is the unappreciated classics," I said authoritatively. "Instead of focussing on the negatives of the seventies, like rebellion and heartbreak and LSD, discotheque celebrated life, love, and the funkiest dance moves this planet has ever seen. It was the best. Of course, most of the people were dancing to it on LSD."

"Are you going to answer it?"

"In a second," I groaned, looking at the call display. "It's my brother-in-law in waiting. Excuse me." I hit the talk button. "Hello?"

"Kiss her, you blockhead!" Boris cheered.

"BORIS!" I roared, spinning around as I heard car tires squeal from the street. I only caught a glimpse of the black Trans Am's license plate as it sped around the corner, out of sight.

"Did Cindy send you to spy on me?" I demanded, but the line was dead, the dial tone humming apathetically in my ear. I sighed and hung up.

"Karen, be glad that you are working *with* a relative. If Randall was working *for* you, I would advise you to just fire him, right now, and save yourself a lot of aggravation. Never let friends or relatives work for you. Look at me. I'm a bitter, cynical mess."

"No, Sidney," Karen laughed, pulling me into one last hug. "You're honest, you're sweet, and you're insightful, and I had a great time." She kissed me on the cheek before going inside. Her words were kind, and her laugh was true, but I was under no illusions of optimism. I knew that this was the only date that I would ever have with Karen Malloy. A kiss can say a lot. That one said "Goodbye."

CHAPTER EIGHTEEN

Angel and I had a blow up a few days later. I guess both of us were in a lousy mood that day. She was still reeling from Clancy dumping her, and I was depressed by the knowledge that a relationship with Karen would most likely be doomed from the start. Angel and I were both snappish and sullen, and everyone else must have been miserable by association. Looking back, it is very hard for me to believe that this explosive incident was not only the turning point in my relationship with Angel, but would also lead to her becoming one of my closest friends. This was especially ironic, as I had so recently assured Angel that shouting matches were the best way to permanently cripple a friendship. I never was certain as to why this fight ended so differently than I had anticipated. Perhaps Angel and I had a subconscious trust with a depth that defied imagination. However, a more likely explanation is that my theory about the fragility of trust was a bunch of bunk. I have always hated the possibility of being wrong. It is unsettling.

In my life, one depression frequently opened the door to the next. My primary reason for asking Karen out was to distract me from the troubles at home: Clancy's drug use, his bickering with Angel, and my own frustrated, overworked existence. I had just wanted a break from it all, and foolishly decided that dating was some sort of mystical cure-all. In the end, I realized that I had only been thinking of myself, not Karen. It would not even have been fair to ask her out again, unless I could bring myself to think of her happiness before mine.

My dad once told me, "Every run of the mill sentimental fool talks about the girl he can't live without. I was one of them. That's not love. Real love is when you care enough about a girl to do whatever is needed to make her happy, even if that means leaving her alone. I married your mother because I thought I couldn't live without her. I was wrong, Sid. I'm not saying that I regret it. To regret my marriage would be to regret you and the lass, and that I cannot do. I love you kids, and I will always love your mother. But I was naive. I fell in love before I knew what love was."

At the time, I thought that he was just being nostalgic, but now his words made a lot of sense. I was not going to make his mistake. I wanted to find that one love that would last, perhaps something similar to what Boris and Cindy had. They had been best friends all their lives.

I suppose the part that irked me the most was knowing that Karen, who fit every single characteristic of my ultimate dream girl, honestly wanted to see me again. She must have thought that I was deep and, therefore, sensitive. She was right about me being deep, which was precisely why I knew that to see her again would be shallow of me. I was not interested in Karen's heart and soul. I was interested in Karen the tall blonde, and I was fully convinced that any relationship with her would be the equivalent of a rebounding fling.

Perhaps what kept my own temper under control was noting how much worse Angel was handling the termination of her own budding romance. Nothing helped to improve my bad moods like regularly seeing someone who was obviously having a worse day than me. It helped to somewhat put my own day into perspective.

Thus far, the new work schedule had worked quite well at keeping Clancy and Angel from lashing out at each other, as they only shared a few work hours each week. Clancy had been reassigned to opening the shop five days a week, and Angel was given the closing shift. There had been no further incidents, and Clancy seemed to be getting over the breakup quite well. He was already in the preliminary stages of dating a chambermaid from one of the hotels, and had even finished paying for his truck's new transmission. Angel, on the other hand, was still absolutely devastated. She did not laugh anymore, and I would frequently see her wiping tears with the back of her hand as she washed dishes or prepared beverages. I was beginning to worry that she was thinking of quitting. She was one of the few employees I had managed to find who did not come into work late, hungover, strung-out, or stoned, and that was reason enough to want her to stay.

Actually, the only time I had seen Angel hungover was on the morning after her drunken, late-night invasion of the restaurant, right after her big fight with

Clancy. I had innocently inquired as to how she had arrived at that state, and was not surprised to learn that she did not remember a thing which had happened that night. She did not even remember how she had gotten home or where her car was, but I was in no mood to tell her. The last thing that she remembered was ordering her first shot and "telling some smelly guy with lousy pick-up lines to get lost." After an indefinite period of blackness, she had awoken on her kitchen floor and sworn off alcohol for all eternity. As she had dully assured me, "If archeologists ever uncover the wine that Jesus drank at the Last Supper, I might have a sip. But just one. Oh man, my *heeeeaaad....*"

Angel had managed to stay sober for the week after her first, and only, bender, but that did not make her any easier to work with. Kat had once even confided to me, "Sid, I'm beginning to miss the bubbliness." Unfortunately, I did not realize until it was too late that Angel's temperament was still very bubbly, but in a much more thermal way. I believe that the most fitting term would have been "nearing the boiling point."

Gavin Malton was a small wiry man in his late fifties, with curly, grey hair, horn-rimmed glasses, and the maturity of a spoiled rotten twelve-year-old. He had been a regular at my restaurant for over a decade, usually coming in for supper after getting off work at the gas station he managed. He loved our marinara fettuccine, but it was an accepted fact that the frequency of his visits was the only compliment that we would ever receive. The man was a crab, a grouchy, cantankerous whiner. Cindy usually served him, having learned from long experience how to keep him happy enough to at least shut him up. Even she could never quite develop a rapport with him, but she could usually keep him nonverbal, which seemed to be the best that we could hope for. I used to pity the man, occasionally wondering what had driven him to such a state of ingrained bitterness. However, after Angel got through with him on a particular night, I never had to ponder such things again. He never came back. I guess that was the silver lining to Angel's storm cloud.

I was in my office that night, figuring out everyone's timecards for their paychecks the next day. It still seemed odd to me that I wrote my own sister's paycheck, but such petty contemplations were about to be forgotten.

Kat burst into the office without knocking, and sharply ordered, "Sid! Here, now!" Kat was usually grammatically correct. Her sentences only got choppy when something was very wrong. I wasted no time in following her out to the kitchen, just in time to hear Angel make a fierce assertion from the dining room.

"Sir, there are a lot of specifications in my job description, but eating the crap off your shoes is *not* one of them!"

Gavin Malton was on his feet by his table, and Angel was right in his face. Both of them were hollering incoherently at each other, much to the delight of the enraptured diners surrounding them. Conflict was such a drawing card in a violence worshipping society.

I had spotted the source of the conflict before I even reached table five. A plate of spaghetti and meatballs was on the blue paper placemat. Gavin only ate marinara fettuccine, and had often harangued Cindy and I, not only on the evils of eating red meat, but also on the evils of operating an establishment that served it. Angel had either mixed up his order with someone else's, or simply prepared the wrong dish. In either case, I knew that it would have been more than enough to set Gavin off. And Angel was not prepared to sit back and listen to him rant. Their faces were mere inches apart, and they were getting louder by the second.

"Whoa, whoa!" I said over the clamour, stepping deftly in between them, just on the off chance that punches were being considered. "Somebody count to ten or take a pill here! What is the problem?"

"This is what you call service?" Malton demanded shrilly, pointing a shaking finger at his plate. "What is that? You tell me what that is!"

It is spaghetti with meatballs, you dumb knob.

"I'm sorry, sir. If we gave you the wrong meal, it will be exchanged, and you will get the replacement for free. Please, just relax."

My soothing tone worked well with most patrons, but this was Gavin Malton. His life's goal was to never be acceptant.

"And what, huh?" Gavin barked in my face. "I do *what?!* Just sit here and starve in the meantime? I do not think so! Is this what you call service in this hole?"

"Sir, please calm down. It was just a mistake, I'm sure."

"I come here for service!" he yelled, pointing a finger in the air, reminding me of an overly charismatic pastor behind the pulpit. "And what do I get? I get slapped in the face with some frizz-factor chick bringing me a plate of junk!"

"*Frizz-factor?*" Angel screamed, shoving past me. Before I could stop her, she had seized a clear, plastic pitcher from a nearby table, and sloshed the full two litres of ice water into Gavin Malton's face.

I could have kissed her. Instead, my position as employer obligated me to kill her.

"Angel, my office, *now!*" I rasped through gritted teeth, dragging her to the kitchen by her elbow. When I had gotten her out of sight, and turned back to my dining room, I could not help noticing that most of the other patrons were trying not to laugh. Had it not been my restaurant, this would likely have been one of those very rare occasions when I laughed my head off. However, it was my restaurant, and I had no clue what to do. This situation was a definite first. For some reason, my first instinct was to lean close to Gavin's ear, and whisper, "*Dude, I think she likes you....*" To this day, I wish that I had actually said that. *That* would have been epic.

"Sir...." was the only other thing that I could think of to say to the drenched little man, cringing under the onslaught of flaming daggers shooting out of his eyes.

"I'm ... leaving!" Gavin hissed. "You, and your whole establishment, can drop dead! All of you!"

"Hey, back off, buddy!" a tall, thirtyish man yelled from table twelve.

"Where are your manners?" snapped an elderly woman, seated at table six with her husband. "The man is trying to apologize to you!"

"Shut up!" Gavin wheezed. "You lost my business tonight, Mr. Pizza. I'm never coming here again!"

Can I have that notarized?

246

That was the only occasion that I ever saw Gavin Malton so angry that he could not say anything else. In fact, he only spent the next ten seconds sputtering senselessly before storming out of the restaurant, kicking the door twice on his way out. I stood very still until I heard the door slam behind him, and then turned to survey the faces of the people surrounding me. There was expectancy in every set of eyes, and the room was perfectly silent. Cindy, Kat, Boris, and Mark were also watching from the kitchen entrance. I realized that this was one of those situations where only I was permitted to break the silence, but knew that it had to be something really good to fix this mess, in any way.

I said it, very casually. "He's gone. You can laugh now."

The room erupted into gales of hysterical laughter, a couple of the patrons even standing to slap me on the back. My employees were laughing harder than anyone, and clapping as well. I needed a coffee.

As I started back toward the kitchen, a native woman with two children called to me from table one.

"You're not going to fire that girl, are you? She got rid of Gavin. You should name a stat holiday after her!"

"I'll give it serious thought," I groaned. "Does anyone want a free order of spaghetti and meatballs? Still hot."

Angel was seated quietly in front of my desk when I entered the office and shut the door, but I could tell that she was still seething inwardly. I sighed heavily as I sat across from her, drumming my fingers on the rim of Sidney's Cup of Wrath, trying to relieve the frigid silence. I wished that the mug was not empty.

"So?" I eventually said, making it clear that the speaker's podium was hers.

She said nothing.

"That was very ... theatrically confrontational, Angel," I said with mixed irritation and admiration.

"Thank you," she replied stonily.

"No, I'm serious, here," I rambled on. "Never since Gandalf the Grey faced down the balrog on the bridge of Khazad-Dum have I seen such a clear depiction of good versus evil. The only problem I have.... My employee was the balrog."

"What, you think this is my fault?" she said, incredulous.

"Well, the part about eating crap off his shoes was a little heavy-handed. You might have been able to settle that more quietly if you hadn't lost your temper. You're one of my staples, Angel. I pay you more than the kids, and I expect more from you."

"Hey, he was in *my* face!"

"You gave him the wrong order! As part of a democratic commonwealth, it's his civic duty to get in your face!"

"Please don't make me angry, Boss," Angel said ominously. "You wouldn't like me when I'm angry."

"I thought you said you didn't know who Lou Ferrigno was."

"I was playing dumb."

"Right. And so this must be you playing calm and collected, hmm?"

"He called me *frizz-factor!*" Angel hissed, leaning forward angrily in her chair.

"Well, then it truly is the end of the world!" I snapped. "Start preparing for the long haul! Write this down. We'll need canned beans, a root cellar, a gas generator, and the book of Revelation. I prefer the New American Standard. And, just FYI, your hair is a bit frizzy today. Try changing your conditioner."

"*Don't ...* mock my hair, Boss," she said menacingly. "I'm not in the mood."

"Do you think I *care?!*" I snarled, surprising myself. "You don't call me anything but Boss, so do you ever think about what that really means? Quite frankly, it means that I am responsible for providing a fair wage, and a safe, equalizing workplace. Your *mood* is not my concern!"

"You don't care about anything but your coffee, do you?" she scoffed, bitterly.

"No. I also care about keeping my hair nice. And, right now, the only thing you care about is your own despondency. Freaking out at patrons is not going to bring Clancy back!"

"I don't want him back!"

"*Then why aren't you happy?!*"

"I *am!*" she shouted, her decibel level contradicting her words.

"Then why are we here?!"

"Because you're in my face about being in that idiot's face!"

"And I'll get in your face every time you attack the customers like that. I'm not making exceptions to the basic courtesy code just because your love life doesn't work out!"

"Well, how about *this?!*" Angel screamed, rising to her feet and slapping her palms onto my desk. "I *quit!*"

I did not like bluffs. I was on my feet as well, slamming a fist onto my old, abused desk.

"How about *this?!*" I barked back in her face. "Your resignation is accepted!"

"Fine!"

"Fine!"

Go back to jail....

Angel turned on her heel and stormed toward the door, while I slammed back down into my chair, snatched a pen, and began furiously scribbling away at the timecards again. I cringed slightly in anticipation of my door crashing shut behind Angel. Slamming doors always unnerved me.

The door did not slam. That was unusual. I had never seen Angel this mad before, but I had assumed that her display of temper would include door slamming, as she stormed out to the kitchen to inform Kat and Cindy of what an idiot I was. Well, I was going to show her a thing or two. Not only was I *not* going to bad-mouth her in front of the others, but I fully intended to take my reproach a step further, and never mention her name again for the rest of my life.

Angel.... How did she ever manage to snag a name like that?

"Boss?"

I was startled to look up and see her still standing in front of the closed door, her flushed face turned just far enough to one side that I could see a look of slight confusion in her eyes. She had not slammed the door. She had not even opened it. Instead, she turned and took a tentative step back toward me. For the first time since I had known her, Angel Bates was obviously thinking very hard about every single word that she slowly stammered out.

"Does this mean you're not … Boss … anymore?"

I had always prided myself on my composure. There was nothing more pathetic to me than a look of slack-jawed astonishment, especially when it was all over *my* face. However, on this one occasion, my cool dignity completely abandoned me. My eyes widened, my mouth hung slightly open, and I dumbly replied, "Yeah. It does!"

One of us must have flinched first, but I cannot remember if it was her or me. All I remember is that she flinched a lot faster than I did. She had vaulted over and slid across my desk, and was in my lap before I could even get up from my seat. I grimaced twice in rapid succession, once as she grabbed the lapels of my vest with both hands, and again as I heard my Cup of Wrath shatter onto the floor. Perhaps it was because her fists were clenching so close to my throat that I half suspected that she was about to head-butt me, but there was just one little factor which would have made that difficult.

I was kissing her.

There was no thought process. My mind was blank. Her soft, warm lips were pressed so tightly against mine, and I had no idea why. I wrapped my arms around her back and pulled her in, tighter and closer, and the only thought that eventually popped into my head was that I was going to have to breathe, sooner or later.

We must have gotten a little too carried away, as the next thing that I remember was my chair leaning too far back, threatening to topple over and spill us onto the concrete floor. As if starting from a dream, I gave a startled and very undignified squawk, and sat bolt upright, so suddenly that I nearly head-butted *her*. I must have startled Angel back to reality as well. She quickly pulled back from my embrace, and gasped, "Wait a sec, I can't quit! I love this place!"

"And I can't accept your resignation," I gurgled. "I need a waitress."

"Hey, I just kissed you." Angel was the only person I knew who could make stating the obvious sound cute. "Why did we do that?"

"Let's call it rebounding," I said dryly. "I just hired you back, and what just happened never happened. Never. Got it?"

"Okay," she said slowly. "But ... didn't you pull me in here to fire me, anyway?"

"No, I pulled you in here to chew you out. Do you remember what Clancy told you about customers, on your first day here?"

"He said the customer is never right," she said reluctantly, "but don't let them know that."

"Exactly," I nodded. "No matter how much your job ticks you off, you can't forget that again. I'm only letting this slide because Gavin Malton is a certified dork, and because you just did me the world's biggest favour by getting rid of him."

"And because I'm a good kisser?" she grinned, tapping the tip of my nose with an index finger.

"Get off my lap, Angel," I growled. "It never happened."

"When was the last time you actually kissed a girl?" she asked impishly.

"Get off … the lap."

"Come on, Boss, we're bonding here," she chuckled, putting her arms around my neck. "We had a fight, and then we kissed and made up. Now's a good time to be perfectly honest. This could be one of those truly beautiful moments in your life, if you'd let it be."

"A beautiful moment…." I mused. "Have you had many of those?"

"Some," she answered with a smile. "Everyone could use more, though."

"Angel," I sighed, "I'm going to tell you just a bit about my life as a boss. I've only done it for four years. And in that time, I have had employees crawl into my house through windows, and bounce on my bed while I am still trying to sleep in it. Employees have called me in the middle of the night, wanting an advance, a raise, a crying shoulder, or the answer to a crossword puzzle. I've put up with a lot, but I'm drawing the line at employees sitting on my lap. I don't have a white beard and a red suit."

Angel finally slid off me, and leaned against the desk, adjusting her skirt.

"Tell me," she said softly. "Tell me about what it's like to be Boss."

"You just saw what it's like, out there," I muttered, gesturing at the door. "Trying to placate everyone, all the time. Trying to be a leader by being a servant. The job's either impossible, nerve-grinding, or hypocritical. I never asked for it. It just got handed to me."

"Wow. You just shared your pain with me. That's a start. Tell on."

"Angel, just because I didn't fire you doesn't make you a confidante."

"Why not? Are we friends, or what?" She folded her arms across her red vest, and drummed her fingers impatiently on her elbows.

I felt as though I was back in kindergarten, when children decided matters of friendship by grabbing the first classmate to pass by and saying, "Will you be my friend?"

"I am your friend, Angel, but I'm also your boss. I don't need to let you into my whole life."

"I think you want to," she ventured. "That's why you kissed me." She tilted her head and raised a curious eyebrow. "Are you lonely?"

"You've been rehired," I replied. "Please go back to work."

"Fine," she sighed, turning to the door. She looked back, with one hand on the doorknob, and commented, "Boss…. If you ever need to talk, you can tell me things. Anything, actually. I'm a good ear." Then she walked out, letting the door slowly swing shut behind her. I sat in absolute shock, frozen in my chair. I had no idea what had just happened, or why. Sure, Angel was cute, but she was no great beauty, not like Karen, or even Spring or Kat, and yet I had just kissed her. Impulsively. And for a long time.

Myers, you idiot. You just kissed an employee! Are you out of your dang mind?

Well, to be fair, she had just quit. She was a free agent for ... thirty seconds or so.

She probably planned this out. Get ready for a harassment suit.

Come on, do you really think Angel's capable of that kind of premeditation?

Hey, you learn how to be sneaky in jail....

My inner dialogue was only ended when Cindy knocked on the doorframe.

"Mmph?" I replied, my voice muffled by the supporting fist pressing into my cheek. The last few years of my life had been a perpetual quest for more coffee, and the need was most dire at that moment.

"You didn't fire her?" I could not tell if Cindy's voice was skeptical or disappointed.

I had to think for several moments before I could reply. My brain did not want to cooperate with my tongue, those old adversaries going at it again, at the most inopportune time.

"We talked it over," I said simply. "We decided that she had been provoked to an unfair extent, she agreed to be more patient next time, and I'm giving her another shot at redemption."

"I know that you're an honest man, bro," Cindy remarked, "because you are the worst liar that I know. Your office is not exactly soundproof."

"*What did you hear?*" I said sharply, sitting up.

"All I could make out was a lot of yelling," she assured me, trying too hard not to smile. "And please tell me that's not your Cup of Wrath smashed on the floor."

"It got … bumped," I quipped, trying to sound casual.

"You broke your Cup of Wrath?!" Cindy was appalled. "Do you have any idea how much that cost me?"

I leaned back in my chair and looked sideways at the crumbled ceramic.

"Judging from the diminutive size of the shards, I'd guess you paid fifteen bucks, embossing included."

"But it's *the thought!* I suppose you'll want a new one for your birthday now."

"Ease up, baby sister. You're going to spend thirty dollars on presents for me in less than two years? You're not letting the checkbook roam free, are you?"

"Was that a yes?"

"Yes. I kind of liked it. It was very fitting for me, don't you think?"

"Sid …. I remember a time when you were happy. Do you remember that?"

I chuckled humourlessly. "It's not easy remembering age three, Cindy."

CHAPTER NINETEEN

Attempting to carry on an average working relationship with an employee whom I had just found myself impulsively smooching was awkward to say the least. Over the next few weeks, it became obvious that Angel was not planning any devious lawsuits, but that did not make the situation any less frigid. The only positive side was that Angel was beginning to speak civilly to Clancy again, most likely because even that was easier than talking to me. One of my biggest weaknesses was completely shutting down communications whenever I was perturbed. Kat once told me, "Sid, you're an oyster, you know that? You have a pearl in there somewhere, but no one's ever going to see it." I was beginning to think that she was right. Aside from my staples, I did not have many friends. Friends required spare time, which required taking time off work, and I was not ready to do that. I often felt that I would have nothing if I did not have my work. Lately, I had started doing maintenance work at the shop on Wednesdays, finding any little chore that needed to be done, or would need to be done eventually. I washed walls, replaced flickering light bars, I even cemented down new black and white checkered floor tiles in the laundry room. The room did not need new flooring, but it was work. Afterwards, I would play my piano, often for hours. I had to be there. I had nothing else, just my pizza shop, and my music, and my coffee.

All around me, the world was moving and changing. Sitting on the piano bench, I could almost feel the whirlwind of change cycling outside that small tinted window.

Boris and Cindy were making wedding plans, and had set the date for the end of November. They had asked Dad's brother, Uncle Reggie Myers, to give the bride away, and Clancy received the assignment of being the MC, much to his delight. The man was a born entertainer.

Randall and Karen had successfully opened the gym, Randall's Ring, and most of my employees had taken memberships. Thus, Clancy and Boris were now sparring partners, as were Kat and Cindy. The boxing ring was apparently becoming something of a spectator sport in Chetwynd, and small crowds often assembled to watch their favourites duke it out. I stayed away from the gym. Karen was too often there.

A few days after our date, Karen had told me that I was "a good friend, but I don't think we'd work out." I could not argue with her. I hoped we could become better friends, but being around her made me uneasy. So, I stayed in my restaurant.

Other bits of local news had been pouring in. Big Ronnie Alders had his second heart attack, and was under doctor's orders to never touch chicken wings again for the rest of his life. He had since developed an addiction to our caesar salad, which I could only hope was a step in the right direction. Due to the rising cost of poultry, the All You Can Eat Wing special had been removed from our menu, anyway.

Gavin Malton had been true to his word, and never returned. He was said to be regularly haunting Milo Manetti's Italian Restaurant and truck stop just outside of town. Hopefully, they could put up with him for the next ten years.

Town councilman Jeffrey Morrow had publically announced that Redmond's Ribs would be open for business by early December. Construction would begin shortly.

Finally, rumour had it that Devon Finn's oldest son was starting to mule crack around town for him. The only age specification for drug use and trafficking was that you had to be old enough to keep a secret. A lot of kids experimented with drugs well before they reached their teens. As a result, some of them never made it out of their teens.

It was a hot Wednesday morning in mid July. I was at the restaurant, alone, and I could not find a single thing to fix up, wash, replace, or even dust. I left just long enough to pick up my mail, and then brought it to my piano to open. The only piece of interest was my contributor's copy of *30 Days Up North*. Sure enough, my entire crew was on the front cover, over a caption that read "Keeping the Peace Region full, one slice at a time." Inside the envelope, Linda Matthews had inserted a handwritten note that said simply *Pam says hi. Linda.*

By The Slice actually had a full, four page spread, with colour photos and even a detailed menu description. The article itself was pretty much what I had expected, a lot of gushing about how fantastic our food, service, music, and sense of family tradition was. Thankfully, only a brief mention was made about how I had come into possession of my business, and no mention was made of my being a "hero" that night. Overall, the article was tasteful and respectful, and just a little bit over the top, but that could only help business. Of course, reading it still turned out to be yet another source of bad memories.

The last thing that I remembered about the crash was trying to wake Dad up. The next memory I had was the sound of weeping. Cindy was crying beside my hospital bed when I awoke. Tears were pooling high in her eyes as she took my hand and kept repeating, "He's gone. He's gone, Sid. He's gone." I did not claim to be an exception to any rules. I went through every stage of grieving, just like everybody else. However, in my case, acceptance was not the final stage. The final stage was withdrawal. A large part of my heart just seemed to shut down. I spent the next four years hoping that hard work and a sardonic sense of humour would help me to start living again. That had not worked. Neither had dating, and, by then, I was desperate enough to actually try talking to someone.

As I mentioned, I had basically been avoiding Angel. I made a point of never being alone with her, and had not had a single conversation with her since she was "rehired." Still, her last words before she walked out of my office had stuck with me. She had told me that I could talk to her, about anything.

After reading the article, I sat at the piano for over an hour and never touched the keys once. My mind kept going over where my life had gone, and the things I would have done differently, if I had actually been given a choice. I also wondered about the choices I had made, and whether they were the right ones.

Cindy had gone to both a grief counsellor and our pastor after Dad died. She said that it had helped, not to eliminate her sadness, but to help her understand that it would always be an important part of her life. She told me that her pain was a reminder of her love for her father. The pain would always stay with her, but once she could understand what it really meant, she did not have to be afraid of it anymore.

I never talked to a therapist. Pastor Ryan told me that his door would never be closed, but I never talked to him, either. When it came to my memories of Karl Myers, I never talked to anyone, not even Cindy. Kat was my inspiration. As far as I knew, she had never visited any counsellors either, and she seemed fine.

It took me a long time to admit that I would never have Kat's strength. I could not just hold my head high and face the pain head on anymore. I needed to talk to someone.

So, why did I want to talk to Angel?

Kat was the closest thing that I had to a best friend, but even she could not hear me out on this matter. We had both lost loved ones, yet I still felt uncomfortable discussing that with her. Whenever I even thought about turning to Kat, I was constantly reminded of the parable of the two blind men. Each one tries to guide the other, but, in the end, they both fall into the proverbial ditch. I guess what I really needed was a vent, someone not close enough to my heart for me to worry about frightening. Kat, Cindy, Boris or Clancy would all think that I was breaking apart if I ever let them know how I really felt inside, and I had spent the past four years trying to be strong for them. Angel was a friend, but, in a lot of ways, she was still a stranger. Sometimes, when I could not trust myself with those closest to me, the friends who did not know me as well were the only ones left to confide in.

My piano was my source of both inspiration and memory. Sitting on the glossy black wooden bench that day, I could not get Angel out of my head. Not only because it was hard to keep our kiss from constantly replaying, but also because she remained such a loveable mystery. Angel was like a good book, one that kept asking questions, but left many of the answers to the imagination of the reader. I could read most people very well. I could tell when they were lying, being evasive, hiding pain, forcing civility, or preparing to lash out. But Angel was a closed book. I realized that opening up to her was the only way that I would ever get her to open up to me, and for some reason that seemed very important.

All right, Angel. You win.

Actually, she had won a long time ago. The night I rescued her and Clancy from the Pine Pass, she had gotten me loose-lipped enough to mention that I played the piano. I had not wanted to tell her that, but I had with barely a thought. Now that she knew, even if I had covered by telling her I "just plinked," I did not even mind as much as I thought I would have.

The strangest aspect of my relationship with Angel was how badly I *wanted* to trust her. Perhaps it was because of how she avoided questions about her past. Her evasiveness made me feel untrusted, which led me to question if that was really how she felt about me. I did not make many new friends. I suppose I needed practice in developing trust.

My insecure reluctance made pressing the seven digits of Angel's home number into my cell phone seem to take forever. It also seemed to take an excessive amount of time for her to pick up, even though it was probably no more than three rings.

"Hello?"

"Angel, it's … Boss."

"Oh." The surprise in her voice was unveiled. "What did I do?"

"Nothing, I was just … calling."

"Did I leave the oven on last night? I know you hate it when I leave the oven on. I'm sure I shut it off."

"Relax, Angel," I assured her, lightly and slowly pressing the ivories in front of me, just enough that the tones could barely be heard. "I'm at the shop now, the oven's off, it's all good. It's fine. Really."

"So, what did I do wrong?" Her surprise was being replaced by anxiety.

"Nothing, you're doing great. Like always. Anyway, I was just calling to … uh, you know … call. You. Hi."

"Boss, you're starting to scare me."

Oh, this is going well....

"Sorry," I groaned. "I'm not good with telephones. They do weird things to my tongue."

"Odd." I could almost see the smirk on her lips. "You usually seem to have great control of your tongue."

I grimaced. "Angel ... it never happened, okay?"

"What? I was talking about your fluency. Why? What did you think I was talking about, Boss?"

You know dang well what.... You know what? Don't even play her game. Just make your point.

"Angel, I trust you."

There was dead silence over the line for a couple of seconds which seemed like a lot more. She had not expected to hear that.

"I don't give out trust very often," I continued. "I just thought you should know that. You're the best waitress who's ever worked at this restaurant. Plus, I consider you a friend. I wanted to tell you that."

"Well ... that's flattering, Boss. And, you're welcome. Uh ... is that all you wanted to— Are you playing the piano?" My fingers froze, still holding one key down as the last note resonated into oblivion. I could not believe that I had just let someone hear me playing, even though a one-handed melody hardly qualified as a song.

"I was just plinking. I do that sometimes."

"Yeah, you mentioned that. Therapeutic, right?"

"It doesn't hurt."

"I believe that. I've got a guitar at home. It's very relaxing."

"That must be nice," I remarked, sounding a lot stupider than I had intended.

"Yeah, it is."

Silence. Again. Heavy breathing on both ends of the phone.

Myers, you're making idiotic small talk. Say what you called to say!

"You know," I commented. "I don't think we've really just had a chat since … Snake Night."

"Boss, if you just called because you needed someone to talk to, that's cool. It's really cool."

Oh, she is good…. Well, here goes nothing.

I closed my eyes, placed an elbow on top of the piano, and rested my forehead against my fingertips.

"You said I could tell you things," I said quietly. "How serious were you about that?"

Her voice was very soft as she replied, "I was serious."

"That night in the pass, you asked for my life story. Do you still want to hear it?"

"I do," she said, almost too quickly.

"I don't talk to people about this," I said clearly. "Do you understand that?"

"I don't blab, Boss."

"Thank you." I took a sip of cold coffee, still wondering why I actually wanted to do this.

"My job is all that I have," I said. "I do it because it was the dream that my dad never finished. He made pizza, so I make pizza. I inherited the business, and I decided to keep it and manage it, because I knew that no one else would be able to do it the way he wanted."

"I'm sorry about your dad," Angel said. "The closest family I ever lost was a grandmother."

"When?" I asked.

265

"When I was nine. She had brain cancer. It was … pretty hard. She just faded, for a long time. By the end … well, she wasn't even Gramma anymore. I know your dad died in a car accident. We can only imagine how horrible that must have been, but still…. You should be glad that he didn't just fade into nothingness, in constant pain, until he would forget who he was talking to right in the middle of a conversation…."

"He died almost instantly," I told her, beginning to cautiously play one-handedly on the piano again. "His truck was T-boned by another one, right into his door. Most of the left side of his body was crushed." I looked up and out of one of the tinted dining room windows. A light breeze had begun stirring the leaves in the row of trees along the street. "It was fast. Very fast."

"Is that what the doctor's said?"

I bit my lip and closed my eyes again. I kept the piano music very low, my fingers crawling over the keys so slowly, like a sleepwalking spider.

"I was there, Angel. I was with him."

"Oh…." Angel gave a heavy sigh, but it was an empathetic one. "Boss, I am not going to say another word. Sometimes … you just have to talk it out."

I did not consider myself much of an oral storyteller, but for the first time in years I made an exception. My mind travelled back through time as I stared at the oak-framed clock on the wall, and I just started talking.

"Do you read many books, Angel?"

"All the time. I love reading."

"I think of every life story as a book. Sometimes, the book doesn't start out the way you want it to. Sometimes, there is an event or tragedy that occurs even before the first chapter, and it leaves the characters in a setting that they didn't choose or want, but still have to live in. And, sometimes, they only figure out how that event truly changed the course of their lives much later, in the last few pages. It's cards. We play them as they're dealt, but we never stop wondering what we could have done to make our hand better. And, if we ever do figure it out, it's too late anyway.

"Four years ago … there was a very popular boy in this town. Josh Kelton, eighteen years old. Rich, tall, built, long blonde hair, handsome as anything. Girls absolutely drooled over him. He was our star basketball player in high school, he had lots of money, a nice house, a big truck, and he was connected to most of the drug dealers in town, so all the best parties were said to be at Josh Kelton's place. Loud music, drugs, booze, girls, the works.

"I knew him. He was a pretty good guy. I wasn't into the drugs, so we weren't really close friends, but we got along. He was a friend.

"One night, there was an amazing spring thunderstorm. Lightning was turning night into day, the thunder was so loud it seemed to come from inside your head. The power was going down all over town. We had candles set out on all the tables here, just in case.

"Josh was having a party that night. When his power went out, he and all of his friends crowded onto the patio to watch the lightning. A lot of them were on mushrooms, and they said later that they had never had such a mind-blowing experience, the most beautiful moment of their lives. Josh was in his element, and stoned. He wanted to share this wonderful time with his girlfriend, Alicia Mann. She was sixteen, with plans to pursue a dancing career. Josh couldn't kick all of his friends out, so he and Alicia decided to drive out into the storm. He had a sweet truck, big green F-150 extended cab on monster tires, total chrome package. Beautiful rig.

"They left just before midnight, and drove all over town. Josh loved speed. He was flying down all the roads in town, no headlights to spoil the lightning, and not a worry in the world. He was high on the moment, and on who knows how many kinds of drugs. Even when the rain started pouring down, he didn't care. The man was invincible, on top of the world. Me and Dad met him at the intersection of main street and Forty-eighth…. We barely even had time to see him coming." I had to stop for a moment to take another swig of coffee, blinking a single tear back where it belonged. My mouth was dry.

"None of us had airbags. Josh had his seatbelt on, so he only smacked his head on the steering wheel and passed out. Alicia went through the windshield, across the hood, and smashed through the canopy window, her body ending up behind the backseat of our Blazer. I didn't even know she was there. The paramedics only found her when they noticed a bloody hole in Kelton's windshield. She never regained consciousness, and died a few hours later in the hospital, full of tubes and needles. Maybe she was the lucky one. Josh burned to death when his truck exploded a minute later…." My voice had trailed off until it was almost inaudible.

"I don't remember much. With the concussion I got, the doctor said that he was surprised that I could remember the previous twelve hours. I hit my head in the crash, but managed to pull Dad out. He was already dead, but I didn't know it yet. I couldn't save him, and I couldn't save Josh.

"A girl named Pam Gregson was working the graveyard shift at the convenience store on the corner. She remembers more than I do. I pulled Dad away from the fire, but Josh's truck blew before I could get him out. Some flying debris hit me on the head again, and this time it was enough to knock me out. Pam saved my life by dragging me away from burning gas, but I don't remember anything until the next morning.

"You know the hardest part? Josh wasn't even drunk. Tests estimated that he had consumed maybe one beer. He was just high. Weed, crack, X, mushrooms, who knows what else. Drugs killed my father, and Josh and Alicia. They had Josh so fascinated with the weather that he couldn't keep his eyes on the road in front of him.

"Do you know how Kelton's friends honoured his memory, Angel? I heard some of them talking outside the hospital the next day. There had to be a dozen of them there, all crying, hugging. And one of them said, 'Tonight, we'll all smoke a joint for Josh Kelton. He'd want us to keep being happy.' And they all nodded, and looked solemn, respectful."

Reciting these memories was making my temperature rise. I needed another swig of cold coffee to cool me down before I could continue.

"There was public outrage. A respected businessman and two rich kids die in a fiery crash, of course people got mad. For a month or so, they demanded 'changes' be made. That was the most specific I ever heard. 'Changes.' They even circulated petitions. This one lady, who obviously didn't know who I was, asked me to sign this petition at a trade show, and gave me this big rehearsed speech about 'recent deaths,' and public safety, and responsibility, and … righteous indignation…. So, I look at this petition in my hand, thinking I'll just sign it to get her to shut up. Then I actually read it.

"It was for a stop light. That was their answer to the problem. They wanted traffic lights installed at the 48th Street intersection. To keep us all safe. To protect 'more innocent kids.'

"I didn't say anything. I just ripped the whole thing in half and walked away. And this lady…. She yells after me. She said that it was people like me who put Chetwynd into the state it was in. It's the people like me…." I had to wipe my eyes with the back of my hand, and lick my dry lips, thankful that Angel could not see me. She was silent on the other end of the line, and I had a brief notion that she might have fallen asleep. Well, that only made it easier to keep talking.

"When you lose a parent … you just get lost. You never realize how much of a compass your parents are, until you're in the woods, and they aren't there anymore. You feel like you have nothing to support you, to guide you. All you have is painful memories, for a very long time. There's nothing else. Then, after a year or so, you start to remember all the good times, the times when 'I love you' was said. But the bad memories…. They never go far away. They're always still there, just lurking out of sight in the shadows, waiting for a trigger.

It's four years later, and I drive past a man in a Blazer. First thought; That's Dad. I see someone on the street, with that hunched over, shuffling walk. That's Dad. And you know what the absolute worst is? I'll be in a crowded room, and I hear a laugh. His. That's Dad. I know he's gone … but I am so desperate to find him again." My voice was ready to break any second.

"Well," I sighed, letting my hand slowly slide from the keys to my lap. "That's my story. Everything before, everything after, it doesn't matter much…. Does it make me any more understandable?"

Listening to Angel's breath in my ear, I realized that she was crying.

"I'm sorry, Boss," she sobbed. "I'm so sorry!" She was roughly two miles away, but I had never felt so close to anyone. I wanted to hug her, and whisper that everything would be all right, as I used to do with Cindy when I heard her crying in the middle of the night. Cindy had cried a lot in the year following Dad's death, and I had to be the strong one who consoled her. In the years since, I never cried more than three or four tears at a time, but not for lack of wanting. Almost every night, I would lie awake in the darkness as the world slept, wishing that someone could be there to hold me as I wept until my eyes had no more tears. However, there was no one to hold me. I knew that real men were not afraid to cry, but, as childish as it sounds, I was afraid to do it alone. There is no greater loneliness than crying by yourself in the dark. In moments like that, you truly have no one and nothing.

Have you been wondering what my greatest fear was? I could not tell Karen, or Cindy, and I would not even tell Angel on this very honest occasion.

I was afraid of being forgotten.

I fought with my fear all the time, trying to get over the loss and find where I had left my own life. Being strong was the only solution. So, I held back the tears, while wondering if that was holding back my heart as well. When the pain became most unbearable in the black of night, I would turn on my bedroom light, sit in front of the mirror on my chest of drawers, and count the tears as they escaped from my stony eyes. One time, I counted six. That was the most.

Angel had no such limitations on her tears. She was weeping unabashedly in my ear receiver.

"Why'd you tell me that story?" she demanded tearfully. "Don't you have any happiness to share?"

That's the thing about life stories, Angel," I replied. "No one cares how it starts, but everyone wants to know how it ends. That's where it all ended for me. I inherited a business, took new responsibility, lost a girlfriend, and it all meant absolutely nothing."

"Boss...." Angel sounded strained, and I could tell that she was desperately searching for some appropriately wise words. I was sorry for putting her into that position. It had not been my intention.

"Boss, what's your reason for getting up in the morning?"

I had to think that question over for some time, lightly stroking the piano keys without pressing them.

"I don't have one," I confessed. "But maybe that in itself is what keeps me going. I have to get up so that I can keep searching for a reason to."

"That's not good enough," she decided. "Getting up and going to work is not living. Think about it, Boss. Where's your joy? What makes you happy?"

"What makes *you* happy?" I returned.

"Friends," she said honestly. "Family. My job. My cat. Sunrises. Starry nights. Helping people. Oh yeah, and Marvin the Martian cartoons. I love that little tyrant."

"I always liked the singing frog. That was the peak of animation."

"That was a classic," Angel giggled her agreement. "See? You do have some happiness. So, embrace that. If you can't see the pleasures in the little things in your life, you miss out on so much."

"Stop and smell the roses, huh?" I smiled grimly.

"It's a tired expression, Boss, but it's still some of the best advice that I've ever heard."

"I suppose," I agreed, downing the last of my coffee.

"Hey, why don't you try something?" Angel suggested. "Just a little experiment, okay? Every morning, as soon as you wake up, just think about one thing that brings you happiness. Just one. It can be a friend, something in nature, a childhood toy, anything. Then, write it down, and think of something else happy the next morning. Keep writing them down, one day at a time. Your list will be your reminder of what makes your life worth all the pain."

"Wow," I remarked. "Which self-empowerment guru taught you that one?"

"Actually, I just thought of it now," she admitted, with some amount of pride. "Dang, that's a good idea! I'm going to have to try that. Okay, I have a pencil and paper and I'm writing 'puppies' at the top. Puppies make everyone happy. Sweet, I just started a Happy List! Your turn. Get a pad."

"Okay, fine," I sighed, deciding that I was willing to try anything at that point. I carried the phone to my office, grabbed a blank notebook and scribbled a quick word in it.

"Done."

"What'd you write?" Angel asked eagerly.

"Money," I said dryly.

"Oh," Angel said skeptically. "Whatever flips your burger...."

"Do you remember your first day here?" I reminded her. "You asked what the job paid, and you said 'Money is one of those happy things.' Don't get hypocritical on me."

"I'm not," she said, defensively. "But, if that's the *happiest* thing in your life, you deserve to be miserable. I can't believe you didn't write puppies! How can you not like puppies?"

"Angel, for Pete's sake, I like puppies!" I said, a bit snappishly. "I'll put it on the list tomorrow. You said just one happy thing per day, remember?"

"I know," she chuckled. "I was just making sure you'd actually do it. Messing with your head, Boss! Ha!"

She had a good laugh over that one, and it was infectious enough to even make me chuckle a bit. When her mirth finally subsided, she let out a long, contented sigh, still suppressing quiet snickers.

"Seriously though, Boss," she said sincerely, "I want to thank you for calling. What you just shared with me … well, it was a beautiful moment. Not the story, but the fact that you … I guess 'honoured me' is the only term for it. You honoured me with your trust, and I know how much value you put on trust. So … thanks. It really means a lot to me. I've had a lot of friends in my life, and I could count on one hand how many of them shared that kind of trust with me. What you just did … it put you on the list. You really are the best boss I've ever had. I mean it."

"Angel … I'm the only boss you've ever had."

"Whatever," she dismissed the obvious. "You're cool. I'm sorry I almost quit."

"And I'm sorry I almost let you," I smiled. "It won't happen again, unless you *really* need it."

"Relax, Boss; This is *me*."

"Yeah, I know. Listen, Angel, Cindy was going to invite some friends over to our place tonight to watch some movies. I think it's a *Star Trek* marathon or something. You wanna come over, around five?"

"I hate *Star Trek*."

"Was that a yes?"

"Yes," she said, complacently. "Who's coming?"

"Well, Kat, and Boris, of course. He's been a bit of a fixture around the house lately. I think Clancy's coming. Is that going to be a problem?"

"No," she sighed. "We're friends. I just don't know how I ever dated him. Is *commitaphobic* a word?"

"No," I said. "But *egocentric* is. Karen and Randall might show up, too."

"Ooh-oooh!" Angel quavered with mock horror. "Be very afraid, Boss. The ex is coming."

"She's not an ex," I groaned. "We had one date. It was an intro, nothing more."

"Boss, what's wrong with you? Did you forget to look at her, or what? That girl is like ... like...."

"...decadent candy?" I guessed tiredly, borrowing Clancy's favourite sexist description.

"Well, yeah, sort of. She's hot."

"She wasn't a friend," I said simply. "Now, she is. If I had dated her, I bet she never would have been."

"Wow, Boss, you're deep," Angel chuckled admiringly. "So, I'll see you tonight."

"Actually," I said slowly, "there's one more thing I need to tell you. Just because we're still confiding. And this one's *really* off the record."

"My ears are open and my lips are sealed," she replied solemnly. "Let me have it."

I had to take a deep breath before I could bring myself to continue.

"I hate pizza."

"*Excuse me?!*" Angel was flabbergasted.

"I hate pizza," I repeated. "I've hated it for years."

"But, *Boss!* You're a ... a pizza boss!"

"Yes, it's tragic," I drolly assured her.

Angel still sounded stunned as she carefully asked, "So ... what do you like?"

I shrugged.

"I kind of like hot dogs. Don't tell Kat. See you tonight."

After I pocketed the phone, I spent a few minutes just leaning against my desk, trying to figure out why I had just unloaded my life's troubles on a fairly new friend, not to mention an employee. I had to admit that I could not have poured out my heart like that to anyone except Angel. She was special, and she was now entrusted with information that, as a rule, I never shared with anyone, and, yet, I was happy that she knew. Talking to Angel had made me happy.

I had nothing else to do at the shop. In fact, I had not had anything to do there in the first place, so I decided to go home and help Cindy, who was planning to barbecue steaks for our guests. However, there was one thing that I knew would torment me all night if I did not attend to it before I left the restaurant.

I sat behind the desk and slid my new "Happy List" across it toward me. Under *Money*, I added a single word.

Puppies.

Angel had told me to write just one word per day. I knew myself well enough to be certain that I would never adhere to that schedule. Maybe she would, but I was too impatient, especially now that I was actually in a good mood.

I'll always miss you, Dad, but telling your story just made something good happen. Thanks.

I ended up spending the next half hour on that list, filling the pages with neat, vertical columns of happiness.

Money.

Puppies.
Coffee.
Piano.
Cowboy boots.
My truck.
Friends.
Dancing cartoon frogs.
Horseback riding.
Aurora borealis.
Mocha.
Hot dogs.
John Wayne movies.
Cappuccino.
Espresso....

CHAPTER TWENTY

Contagious was one of the best words I could think of to describe Angel. Every afternoon when she came into work, she would tell me the newest happy word that had been added to her Happy List. I was not sure if that was just her attempt at keeping me happy, but it did get the rest of the staff, and quite a few patrons, asking questions. Suffice to say, one thing led to the next, and over one hundred people of all ages had begun writing Happy Lists within the month. Angel's theory of life appreciation, which had seemed simplistic enough to be a first grade homework assignment or the advice of a motivational speaker, had become the newest craze in Chetwynd. One wannabe four-twenty gang of teenagers had even declared that they were all going to start recording their fondest stoner memories on "Happy-High Lists." Angel was officially the founder of a revolution, albeit one that was most likely to fizzle out in a matter of months. Angry revolutions can drag on for years, or even centuries, whereas happy ones have a much harder time keeping momentum; e.g., the disco era. Personally, I blamed a cultural obsession with violence, stemming from the classic Greek tragedies and rap music. How did a guy like Oedipus ever survive long enough to be king, anyway?

I was not a revolutionary. In twenty-six years, I had never even changed my barber. Change was annoying. It required readjustment. I did not even like it when Cindy bought the white toothpaste instead of the striped stuff. Thus, I did not add to my Happy List after the first writing session. Writing it had made me feel better, but I was not about to delude myself into thinking that puppy dogs and rainbows in a notebook would be enough to take the storm cloud out of my life. If there was just one thing that I had been sure of for the past four years, it was that I would never truly be happy until I could love the smell of rain again.

The deepest problems in life cannot be solved by meaningless words on paper. Problems remain until feelings or mind sets can be changed, and sometimes it can take a lifetime for that to happen.

Unfortunately, my life was destined to transition, whether or not I wanted comforting monotony. Angel's innocent sincerity was so annoyingly effective, I had actually begun sharing my feelings with her. That definitely made change inevitable, which was enough to make me surly. Clancy probably summed me up the best when he once said, "Sid, you get mad at yourself for being happy. Believe me, no one else does that!"

My life would be forever changed before the end of the year, but the change occurred slowly at first. Over the next three months, my friendship and shared trust with Angel grew deeper. I realized that it was absurd to try living my life like a clam, as Kat had said. It had felt good to confide in Angel, and she had assured me that, anytime I needed to, I could call her. So, I did call her. I had never known anyone who was so easy to talk to. Sometimes, we would just chat for an hour about nothing in particular, and, on other occasions, she would tell me to quit hem-hawing and just spill my guts. My feelings and emotions had been bottled up for so long, and pouring them out was such a refreshing experience. We talked about my dad a lot, and Angel asked many questions about him. I told her everything that I could remember about growing up on the acreage, about how much I missed the horseback riding, and Dad's piano playing.

Once, I told Angel about how betrayed I had felt by Clancy's secret drug use. I had other friends who used drugs, but none of them were ever bashful about it. If Clancy was ashamed of his habit, perhaps even pained, why had he not trusted me enough to ask for help? Angel had no answer for that, but, again, just telling her made my life seem that much more tolerable.

One Thursday evening in late October, Angel and I actually went for coffee at a nearby diner after work. We talked for a few minutes about funny things that had happened in the restaurant during the previous week, and Cindy and Boris's rapidly approaching wedding. Then, the conversation drifted to the newest restaurant in town, Redmond's Ribs. The building construction was almost finished, with the grand opening set for December first. For the first time, I told Angel about one of my greatest concerns. I was afraid that the new restaurant would put mine out of business. Angel and I had spent a lot of time discussing personal issues, but that was the only time that I had told her something that even I knew was most likely just paranoia. It made me realize how much I trusted her confidence.

From that moment on, I never again felt bad for confiding in Angel. I wanted to keep our relationship as honest as it was right then. I was tired of my own secrets. I would have taken her back to the restaurant and played the piano for her, and everyone else, that very hour, but I never got the chance. Something else happened first, something that would change my life even more. My cell phone rang.

Angel was clearly disappointed that our conversation was being interrupted, particularly by a Gloria Gaynor tune.

"Who is it now?" she said, annoyed.

I flipped the phone out of my brown leather jacket, and checked the call display.

"Ah crap, it's the shop," I moaned. "I hope they didn't get a rush. I'm starting to enjoy taking a few evenings off." Kat, Boris and Cindy were the only ones left at work that night, but I had told them, as always, to call me if it got very busy. Still, I really hated having to put my vest and tie back on once my shift was over.

"Hello, talk to me," I muttered into the phone.

"Sid, we got a problem." Kat sounded more disturbed than I had expected. Usually, when I had to be called back in, she just sounded apologetic.

"Why, what's wrong?" I said, already feeling a tense knot growing in my stomach. I had known Kat all of my life, and could read her voice as though it was my own.

"Boris just got beat up on a delivery. Some drunk bastard didn't like the price of his pizza."

"Is he okay?" I asked quickly.

"He's back here now. I didn't know what to do."

"I'm on my way," I answered, already throwing a five-dollar bill on the table as I stood up and put the phone away.

"What's wrong?" Angel wondered, looking concerned.

"I've gotta go," I said quietly. "Sorry."

"Boss!"

"I'll talk to you tomorrow," I called, hurrying out to my truck.

So much for communication....

Boris was sitting alone at a patio table on the dark veranda when I arrived back at my shop. There was a chill breeze skittering the first fragile autumn leaves across the interlocking red bricks, but Boris did not seem to care. He was holding a bag of ice to his swollen cheek, and his lower lip was split. Even in the dim light of the street lamps, I could see the drops of blood that had soaked into the front of his white tee-shirt. He suddenly reminded me of Dad. I forced myself not to think about that.

Boris stared with empty eyes into the black street, his breath sounding shallow as it seeped through his slightly gritted teeth. He was clearly in some amount of shock, still. I did not say anything. I sat beside him, and put a reassuring hand on his shoulder. Neither one of us spoke, we just kept watching the road. It was almost eleven o'clock, and the streets were void of traffic. The parking lot was also vacant, so I assumed that no one was dining inside.

"Sorry to interrupt your date." Boris had to whisper in an effort to keep his adrenaline loaded voice from quavering. He was obviously embarrassed by his shaky state, even though I knew that it was just a reflex action.

"It was coffee, Boris. Not a date. Are you okay?"

His voice was very shaky. "I didn't even provoke him, Sid. I was polite. I just told him what the price was."

"Whose place? Do we know him?"

Boris shook his head. "It was Prairie Falls Tavern, some big guy. I think he's with one of those gas line maintenance crews that are always at the hotels."

"What was the order?"

"Just a medium sausage and onion, fifteen bucks. He was just sitting at the bar with three other guys, and when I told him the price, he just started swearing and yelling, saying we were crooks for charging so much. His friends were kind of cheering him on, so he slaps the pizza box onto the floor. I was going to just pick it up and leave, but as soon as I turned around, he yells 'Don't turn your back on me!' and backhanded me across the back of the head." His voice was steadying, but now sounded angrier.

"It knocked me around, right against the bar. I just about bashed my head on it, and I fall to the floor. He tried to kick me in the ribs, but he hit my forearm, so I didn't really get hurt there. But then he pulls me to my feet, and just starts decking me. He slugged me about three times before the bouncer tackled him. And I'm just standing there…. I didn't do anything. Nothing. The guy could have killed me, and I just stood there!" His voice was livid with frustration.

"Mac Denham?" I asked curiously, after giving him a moment to simmer down. "Was that the bouncer?"

"Yeah, I think so," Boris nodded. "You know him?"

"I went to school with him. He's a good guy."

"I know," Boris muttered. "He threw the guy outside, and asked if I wanted to call the cops, press charges. I said no, and I just … came back here. I mean, what else could I do?"

"No, you did the right thing," I said, rubbing my face, frustrated. "You'd better just go home, man. I'll help them close up. Look, he attacked you. It's not your fault. You've got every right to file assault charges. I know I would."

"No, I can't," Boris moaned. "What's the point?"

"What do you mean, can't?" I demanded. "Why not?"

Boris shrugged in disgust.

"He was drunk."

I could only stare at him as I slowly stood up.

"Did he pay for the pizza, Boris?"

"No," he snorted. "Of course not."

I took a long breath, looking up at the stars.

"Let's go," I said in a low monotone.

"Where?"

"We've gotta go talk to Mac, figure this out."

"Ah, come on, Sid!" he complained. "I don't wanna go back there. It's humiliating enough, already."

"You can wait in the truck if you want," I said. "Are you coming, or not?"

"Fine," he sighed, tossing the ice onto the table. "What do you mean, 'figure this out?'"

"No one paid for the pizza," I said evenly. "And no one had just cause to get it free."

"So? We're out fifteen bucks. The world will keep spinning."

"And there's a lot of other drunks at that bar who just got ideas about how to get free take-out. Someone owes me fifteen dollars."

"Sid, this is crazy," Boris snapped, following me into Sid's Rig. "Just let it go."

"It's my money," I said, firing up the truck.

"Well, I'm staying in here. I'm a mess."

We did not talk on the drive to the tavern. There was not much else to say. Boris still looked angry, whether at me, his attacker, or himself, I could not tell. I was completely emotionless. My heart felt as though it had completely shut down again. I just felt cold, but not because of the weather.

Money was at the top of your Happy List, Myers.... Angel was right. You should have written 'puppies' first.

Prairie Falls Tavern was designed in replica of an elegant wilderness hunting lodge, a large log cabin on the western outskirts of town. The architecture suggested that it was a classy establishment, but the clientele had a tendency to shatter that illusion of grandeur, not to mention the occasional plate glass window.

The burly Mac Denham was having his smoke break in front of the building, hunkered down on a stool beside the front entrance, two heavy oak and glass doors, rather ornately engraved with rocky mountains and coniferous trees. Most of the windows were frosted with wildlife scenes, mostly sandblasted moose and elk in valleys. In a different town, Prairie Falls Tavern would have been a nice place to unwind after work. Boris was not the first one to be innocently assaulted there.

Mac Denham was a long time bodybuilder, well over six feet tall, with a shaved head and full red beard. He was most often seen in an Edmonton Eskimos football jersey with a heavy gold chain around his thick neck, black biker pants, and a green headband. He recognized me as I stepped out of the blue truck, and stood up with an acceptant sigh, flicking his glowing cigar butt into the dark shrubbery around the gravel parking lot. He shook my hand as I walked up the wooden boardwalk, the dull pounding of country music emanating from inside the bar.

"Hey, Sid."

"Been awhile, Mac," I said calmly.

"I figured you'd stop by," he acknowledged, leaning against a rustic hitching rail. "I'm sorry I couldn't help more. I was at the other end of the room with two guys arguing about the pool table."

"You did what you could," I soothed him, leaning against the railing, beside him. "I didn't come here to blame anybody."

"Well, what can you do?" he snorted, irritated. "He was drunk. All I could do was toss him out on his ear, the idiot."

"Where's the pizza?" I asked quietly.

"Ah, he took it with him. I wish he'd leave."

"What, he's still *here?*" I demanded, disgusted.

287

"Over there." Mac pointed to a large, sulky man sitting on the tailgate of a green, old model Ford pickup. "He's still waiting for his friends to come out. I'm not letting him back in. Name's Phil Vardega, one of the crew guys."

I had not noticed the man on the tailgate until then. I looked him over, a muscular Hispanic man, completely dressed in denim, with a black ponytail, red head-scarf, and week's growth of scruffy goatee beard. The pizza box was sitting open on the tailgate next to him. He had been eating a slice, but was now standing with his back to us, using his broad shoulders to shield his cigarette and lighter from the wind, which was rapidly getting colder and stronger. Clouds were rolling in from the east, blanketing the stars.

"Cover me," I said dryly, as I began walking across the gravel.

"Sid, what are you doing?" Mac said nervously.

"He never paid for that," I muttered, not looking back. Over the whistle of the wind, I could hear Boris finally wrenching his door open to get out.

Yeah, seeing your employer getting stomped into a bloody pulp is too good to watch from the cab.

The gravel was crunching under my cowboy boots as I crossed the fifty feet of parking lot to the green truck, but the howling wind drowned out the sound. Phil Vardega was still trying to get his lighter working, and did not see or hear me until I spoke to him. I think I startled him.

The man was taller than me, stronger, and obviously violent. To this day, I am amazed that I was not the least bit intimidated. I still just felt cold.

"Mr. Vardega?"

I only wanted to talk to him, reason with him. He was eating food that he had stolen from my restaurant. All that I wanted was the fifteen dollars that he owed me. Life is just never that simple.

He turned around, and I hit him. I gave him no reason or warning. I just drove a fist straight into his nose, feeling the cartilage snapping and crushing under my knuckles. Blood exploded from the smashed nostrils, warm droplets pattering onto my leather coat. His eyes immediately flooded with tears, blinding him, and he let out a pained cry. I should have stopped right there, but I did not even slow down. As Vardega staggered back, trying to stem the flow of blood with his hands, I stepped in with arms spread wide, and slammed both of my palms onto his ears, driving air into his eardrums like icepicks. Vardega gave an agonized scream, trying to clamp his own bloody fists over his ears, but I was not finished yet. Sliding my hands past his earlobes, I interlaced my fingers around the back of his neck and dropped my elbows to my sides, forcing him to double over, and my right knee was coming up just as his torso was coming down. The smashing contact blew the wind out of him, preventing his screams from escaping. His back was exposed, so I clasped both of my hands together into one huge fist, heaved my arms over my own head, and drove the hammer-fist into his spine. Vardega was slammed to the gravel, which gashed into his already bloody chin. He moaned and began to draw one leg up under himself, trying to stand. Still feeling nothing but ice, I dropped one knee onto his ribs, allowing my full crushing weight to pin him to the ground. He tried to scream, but could barely breathe. Driving his face down hard into the gravel with both hands, I leaned down close to his ear. I had to take a moment to catch my own breath.

"Do yourself a favour," I finally rasped, still grinding his cheek into the tiny rocks. "Don't get up."

His leg stretched back out in the dust, and he lay still, struggling to draw breath. I guess a person can be emotionless and irrational at the same time, because what I did next still makes no sense to me. I pulled my own wallet out of my black Wranglers, and threw fifteen dollars into the dirt by his bleeding face.

"It's on the house, sir," I said, stepping on his back as I stood up and walked back to my truck, hands in my jacket pockets.

The entire attack had lasted under five seconds. Uncle Reggie had told me that if my opponent ever knew what was happening, I had already failed. Phil Vardega never knew who had hit him.

Mac and Boris could only stare in disbelief as I walked past them without saying a word. I silently handed my keys to Boris, and began walking home. I knew he would leave the truck at the restaurant when he picked up his car. I just had to walk away, and keep walking. My friends watched me go, but I did not look back. I let the darkness swallow me.

That was my first fight, and I had won. There was no thrill of victory, no Sousa big band march to welcome a hero. My cheek had a small, burning speck on it, that I knew must have been a drop of Vardega's blood. I could not bring myself to wipe it off. I had to keep walking, back into town, down the North Access Road that led to my place of business. There was some traffic on the streets now, mostly roaming police cars, partying teenagers, and the changing shifts from the lumber mills. Only a few hotels, restaurants, and convenience stores were still open, plastered with black and orange Hallowe'en decor. Of course, the bars were still open as well.

I still could not feel anything. I could barely think. Less than an hour before, I had been baring my soul to Angel, and now I was closed up tighter than ever.

You know what you are, Myers? You're a clam with feet. You're not an oyster. You don't have the benefit of a hidden treasure. You're a clam.

Boris must have driven a different road, or talked with Mac for awhile, because I never saw him drive past me, which was just as well. I needed to be alone to digest what had been done, and even having someone I knew drive by would have disrupted that.

Every inhalation was crisp and cold. There would be frost that night, but I could not smell snow yet. Winter had come late the past few years, with actual snow accumulation holding back until mid or late December. I decided that I wanted snow to fall before I got home. For some reason, Bing Crosby's *White Christmas* was stuck in my head, in between constant replays of the fight.

Was it worth it?

"I don't know," I said to myself. "Ask me in the morning."

I had to walk past By The Slice, but I did not see anyone. I stopped only long enough to lock the doors on my truck, which Boris had dropped off in the back parking space behind the building, and then I just walked the rest of the way home, and went to bed. There was no snow.

I fell asleep relatively quickly, but awoke around three in the morning, with only one burning thought in my mind.

I hit the wrong guy.

By four-thirty a.m., I was in my garage, wearing only a grey tee-shirt and sweat pants, pounding an incessant rage into the punching bag. I wanted to give a furious roar with every icy blow, but forced myself to suppress them behind clenched teeth.

When Cindy's nudging toe woke me the next morning, the concrete floor was very cold, especially on my bare feet. I still felt sick.

CHAPTER TWENTY-ONE

A man to man fist fight is a secret, and often not so secret, dream of most males on this planet. Whether as a test of manhood, or as some fantastic quest for justice really depends on the ego and mind set of the male. I had spent the last few years of my life trying to get by without ego, so could only assume that my fantasy was justice.

Phil Vardega had been the ideal scenario. He was bigger and stronger than me, irrationally violent, and had attacked my friend without provocation. So, I had fought him, and defeated him. I had taught him a well deserved lesson.

I told myself that a dozen times the next morning, but it did not change the fact that I did not even want to get out of bed. I wanted to stay locked in my house, under the covers for the next year or so.

What have I done? That was the question that was running laps in my head throughout the morning, as I sat alone at the kitchen table in my pajamas and bathrobe, eating dry cornflakes. We were out of milk.

Does Cindy know?

My sister had gone out for breakfast with some girlfriends, and I could not help wondering what Boris had told her when he brought my truck back to the restaurant the night before. I had never seen him look as shocked as he did when I had handed him the keys and walked away into the night.

I had to be at work by eleven, but I was still sitting at that table at ten o'clock, when Boris burst in, uninvited. He was wearing jogging clothes, and had probably made the spontaneous decision to confront me as he passed by the house on his morning run. His oversized red sweatshirt was damp, and his thick wavy black hair was dripping sweat down his bruised face. I tossed him a clean dish towel as he slumped into the chair across from me. He accepted it without a word, vigorously towelled his matted hair, mopped his forehead, then tossed the towel into the sink. Cindy would have freaked out if she had seen that. Boris leaned back in the chair, still breathing heavily from the exertion.

"You okay?" I asked, sipping a glass of orange juice.

"Better," he said simply.

"Have you had breakfast?"

He nodded.

"Do you want more? We're out of milk."

"No," he said quietly.

I munched through another spoonful of cereal before asking, "Do they know?"

"I didn't tell anyone."

"And they didn't ask?"

"I told them you talked to Mac. Cindy did call me this morning and ask why you were passed out by the punching bag again."

"And you said …?"

"I told her you were a tragic and tormented soul, and she should set you up with one of her girlfriends before you officially became a confirmed old geezer."

"Thanks."

"Don't mention it." He folded his arms and waited, for what I did not know. I had cereal to finish. I did not even like cornflakes.

"Did you talk to Mac?"

"He went and got Vardega's friends to carry him home, or whatever they were going to do with him. They had no idea what happened, Vardega had no idea what happened, and they were too drunk to care. I just … kinda stayed out of sight."

"I hope they made it home okay," I said mildly, almost smiling.

"Shooter waitress called them a cab."

I snorted. "In that case, I hope the cab driver made it home okay."

Boris sighed, reached across the table, and took a long swig from the orange juice bottle, another thing that Cindy would have freaked about. Then, he stared at me and slowly shook his head.

"We should have done something else, Sid. It was just wrong."

"You had the option of calling the police," I said sourly. "You didn't."

"I'd just been beaten up! I was in shock, numb. I probably would have called them after I settled down. Now what am I supposed to do? Report two assaults?"

"If you want," I shrugged. "Do what you think is best."

"Yeah right," he snapped. "Mac told me that if the cops asked questions, he was going to say that Vardega attacked you, and you fought back."

"I never asked him to do that," I pointed out. "If cops talk to me, I'll tell them exactly what happened. He had to learn."

"Yeah, Sid?" Boris was angry. "Learn what? How to sucker punch?"

"He already knew that."

"Sid, he was *drunk!*"

"I know he was drunk!" I snarled. "I am sick of that being the dismissive phrase everyone uses. Phil Vardega lives his life counting on that phrase to get him out of trouble. Beats his wife, crashes his car, slugs the pizza guy, it's not his fault, he was drunk! The beer made him do it. That's his excuse, his alibi. People roll their eyes, but all they ever say is 'He was drunk!' We let people like him get away with it until someone dies, and then we charge him with vehicular manslaughter. There's no justice."

"You call what you did *justice?*" Boris demanded. "You viciously attacked an unsuspecting man!"

"It was not vicious," I said coldly. "I gave him a quick takedown. He'll catch his breath, stick a rag up his nose, and sleep off a hangover. He got off easy."

"Easy?! You broke his nose!" Boris choked. "Flattened it! How is that *easy?*"

"I'll tell you how!" I snapped. "The human face is unbelievably vulnerable to someone who knows what to aim for, and, quite frankly, I'm one of them. A dozen exposed areas, all easy to inflict extreme pain on, and all non-lethal. Eyes, nose, ears, lips, hair, jaw, teeth, cheekbones, tongue. Any of these can be very painfully broken, gouged, slashed or cut right off, and the recipient can still lead a long, happy, tragically scarred life. I could have made his face into a monster mask, and I restrained myself to breaking his nose. And maybe it will make him think twice before he does anything that stupid again, so, yes, he got off easy!"

"Sid, are you listening to yourself?!" Boris yelled. "You're justifying! I've known you all my life, and I know the kind of crap you've been through. Karl, Spring, getting stuck with the restaurant. I've watched you get angry, get frustrated, but I've always been proud of you, because you were strong and could handle it. You, and Cindy, and Kat, you showed me what strength was. I learned from you, Sid! What am I supposed to learn now?"

"How to survive," I said irritably.

"No one's life was in danger except Phil Vardega's!" Boris roared. "You're telling me what you know about non-lethal hits, so listen to what I know! I know that the line between lethal and superficial injuries can be a very fine one. A boxer can get his face pummelled off for twenty years, and lose a few brain cells, and someone else can take a single punch to the jaw and drop dead with a ruptured artery. Are you sure you only winded that guy? The Great Houdini died from a single punch to the stomach, days after it happened. Better watch the obituaries, Sid. What's happened to you, man? Don't say you haven't changed. You've changed."

"Okay, fine," I growled. "I crossed a line. We all do it, sometimes."

"No, we don't," Boris shot back. "People don't cross lines. We erase them, and step over where they used to be. That way, we can look back and see nothing but a clean slate. It's delusion, Sid. Nothing more."

"Boris…." I sighed, rubbing my forehead. "You're my friend. Okay? I did it for you."

Boris shook his head sadly, standing from the table.

"That's the really sorry part, Sid. You see, I think you did it for you. You gave Vardega the revenge you never got to give Kelton. Revenge, pure and simple. It's kind of pathetic, really."

I was left at a loss for words as he headed for the door.

"Get your life figured out, Sidney," he called over his shoulder, as he resumed jogging out the garage door, "before whatever it is that's gnawing at you eats you alive. Thanks for the juice." The door slammed, making me wince. My cereal suddenly tasted like wood chips.

Thank you, Boris. I was miserable this morning. I feel much worse now.

My truck was still at the restaurant, and Cindy had taken hers as well, so I would have to walk to work. I did not want to leave the house, but it was Friday, the busiest day of the week. Dad never missed a Friday, so neither would I.

What would he have done last night?

Karl Myers would have called the police and had Phil Vardega arrested for assault. Charges would have been laid, and Vardega would likely have spent time in jail. My father would have been just as angered, but he would have followed the letter of the law. I had not done that.

Great, Myers, you're a vigilante. Happy now?

Although I did not want to leave my sanctuary, I knew that work would be a welcome relief from this latest moral conflict. As I dressed and began walking to the restaurant, I began to understand how unhealthy my whole outlook on life was. I never dealt with problems, I just went to work so that I could forget about them for a while. My job was my solace, my refuge. What was starting to really bother me was the realization that I did not run my restaurant. It ran me.

I had been trying to take Angel's advice about finding pleasure in the small things around me, but it was very hard that morning. It should not have been. I loved early autumn, and that day was beautiful. Cool without being cold, grey without being dull. The sugar coating of frost was slowly de-crystalizing as the sunlight made its slow passage over rooftops and blades of grass. There is no other smell in the world like that of frost burning off in the morning sun. The crunching carpets of red, orange, and yellow leaves that covered the sides of the roads were virtual time-machines to pleasant memories. Spring and I used to walk together in the fall, scuffing our shoes to send the leaves skittering all around us, like ripples on a still rainbow pond. When Cindy and I were very young, we would help Dad rake the leaves into a huge pile, and then take turns burying each other under it. When Hallowe'en arrived, we would hide in leaf forts with water guns and snipe at trick-or-treaters. Boris was no more than five years old then, and I will never forget how he ran to his mother, with terrified tears running down his Batman mask, crying that, "A zombie mutant leaf pile just horked on me!" Actually, that was the memory that finally allowed me to crack a smile, just as I walked into By The Slice. Three dining room tables were occupied by patrons, and Becky, in her tan vest, bow-tie and slacks, was serving them from our breakfast menu, silent as always. When I came into the kitchen, Clancy was preparing one of his famous Mexican omelettes, his own invention which had been quite a hit with our breakfast regulars.

"Hail to the chief," he said briskly, saluting me with his left hand. "How was your date?"

"It was coffee," I said, tying on an apron.

"Yep, I believe you," Clancy said with a solemn nod. "Relax, Sid, I'm not going to come after you or anything. Me and Angel are history. Go for it."

"It … was … *coffee*," I repeated, putting exaggerated emphasis on every syllable. "I have coffee with Kat all the time. Why is everyone suddenly assuming this was a date? I don't date employees."

"Oh." Clancy seemed disappointed. "I guess we're all just impatient for you to get married, and I think you're setting your standards way too high."

"What?" I had not heard that one before.

"Oh, come on, Sidney! You walked away from Karen Malloy, who was, to be honest, about the most decadent candy I've ever met. Like, *sweeeet!*"

"It wouldn't have worked," I said, pouring fresh coffee into a floral patterned ceramic mug. I really missed my Cup of Wrath. "Karen was out of my league."

"Oh…. Can I have her, then?"

"Knock yourself out. And I've told you to clean up the counter as soon as you finish cracking the eggs. Look at that mess."

"Sorry," he said sheepishly, sliding the puffy eggs and cheese from the skillet onto a waiting plate with a side of toast. "Becky! Table nine is up! Say, Sid, how's Boris? I heard he got whacked last night."

I took a sip from my mug. Becky actually made decent coffee.

"Pretty much," I said. "He's okay, couple of bruises."

"So? Who was the jerk?"

Me.

"Just some drunk crew guy," I replied dismissively. "Wipe down that counter before those egg whites poison something." I tossed him a damp cloth from the dish sink. "Bleach it."

"Did you see the guy?" Clancy asked, curious. "Kat said you and Boris went back there to straighten it out."

Well, that would be one way of phrasing it....

"I saw him," I replied. "He never talked to me."

"Did he pay for the pizza?"

"No, I told him it was on the house."

"*What?!* Why would you do that?"

I pondered that for a moment, still unsure of my own reasoning.

"It's good PR." I began weighing out dough for sheeting.

"Uh ... Sid?" Clancy looked vaguely disturbed as he stared at me, still holding the platter for table nine.

"Yeah?"

"Your knuckles are cut. You've got … cuts."

I looked at the back of my right hand. The knuckles of my index and middle fingers had split upon impact with the bridge of Vardega's nose. They had not bled much, but the cuts were clearly visible. I looked back at Clancy. "I must have hit something."

"Uhhh…." He did not look convinced.

"I was on the punching bag last night. It's therapeutic."

"Okay," he said, still uncertain. *"Becky! Table nine!"*

Becky came in from the dining room long enough to snatch the plate and tray from Clancy, and was gone just as suddenly.

"Thanks, Becky!" Clancy and I both blurted, trying to get the words out before she disappeared again. If she heard us, she gave no indication of it.

"That girl really is a ghost," Clancy said, shaking his head. "She's been here for months, and all I've ever said to her is 'Hi,' 'Bye,' and 'Thanks Becky.'"

"Well, you'd better start," I remarked. "You have to escort her down the aisle at the wedding. Boris's cousin Judy can't get the weekend off, so Becky just became a bridesmaid. She's paired up with you for the march."

"What? I thought Kat was the maid of honour."

"She is."

"I'm the best man, Sid. The best man escorts the maid of honour. Right?"

"Right. Didn't Boris talk to you on Wednesday? Plans changed."

"Changed, how?" Clancy asked, suspiciously.

"Well, apparently Boris's cousin Mike *can* make it for the wedding now, so, uh ... you've been pre-empted. You and me are just plain old groomsmen."

"Boris gave my position to *Mike Landley?*" Clancy was disgusted.

"What's wrong with Mike? He's a good guy."

"Sid, he's from *Winnipeg!*"

"No one's perfect," I commented, running the first ball of dough through the press.

"That's in Saskatchewan or something! Boris only sees him once every two or three years."

"So?"

"So, I'm practically his best friend. I deserve to be the best man."

"Quit your whining," I chuckled. "Boris has always been close with Mike. He was Mike and Laura's best man three years ago, so it's kind of an honour debt. Anyway, the guy's flying in all the way from *Manitoba,* and what? You're just going to make him sit with the guests?"

"I guess not," Clancy grumbled, scrubbing the raw egg from the counter. "So, who else do we got in the party? Any other surprises?"

"Angel and Louise Park, Cindy's best friend from Fort St. John. And Boris asked Randall to be a groomsman, too."

"Is your uncle Reggie giving the bride away?"

"Yeah," I said, twirling the pizza crust over my head. "Cindy said he was the only one who she would let do it. He's thrilled. He and Aunt Jessie never had kids, so Cindy's always been like a daughter."

"Who gets Louise? As I recall, she was pretty fine."

"Randall. I'm walking with Angel. And we had to get Father Makkie to do the ceremony. Boris and Cindy both wanted Pastor Ryan to perform it, but, apparently, Boris's grandmother won't even show up unless the officiator is Catholic."

"Ouch," Clancy cringed. "Gramma Morris on the warpath. Scary thought.... How's the rest of his family dealing with the fact that he's marrying a Baptist?"

"Most of them don't seem to care," I said. "But, there's always someone, from either side, who's going to get all denominational on us."

"I don't want to knock your religion," Clancy ventured, "but sometimes I'm really glad I'm not a church guy. A lot of the ones I've met seem really … sanctimonious, I guess. Or just plain bitter."

"I know what you mean," I grunted. "The finest people I know are Christians … and so are some of the stupidest people I know. My faith is probably the most important part of my life, but some people really try to complicate it."

"You think faith is simple?"

I nodded. "Faith is just knowing that impossible is a really big word. That's pretty simple to me."

"You believe in heaven and hell, too?"

"It's kind of par for the course."

Here it comes....

Clancy asked the expected question. "And you think that God can be loving and still send people to hell?"

I threw another ball into the press.

"I believe that people get what they want. Either an eternity with God, or an eternity without Him."

"So, just looking at me, drugs and all," Clancy challenged, "where am I going?"

"I don't know," I said honestly. "I can make all kinds of guesses and unauthorized judgements, but only God knows your heart. It's between you and Him. We need more ground beef cooked, we're almost out."

Clancy laughed. "Sid, if all preachers kept their sermons that short, I'd be in church every Sunday."

When Boris arrived for duty that afternoon, I called him into my office. Again, I kept the sermon short.

"Last night," I said, leaning against my old desk and folding my arms, "you proved that you are a better man than me. I am very glad that you are marrying my sister. There's two deliveries in the warmer for you."

"Yeah, sorry I'm late."

"It's okay."

CHAPTER TWENTY-TWO

Even after I talked to Boris, it took me a few days to realize that my life had officially reached a new low. My attack on Phil Vardega was not a matter of defending a friend, or even of vengeance. It was pure hate, a hatred that was so deeply ingrained in me that I scarcely noticed it anymore. I had not been emotionless. The cold that I had felt was not the weather. It was icy rage. I had felt it before. It was the reason that I felt cold when I remembered Josh Kelton. It was the reason that my punching bag felt like a block of burning ice with every blow. In those moments, I was truly cold-blooded, and it scared me.

A lot of men fought in my little hometown. They would get drunk, beat someone up, or get beaten up, and the next day they would laugh about it on their coffee breaks. Hating people they barely knew was commonplace. Talks of retribution made conversations lively.

I did not want hate in my life, but I knew that it was not something that I could just turn my back on. I hated every man I saw staggering into or out of a pub.

I wanted to hurt every one of them, as they fumbled with the keys to the car they were about to drive home through the black of night. I never considered helping them. Usually, I considered wresting the keys from them, and punching them if they resisted. Every one of them was guilty of murder, in my mind. They were all responsible for my father's death. I had let hate go unchecked for too long, and now it had finally caught up with me. I had taken the next step. I had hit one of the men that I hated, and now I absolutely hated myself for it. There had been no glory, no honour, no justification. Whereas I had previously just spent my life being annoyed with the world around me, now I could not look out my window at it without being faced by my own mirror image of self-loathing. The town that I lived in and the people who lived around me were not my problem. I was my own problem, and I did not believe that I could help myself. The situation seemed hopeless. Suddenly, everything felt like it was entirely my fault. I had always blamed Kelton, and his drugs, for the deaths of three people, including himself, yet now I only wanted to blame and hate myself. There was no space for love in my life. I had allowed bitterness to get such a hold on my soul that I was in a perpetual search for someone to blame. Someone had to be held responsible, and someone had to be hated. Forgiveness was never once considered. That was not even an option.

In the end, I decided that the only person I could turn to was the one woman who seemed to live a life of complete love and empathy. I had seen Angel Bates get mad, and even try to hold a grudge once, but wrath just never seemed to be able to stick to her. Her joy for life would not allow it.

Angel had passed the same unspoken test that my other staples had passed years before. I thought of her more as a friend than an employee. Big business owners had told me that it was better to isolate employers from employees, that fraternization was fiscally reckless. Well, my shop was not a big business, and never would be. It was a small, family business, and a groundwork of friendship had kept it thriving for almost thirty years. Right then, friendship seemed like the only thing I had left, and I trusted Angel more than anyone else, although I did not really know why. Sometimes, I still wondered if she was on the lam or probation, but that was a minor issue. Friendship was about overlooking imperfections.

It was the following Monday, and I had just returned home from the morning shift at work. I was still working every day, but was gradually beginning to accept the fact that Kat and Clancy could handle most of the evening rushes without me.

I was lounging on my sofa, staring at the blank TV screen in my living room, when I remembered that it was also Angel's day off. I decided to give her a call, if for no other reason than that her cheeriness was a much needed contagion.

Just my luck, she was crying when she picked up the phone.

"Hello?" she hiccupped, sniffling audibly.

"Angel?" I was obviously startled.

"Hey, Boss," she croaked. "What's up?"

"Are you okay? You sound like you're ... you know...."

"Yeah, I'm bawling, okay?"

"Dare I ask?"

She blew her nose loudly into the receiver.

"I'm just watching my favourite show. It always makes me cry."

"So ... they're happy tears?"

"No! It's so *sad!*"

"You're watching *Melrose Place* reruns?"

"Boss! *The Littlest Hobo!* It's so sad. He does so much for everyone he meets, and he doesn't even have a *home!* It's *sad!*"

"Yes, the dog was amazing, but don't let him romanticize you. I met a couple of hobos, once. They were trying to drink antifreeze."

"Quiet, Boss, it's the end credits! I don't wanna miss the song. '*Maybe tomorrow ...!*'"

"Yeah, I can hear it," I cringed, pulling the blaring cell phone away from my ear. "How loud have you got that thing?"

"Sorry. Surround sound. It's wonderful, isn't it?"

Surround sound? She has surround?

"So, talk to me, Boss," she rambled. "What's your favourite show?"

"Present, or are we still in the eighties?"

"Let's stick with the eighties. I loved the eighties."

This girl truly is your exact opposite, Myers.

"I'm not sure," I answered. "Probably a toss-up between *The Cosby Show* and *The A-Team.*"

"You are so unpatriotic, you know that?" Angel snorted. "Where's your Canadian content?"

"Does *Smith and Smith* count?"

"Yeah. What's up?"

"Huh?" I grunted stupidly.

"You called me."

"Oh, right…. Uh, how are you?"

"Better than you," she quipped. "Otherwise, you wouldn't have called me."

I groaned, scratching my hair fitfully.

"Angel, I'm sorry. It seems like I only call you when I need to gripe about something. This was never in your job description."

"I call it trust, Boss. It's a happy thing. What's wrong?" She wanted to know. Angel really cared about my issues, and usually managed to give me a bit of a boost with her replies. On that day, however, I was still too overwhelmed with what had happened less than a week ago. I did not want to burden Angel with my imperfection. To do so would be to risk condemnation, or, worse yet, condescension.

"Why are you so happy, Angel?"

"You say it like it's a bad thing."

"Sorry, I should say it differently…. *How* are you so happy?"

"Boss … do you know how to have fun, or not?" Angel seemed to trust me. Thus, I could not quite bring myself to answer, "Of course. What kind of question is that?"

"Sort of," I groaned. "That's where you do stuff without having to force a smile, right?"

"Look, Boss, I know that you've been a certified workaholic for years, and that's just you doing your job.

Now, as much as we both love it, this is a pretty boring town, so what do you do for fun?"

"Well, most people seem to do drugs."

"Right. Are you doing anything right now?"

"I'm sitting down."

"You're going to have fun. That's an order. Be at Randall's gym in an hour." Then, she hung up.

"Okay," I slowly confirmed to the dial tone. I always was better at taking orders than giving them.

Needing the refreshment of the open twilight air, I walked to the gym with some workout clothes in a brown shoulder bag, pondering why I did not just hand the business deed over to Angel right then. Judging from the way that she had all of us wrapped around her finger, she would be a born leader. As for myself, my unquestioning obedience to her would likely earn me employee of the month status about twelve times per year. I never asked for any of this.

Randall Harrigan was better than I was at kicking back and proudly watching his business thrive. Behind the front desk of his gym, he was lounging in a jogging suit and a very comfortable padded recliner when I entered. Angel was nowhere to be seen, and her car had not been in the parking lot. Several other cars had been there, however, and most of the treadmills and workout stations were occupied by sweaty, cotton-clad citizens of various ages and fitness levels. Randall had a radio on the small beverage table beside his chair, softly playing country music, just loud enough to create a homey atmosphere. He was flipping through a fishing magazine, so he did not notice me until I rapped my knuckles on the metal wraparound desk.

311

"Sid, you rodent," was Randall's cheery reply, heaving himself out of the recliner. "You don't have a membership here yet. It's about time. You want day, month, or year?"

"Day for now," I sighed, picking a pencil eraser off the desk and bouncing it off his head. "Looks like you're keeping busy."

"Dream come true," he grinned. "Are you sure you only want a day? I mean, you kind of owe me for…. Well, I could think of something if I really tried. I set you up with my cousin."

"You still owe me eighty bucks from high school," I snapped. "Put me down for free today, and we'll call it even."

"What eighty bucks?" he asked, suspiciously.

"Biology class, grade eleven, Mrs. Williston giving us a lecture on bacterial infections. You said you could get that exchange girl to go out with you in fifteen words or less. We bet a hundred, but I still owed you twenty bucks from that pie-eating bet at the fall fair. You used twenty-three words."

"Fine, you're in free," he grumbled, scribbling my name in a ledger. "You never forget anything, do you?"

I smiled slightly. "Only once, Randy. Never again. I'm hanging onto the memories."

"Have fun, you skinflint," he chuckled.

"Thank me," I said, striding away. "You just saved eighty bucks."

"I'll bet you don't remember her name!" he called after me.

"Charlene Mendelsohn, seventeen, psychology major from Frankfurt, red hair, pale green eyes," I said flatly, walking into the locker room. "Five feet, eight inches, 34-23-34."

"Wow," I heard Randall grunt as the hydraulic door hissed shut behind me.

I donned a black sweatsuit and sneakers, but the only empty areas of the gym were the boxing ring and punching bags. I had no sparring partner, and no real desire to box anyone there, anyway. I went to the punching bags.

I only ever tried to cataclysmically destroy my own punching bag, in the contained safety of my battlefield garage. On the few occasions when I attended public gyms, thirteen-year-old girls had approached me and told me that I was punching like a girl. Thus, when Angel finally strolled in, I was only giving the bag a few half-hearted slugs, not even working up a sweat.

Angel was wearing a pale violet blouse that shimmered in the florescent lighting, dark slacks, and semi-casual black shoes. She was not dressed for a workout, and carried no gym bag.

"Boss, what are you doing?" she asked, walking over to me.

"I'm punching a bag," I said. "Why is that confusing to you?"

"What, you think we're here to *workout?*"

"Forgive me if that was an unreasonable assumption," I said dryly, peeling the tape wraps off my hands. "You had a better idea?"

Angel just smiled and handed me the white Styrofoam dixie cup she had brought in. For a brief instant, I thought she had brought me a coffee, but the cup was too heavy. It was also too shiny, and jingled as it passed from her hand to mine.

This is a bit embarrassing for me to admit, but, over the next few hours, Angel and I fed every single quarter in that cup into Randall's two arcade games. We raced digital motorcycles for the first hour, then blasted digital dinosaurs with our plastic pistols until we ran out of coins. We were yelling at the onscreen characters, and each other, and quite a few people, Randall included, could only stare at us and shake their heads.

"*Die, you scum-sucking reptilian freaks!*" Angel shrieked, emptying her pistol into a fast slashing deinonychus.

"You have called down the wrath," I growled, double-tapping the hard skull of a pachycephalasaurus. "*Here comes the thunder!*" It was the most infantile behaviour that I had displayed in years, and I had never had so much fun in my entire life. An extended moment of pure happiness was mine, and the games had very little to do with it. It was the effect of Angel.

I think that was the day I realized that Angel was my best friend.

CHAPTER TWENTY-THREE

I used to play baseball. In fact, I played all the way through my secondary school years. I used to be on a boxing team. I used to ride horseback, and was even a member of the local gymkhana for a couple of years in junior high. I used to do things. It all ended once I started working at By The Slice.

My social life seemed to just dwindle away. Friends from school moved on to colleges in other cities, then to jobs in other provinces. A handful of them came back for visits. One or two even called me a few times a year, but the bottom line was that most of my previous friendships had slipped away, and I never had time for new ones. I never allowed myself to have time. Time was something which I considered reserved for work. I could never bring myself to consider it a luxury.

Karl Myers loved his restaurant, and he loved the work. Looking back on my life, I realize that he only took three or four vacations after I was born, and I am certain that none of them lasted more than one week. Now that I was trying to continue his dream, I pushed myself to run the business just as he had, and that included being there all the time, only taking a few evenings off. My last real vacation had been a road trip down through the Rockies with Dad and Cindy during my tenth summer. I remembered very little of it, except the part where a bighorn sheep committed suicide by stopping in the centre of the road to stare dumbly at our approaching station wagon. Cindy was slightly traumatized, but I remember asking if we could cut off the horns and take them home with us. Dad said no. Thanks to my sister, that was probably the only bighorn sheep to ever get a proper funeral along that back dirt road, albeit only buried under some dead foliage in the ditch. Dad was always there for us when we needed things like that done.

For some reason, Angel had sort of taken over Karl Myer's role of looking after me. I was her boss. I was supposed to be the one responsible for her well-being, but, instead, she kept on being there for me. Her kindness, beyond anything I deserved, made no sense to me. I had never had a friend like her, and I still could not understand her at all. Furthermore, I did not care.

Did romance ever cross my mind? Of course. I was aware of my ethical responsibilities as an employer, but it was hard not to wonder about the potential of a friendship that deeply rooted. However, I was completely satisfied with our relationship, because it was the best one that I had ever had. Certainly, I still had questions. Where did she come from? Why did she come to Chetwynd? Why had she never had a job? All of these questions, and many more, were constantly in the back of my mind, but, out of all of them, only one burned into me with such intensity that I decided that I would never be able to sleep at night if I did not confront her with it.

I was not confrontational, and I was certainly not in the habit of becoming so, simply for the purpose of satisfying a point of curiosity. The question itself was nothing short of trivial, so I am still amazed that it led me to make the choice that I did, and also that it was followed by such an incredible revelation.

Where did she get that violet blouse she wore to Randall's gym? Yes, I know how ridiculous, and possibly disturbing, that sounds, but, in the two days following our night at the arcade, that same stupid question would not go away. Angel had worn a violet blouse that was, unless I was mistaken, made from real silk. I could count on two fingers the women I knew who owned a shirt like that. One of them was a major crack dealer in town, and the other was from a very wealthy family, something to do with inventing the plastic caps for ball point pens, if I remembered correctly. In either case, the shirt equalled money.

It was early November, almost six months to the day from when Angel was hired. As a boss, it was not my business to go to her house on that cold Wednesday morning, but, as her friend, my curiosity was just about driving me nuts. Besides that, I did not have much time. Cindy, Kat, Becky, and Louise Park were coming to get Angel at noon in Louise's SUV for what they were calling "Girls night out," to Grande Prairie, to pick up the wedding dress and bridesmaid's gowns. Boris said that he was renting all the groomsmen's tuxedos, with the exception of his own, which he had somehow owned for five years without my knowledge. He said that he had ordered matching single-breasted, two button shawls, which was a bit of a pity, in my mind, anyway. My preference ran to the three buttoned, notch collar variety. Oh well, it was his cash, his choice.

The wedding was less than three weeks away. The flowers were ordered, the caterers had been hired, and the reception hall had been booked. Invitations had been sent, and we were trying very hard to keep the guest list at one hundred or less, which was pretty much impossible to do, considering the very traditional and, dare I say, prolific Catholic family on Boris's side. My only family, besides Cindy, was Uncle Reggie, his wife Jessica, and Grandma Adele Myers. My mother's side of the family was unknown to me. I had no idea if I had living grandparents, cousins, uncles or aunts on my mother's side, a family that I believe was named Wellington, although my dad had once told me that they were about half French, in spite of the English name. I guess the mix of Irish, French, and English was a recipe for disaster.

I am not sure which fraction of my heritage was feeling dominant that morning as I drove to Angel's duplex, but I did not think that it was the French. I felt a bit uncertain of my decision. I had never been invited to Angel's home, and, now that I was about to just show up on her step and ask about a shirt, I felt like an unwise minion barging in on a wrathful, meditating high priest to request small change for the soft drink dispenser.

Angel was clearly startled to see me when she peeked out from behind her door, wearing a casual pink tee-shirt and grey sweat pants.

"Hi, Angel," I said pleasantly. "Lovely morning, isn't it?"

"Hey, Boss," she answered, puzzled. "Am I in trouble?"

"You wear really nice shoes," I observed, watching for her reaction.

"Seriously, Boss," she groaned. "I would have expected a come-on like that back in grade seven. Not from you."

"That wasn't a come-on," I replied. "It was a noteworthy observation. You always wear nice shoes. I think that's interesting."

Angel sighed. "You're not making any sense, so you might as well come in." She swung the door wide, and bowed jokingly as I entered. The white porch was dimly lit, but warm and homey. The brown closet doors were closed, but my gaze was immediately drawn to a varnished-wood boot rack, with four large shelves neatly lined with rows of glossy leather boots, athletic shoes, loafers and sandals. Throughout the course of my life, I had probably never owned that much footwear, even counting my baby booties. The apartment was spotlessly clean, as well.

"Nice place," I mused.

"My humble abode is honoured by the presence of an authority figure. Should I curtsy or genuflect?"

"Neither," I smiled. "I wouldn't want you to scuff those nice shoes."

"You seriously came here to tell me I have nice shoes?"

"Pretty much," I nodded absently. "It's an impressive collection."

Angel shrugged as I followed her up the light blue carpeted stairs to the living room. "Well, any girl likes a good compliment session. Please continue, if that's really what you're here for."

"You wear nice clothes, too," I expounded, settling onto a bone-toned leather sofa and crossing my legs, taking in the whole room in a glance. Like the porch, it was immaculate, spotless, and lavish, but there was definitely something missing. It took me a moment to figure out what it was. "I really liked that black fleece you wore to work one day."

"Sleeveless, rollover collar?" she guessed.

"Yeah, that one."

"I like it, too," she agreed. "It's one of my favourites, but I only wear it with—"

"—the beige skirt," I interrupted. "Leather, above the knee."

"How did you know that?"

"Because I only saw them once, and you were wearing them together. You never wear the same clothes twice."

Angel pressed her back against a bookcase, her reddish hair falling over her shoulders as she cocked her head off to one side, as she always did when trying hard to figure me out.

"Sidney, are you hitting on me?" I could not tell if the notion was pleasing to her, or troubling. It was also such a bizarre thing to hear her speak my name that, for a moment, I could not answer.

"No," I eventually assured her. "Believe it or not, I'm not. I've just been noticing your clothes, that's all."

"Boss...."

"Are those nails manicured?"

"You know," she sighed impatiently, folding her arms behind her back, "I could stand here playing 20 Compliments from now til Kingdom Come, but are you making a point?"

"Nice shoes," I rambled. "Nice clothes. Nice nails. New car. High rent apartment. Hairstyles that you could wear on a red carpet. And now I'm looking at an oak dining table in the kitchen, a plasma TV, and I'm sitting on a slippery leather sofa."

"I like my apartment shiny," she said dismissively.

"Very shiny," I agreed. "Not having any roommates must help keep it that way."

"Silence is one of those happy things."

"You have everything," I pointed out. "Except for one thing. Pictures. Family portraits, grad photos, childhood memories. No picture frames, no Polaroids on the fridge. Is that a happy thing, too?"

"Do you watch *Law & Order?*"

"Religiously. Why?"

"Because all you've done is cheap detective work since you walked in, and you still haven't told me why you're here."

"Well, forgive the curiosity," I said irritably, scratching my hair. "Angel, you're a great friend, but I feel like I need a forensic degree and a copy of your psychiatric assessment to even know who you are. For some reason I can't even figure out, I trust you, but you don't want to tell me anything. Do you even have a middle name? I don't know your middle name."

"What's yours?" she asked, playfully.

"See? There, you're doing it again! I don't care what your middle name is, I just asked because I knew you'd turn the question around and give it back to me. I think it's an ingrained reflex for you to deflect personal questions. I don't know why, and maybe it's none of my business. There are things in my past that I don't talk about either, so I can respect that. However, as your employer as well as your friend, there is just one issue that may be my business." I leaned forward and folded my hands, resting my elbows on my knees as I looked at her over my fingertips. Angel's brow was clenched nervously, and she could not hold my gaze. She knew what I was going to say. I realized that I might be about to push her away forever, but I grimly decided that even her friendship was meaningless if she refused to trust me. Trust could not be forced, but it should not have been one-sided either.

"Angel, you can't live like this from what I pay you."

Angel blinked.

"That was my opinion," I said flatly. "It wasn't a question, so, technically, you don't have to say anything. I just want to know if you trust me."

Angel was torn apart inside. I could tell by the look in her brown puppy eyes. Part of her wanted to tell me everything, but she had held herself and her past hostage for so long that she was afraid of the hidden consequences of letting them go. In that way, the two of us were exactly the same. Insecurity was the greatest barrier between us and those we cared about the most.

Angel did not blink a second time. She was staring right back at me, as if each of us was daring the other to flinch first. Even as she pushed herself away from the bookcase and walked toward me, eye contact was never broken. She slowly sat to my right on the sofa, and placed her palms on her knees, her eyes looking right into mine, but her resolution was wavering. Then, she looked away.

"Jolene," she said quietly, looking down at the white sock she was lightly tapping against the lion's paw leg of the glass and oak coffee table.

"Excuse me?" I was not sure if I had heard her correctly.

"Jolene. Angela Jolene Bateman."

"Angela? *Bateman?*"

She nodded, a slight, jerky motion of her head.

"I had it legally changed to Angel Bates when I turned eighteen." She turned to face me, leaning back into the cushions. "Your turn."

It was my turn to blink, several times, in an attempt to make the world make sense. It did not.

"Sidney Karl Myers," I replied. "Dare I ask?"

"I have money, Boss. A lot."

"You're rich," I clarified.

"Oh yeah, I'm loaded," she assured me. "You're not surprised?"

"Well, it does explain a lot," I said, shaking my head. "Except why you're working for me, for ten bucks an hour."

"Boss, is it too much to ask to have some semblance of a normal life?! Is that too much to ask?" She was suddenly angered. For an instant, I thought I saw frustrated tears in her eyes.

"Hey, take it easy, it was just a question," I said defensively, holding my hands out, placatingly. "You have to admit, it just seems weird."

"Sure," she snorted, crossing her arms. "My whole life is weird. Why should my employment status be any different? Hand me that pad, will you?"

I glanced over at the small glass side table by my elbow. A yellow pad of lined paper was set there, filled in heavily with rows of neatly handwritten, although apparently random, words. I did not realize what it was until I read the first word in the top, left-hand corner.

Puppies.

"Your Happy List?" I guessed, passing it to her. She snatched it from me, and began searching the coffee table for a pen.

"Yes, I'm suddenly in a 'de-happy' mood." She found a pen and began tapping it irritably against the edge of the pad. "Do I still get my raise?"

"What?"

"You said that if I lasted a year, my wages get hiked up to twelve an hour. Do I still get that?"

"Money is one of those happy things," I soothed her. "You don't get it until May, but you get it."

"Throw me a happy word, Boss," she muttered, scratching her forehead with the pen. "I'll tell you anything you want to know, but not until I get a happy buzz. Word or phrase, whatever. Just give me *something.*"

"Caviar," I said dryly. "Beluga."

"I've already got that," she snapped. "Number thirty-seven."

"Favourable profit margins."

324

"Okay, I didn't have that one," she confessed, flipping over several pages and scribbling the phrase onto the end of the list. "And, to be perfectly honest, I don't think I ever would have thought of it."

"You're welcome," I smiled. "Happy yet?"

"No," she sighed. "But, I'm close enough. I'm sorry. I should have told you about all this a long time ago. I'm just so used to hiding."

"From what? *The Enquirer* photographers?"

"Not quite, but almost. Normality was never an option for me."

Normality.... Good word use.

"I was just a kid, Boss, and my face was all over the TV. Everywhere I went, people would point at me. I mean, how rude is that?"

"Whoa, whoa!" I said sharply. "Back up a few steps! You were a *child star?!*"

"Sort of," she nodded. "What, I thought you were here because you remembered my commercials."

"Commercials? No.... What commercials? Whoa. You were in *commercials?* Like, on TV?"

"Come on, Boss! The Redmond's Ribs ads."

Had I been drinking water when she said that, she would have been drenched.

"You were Little Maple?!"

"Yeah, yeah...."

"*Little Maple?!*"

"I said yes! That's where it all started. I never asked for it. Daddy wanted his little girl in his commercial."

"*Little ... MAPLE?!*"

"Quit saying that!" she growled.

325

"Angel, you're a *bona fide celebrity!*" I gurgled. "I still remember your lines, for Pete's sake! 'Mmm, maple roasted ribs are the *nummiest!*'"

"Don't do that," she moaned. "I thought you were supposed to be unflappable. I hate that dumb line."

"Sorry," I said, trying to remember how to breathe. "I'm just a bit … utterly flabbergasted, that's all."

"Well, snap out of it!" she said tersely, holding a thumb up in front of my face. "Focus, Boss! How many index fingers am I holding up?"

"None."

"Good. You're awake. Act like it!"

"Angel…."

"I don't want to talk about it!"

"Okay," I said weakly, shrivelling into the couch.

Angel leaned back into her armrest, pouting slightly.

"You think I'm living large here, Boss? A duplex and a big TV? This is incognito for me. Believe me, if I wanted to, I could live a lot bigger. I'm living small. Itsy-bitsy." We sat in awkward silence for about a minute before Angel asked, "When's your sister coming to get me?" I checked my watch. It was ten o'clock in the morning.

"A couple of hours. You have to answer this one…. Any movies?"

Angel groaned and sat up slightly.

"*True North Justice,* 1989," she sighed. "I was Donald Sutherland's kidnapped granddaughter. You want some popcorn?"

Donald Sutherland…. Crying at the movie theatre…. Well, that part suddenly made sense.

I let out a long breath. "I think I need some popcorn." *And two extra strength acetaminophen and a tranquillizer dart, please.*

"Good!" she said brightly, suddenly back to her standard cheery persona as she hopped lightly over the couch back and jogged to the kitchen. She jogged everywhere, as though time was of great value, even in her own home. My waitress was a former movie star. She was an early eighties cuisinary icon. Something that I had told Karen Malloy suddenly resurged into my memory.

Do you ever wonder why unemployed actors always end up as politicians, animal rights activists, or waiters? Because those are the jobs that demand natural born actors. It let's them hone their craft, it just doesn't pay as well.

Ten dollars an hour, to be exact, with a two dollar per hour raise in May.

"I said you looked familiar," I called after her, recalling our first meeting. "Day one, I told you that. And you looked down at the floor of my office, and I believe you scuffed your toe on the concrete."

"Have you ever thought about linoleum?" her voice responded from the next room.

"No. I keep my overheads low."

"Did you ever see that one?" Angel shouted, her voice all but drowned out by the clattering of pans on the stove top.

"Which what?"

That is likely the worst verbal response I have ever given to anyone, grammatically speaking.

"The movie."

"Sorry, I'm a typically pathetic Canadian," I croaked. "I only watch American movies. Or old kung-fu."

"Well, you should. It's a classic. Donny's a Mountie, and there's this one scene where he pries a henchman's teeth out with a crowbar to get him to tell where they're hiding me. It's brutal."

"*Donny?!*"

"Yep," she said proudly. "He says I'm the only one who's allowed to call him that. We still write."

My waitress gets birthday cards from Donald Sutherland....

Angel was making a lot of noise in that kitchen, somewhat unusual considering that she had just told me that silence was "one of those happy things." I guess she only liked her own noise.

"Angel?"

"Yo?"

"What are you doing?"

"I'm making popcorn."

"Yeah, but why is making popcorn so loud?"

"Kettle cooked, Boss. Air poppers are for wimps."

"I use an air popper."

"Kettle cooked tastes better."

"Okay." Who was I to argue with a celebrity, particularly a celebrity who referred to one of Canada's most noted actors as "Donny?" I did not realize that I had settled into a stunned silence until Angel looked in from the kitchen, leaning on the doorframe.

"Say something, Boss. You're making me nervous."

"I might be distantly related to Mike Myers," I said blandly.

She actually giggled a little at that. "Say something else."

"Is 'nummiest' a word, or did they just make it up?"

"I was five, Boss. It was supposed to be 'yummiest,' but I screwed it up, and everyone thought it sounded cute."

"Very cute. How exactly do they 'maple roast' those ribs?"

"Nope," she said smugly, shaking her head and wagging a finger at me. "That's the company's big red book. If I told you, I'd have to kill you."

"Hey, I told you the secret ingredients in Kat's spicy pizza sauce," I reminded her.

"Savoury and horseradish? Not good enough."

"You forgot the Habanera sauce."

"I'm still not telling you," she said primly, with a wide smile.

"You're popcorn's burning," I said snappishly.

"Oh, shoot!" Angel ducked back into the kitchen and resumed clattering. Well, there was one thing that she was right about. Her popcorn already smelled better than mine did.

Little Maple. Maple roasted. Angela. Jolene. Bateman. Kettle cooked popcorn. Donald Sutherland. Eighties cultural icon. This was too much information to process in a single day.

Angel's voice carried over the clamour once more.

"You can't tell anyone. You know that, right?"

I looked up at the hanging lamp over the couch, and shook my head groggily, still having a hard time believing everything that I had just unearthed. My thoughts began moseying aimlessly as I found myself wondering why people shook their heads when overwhelmed. Head shaking usually denoted negative, whereas head nodding implied affirmative; so, when someone did a head shake, were they saying "No, that's not true, you're lying?" Perhaps they simply did it as a wake up mechanism in response to the insistence of some part of their subconsciousness which was firmly persuaded that they were still dreaming. I also found myself wondering if anyone except a pizza guy would sit around and wonder about things like that.

"Boss, I said you can't tell anyone."

"Yeah, I heard you. You mind telling me how you managed to keep a secret like that for so long?"

"Dropping out of the public eye isn't hard," she replied, "especially when you're just a kid. You just go home and never leave. I was home-schooled ever since the fifth grade, and I barely kept in contact with my old friends."

"So, what? You just became a hermit?"

"Some people actually don't like living in a spotlight. You like lots of butter?"

"Yeah. Please." Manners suddenly seemed very important.

"Good. Me too."

"But, Angel, what about high school? Hanging out at the mall? Prom? Dating?"

"Hey, I dated a lot," she assured me. "I just broke it off when I figured they were after my money, or wanted what I wasn't about to give them."

"Are you a Christian, Miss Bates?" I could not help inquiring.

"I'm still a virgin, if that's what you're wondering."

I cringed. "I wasn't!"

"Yeah, right. Salt?"

"Just a bit. Why did you move here? Actually, where did you move from?"

"Born and raised in Toronto. We moved to a country home outside of Edmonton when I was thirteen. I guess my parents wanted to help get me away from all the publicity, but it didn't help much. People kept coming to the door, perfect strangers acting like old friends. I just got sick of it."

"But, why Chetwynd? Of all places, why here?"

"Partly because it's hours away from the nearest major city, but mostly because I had never heard of it. And neither had anyone else."

"Good point," I admitted.

I'm talking to a movie star, and she's making me popcorn. I always figured that if I met a movie star, I'd be serving her a lobster or something. Good grief, I KISSED a movie star!

Okay, reality check, Myers. It was a supporting role in a late eighties Sutherland movie you've never heard of.

Yeah, but still....

Angel returned from the kitchen with two ice cream pails, each one filled about half full of popcorn. She handed one to me and slid back onto the couch, cross-legged, with the pail between her knees.

"You didn't have to use the good china just for me," I said mildly, sampling a few kernels.

Angel laughed and snapped a piece of popcorn high into the air, catching it in her mouth.

"Kettle cooked tastes *better*," Angel clarified. "But it's only *perfect* when you eat it from an ice cream pail.

Come on, everyone knows that. Did you want to know anything else?"

"Hey, a few minutes ago you said you didn't want to talk about it."

"Yeah, but I just realized how much I trust you," she said kindly. "Actually, it feels good to let all of this out. It's been forever since I've been able to talk to anyone about who I really am. Fire away, ask anything."

"To be honest," I confessed, "now that I'm over my … star-struck jitters, I really don't know what to ask you. Your life is your story, not mine."

"Ah, Boss, that's such a beautiful thing to say," she smiled. "Two million."

"What?"

"You didn't want to be so rude as to come right out and ask how much money I have," she expounded patiently. "It's two million dollars."

"Okay, I *was* wondering about that."

"I thought your curiosity would be just about killing you by now," she chuckled, her mouth full of popcorn mush. "But thanks for not asking. I appreciate that. You like the popcorn?"

"It's great," I said. "Different from air popped, somehow."

"It's squeakier," she explained, licking her fingers. "You know, from the oil. It squeaks. I had one boyfriend who couldn't eat it because he said it was like fingernails on a chalkboard in his mouth. Wimp."

"Is that why you dumped him?"

"Sure, like I'm supposed to build a meaningful relationship with a guy I can't even share a pail of popcorn with? No thanks."

"You base relationship success on popcorn? That almost sounds shallow, Angel."

"We all have our weak points," she shrugged. "I'll bet even you're shallow in some way."

"I'm not," I said glibly.

"Yeah, I've heard *that* before," Angel snorted. "Are you telling me that you've never once asked a girl out on a date, basing the decision mainly on her.... Oh, how shall I put it ...?"

"Contour?" I supplied.

"Well, I never would have used that exact word, but, yeah. Contour."

"A few times in high school."

"How'd that go for you?"

"One didn't show up, and another one ran into an old boyfriend halfway through our date. Apparently, his contour had improved since she last saw him."

"Ouch," Angel winced.

"Darn gym monkey," I grumbled. "Okay, fine. I'm shallow."

Angel gave me a consoling pat on the shoulder.

"Don't worry, Boss. I think your contour's just fine."

"Thank you," I grimaced. "So is yours."

Myers, you did not just tell an employee that she has a nice body.... IDIOT! Change the subject!

"Angel ... why did you hate your life so much?"

Very good. That sounded deep. The low voice and eye contact helped.

Angel did not answer until she had swallowed her popcorn, which was a definite improvement from watching her chew it with her mouth open. This girl had lived alone for too long.

"I guess mostly because I never chose it," she answered quietly. "After Little Maple, my whole life looked like it was being written out for me. I met other rich kids, and some of them seemed fine, but … I don't know. They just didn't seem real. I wanted my life to be real." She set her popcorn on the coffee table, then turned to face me, sliding one arm onto the top of the couch back and resting her head on it.

"That's how you feel."

"I'm sorry?"

"You never picked your life. It got handed to you when your dad died."

"I like my life. It's fine."

"But you never chose it," she insisted. "I know you, Boss. You wanted to be a cop."

I could only close my eyes and cup my face in the palm of my left hand.

"Okay, I give up," I muttered. "*How* did you know that? *How?*"

Angel grinned. "I'm like Boris. I'm a pizza girl; I know everything. You'd be a good cop."

"Gee, thanks."

"Okay, your turn. What did *I* want to be?"

"A rodeo princess."

"*Please,*" she croaked, rolling her eyes. "Take a real guess."

"A rodeo clown?"

"Close enough," she giggled. "I wanted to work in a tire shop."

"A *tire shop?*"

"I like tires. You like guns. To each, their own."

"So, why aren't you at the tire shop across the street from my shop?"

"They weren't hiring."

I shook my head for the hundredth time. "A tire shop...."

"Tires are cool. They're the greatest invention since the wheel. And I love the coveralls."

"You know something, Angel?" I remarked. "I just realized that you're weird ... but in a really nice way."

She laughed. "It's who I am, Boss."

"I never said I liked guns."

"Get a grip. Everybody who wants to be a cop likes guns. That's why people become cops. Sure, they all have vague notions about law, justice, and the Canadian way, but the real drawing card is the guns."

"You don't like guns?"

That brought a snicker. "Boss, I own three rifles."

I paused to stare cautiously at her. "Now, you're scaring *me*."

"A bolt action .308 with a scope, a 30-30 Winchester with open sights, and a 12-gage riot gun. Burglars, *beware*. Wanna see them?"

"The guns, or your collection of dead burglars?"

"I'll be right back." She clambered over the couch again and resumed her jogging, this time up the stairs to her bedroom.

A fame-hating, former child star, pizza shop waitress with tire ambitions and a coverall fetish is about to walk into this room with an armload of rifles.... This was beginning to sound like one of those bizarre fantasies that people only revealed to their psychiatrists.

Angel definitely looked the part of a warrior princess as she came back down the stairs, arms wrapped around her three-piece home security system.

"Check this action out," she said, tossing the shotgun at me.

"Nice," I said, catching it gingerly, inwardly cringing at her lack of basic safety procedure.

"Just make sure you point it in a safe direction," she wisely counselled me. "It's loaded."

Are you insane, lady?!

I slowly jacked the five slug rounds out of the weapon, and set them in a neat row on the coffee table. My waitress was a truly scary woman.

"Relax, Boss," Angel commented, checking the lever action on the 30-30. "I think the safety's on."

"That's very comforting," I sighed. "By the way … they're opening a Redmond's Ribs here. I'm assuming you knew that. I mean, you have to drive right by the big sign on your way to work."

"Of course I knew. They've got over one hundred twenty restaurants in eight different countries. I can't help where they decide to set up shop."

"So … they don't know about you?"

"Yeah, right," Angel grunted, sitting beside me again, setting her rifles down on the carpet beside the couch. "I'm not going to let them use me as a dang promotional tool. I'm just hoping they don't recognize me. Not that I'm ever going in there, but it's a small town. It's hard to hide from the people in it."

"You could grow a beard," I suggested.

Angel glared. "That's not funny."

"It was a joke," I said weakly. "And you're absolutely right. It wasn't funny. Not funny at all. Sorry."

"Boss, you're getting all submissive on me," she pointed out, crossly. "I'm still your waitress. I'm a girl trying to earn a living, you're the boss. Get back to being sarcastic."

"I prefer to think of it as sardonic. And I can't right now. You're a movie star, or were. I'll be fine tomorrow, but, for now, I'm a slack-jawed imbecile. This is a big revelation, okay? Bear with me."

"Then let's change the subject," Angel decided. "Do you like that shotgun?"

"Love it," I said admiringly, hefting the gun up and levelling the sights on Angel's mountain goat calendar on the far wall. I lined the barrel up between the goat's eyes, and held it there for a long time.

"Do you have a gun?" Angel eventually asked, causing me to flinch, startled.

I slowly lowered the shotgun. "No."

"Do you want that one?" Angel wanted to know, smiling teasingly at me.

"Are you serious?" I asked, skeptically.

"Yours if you want it."

"Very generous," I said appreciatively, setting the gun on the coffee table with the slugs. "But you have two million dollars. That's your best home defence."

She looked disappointed. "I can buy a new one, Boss. I've got a few bucks saved."

"Thanks anyway," I smiled. "I don't need a gun."

"Suit yourself," Angel said reluctantly.

"If you ever need to shoot somebody, don't say I didn't offer. This is a tough town."

"If I ever need something or someone shot, you'll be the first person I'll call," I assured her.

"Who were you aiming at?" she asked quite suddenly, looking strangely at me.

"What?"

"You were sighting in on the mountain goat, but I was watching your eyes. They were hard. You weren't seeing a goat. You were seeing someone you hate."

"I hate mountain goats," I said dryly. "They smell."

"Boss...." Her firm voice was unsettling. "I've been very honest with you. I expect the same."

I leaned back to stare at her. Angel could read me so perfectly. I could not even hide my secret feelings from her. I had to draw in a long breath before I could reply. I considered myself an honest man, but I was about to delve into the realm of my darkest, hidden honesty.

"You once asked me what I needed out of life," I answered. "Do you really want to know?"

"I do," she said seriously.

"After you know ... you'll wish you didn't," I said plainly. "For years, I've only wanted one thing. And I can't have it."

"Can't is a big word," she reminded me. "You told me that."

"I want to kill a man who's already dead."

My words were low and cold, and my face was a carved stone. Angel slowly sat up in surprise, her lips parting slightly. A knowing light seemed to dawn in her eyes after a moment.

"Josh Kelton," she said slowly. "He's that one person you wanted to fight, isn't he? In the Pine Pass, you said you only ever wanted to get in one fight in your life. Just one."

"Josh Kelton," I nodded. "He made me mad."

Angel sighed deeply, closing her eyes and rubbing her forehead with the fingertips of her right hand.

"Revenge will not help," she said assertively, without opening her eyes. "You know that, Boss. You're smart."

"Revenge can't help," I shrugged. "The time for it has passed. Don't worry. I told you that you wouldn't want to know."

"Actually, I'm glad I know," she said, with just a hint of defiance in her tone. "Maybe now I can help you."

"Thanks anyway," I said calmly. "I'm fine."

"Don't you dare try to brush me off like that!" Angel hissed with startling ferocity, leaning toward me with livid, burning eyes. "I've seen what hatred can turn decent people into! You're my friend, and I will *not* let you do that to yourself! Get it?"

I stared at her in utter astonishment as she flopped back onto the leather cushions and looked up at the ceiling, still seething. After a moment, she closed her eyes again and pressed her lips together, slowly collecting her scattered fragments of composure. After nearly a minute of frozen silence, she began speaking, slowly and very quietly, never once opening her eyes.

"I started looking for a hideaway nearly three years ago. I just couldn't stay with my family, living a life that wasn't mine. So, I drove around Alberta. Then Saskatchewan. Then BC. Then back to Manitoba, Ontario, all over Canada. I looked for roads that weren't paved, the kind that led to seclusion, sleepy little towns that either wouldn't know who I was, or wouldn't care.

Sometimes, I'd drive for weeks, eating in restaurants, sleeping in motels, barely speaking to anyone, except to get the 411 on the towns. I had to find a place for me.

"Then I drove through this tiny little town in southern Alberta, down in the badlands. It was a little hole of a place, not much more than a few houses and a grain mill. Charming spot, even beautiful, but I'm no farm girl. I just stopped by for a meal one night, really late, and then left. But the funny thing is that I stopped my car by this lonely old church on a grassy knoll outside of town, just to check my map. And I noticed that I was parked in a shadow. There were no trees, and the church was lit up by this one lamp stand, so I had no idea where this shadow was coming from. The lamp stand lit up the whole church, knoll, and just about everything else. I shut off my car, switched off the lights, and got out to look around.

"It turns out that I was actually in the shadow of the lamp stand. It was more like a short street light, but the supporting arm and light were on the church side of the pole, not over the road. For some reason, the lamp was kind of pointed back down toward the pole that held it in the air, so the shadow from the pole lay across the road.

"I didn't think much of it, until I began wondering how that pole alone could throw a shadow over my whole car. It was only twelve, fifteen feet high, maybe, and maybe ten inches in diameter. I looked hard at the shadow, and realized that it got narrower near the base of the pole, so it actually widened as it got further down the hill. But then I turned around to go back to my car, and that was when I couldn't believe my own eyes.

"That little hill just dipped down a few feet to the dirt road, and then there was a big, low valley on the other side of my car, a cow pasture, I guess. That shadow blacked it out, completely. It stretched all the way down and across the valley, and up the sides of the hills on the far side. Boss, that shadow had to be four miles long, and nearly three miles across the far end. I would never have believed it if I hadn't seen it. It was the most amazing thing I've ever seen. There was a light on a hill, a light that should have lit up everything, all around it, and one little pole was all that was needed to kill it.

"A little flicker of light can shine through a lot of darkness, Boss. But just a little sliver in just the right place can make all that blackness come right back. If you've ever learned a better life lesson than that, I'd love to hear it."

Her head was still tilted back as she finally opened her eyes. My gaze was transfixed on the profile of her face. I could think of nothing to say. Any response would have shattered the magic that her low voice had created, and to do that would have been just plain murder. I was too awed to even realize that I really needed a coffee. That realization would come later. For the moment, it had to wait in reverent silence, just like me.

Angel slowly shifted her weight on the couch, as if stirring from the hazy mists of a dream. She blinked a few times, and then turned to face me. Her eyes were so big and brown as she looked into mine, and asked, "Do you want something to drink? I'm thirsty." That was my cue to reanimate.

341

"I need a coffee," I said, wondering why my voice had to struggle to rise above a hushed tone.

Angel smiled and gave me a hug. I did not know why she did it, but it felt good to embrace her.

"I don't have any," she whispered in my ear, and then she started giggling uncontrollably. I did not think that she was laughing at me, but, with Angel, who could be certain? She sat up, releasing me, and just laughed. And I laughed too. Not as long as she did, nor as heartily, but I actually laughed. I missed my own laughter. I missed the happiness that Angel had been wise enough to never let go of.

We both leaned back into the couch as our laughing died out, and we just sat there, grinning stupidly at each other.

"You can say it," Angel chuckled, her cheeks glittering with mirthful tears, again proving that my life was a pop-up book to her discerning eyes. She could effortlessly read my eyes and face, and she could read my soul between the lines.

"You're my best friend," I said quietly, trying not to smile while saying something that important.

"And you're mine," she murmured. "Can I have my raise now?"

"No."

"And you know what else?" Angel sighed, reluctant to release the peaceful moment. "Your sister's coming here pretty soon, and I've still got to get showered and ready to go."

"Then I'd better leave you to it," I said complacently, rising from the couch and stretching my stiff muscles. I looked back down at the short girl sitting on the leather furniture, and I said simply, "You have to say it."

"Say what?" she asked, leaning forward and propping her chin on her fist.

"I'm not kidding," I said seriously. "I'm not going to believe you unless you say it."

Angel grimaced, but took an obligatory deep breath, as though she had to get into character.

"Mmm," she cooed, "maple roasted ribs are the *nummiest!*"

Well, I was convinced.

I had thought that the day had already held enough surprises, but Angel still had her biggest one up her sleeve. I had walked out the front door, and was about to get in my truck, when I called out to Angel, as she stood in the doorway.

"You know, we should get your dad to come up here. Maybe he could make a commercial for By The Slice, get us some publicity."

"Why in the world would he do that?" Her stare was blank.

"That's what TV producers do, right?"

"Who said he was a TV producer?"

"You did."

"No, I didn't. I said it was his commercial."

"*Excuse me?*" I am sure that my face was paper white.

"Oh, didn't you know?" she said airily. "Daddy's name is Redmond Bateman. Later, Boss." Then, she closed the door.

CHAPTER TWENTY-FOUR

I told everyone that I was taking the next two days off work. Yes, you heard right. I was going to take off Thursday *and Friday*. What else could I do? I was in shock. It had been hard enough to face Angel the day after I kissed her. To work with her immediately after realizing that her father was potentially going to put me out of business would have been absolutely impossible. I hardly knew what to feel. I was flabbergasted, awed, confused, betrayed, terrified, irritated, inspired, and sworn to secrecy. A few times, I was pretty certain that I felt my left eye twitching. Forget coffee. I was planning on switching to double espressos with lots of sugar and frosted cinnamon rolls on the side. Cindy had often told me that caffeine would kill me, and, if she was right, I wanted it to do the deed before my restaurant went under. I still felt that my restaurant was all that I had. The lives of my friends would go on without me, and the fact was that I did not deserve them, anyway. I could not appreciate them enough. I was too obsessed with my work, and, now that my business was facing a legitimate threat, I was absolutely despondent. Without my restaurant, I would truly lose Dad. I had tried so hard to keep his spirit alive in that restaurant, and now the father of my best friend was about to take that away from me.

No, I was not suicidal. I believed too strongly in the existence of hell to risk that, but I was still looking for a reason to get up in the morning. My restaurant was not a good enough reason, but sometimes it was all that I had.

I wanted to be at work, now more than ever. Sitting on my living room sofa in my old blue bathrobe for two days straight, watching reruns of all the shows that had seemed so hilarious when I was nine, was not the way that I wanted to be spending my time. Yet, there I was. It was Friday evening, just after five, and already it was getting dark. The days were cold and short, and we all knew that the first snowfall was overdue. This time of year was usually Boris's prime time. With the first major snowfalls tempting people to stay in the heated comfort of their homes, his deliveries nearly doubled during the winter months.

I often missed the days before I was the owner, or even manager, when my primary job was pizza delivery. There was a freedom in that job, even a rapport, which I had not experienced since I became the boss. There was nothing like being able to get out of the kitchen every few minutes, to drive the streets of Chetwynd with the radio on. Of course, I had to deal with customers who were a lot more inebriated than the ones who generally came into the dining room, but when one was as skilled as Boris and I were in the use of charming and confusing words, it was amazing how well drunk people would tip.

I missed the love for my job that Boris and Angel and all the others still possessed. I needed my work. I did not love it anymore. My staples and students still did, no matter how stressful it occasionally became.

Certainly, there were times when it was hard for them to love the job, too, such as the incidents with Gavin Malton and Phil Vardega. Even when life was considerably less dramatic than those occasions, a life of servitude could still be straining. I will never forget Boris's words during such a moment of job frustration, over a year earlier.

"I spend my life fighting the stereotype," he had ranted. "You think it's easy? There are certain truths that people just do not want to face. Not every old person is wise, not every deaf-mute deserves to win, and not every pizza delivery guy is a zit-faced hack!"

Still, he and the rest of my staff managed to enjoy their work. They were like Karl Myers. They had servant's hearts. No one else could successfully work in that restaurant for any amount of time. The job would never make anyone rich. Most honest jobs that required good manners and a love for humanity never did. Yet, my staple crew was happy, because they could see the side of the service sector that I no longer let myself see. I did the job because I was obligated to it, and to Karl Myers' memory.

My father was a brilliant and simple man. Giving people good service, smiles, and the occasional tune on the piano was all that he needed to be satisfied with his life. I had tried to follow in his steps, but I could not bring myself to play the piano for anyone, and, since Dad's death, smiling had become such a nuisance that I usually confined myself to the kitchen and my office. I let my happy workers take care of the dining room.

Now, even my kitchen was daunting. My waitress was terrifying me, and I had not shaved or gotten out of my bathrobe in two days. Furthermore, I now had something else to blame Angel for. Not only had she betrayed me by concealing the fact that her father was the greatest single threat to my current livelihood, but she had also gotten me addicted to *The Littlest Hobo*. Dang, that dog was a genius.

I honestly did not realize how bad my life had become, until the doorbell rang during the final five minutes of a *T&T* rerun, and I was suddenly in agony over the prospect of missing the ending while answering the front door. At that moment, I began to understand that I had officially derailed somewhere along the line. Before answering the door, I shut off the TV and took the batteries out of the remote control, dropping the double-A's into the kitchen garbage can on my way to the porch.

And, as living proof that your problems will follow you home, Angel was standing in my doorway.

She looked cold. There was a chill wind blowing, and she only had a light denim jacket over her white uniform blouse and black skirt. I could only assume that she had come directly from work to my house, although her car was not in the driveway. She had walked all the way.

347

"Hey, Boss," she said, her cheery voice sounding just a little more cautious than usual. "Did you miss me?"

"No," I said, honestly and sarcastically at the same time. I wished that I was wearing socks. My feet were cold.

She smirked. "Right. How are you?"

"Angel," I sighed, slumping against the doorframe, "two days ago, I realized that your family business is probably going to put my family business out of business. How are you?"

"Boss!" she protested. "The place hasn't even opened yet. Are you sure you're not overreacting?"

"You, of all people, should know the cost of your dad's success, especially in a small town."

"But people still need pizza," Angel pointed out.

"People don't need anything," I growled.

"Do you hate me, now?" The question hit me like a hard fist to the stomach.

"Crap, I'm sorry," I groaned. "I'm an idiot, a big baby. Do you want a raise?"

"Yes, actually."

"You got it," I assured her. "Starting first thing … next May."

"You came to me," Angel reminded me. "You knocked on my door, and you asked about my life. What'd you expect? Dishonesty? Evasiveness?"

"A little of both, frankly. Look, I told you your story was your own. I guess now I'm wishing that we'd kept it that way."

Angel shook her head. "Secrets aren't good for friendships. My only regret is not telling you sooner."

"That's great," I muttered. "But now that I know, I wish I didn't."

"Why?" There was the five-year-old again.

I forced myself to look her right in the eye as I replied, "Because I might be tempted to blame you. That's irrational, sure. But it's human nature. You know that."

"I know," she acknowledged. "But I'm still a woman, so I'm obligated to be offended by that."

Please, somebody just shoot me.... Not a kill shot, just something to put me in the hospital for a couple weeks, with some well-deserved sympathy and cards.

"Boss...." Angel was biting her lip, some gestures that made my brow furrow with more anxiety than I had experienced in months.

"Come for a walk with me."

"You're ... still offended, right?" I asked cautiously. She did not sound offended. Angel had to be the most inscrutable person I had ever met.

"I want you to come for a walk with me, okay?"

"Look, we had coffee once, and I've been trying to quell dating rumours ever since."

"Are you coming, or not?"

"I'm in a bathrobe."

"I'll take that as a yes. Get dressed." In spite of her youth and short stature, Angel would have made a really intimidating elementary school principal. Her low-toned voice was one of the most commanding that I had ever heard. I went back inside without inviting her in, and got dressed.

Angel had not waited for an invitation to come into my kitchen and start digging through the fridge.

When I entered the room, wearing an old grey work shirt, jeans, and a brown winter jacket, she was bent over behind the open refrigerator door, investigating a casserole dish of leftover rotini alfredo.

"What are you doing?" I growled, zipping up my jacket.

"It was a busy shift," she mumbled through a forkful of cold noodles. "I didn't have time to eat. That's what happens when you skip a Friday."

"You're eating my noodles," I pointed out.

Oh crap, I'm becoming Angel. I'm stating the obvious

"Hey, two days ago, you called me your best friend," she reminded me, pointing the fork at my chin. "Even if you feel a bit betrayed, that still gives me unlimited access to your refrigerator. Friendship's all about sharing, Boss. That's why there's no 'I' in 'friends.'"

I did not say a word. And, believe me, it was hard, but I was not going to state the obvious again. I grabbed one of Cindy's knee-length winter jackets from the coat hooks in the porch, and tossed it at Angel.

"Put that on," I instructed, trying to maintain some amount of civility, as I put on a blue ball cap.

"Why?"

"Because you'll catch your death if you don't," I replied, sounding more like a concerned parent than I had meant to.

Angel looked skeptically at the heavy, lime green coat in her arms.

"Don't you have anything in red?" she asked. "I like red."

"I know you like red. Wear green. Let's go."

"Hey, I'm eating here," she reminded me, still chewing with her mouth open.

I pulled open a cabinet drawer, and tossed her a fruit and nut energy bar from inside. She caught it with one hand, almost dropping the casserole dish.

"You came here to walk, let's walk," I said, heading for the door.

"Eew, does this have walnuts in it?" Angel asked squeamishly, studying the bar in her hand carefully as we walked out into the windy night.

This was not a pleasant autumn walk. Most of the dead leaves had long since drifted away to wherever the wind carried dead leaves in mid-November. The weather report had said that the temperature would rise to well above the seasonal average overnight, but, at that moment, the air still felt and smelled like a prelude to a heavy snowfall. The world around us was dark, except for the rhythmic flickering of early residential Christmas lights, some of which had been left on all year. One by one, the street lights were also coming alive, and the roads were moderately filled with cars returning their weary drivers from work, the bouncing headlights pointing the way home. In spite of the illumination, the whole town still seemed dark and cold. Angel and I both kept our hands in our pockets, trying to evade the biting wind.

I had thought that Angel had needed to talk to me, perhaps in an effort to bridge the rift that had so suddenly divided us, but, surprisingly, she did not say a word as we left my home block and then the subdivision. We were already walking in the grassy ditch along main street, following a parallel dirt bike trail, when I ventured, "Where are we going?"

Angel crumpled up her empty candy bar wrapper, and flicked the foil wad into the steel mouth of a culvert buried under the road. I did not even have the energy to chide her for littering.

"Redmond's Ribs," she said innocently. "Do you have any matches?"

"That's not funny," I snapped, kicking a rock down the trail ahead of us. "Where are we going?"

"Redmond's Ribs," she repeated. "I want you to see it."

"I've seen it," I said, watching my own breath curl into the cold air.

"Not this close, you haven't," she assured me.

"What, you want me to break into a construction site?"

"No. We're just going to scale the fence. You can climb, right?"

"Are you drunk again?"

"Nope," she smiled sweetly. "I'm sworn off the stuff. Anyway, I hate lime, and salt is bad for you."

"Good girl," I sighed, nervously scratching the back of my head. "I'm not breaking into a construction site. Or climbing a fence."

"Whatever," she said dismissively. "That's where we're going."

"Why?" I demanded, as we crossed a rickety wooden footbridge over a small creek.

"Because I want you to see something," was her patient reply.

I gave up, knowing very well that she was taking a secret delight in keeping me in suspense. I changed the subject.

"So, what's he like?" I asked, keenly interested.

"My dad?"

"No. Donald Sutherland."

"Tall," she said simply. "And cool."

"Wow," I said drolly. "Your vivid descriptions are pure magic to the senses."

"You know what your problem is, Boss?" she demanded, pointing a finger in my face. "Sarcasm is *your* ingrained response to life, just like deflection is for me. Usually, it's funny, but sometimes you have to know how to turn it off. Okay?"

"Hey, you're the celebrity. You'd know."

"You're actually going to hold that against me, aren't you?" she said angrily, stopping on the trail, and crossing her arms. "I never made myself out to be anything that I'm not. I just didn't tell you everything about my past, because you didn't need to know, and I wanted to be treated like a normal person! Do you know what it's like to know that you'll never be considered ordinary? It stinks. So, don't get all huffy at me for wanting my own life! I'm trying to do you a favour here, and you're throwing it back in my face!"

I stood and watched as she stormed off down the trail. However, she only went about ten feet before stopping again. Then, she turned around, marched back up to me, and slapped my face. It was more dramatic than hurtful, but it still surprised me. I blinked.

"Dare I ask?" I cringed, rubbing my jaw gingerly. My cheek was hot and tingling.

353

"That's for not accepting the shotgun I offered you," she explained primly. "It was meant as a goodwill offering. Am I fired?"

"No," I said. "You probably need the money…. And that was a joke, not sarcasm."

"Yeah, I know," she nodded understandingly. "Come on, it's getting colder. What's holding you up?" She grabbed my elbow and began tugging me along behind her. Any other boss on the planet would have terminated employment by now.

"What favour?" I asked, wrenching my arm out of her grasp. I could see the Redmond's Ribs building ahead of us, to our right. "You said you were trying to do me a favour. What favour?"

"That," she answered, pointing at the nearly completed restaurant. The trademark white brick building and low red roof had been completed only days before, and all of the glass doors and windows had been put in, as well. That left only the furniture and some of the cooking appliances to be moved in and installed. Even the red and blue logo had been hung up over the double front doors, with the larger roadside sign scheduled to be raised before the next weekend. It was a beautiful restaurant, more than three times the size of my own. From my previous visits to other Redmond's establishments, I knew that the inside included a large dining room, and an adult's sports lounge. The play area for children was more like a theme park, complete with air hockey, fooseball, coin-operated stationary rides, and an arcade. The restaurant was a mini-mall, and it was going to blow mine out of the water.

"How is that a favour?" I muttered, as we stood in front of the main entrance, looking through the links of a makeshift chain-link fence encompassing the site.

"Just look at it," Angel insisted, her face somewhat enraptured by her father's accomplishment.

"It's beautiful," I said dully. "And it's cold. Angel, what is this about? You don't seem like the type who would rub salt into already tender wounds, so what's the deal? Are you trying to offer me a job, or what?"

"That's not a bad idea," she admitted. "You'd do good here. But, it's too late for that, now."

"Angel…."

"Boss, just look at it. Look at the fence. Just look."

"I've looked."

"Look again," she ordered. "What's missing?"

"My job security."

"On the fence. What's missing?"

"I don't know," I groaned. "How am I supposed to know what's missing? I'm not an architect."

"Think back carefully," she replied coolly. "What did you see, every time you drove by here? What words did you read, that secretly terrified you?"

I had to blink again. Then I blinked several more times. She was right. A sign on the front gate was missing. My mouth opened slightly as I tried to decide what that meant.

"The sign," I said slowly. "There was a sign there."

"And what did it say?" she asked calmly.

I turned to stare at her, not knowing what to think.

Impossible….

"'Grand opening, December first.'"

355

Angel just smiled, and placed her hands on the fence, wrapping her fingers through the metal links. Then she began to speak quietly, almost hypnotically.

"The Chetwynd branch of Redmond's Ribs was ordered to halt construction at exactly nine o'clock this morning. No explanation was given, except to say that the order to pull all funding from the project had come directly from franchise CEO Redmond Bateman and the Toronto board of directors. Project investors and construction contractors are being contacted in regards to reimbursement for building and zoning contracts already paid, and a non-specifying letter of apology is being drafted by the Redmond's Ribs public relations department. It is addressed to the district of Chetwynd, its mayor and council. Basically, it says, 'Sorry for getting your hopes up, the situation is beyond our control.' A compensatory package is also being offered, quite generously, I may add. The building itself will most likely be donated to the community, perhaps as a youth centre or other recreational facility."

Angel took a deep breath, then turned her back to the gate, leaning against it as she looked up at the first stars appearing in the black sky, shining dimly through the glow of the street lights. I could not flinch. I was frozen, and the weather was not the cause.

"Public outcry is expected," she murmured, almost as though she had rehearsed this speech, or even given it before. "Boy, are they going to be *mad*. This generally dies out after two to four weeks, as anticipation begins to develop as to the vacated building's new usage. Town meetings will be held, and the building's fate will be decided. Demolition will not be an option at this advanced development stage, unless no suitable purchase option is made. Personally, I think it would make a great bowling alley.

"Local hiring and training of personnel has already begun. Therefore, the preselected restaurant management team will be the most disappointed and angered. However, they will be offered similar postings at any of the sixteen Redmond's Ribs establishments currently under construction in Canada, the United States, Mexico, England, Germany, and Australia. Should they prefer to wait six months, they will have the option of managing the first of the franchise to be opened in Scotland, and, yes, a recipe for maple roasted haggis is being developed as we speak. Needless to say, we're very excited about that." She finally fell silent, and I could only stare dumbly at her for a full minute.

"Holy crap," I said blankly. No other words would form on my tongue.

Angel shrugged.

"I made a call, Boss."

"Holy … cow."

I was stunned. Angel had pulled the plug on my competition. I could not believe it. It was absolutely unfathomable. This was far beyond helping out a friend.

"Angel, you can't just … kill a major business development, just like that."

"I didn't," she said flatly. "My father and the Toronto board of directors did."

"Angel, *how?!*"

"I just made a call."

"And said what?"

357

"I told Daddy that I did not want to risk public exposure in my new, private life, and that having the business, which my very image was once representative of, located in such close proximity to me made that risk much more imminent. Also, I told him that the completion of his restaurant would threaten my own employment status." I had never heard Angel speak with such fluency before. Then again, she had been an actress. I suddenly wondered which part of her persona was real, and which part had been playing a role.

"How can they just shut it down?" I demanded. "I thought it was privately owned!"

"Relax, Boss. It's taken care of."

"Angel ... this is nuts."

"No, nuts are what's stuck in my teeth right now," she grumbled, running her tongue across her upper molars. "I told you I hated walnuts."

"Sorry."

"You're forgiven," she nodded, acceptantly. "And, you're welcome."

I closed my eyes and pressed my palms and forehead against the icy chain link gate, the contact with the metal causing the scar on my right temple to itch and burn.

"You did that for me?" I had to swallow the lump in my throat. I still could not believe it.

"Partly for me," she pointed out quickly. "I didn't lie to Daddy at all. But, yeah, partly for you, too. And for your dad. He'd want you to keep By The Slice going strong."

"Why?" I whispered, my eyes clamped shut.

Angel's low voice was soft in my ear.

"Because I love my job. Because I love all of you at the shop. You, and Cindy, and Kat, and Clancy, and Boris, and Becky, and Mark, and…. Well, Clayton's a bit of a twit, huh?"

"Yeah," I croaked. "Remind me to fire him tomorrow."

Angel's cold hand reached over to touch mine, her small fingers interlacing mine against the fence.

"You guys are my family," she said. "My new family here in Chetwynd. I love this town, drugs and crack-heads and drunks and dealers and the whole bloody mess. I love it. It reminds me of what my grandpa told me, years ago. He said, 'Angie….' That's what people used to call me, Angie. 'Angie,' he said, 'the world is not beautiful, but life can be. You have to make it beautiful by being beautiful, and that has nothing to do with what you look like.'

"That's why I'm happy, Boss. It's how I make my world happy. It's life, Sidney Karl Myers. Life is one of those happy things."

She turned and looked up at me.

"So, what the heck is wrong with you?" she demanded.

I cringed at her abrupt mood swing.

"Excuse me?"

"You need to tell me what it is that's eating you, Boss."

"I believe I already have."

"No," she said, quite positive. "You've had painful experiences, you've lost loved ones, but that does not explain you, not quite. There's something missing, still."

"Angel ... I think I've told you everything."

"Then why do you still hurt so much, Boss? The pain that I see in your eyes…. It's guilt. Why do you blame yourself?"

"I don't know, Angel. I have to. Ever since it happened, I've just known that some part of that night had to be my fault. I had a part in it, like I had guided Kelton into our truck. It had to be me."

"Kelton killed himself, Boss. He killed everyone who died that night."

"So ... why can I never accept that?"

She sighed helplessly. "Survivors guilt."

"Have you ever had that kind of guilt, Angel?"

"No."

"We aren't always responsible for the things that happen to us. We can get hurt, but knowing that we were the ones wronged helps us to get through. We can hide from that. What we can never hide from is ourselves. The possibility of our own crimes cannot stay behind us forever. Our wrongs will find us, sooner or later, and that is where the true torment is. That's the pain that can stay with you all your life."

She shook her head, slowly, and put a cold hand on my cheek.

"You did your best, Boss. In the end, no one can ever ask for more than that from you. You did what you could. Guilt is normal, but you don't have to carry it. That's a choice that you make."

I hugged Angel, right there in the shadow of that massive restaurant that would never see its grand opening. That hug lasted for several minutes, without another word being spoken.

The weather forecast was right. A warm chinook wind was coming in from the east. I could hear the change even before I felt it. Cold wind whistles. Warm wind breathes. I could hear that soft wind breathing down from the sky, and the very sound of it warmed me, almost as much as Angel's tight, tearful embrace.

I sometimes wonder what would have happened, had the doors of Redmond's Ribs actually opened. Certainly, my business would have suffered initially, but the question of whether or not the damage would have been irreparable still lingers in my mind. Perhaps my restaurant would have been forced to close, but I do not really believe that, anymore. As Angel had assured me, people still needed pizza.

That night stands out in my memory as "one of those truly beautiful moments," as Angel would have called it. I am very glad that I had that moment, because the two weeks that followed were the longest of my life.

CHAPTER TWENTY-FIVE

The existence of coincidence has been a major topic of discussion by philosophers, educators, scientists, physicists, and theologians for centuries. An event occurs. Like ripples on a pond, thousands of consequential events occur. Is it possible to avoid the initial event, or is there a driving force behind the universe, a storyteller who scripts the plot of life to wherever it must go, no matter how grim or tragic? No single answer will ever satisfy everyone, so the debate will continue into the future. I did not know what to believe. I believed in a God who knew our futures, but I also believed that we had been given free choice, regardless of how contradictory that sounds. Aside from that, I tried not to ponder predestination too much, simply to avoid the headaches. I had told Linda Matthews of my belief that the theory of cause and effect did not allow for accidents. However, I still often found myself wondering what would have happened if Dad and I had left the restaurant just five minutes earlier.

Five minutes could have changed so much, then and four-and-a-half years later. The day after Angel and I walked to Redmond's Ribs, I came to work around four o'clock, although I had told Boris and Clancy, the only ones on duty that day, that I would not be in until five. I chatted with Boris, and then, at 4:08 p.m., I walked into the back laundry room. To this day, I wonder how much hardship could have been avoid if I had waited until 4:13.

The theory of coincidence was the furthest thing from my mind that Saturday afternoon when I entered my place of business. I was in heaven. Redmond's Ribs was no longer a threat to my livelihood, and, as the instigator of its termination, Angel had proven herself to be the absolute best friend that anyone could ever have. The girl had guts. It takes a good amount of grit to demand that the rug be pulled out from under a half a million-dollar business venture.

Aside from that bit of soul solace, I had something else to be happy about. Boris and Cindy were going to be man and wife in two weeks. Apart from the joy that their joy would bring to everyone, the occasion also marked the first time that I would finally have my house to myself. I loved my sister more than the air I breathed, but, after twenty-two years under the same roof, we were both looking forward to having our own lives for once.

Boris was just finishing taking an order when I entered the kitchen. He hung up the phone as I checked the pizza oven, which had become a force of habit, to see if anything was cooking or burning. I could not walk into that room without opening the oven.

"Sid," Boris greeted me, writing the price at the bottom of the order slip. "You're early."

"What is it?" I asked, in reference to the order.

"Four large pizzas and two tables, reserved for tomorrow night at six. There's nothing else up, so quit checking the oven. It's like a nervous tic with you."

"When you and Clancy stop burning pizzas, I'll stop checking the oven," I chuckled. "Busy?"

"Steady," he said. "Clancy said he and Becky had a pretty busy lunch hour. They did about three hundred dollars already today."

"Excellent," I grinned, washing my hands in the dish sink. "Life is good."

"You're in a good mood," he noted, almost suspiciously. "Did a doctor prescribe that?"

"Nope," I said cheerily. "Business is booming, I have great friends working with me, and I'm thinking of buying a puppy. Puppies are happy things. Don't you wish you had a puppy, right here, right now?"

"Sure, I guess," Boris said cautiously, looking as though he was facing a madman. "I thought you said you hated puppies."

"No way!" I exclaimed. "When did I ever say that?"

"Right after you and Spring broke up," he reminded me, hanging the order up over the prep table. "I told you that you should buy a puppy, and you said that puppies were 'pukey, poopy pooches,' or something very similar to that."

"I had just broken up." I dismissed his recollection with a waving gesture. "I hated everything for a while. I'm fine now. And I'm going to buy a puppy."

"You're going to miss Cindy, aren't you?" he chided me, leaning against the counter and folding his arms, assertively. "You'll need a dog for company."

"It's not like she's actually going anywhere," I snorted. "You're two blocks down the street, and you've already made it pretty clear that you're going to be barging in on me all the time."

Boris laughed. "Hey, if you think I'm bad about that as a friend, just wait until we're actually *family!* I'll be in your fridge every single day."

"I don't doubt it," I smiled. "You and Angel, both."

"What?"

"Nothing. How's the wedding plans?"

"Actually, I wanted to talk to you about that," Boris sighed, running a hand through his dark, wavy hair. "We've hit a snag."

"How big a snag?" I asked slowly.

"Sid … you know how every couple has a special song? That one song that means something extra to both of them, that kind of defines the whole relationship?"

"Yeah."

"Good. Cindy and I…. We don't have one. We can't decide on which song to play for the first dance."

"Oh…." I said, never having given much thought to their differing musical preferences before. "Did you have any that you both … sort of like?"

Boris groaned and pulled a crumpled wad of paper from his trousers pocket, flicking it at me.

"That's our list of favourites, hers and mine," he explained, as I straightened the creases out of the mashed up sheet. "There's not much overlap."

"Celine Dion, Charlotte Church, Tammy Wynette, Faith Hill, Clay Aiken, John Michael Montgomery, Jewel," I read aloud from Cindy's list, then glanced further down at Boris's selections. "*The Eagles, The Rolling Stones,* Tom Petty, *Pink Floyd, The Smashing Pumpkins,* and Jim Morrison…. Okay, you're in trouble."

"I know," he croaked. "That's why we need you. We need mediation."

"You want us to play *Hotel California* for your first dance?" I said in disgust, looking at Boris's song choices. "Are you out of your mind?"

"I'm getting there," he said weakly. "That's why we need a mediator. It's hopeless."

"No way, Boris," I said harshly. "Your mess, not mine."

"Come on, Sid!" he pleaded. "No one knows me and Cindy better than you. You have to do this for us." "So … you want me to pick a song that's perfect for both of you. Is that it?"

"Yes," Boris said eagerly. "You don't even have to tell us what it is, just get the DJ to put it on for the first dance. You'll find a good one. I trust you."

"Okay, whatever," I said, rolling my eyes. "I'll find something perfect. Where's Clancy?"

"Having a smoke break."

"Good. When Kat gets in, tell her we need a new batch of spicy pizza sauce mixed up. Angel told me you were almost out, last night."

"Are you two hanging out a lot, lately?" Boris called after me as I strode into the back room to get my vest and tie. As I passed through the doorframe, I absently glanced at my watch.

4:08 p.m.

My timing was impossibly bad. Clancy did not expect me to arrive for nearly an hour, and obviously had not heard me talking to Boris. Otherwise, he never would have been standing by the rear exit with Devon Finn.

I saw them before they saw me. The washing machine was working its way through a load of dish towels, so they never heard me approaching. I stopped abruptly in front of them, about fifteen feet away. I froze, almost in mid stride.

They had been talking, but I will never know what about. Devon, clad in a grey hooded sweater and brown corduroy pants, saw me first. His mouth clamped shut, and he returned my blank stare. It took Clancy a few more seconds to notice that his friend had clammed up. When he followed Devon's gaze and saw me, his mouth fell open. My mouth was open as well. No one moved, or spoke, for ten very long seconds.

"Sid...." Clancy said, almost despairingly, but it was already far too late for explanations.

Devon held a handful of ten dollar bills in his right hand. Clancy's right hand held a small zip-lock bag, partly filled with white powdered cocaine. It was the kind of timing that a police narcotic's officer could only dream of.

"Office," I said softly, never blinking. "Now."

Clancy's head was ducked low with shame as he began to walk past me. I stopped him with my left hand held out, palm up, in front of his chest. He immediately placed the drugs in it, and then walked out of the room.

I took a few slow steps toward Finn.

"Yours?" I asked, holding up the bag in front of his eyes. It was a stupid question, but I wanted to hear his response.

"Never seen it before," he said evenly, tucking the cash into his pocket. "I guess I'll pay Clancy that money I owe him later."

"You're in an employee only area," I said. "Please leave."

"Sorry, I was just stopping by," Devon said, sheepishly. "See you later."

"Call anytime. We deliver."

Devon was whistling as he turned and walked back outside. I watched until he was out of sight in the back parking lot. A gust of chinook wind blew in the door, rustling the fresh uniforms hanging in the open closet.

Don't you ever set foot in my restaurant again.

There was an employee's washroom by the back door. I took the bag into the stall, dumped the coke into the toilet, and flushed it away, cramming the bag deep into the garbage can.

I found my black vest and tie, and took my time in front of the mirror beside the washing machine, as I carefully did up the three buttons and tied the square knot, which I preferred over the triangular. Then I walked to my office, passing Boris without a word, and shut the door behind me.

Clancy was sitting in the folding chair across the desk from my more comfortable padded seat. His eyes were closed, and one hand was supporting the weight of his head, fingertips pressed into his temples. He had nothing to say, absolutely no defence of any kind.

So busted....

I leaned against the wall to his left, rather than sitting across from him, and drew a long breath. I did not want to sit. He could not look at me.

"I did warn you," I reminded him, in a very low voice. "The day that I found out you were a user, I warned you about letting drugs interfere with your work. Do you remember that?"

"Yes," he sighed. "I remember. Sid, I am so sorry. I blew it."

"Everybody's sorry when they get caught," I muttered. "Frederick was. You remember him? A few years ago?"

Clancy nodded, still looking at the floor.

"I fired him on the spot for smoking a roach on his break," I continued. "You know what he said?"

"'Everybody does it,'" Clancy answered, almost inaudibly.

"That's right," I agreed. "It seems he was close to right, too. It is getting so, so hard … just to find people who will work here without breaking the rules, heck, without breaking the law. You know I'm not going to turn you in. You know that, right? I should, but I'm not going to."

"So, why don't you?" he asked, sounding weary.

"Because I probably just committed a crime by destroying evidence," I snapped.

Clancy looked up at me, surprised.

"Did you really think I'd just give it back to you?" I said irritably. "I flushed it. It was in *my* workplace. Now, it's in the public domain of the sewer system. Where it belongs."

Clancy was a man floundering helplessly in poor excuses as he said, "I wasn't going to do it here. I'd never do that to you. I was just going to put it in my truck and take it home for tonight."

"I believe you," I soothed him icily. "You're dumb, but you're not that dumb."

"Sid, I'm sorry. It was a stupid mistake, okay? It won't ever happen again. I promise."

I turned my back on him, and abruptly slammed an angry palm into the wall, suddenly furious at the position I had been thrust into. Clancy jumped slightly, startled.

I placed both of my fists on the wall at eye level, and rested my forehead against them. My tight pressed lips were contorted with anger. I did not want to look at Clancy as I spoke.

"How stupid can you be?" My quiet voice did little to mask my rage. Fury was poured into every boiling word.

"Sid, I said I'm sorry!"

"How stupid can you be?! Huh? Answer that!"

"I was stupid!"

"How stupid?"

"More than I ever have been before, okay?" he rasped. "Happy?"

I spun around and slammed myself into my chair, looking him right in the eye, with my palms pressed onto the surface of the wooden desk.

"Yeah, you were stupid!" I said in a rush of frustration. "We've been friends forever, and we've worked together for years. You're one of the best I've got here. And I believe you when you say you'd never do drugs at work, but you know what? My *belief* doesn't matter anymore! I'm your boss, but I'm also your friend. So, as a friend… I'm asking you to put in your two-week notice. Right now."

Clancy was appalled, his eyes and mouth wide open.

"Sid, please…. Is this really that big of a deal?"

"It's the hardest decision I've ever made here," I said stonily. "But, the decision's made, and two weeks is the offer on the table. You can put in your notice, or I can fire you now. Your choice."

"So, that's it?" Clancy was livid, as he leaned forward in his chair. I had never seen his face turn so red. "Almost six years here, and you want me to walk out? Just like *that*?"

I nodded. "Just like that."

"Six … *years*, Sid! This is my first mistake."

"And it's a doozy," I muttered. "Bad timing. Extremely bad, Clancy."

"I *know*! But it's a few grams, Sid! Everybody in this town does it, and I don't see *them* getting fired."

"They don't work for me," I said coldly.

"Sidney, this is not being fair! You're cracking down on *me*, since *you* hate drugs! Just because I use—"

"Just because you *bought*!" I yelled. "You purchased illegal narcotics, *in the workplace*! You were inside the building, *not* in the parking lot, not even on the back stairs! Is it *possible* for you to be that stupid? That *desperate*?"

"He's leaving town for the weekend, okay?" Clancy snapped his explanation. "I needed some lines for a party tonight."

"And Devon's your only possible supplier?" I demanded, incredulously. "There's a couple dozen dealers, at least. Are you telling me you have *loyalty* issues?"

"He's my friend! He gives me discounts. So, yes, he's my preferred source. In your own words, it's fiscally advantageous."

"Well, fiscally advantageous reasoning just sent you to the classifieds," I snarled, tapping a pen fitfully against my coffee mug.

Clancy was on his feet, and yelling back in my face. "I thought you were my friend!"

"I am. *That* is why I'm offering you an extra two weeks pay, instead of just kicking you out, right now. And you know that I would be perfectly justified in doing that."

"Sid!" He was angry, but now flustered as well.

"Sit, Clancy." I held my voice low again.

Clancy actually looked tired as he slumped back into the chair, his rage seeming to drain away as quickly as his energy. He shook his head, hopeless.

"This job is all I've got. It's all I've ever had, since high school."

"I know," I said, looking up at the ceiling, and shaking my head. "I'm sorry, too."

"Six ... *years* working together, Sid. And friends forever before that."

"Make your choice," I said, unflinching. "Two weeks, or I fire you. Not many workers on this planet ever get that choice."

He stiffened, and gave me a hard, heated stare.

"You really think you're better than me, don't you?"

"Choose."

"Not until I'm finished," he said firmly. "My job is over, either way, so the least you can do is hear me out."

I sighed heavily, then checked my watch.

"Two weeks," I said simply. "Two minutes. Even if I get mad, just say what you will. Go."

Clancy started. "I've used since junior high. The first few years, I was ashamed, so I hid it. I'd buy in secret, and use in secret. Around graduation, I took a good look around and realized that I was far from alone, and no one else seemed to care about hiding anymore. That's when I started the partying. Out of respect for your feelings, I never told you. I knew you'd judge me. I didn't want to end up on your hate list.

"Drugs are recreation for me, okay? They're peace. You take a walk down the streets of Vancouver, Toronto, and you'll see kids who are seriously strung-out junkies, and, for them, it's life. It's all they've got. I work for a living, I earn my keep, I pay my way, and you'll judge me as hard as you'd judge them?"

"Harder," I shot back. "Kids on the street don't care if drugs are killing them. They figure something else will get them first. You're not trying to relieve the pain of an impoverished life. You're just playing Russian roulette for kicks."

"Get real, Sid! Wake up! A few doobies, a couple lines. It's not heroin. Smoking a joint is not the same as putting a gun to my head!"

"Maybe you're not putting the gun to your own head. One minute."

Clancy snorted. "Oh, you *are* getting mad. You *really* think you're better than me."

"Fifty seconds."

"You think you're righteous, Sid? Huh? Holy? You go to church, don't use, don't drink, don't cuss, don't sleep around. But, so what? Look at you! Playing the goody-goody, 'I'm Sidney Myers, I'm perfect,' and yet you have more hate in your life than anyone else I know!"

"Time," I reminded him in a whisper, trying to bite back my temper.

"You say you love God, but you hate your neighbour," he murmured, almost smirking. I pressed my lips together to keep from shouting defiance at him, but my eyes were in flames.

"Five seconds." My voice was almost inaudible.

He smiled, without a trace of amusement in his eyes.

"I'll take the two weeks."

I leaned back in my swivel chair, and took a sip of two day old coffee.

"Take the rest of the day off," I instructed, emotionlessly. "You're in at three tomorrow."

He raised an eyebrow, and snorted derisively.

"Are you sure, Sid? It's Saturday."

"Get out."

Half an hour later, Kat came into my office to ask if Clancy had called in sick. Although I had intended to keep silent, I was frustrated, and ended up telling her everything, and then asked her not to tell anyone.

Kat was very surprised. She had not known that Clancy used drugs, either.

CHAPTER TWENTY-SIX

I was not in the mood for a wedding.

The hardest part of my life at that moment was trying to hide every aspect of it from Cindy. Yes, that meant that my line of communication with my sister was shutting down, but I kept telling myself that it was for her own good. Cindy was living in a love struck dreamworld, and, quite frankly, I wanted her and Boris to stay there for as long as possible. I did not want them to have the issues that I had. My assistant prep cook was leaving and participating in drug trade, and there was no way that I was going to let Cindy or Boris find out until after the wedding. I had not seen my sister so happy since before Dad was killed, and I was not going to risk having that joy taken away. I had seen too little joy in the past few years. Cindy was happy, and she was going to stay that way.

Actually, I had seen very little of Cindy for the past week, except at work. She and Boris spent every spare moment together, and I usually only caught glimpses of them as the Trans Am sped past the house or restaurant. That was just as well. Angel was the only person who could read my feelings better than my sister, so Cindy definitely would have known that something was wrong. I tried to keep her distracted, which was actually not all that difficult. We seemed to have different well-wishing friends over at the house every single day, so the air was never void of idle chit-chat and generic words of congratulations. That made it easier to avoid any meaningful conversations, which would have led to uncomfortable questions. I hated myself for doing that. Cindy was about to make the biggest change of her life. In a strange way, I felt that her marriage would be the end of our last fragment of childhood, a tiny, nostalgic piece of our younger days which we had secretly clung to throughout our adult years. I wanted to tell her how much she meant to me. I wanted her to know that her big brother would always be there for her, even if she and Boris eventually moved on to another town or province. I wanted to pour out my heart to her, all of my frustrations and fears, but I could not. For Cindy's sake, I still had to be strong, and, for the moment, that meant being evasive.

It was almost three days after Clancy put in his two weeks notice that I learned how dangerous it can be to always play the role of unwavering strength. Every person is possessed with both great strength, and great weakness. To ignore one in favour of the other creates an imbalance in our human nature. And that imbalance can be catastrophic.

I cannot even remember who was at our house on that cold Tuesday evening, around eleven o'clock. I remember that there were four of them, plus Boris and Cindy. Most likely they were old high school friends, but I do not remember anything else about them. I do not know why. All of us were gathered around the table, sipping hot chocolate. I kept my mouth shut, listening to the excited prattle about the wedding, allowing the joy in that dining room to seep into my parched heart. It felt good to just sit back and slurp down the marshmallows in my cocoa, watching everyone else being so happy.

I welcomed the distraction. For the past three days, all that I had been able to think about was Clancy and Devon Finn. Clancy and I had barely spoken since he left my office, although he had asked me not to tell anyone that he was quitting. He, too, was reluctant to dampen anyone's spirits, particularly because his last day of work was the Thursday before the wedding.

I wished that it did not have to be this way. Clancy was a lifelong friend, one of the closest that I had, in spite of our age difference of five years. I did not want him to leave, but his conscious actions could not be overlooked this time. As I sat at the table, a hundred memories of Clancy fought to resurface in my mind. I remembered an occasion five years earlier, when he and I had unknowingly asked out the same girl, who agreed to see both of us on the same night. I smiled as I remembered back about ten years before that, when Cindy and I had taught six-year-old Clancy how to ride horseback at our old acreage. He had been so thrilled and nervous that he could not stop giggling throughout the course of the trail ride.

I had recommended Clancy to Dad for employment, more than five years before. I had helped Clancy move into his new trailer after his parents and grandmother moved back to their hometown of Regina, Saskatchewan. I had rescued him and Angel from their disastrous final date. I had been his friend, and he had betrayed my trust. I could not imagine disregarding the value of trust in the manner that he had. It just did not make any sense. Even my closest friends could still be a mystery to me.

Devon Finn was a mystery, as well. I did not know him very well, and had not even when we were in school together. Rumour had it that his father, whose name I never did know, had been an alcoholic, a dope pusher, and a vicious wife-beater, and had died over a decade before, under suspicious circumstances. Devon was left alone to be raised by his mother, Amelia Redbird-Finn. I knew her better than I knew her son, and, even then, only because she had worked at the local drug store for as long as I could remember. People said that she was a sacrificial protector, one who would put her own face between Devon and his father's fist, selflessly and frequently putting herself in peril to protect the boy. That may have all been nothing but gossip, but, to me, she seemed like the type of woman who would do her absolute best to raise her son well. However, even that had not been enough to keep Devon from following in his father's footsteps. I had read that abused children often bond more strongly with the abusive parent, in an unconscious effort to win favour and love. I believe that this was the case with Devon, but, like I said, I never knew him well enough to be certain.

Perhaps it was the swirl of shocking rumours about his past that kept me from ever hating Devon. I absolutely despised most drug dealers, but I could only ever feel sorry for Devon. He never seemed like an enemy. He was just another imperfect human being, one who made mistakes like everybody else. It was obvious that he loved his own children, and even seemed to treat his common-law wife, Debbie Browning, quite well, although she always struck me as being the most despondent woman that I had ever seen. I think she hated what Devon did for a living, but stayed with him for the sake of their children.

Drug dealers in Chetwynd often attained such a degree of notoriety as to become borderline celebrities, particularly popular amongst young people. To be invited to a crack party at a dealer's house was an honour badge to many teenagers. The police and drug awareness programs did their best to bring some amount of order into the chaos, and drug busts were common. However, few of these operations were successful in the area of deterrence. Drug dealers were rebels, and young people worshipped rebels. The drugs that were sold were dangerous, which made them intriguing and irresistible. Perhaps those were some of the reasons why Devon had begun trafficking. He longed for the adoration, and the danger.

All of these notions and ponderings were abstractly wandering through my head, as I tuned out the chatter of my guests that night. In fact, I was so absorbed by my thoughts that I did not realize that my cell phone was ringing, until Cindy, seated across the table from me, ventured, "Are you going to answer that?" I started, and sheepishly excused myself from the table, stepping into the front porch before answering the phone, silencing the *Bee Gees* jingle with the press of a button.

"Hello," I said brightly, trying to sound jovial and matrimonial.

There was silence on the other end of the line for a long time, but I could hear heavy breathing. The voice which finally spoke was so low and laboured that I could not even tell if it was male or female.

"No one cares, Sidney. Nobody." The voice sent a chill shiver down the back of my neck. It was known to me, familiar, but there was something very wrong with it. I could hear an almost unfathomable pain in every syllable.

"Hello?" I said carefully, brows furrowed, perplexed.

"They cared. Before. So did you. You used to care. But … everyone stays away now…. They don't talk about it. You don't care, Sidney. I still do."

"Who is this?" I demanded. "Is this a joke?"

The voice droned on as though I had not said a word.

"It is a long time. Not long enough, though. To everyone else, it's just one year later than last year. Next year, too. Next year's a year later than that. Years … they're so long. They're just ring around the rosy to you. Just going around the sun. Three years … around the sun. I'm the only one who cares."

There was a long moment of breathing, each gasp sounding more ragged than the last. I did not know what to say, but my stomach had already knotted up tightly. The voice was so known to me, yet it was not the same. It was not right, and had begun to grow shakier.

381

"What happened, Sidney? Why'd you forget? You forgot … to care. You shouldn't. He wouldn't have forgotten. Not ever. Friends … they remember. Care. They help."

"Friends remember?" I said puzzled. "Remember what? Who is this, and what am I supposed to remember?"

There were tears in the voice now. Bitter, confused tears. "I'm tired … so tired…. It's not good here. I need to always remember, always care. Death…. I can't let it win. Can't."

"Look, I don't know who you are," I said slowly, my low, even tone covering up the fact that my mind was racing frantically, "but if you're planning to … hurt yourself…. Please, just talk to me. What do you need? Is there any way I can help?"

"No one helped."

"Then let me, now. Please. Just tell me who you are."

"No one could help. They couldn't. I couldn't! Just like Karl. You couldn't help then. Not him, either. You just watched. You all did. And now…. Too late. Late for us. No one's coming back." The voice broke into sobs.

Ask questions, Myers! Keep talking.

"Listen to me," I said, slowly and emphatically. "*What* … did I watch? Why is it too late?"

"You knew then…." As the voice trailed off, there were more sobs, but, in between them, I eventually caught one word, whispered so quietly that, at first, I thought it was simply background noise.

"Roger…. Roger!"

Horror crept over me as I realized what was happening, already imagining the worst.

Too late?

"Kat?" I asked, with quiet astonishment. "Kat? Are you still there?"

"Three years!" Her voice was still shaky, and seemed to be getting weaker by the second. "Today, three.... Too long, and no one cares.... I know you're happy. So happy...."

Roger MacDonnell died three years ago today....

"Kat, what's wrong?" I asked urgently, my voice rising involuntarily. "Are you okay?" She did not sound drunk. There was something much worse in her voice than alcohol.

"Sidney...."

She was pleading with me. I did not know what she wanted.

"I think ... too much.... Too ... many.... Please, Sid...."

"Kat!" I barked, frightened. "Listen to me! *What's ... wrong?*" There was no answer. Even the breathing was barely audible now.

"Kat, talk to me! Tell me what's wrong!"

Silence.

"*Kat!*" I looked sharply at the call display. She was calling from home.

"KAT!" There was no sound. Everyone in the next room had stopped talking, in an attempt to figure out what I was shouting about. There was absolute silence.

"*Shit!*" I hissed, grabbing a jacket from the pegboard, and hitting the door to the garage at a flat out run.

The drive to Kat's apartment usually took me six or seven minutes. That night, I made it there in less than three, shouting a few directions and scattered bits of information to a 911 operator. I slammed the truck into park, right in front of the glass-doored entrance, and shoulder slammed the sticky driver side door. It popped open with such force that the hinges screamed and banged. I punched in the entrance code on the keypad next to the door, and took the stairs to the second floor three at a time. An old man was easing his way down the staircase, leaning heavily on the railing, and probably thought that I was the rudest man in the world for shoving past him without slowing. I did not even have time to care.

Kat's door was unlocked, almost as though she was expecting me. I burst in without knocking, and began frenziedly looking around the kitchen and dining room. I could not see anyone.

"Kat?" I called hoarsely, still winded from my dash up the stairs. "Kat, where are you?!" I ran into the living room and hit the light switch. At first, I thought that the room was vacant as well, until I glanced over at the treadmill, partially blocked from view by the sofa. That was when I saw her bare foot.

Kat was in a fetal position on the carpet, between the sofa and treadmill. She wore only a pale blue nightgown, and her loose black hair covered most of her face, but I could still see the tear streaks running down her cheeks as I dropped to my knees beside her. She was so still, and that terrified me.

I was still holding my phone, and she was clutching hers, the receiver beeping audibly from being off the hook too long. On the coffee table, an expensive bottle of Dom Perignon stood uncorked, beside two tall wine glasses, one full, the other nearly empty. Next to them, a small plastic bag lay open on the chessboard, filled with a glittering white substance, almost like clear sand. A spoon was set on top of the bag.

"KAT!" I shouted, placing a hand under her cheek, and turning her face toward mine. Her head and neck were limp, and weighed heavily in my hands. Her entire body was limp.

Kat was not breathing.

CHAPTER TWENTY-SEVEN

The longest hours of my life have been spent in a hospital.

Some people have sat in hospitals waiting nervously for joyful news. "It's a boy," or, "The operation was a success. She's going to be fine." Then, there were people like me, who sat impatiently in waiting rooms, praying that our loved one would even survive. The only good news I could hope for was "She'll live." Even that was only good news, not joyful news. The gladness felt over not losing another friend would only be diminished as I helplessly tried to figure out what I should have done to prevent this. The cause of Kat's actions would torment me for a long time. Torment was all that my heart would allow. Joy was not an option.

Kat's a user, too? Is there anyone else I should know about?

I do not know how many hours I sat silently in that unpadded seat in the empty waiting room, staring at the covers of old magazines, never picking up a single one. My entire being was awash in guilt and grief. How could I have missed it? How could I not have known how much pain Kat must have lived with? She was so strong to the naked eye, but, in my heart, I should have known what she was going through. We were the same. We both tried to be strong for the benefit of the loved ones around us. We tried to ease their pain, but never really dealt with our own. Besides that, Kat had lost someone who was even closer to her than my father was to me. I was a fool to believe that she was that strong. No one could be that resilient to pain, not if they truly loved the one they had lost. Roger MacDonnell had been Kat's entire world. I should have known.

The ticks of the clock on the wall seemed to be minutes apart. I must have sat there for at least two or three hours, but I never actually looked up at the clock or down at my watch. I just sat and stared, gazing vacantly, and seeing absolutely nothing. All I could do was remember the last time that I had been in this building. Nearly five years ago, I had awoken here, with Cindy weeping at my bedside. Looking down the corridor, I could even see the recovery room I had been in. But now, there was no knot in my stomach. My stomach felt empty, just like the rest of my body and soul. I was alone. The lone nurse with the short grey hair and large glasses behind the reception desk, who never once looked up from her paperwork, was no company. The bustling world of humanity was far away from me, with its billions of people who did not know the name of Katherine Moira MacDonnell. Billions of people who would not care, even if they did know. I wanted to hate them all for their ignorance, but I could not. I was too tired.

"Mr. Myers?"

A doctor was talking to me, a tall, bearded Inuit man in his fifties, with short-cropped black hair and a clipboard in his hands. I had not even noticed him approaching, and now that he was standing before me, speaking my name, all that I could do at first was wonder what was written on his board.

"Yes, sir," I replied dully, standing and stretching stiff muscles. For some reason, I almost said, "May I take your order?"

"I'm Dr. Jacobs," he said in a low, soothing voice, which I was certain had been perfected over many years of dealing with agitated, frightened people like me. "You came in with Katherine. You're a friend?"

"Is she okay?" I thought that my heart would not beat again until he gave me an affirmative reply.

"She's still under observation," he said. "We'll keep a close eye on her until morning, but she should be all right. We got to her in time."

"I'm sorry," I clarified, fidgeting. "What…. What do you mean? What kind of observation?"

"Just monitoring her vital systems, making sure that everything is still running strong," he assured me. "Her heart rate is almost back to normal. She'll need a lot of rest, but the real danger is past."

I closed my eyes, wanting to hug this perfect stranger in front of me. For the first time in hours, I began to feel calmer. "Thank you," I said quietly. "Very much, thank you."

"I just need to ask you a few more questions," he said, unclipping the pen from the top of the board. "Just for clarification. You said you found her on the floor, correct?"

"She called me," I said, having a hard time remembering even the simplest details. "I know her voice. Something was wrong, so I went to her place and found her."

"When she talked to you, what struck you as odd, specifically?"

"Kat is fluent, always. She loves the English language. I've only heard her get … a bit incoherent when things are going wrong. When she called, she was … gone. She was talking in a really strained voice, and what she said…. It was all jumbled. Sad, and angry. It took me forever to make any sense out of it. That's what really scared me. Kat knows how to talk. And, suddenly … she couldn't."

"You didn't wait for the ambulance. Why was that?"

I shook my head. "I saw the bag and a bottle of wine, and Kat …. I thought she wasn't breathing. I tried CPR, but those drugs … whatever they were, I thought they might … you know, do something to her heart. All I could think was that I had to get her here."

"You carried her?"

"To my truck. Then I called here again while I was driving."

Dr. Jacobs was constantly writing on his clipboard.

"Does Katherine … have a history of drug use? Any at all?"

I did not know what to say. I barely knew how to speak at that point.

"I don't know," I admitted, flustered. "I didn't think so, but … Doc, you think that you know someone, and

389

then you don't, and you don't know what to … what to believe, or think. It's just...." My voice trailed off, my mouth unable to form another word.

"You've never seen her take drugs before?" he said, slowly and clearly.

"I just saw the bag on the table. I gave it to…. I don't even remember. A nurse or a paramedic, or someone. I can't remember."

The doctor smiled slightly. "You gave it to me, Mr. Myers."

"Did I?" I was an official basket case.

"Are you all right, Mr. Myers? Would you like us to call anyone?"

I had not made any phone calls yet. Calling someone had not even occurred to me. Now it was very late, much too late to make distressing phone calls.

"No, I'll take care of it," I said, not sounding very dependable. "That bag was not coke. I know that much. What was it?"

"Mr. Myers, you seem to believe that Katherine was not a habitual user. I believe that she did not even know *how* to use the drugs. I have seen drug overdoses frequently in first-time users, especially unsupervised ones. They often purchase or receive the drugs, and then try them out alone, at home. People tempted to use for the first time, especially to treat a secret pain, often want to keep it a secret, out of shame. They do not even seek advice on how the drug is designed to be used. To them, a spoonful appears no more harmful than a spoon of sugar. Many do not realize how sensitive the dosages can be until it is too late."

"I saw a spoon," I remembered. "It was on top of the bag. I figured she had smoked off it."

"Did you see matches, or a lighter?" he inquired, raising an eyebrow.

"I…. Ah heck, I don't remember. Crap, I'm sorry."

"It's okay," he said placatingly. "Perhaps a different sense would help. People often remember what they smell better than what they see, hear, or feel. Did you smell anything? Perhaps a smoky, sweetish smell?"

"Swedish?"

"*Sweet,*" he enunciated.

"Oh … um…." I tried to think hard, to focus my thoughts on my sense of smell. Kat's apartment had seemed normal in every way. That was odd, now that I thought about it. "No. I didn't smell anything."

"Was there a fan on, or a window open?"

"No." I was fairly certain of that. "I couldn't hear a fan, and it's too cold to have a window open. The room was nice and warm."

Dr. Jacobs nodded knowingly. "That's what I thought. It would have been quite difficult for Kat to overdose on a smoked dosage, and, even if she had managed it, the room would have been rank with the smoke."

"Doc, what was it?" I said. "I touched her face when I started the CPR…. Her skin was absolutely on fire."

"That is called hyperthermia," he explained. "Drugs of this sort accelerate the cardiovascular system to a dangerous level when used in such high quantities, or when taken from a particularly potent batch. Body temperature rises, and, if not treated immediately, convulsions can begin, which can lead to a coma, or death. We had to give Katherine an ice bath to get her body back to a safe temperature. But she may have been within minutes of requiring medical anti-convulsant treatment when you found her. I am surprised that she was even able to call you at that stage."

"What was it?" I repeated.

"We'll need to run tests to be certain," he reminded me, "but, based on visual identification, Katherine's symptoms, and the apparent lack of smoke … I believe that she orally ingested crystal methamphetamine."

"*Meth?!*"

He nodded grimly. "Most likely, she used the spoon to try to eat it, but found it too bitter. She probably mixed it into the wine after that. Either way, she did not know what she was doing, which leads me to believe that she was a first time user. You told the attendant that she lost family?"

"Her husband. It was three years ago today…. Well, yesterday. No one else remembered."

"I'm sorry."

"You said she *ate it?*"

"I believe so. Or drank it. Meth dissolves instantly in liquid, which would explain the wine."

"Couldn't she have snorted it?"

"She wouldn't have needed a spoon for that. Besides, I checked her nasal cavities. They were clear. Believe me. She ingested it."

"How much?"

"All I can tell you at this point is 'too much.' Ingestion takes much longer for the rush to hit, as it can take twenty minutes or so to access the blood stream. Some inexperienced users think the delay means that it isn't working, so they take more. Smoked or injected dosages give a rush almost immediately, and are easier to measure the intake amount. If she had known anything about crank, she never would have ingested it without careful measurement. This *was* her first time, and could have been her last."

"It had better be her last," I muttered.

"Well, she is fortunate to have a friend who can read her voice over the phone. Very fortunate." He held out his hand. "Thank you, Mr. Myers. I am sure the police will need to take a statement from you as well. I did have to inform them."

"I figured as much," I said miserably, shaking his hand. "Thanks again. Can I see her?"

He hesitated. "I don't think visitors would be a good idea just yet. Katherine needs complete rest."

"Doc, please. Just for a minute. She's a life friend."

"Katherine's heart almost stopped, Mr. Myers," Dr. Jacobs' voice was unflinching. "Her entire cardio system is recovering, but it is still weakened. Even an emotional reunion could upset the healing process at this point."

"Of course, I'm sorry," I sighed, rubbing my sore, bleary eyes. I needed a coffee.

"Don't be," he said kindly, putting a hand on my shoulder. "You saved her life."

Sidney the hero....

"Who has meth in a town this size?" I intoned, to no one in particular. "I thought that was a big city drug."

Dr. Jacobs gave a brief chuckle. "That's a question for the police, not me. But I can tell you this. Methamphetamine is completely synthetic. Any kid with a stockpile of cold medication, some ether, and a coffeepot can cook up that nasty stuff."

Only one name was immediately in my head.

Devon Finn ... a chemistry whiz with no ambitions except being a wannabe dope pusher....

Well, it seemed that Clancy had been right. Devon's business was expanding.

Dr. Jacobs had just one more question.

"What was the wine?"

"Sorry?"

"The wine on the table. Did you notice what kind it was?"

"Actually, yes," I said, suddenly surprised. I had known instantly what that bottle was. "It was the Dom Perignon. I recognized it. Roger gave it to her on their first anniversary. It was like thirty years old, from a collector he knew. Kat said she would never drink it, it was too valuable. She was going to keep it forever."

"But she was drinking it?"

"It was open...." A sudden fear hit me. *"Why?* Why would you want to know that?!"

"Perignon is celebratory, Mr. Myers," he said soothingly. "If she was trying to feel better, perhaps she simply wanted to make her first drug use more enjoyable, a festive occasion to ease the pain in her heart."

Or maybe she wanted to leave us a sign that she was ready to go....

The rest of the night was a sleepy blur. A young RCMP constable, Maurice Goodman, arrived to ask me most of the questions that Dr. Jacobs already had, but he also wanted to know if I had any idea as to who Kat's supplier was. I told him that I honestly did not know, that this was the first time I had even been aware of her drug use. I do not think that he believed me, but he definitely seemed disturbed by the fact that crystal meth was being locally distributed. I wondered if this was the first time that it had shown up in Chetwynd.

"Tina's in town," he muttered with a thick Quebec accent. "There goes the neighbourhood."

After thanking me for my cooperation, Constable Goodman asked Dr. Jacobs when he could talk to Kat. The doctor gave him the same answer that he had given me. Kat would have no visitors until she was fully rested. Then they both told me that I should go home and get some sleep, and that I would be immediately contacted if there were any developments. My response was to sit back in that hard chair and ask if they had any coffee available. I was not leaving.

I sat in that hospital all night long. Occasionally, I would start to doze off for a few minutes, but mostly I just sat and flipped through old fishing magazines. New doctors and nurses arrived as morning drew nearer. Eventually, a handful of patients began to come in for early appointments, but it was not until nearly ten o'clock that I went outside to deeply breathe the cold, fresh air in the parking lot, and watch the late sunrise. It was a beautiful time of the morning, and I wished so badly that Kat could be standing next to me, watching those first golden rays melting away the redness of the eastern horizon over the frosted blue mountains.

God, help.

It was the shortest prayer my mind had ever petitioned God with, but I knew that He understood.

It was a cold sunrise, but I could not help feeling just a little warmer.

Of course, I still had calls to make, but I had no idea who to call first. Kat's parents in Red Deer seemed like an obvious choice, but I did not know if hospital protocol required the doctors to call them, so it was possible that they already knew. Boris and Cindy would have wondered where I had gone, but, as it was a Wednesday, they would most likely still be asleep for a couple more hours. For some reason as I stood there in the parking lot, glaring at the cell phone in my cold and clumsy fingers, I was unable to come to any decision. Never before had I hated the telephone so much. I put it back in my pocket without calling anyone.

After a few more chilly minutes, Dr. Jacobs walked out the front entrance in a heavy red jacket, stood next to me, and lit a cigarette, after waiting for my permissive nod. Perhaps my exhaustion was to blame, but I found the sight of a doctor smoking to be so ironic as to produce a few chuckles. The doctor grinned, pocketing his lighter, the cigarette clenched between his incisors.

"We all have our vices," he said. "I spend my life telling children to never do what I'm standing here doing."

I nodded. "Mine would have to be coffee. I'm probably more addicted to it than a lot of people are to drugs or alcohol." I covered a yawn with a fist, and fitfully scratched my hair. "Why do you think that is, Doctor? Why do we … get involved with the things that we all know are eventually going to control us?"

He shook his head and took a long drag from the cigarette, slowly whistling the smoke back into the chill air. "Almost every addiction starts as a solution to some daily issue that we want to deal with, but don't know how. We don't like getting up early, so we start drinking coffee to help wake us up faster. We get headaches from the stress of our jobs or our relationships, so we sooth ourselves with cigarettes, or a beer after work, or something else that helps to alter our way of looking at life. Then we feel better, until the caffeine, or nicotine, or alcohol wears away. Some people are smart enough to know then that they need something else to solve their problems, and it's usually some personal, emotional component that's missing. They get their lives figured out, and make the best of them, but the rest of us.... We just need something else to look forward to, rather than being content with the present. Sometimes the buzz, the rush, is the only thing we have."

I looked out over the evergreen treetops at the rising sun in the pale grey sky.

"And it becomes our reason for getting up in the morning," I sighed. "That's not good enough."

The doctor shrugged his shoulders dismissively. "That's the funny thing about humans. We're the only species on the planet who will readily settle for 'not good enough.'" He took one more deep inhalation, the cigarette tip flaring up into a glowing red as it was turned into a long, suspended ash. The doctor then flicked it expertly into a nearby ashtray.

"Nice shot," I commented.

"You want some advice?" he said casually, jamming his chilled, clammy hands into his jacket pockets.

"Hey, you're the doctor," I said wryly.

"Go home. Katherine will probably be fairly well rested by this afternoon. You can come back and see her this evening. Get some breakfast, get some sleep."

I hesitated, looking at my parked truck, the windows adorned with the works of Jack Frost, and then back at the glass doors leading back to the waiting room.

"I don't want to leave her," I admitted. "Ever."

"She's fine," he said flatly. "Vital signs are strong, cardio is almost normal, temperature is healthy. She's just sleeping. She needs the rest, and so do you. Go home. Doctor's orders."

I gave an acceptant nod and slowly trudged across the parking lot, yanking the driver side door open.

"Did you know I once had a snake living in this truck?" I called back over my shoulder. "I thought my life was weird *then.*"

I could hear the doctor give a short, bemused laugh as I wearily climbed into the cab.

"Go home, Mr. Myers."

"Thanks for everything," I said loudly, firing the ignition and slamming the door.

Wednesdays shouldn't have to be like this, Myers.

My house was still dark and silent when I entered the porch, letting my brown winter coat slip off my shoulders, onto the floor. The dining room was quite the opposite of the bright, vibrant atmosphere I had bolted from the night before. My mug of cocoa was still sitting on the table, stone cold, with a sticky mat of melted marshmallow over the surface. It was not coffee, but I still downed the whole mug in one long, sweet slurp, and then slowly walked upstairs to Cindy's room. She would still be sleeping, but I needed to see her.

Her door was open, and I could just see the top of her tussled blonde head protruding from the pile of warm blankets which covered most of her face. I walked in quietly and knelt by her bedside. Her even breathing was the only sound in the drape darkened room. I watched her sleep for a moment, and then began gently stroking her hair. She stirred in her sleep, and muttered something tired and nonsensical.

"Hey, baby sister," I murmured, pulling the comforter down over the tip of her nose with one finger. One of her sleepy blue eyes slid open, and looked up at me.

"Where'd you go, Sidney?" she mumbled, still half asleep.

"I had to go see Kat," I said. "Wake up, okay? I need to talk to you."

"Is Kat okay?" Cindy asked groggily. "We just heard you yelling at someone on the phone."

"Kat … Kat's fine," I assured her. "She just needed some attention, I guess."

"So … you yelled at her?"

"I didn't mean to."

"Sid, what's wrong?" she asked, pushing herself up until she was sitting against the headboard, blinking sleep out of her blue eyes.

"I love you, baby sister," I whispered, trying to swallow the lump in my throat. "You know that, don't you?"

Cindy looked at me, surprised.

"Of course," she said slowly.

"I am so happy for you," I choked out. "Your happiness…. That's all I've ever wanted for you. I'm proud of you. You and Boris. Dad's proud of you. I just wanted you to know that. And I will always be here for you, for both of you. If you don't want to stay at the shop, if you need to move on … I'll always still be here."

"I love you, too, Sid," she said, quite puzzled. "Did something happen last night?"

I blinked a tear back, and nodded. Cindy looked alarmed.

"Sid, tell me."

I reached out my hand and cupped her warm cheek in it. She put her hand over mine, and squeezed it, beginning to be afraid.

"Kat had an accident last night," I said hoarsely, mist settling into my eyes. "But she's fine now." My voice broke, unable to hold steady for a moment longer.

"Sid…."

I closed my eyes as the first tears began to roll down my cheeks.

"She's going to be fine," I sobbed, almost trying to convince myself.

For the first time in years, I really cried. Cindy pulled me into her arms, comforting me as I wept until I had no more tears to shed.

I would never have believed how relieving it was to let someone else be strong for me. Just for those few minutes, I was weaker than any baby, and I have never known such peace.

CHAPTER TWENTY-EIGHT

I never did make any calls that morning. I decided that Kat was going to get better, and that informing anyone else of what had happened would be entirely her decision to make.

Of course, I could not sleep after I got home. I was too tired. Actually, absolute exhaustion is a better term for how I felt. Sleep was not possible.

Cindy had no problem with making up for lost sleep. After we had talked for nearly an hour, I went downstairs to watch some TV and eat breakfast, while Cindy fell right back asleep, and did not emerge from her room until Boris came to pick her up around one o'clock in the afternoon. I did not know where they were going, but I needed the time to be alone, and they both knew that. They had agreed to not let word get out about Kat's condition for the time being.

Meanwhile, Kat slumbered on in the hospital. At four o'clock, I called to inquire after her. The nurse who answered told me that Kat had awoken briefly a few hours earlier, but had only said a few tired words to a doctor before dozing off again. She had said that she felt "sick, but okay." She also asked how she had gotten there.

The day passed slowly. Nobody called, or stopped by to visit. I just sat on the couch, vacantly watching the movie channel. It was not until seven-thirty that the exhaustion of my previous, sleepless, thirty-six hours finally caught up with me. Toward the end of *To Kill A Mockingbird*, quite possibly my favourite movie of all time, my eyelids were weighted down, and I was asleep before I could find out whether or not the young Robert Duvall managed to save Jem and Scout again.

When the phone next to my elbow on the lamp table startled me awake, it was pitch black outside once again, probably almost ten o'clock, although I could not see my watch. I sat up groggily, and answered it.

"By The Slice." My voice was a croaky whisper.

"Mr. Sidney Myers?" I recognized the voice of Dr. Jacobs.

"Yes."

"Katherine is awake. She says that she will not talk to anyone until she has seen you."

My deep sigh was a mixture of weariness and sweet relief.

"Tell her I'll be there in five minutes."

When I got back to the hospital, I was told that Kat had been moved to a room of her own, and was waiting for me. As I followed the nurse's direction down the hall, I was surprised to see that Constable Goodman was already there, talking quietly with Dr. Jacobs outside the closed door to Kat's room. They spotted me as I approached, and the young police officer motioned for me to join them. He looked upset, his thin lips pressed tightly together, arms crossed.

"Katherine says that she will talk to us," he said, "but not until she has spoken to you in private, Mr. Myers. Do you have any idea why?"

I could understand that the constable had a job to do, but I was still exhausted, and his impatient tone irked me.

"Because I'm her boss," I said irritably. "Who do *you* call when you get in trouble? Just give me a few minutes."

"Be calm," Dr. Jacobs advised me. "If you get her excited or antagonized, I will have you removed."

"I understand," I acknowledged. "I'm too tired to be excitable."

When I first entered the room and saw Kat, I could not be sure that it was really her. Her face was deathly pale, and an IV line was feeding fluid into the back of her hand. Her black hair was tangled and hanging loose over the shoulders of her green hospital gown. Even her eyes were not as they should have been, sunken and bloodshot, with dark, puffy eyelids. Her lips were chapped, and her tired tongue kept trying to lick some moisture back into them. Every small movement she made seemed more like an involuntary spasm. In spite of it all, she managed a weak smile when she saw me.

"Hey, Sid." She spoke in a quavery whisper, as though she had just awoken from a bad dream. Her hands were trembling, but she did not seem to notice.

"You almost missed our Wednesday chess match," I said with a quiet smile, sitting in the chair beside her bed.

She actually chuckled a little. "You'll never win anyway, cowboy. You're good at math, but you're just not that good." She held her hand out to me, and I held it firmly between both of mine. Kat was trying not to cry, and trying to sit up. "It's okay," I shushed her, placing a gentle hand on her shoulder and applying just enough pressure to ease her back down to the pillow. "Don't try to get up. It's over. You're going to be fine. And you're not supposed to get upset or excited, so just relax. I'm here."

"I wasn't going to…. You know…." Kat tried to persuade me. "I mean, I wasn't trying to—"

"I know," I said soothingly. "I know. You were just hurting. You wanted the pain to go away. No one can blame you for that."

"You came for me?" She could not remember.

"Yeah, I brought you here." I nodded.

"Was I …?"

"You were sleeping," I said coolly. "You needed a rest."

"I'm so sorry, Sid." In spite of her best efforts, tears were beginning to slide down into her ears. "I'm sorry."

I closed my eyes.

"You scared me, Kat." Kat's eyes were brimming as she turned away to stare out of her dark window, settling her tired head back into the pillow.

"I'm tired of being strong, Sid. I'm just so tired…."

"It's okay to be tired," I said. "I'm tired of it, too. That's why you're here. You are going to stay here until you are strong enough to be strong again. I'm the only one who needs to apologize. I'm sorry I never helped you carry your pain. I should have helped you to cry."

"You were always there, Sid," she whispered, so quietly that I could barely make out the words. "This is not you... not your fault.... My bad...."

"There's a man outside," I said quietly, trying to distract her. "He needs to talk to you."

"That cute cop?"

I smiled wryly. "The cute cop, yeah."

"I figured he would," she sighed. "Oh, crap. Am I in trouble?"

"I don't know," I admitted. "Not as much as whoever sold you the stuff, most likely."

There was a strangely uncomfortable silence, before I ventured, "So ... who?"

Kat groaned, and placed a hand over her eyes, rubbing the tears away with her thumb and forefinger.

"Please don't ask me that," she sobbed quietly. "Not now. Please, not now."

"Was it meth?" I asked, puzzled by her secrecy. "Is that what they gave you? Crystal meth?"

She nodded. "He.... The guy said it had helped him when his ... well, to get over loss. I didn't know how to take it."

"Kat...." I was hesitant to ask this question, but it was one that had been gnawing at me all day. "Did Clancy know?"

Kat looked at me with an expressionless, misty-eyed, face.

"I'm ready to talk to the cop." Her response was curious, but I slowly stood and turned toward the door. I did not want to upset her by pressing the matter.

"Hey, Sid?"

I looked back at her, lying there so helplessly. She gave a teary smile.

"Thanks," she quavered softly. "I'm alive."

"Never ... again," I said coldly.

She nodded, jerkily.

"Never again."

There was a chair in the hall near her door. After Dr. Jacobs and Constable Goodman went into the room, I slumped down into it, feeling more exhausted than ever. It was not my intention to eavesdrop, but I realized that I could make out their words from where I sat.

The first to speak was the constable. He was introducing himself, and saying that he was glad to hear that she would be well soon. Kat's response was unintelligible, but sounded like a thank-you.

"Katherine, it is my sincerest wish that you will help me find out who hurt you like this," Goodman said. "The drugs you took are very dangerous. They could hurt other people as well. Many other people."

"I know," Kat said. "It was a stupid thing to do."

"I understand," the constable said kindly. "I know about your husband. I'm very sorry for your loss."

"Thank you."

"Katherine, you are not a drug user. You are no addict, and you're not reckless. You were desperate. This was your first time, wasn't it?"

"Yes. It was."

"I do not want anyone else to be hurt by this drug. Will you tell me where you got it?"

Kat sighed, but did not reply.

"Please, Katherine. You can stop this drug. We can end it right now."

"I don't know where it's from."

My heart almost stopped.

"What?" Goodman was not getting the answer that he had hoped for.

"I'm sorry. I didn't buy it. I just found it."

"You found it?" The skepticism in Goodman's voice was unmasked.

"Yeah. Found it." Kat's voice was becoming slow and thick from exhaustion. "There's a bench. It's the one by ... the drug store. I was walking last night, thinking about Roger, and I saw the bag under it when I sat down. Old Rob Gorman and a few other drunks have fallen asleep there. I've seen them.... I thought it must have fallen out of someone's pocket. I was so sad ... I just took it home. It was stupid."

"So," the young officer said slowly, "you have no idea who it came from? No idea?"

"I'm sorry. I don't know."

Kat, what are you doing? Tell them!

"Katherine ... I certainly hope that you are not trying to protect anyone. Your loyalty would be very misplaced. I have known many drug dealers. Not many would do the same for you. Are you positive that a drug dealer is worth it?"

"I would not protect a dealer," Kat's tired voice managed to sound firm. "I consider them a low form of life."

"You're sure?" Goodman was letting a slight amount of his frustration seep into his voice.

"I'm sure. I wish I could help more."

"No, that's … quite all right," Goodman sighed. "Thank you for your cooperation. I do hope that you have a speedy recovery. By the way…." I could hear him fumbling around, apparently finding a card to give her. "If you do happen to think of anything else, I would be only too happy to talk to you again. Please, call anytime."

By then, I was already striding rapidly toward the exit. Kat had just verified my darkest suspicions.

Clancy Grover lived in a rented mobile home in the Evergreen Trailer Court, at the opposite end of town. I left the hospital and drove to his home, easing into his muddy driveway at just after ten-thirty.

You have some explaining to do, friend.

Every light in the brown trailer was shining brightly onto the brown, winter-killed grass in the front lawn, and the driveway was crowded with three cars and Clancy's beloved truck.

It was a Wednesday evening. Clancy was hosting a party. I could see people moving around inside, most of them carrying beer bottles. One of the girls, a pretty redhead who looked to be no more than sixteen, appeared in the living room window, wearing cutoff blue jeans and a white tank-top. She held a beer bottle in each hand, and seemed to be dancing with herself. As I watched through my windshield, Clancy danced into view in his favourite Vancouver Canucks jersey, just long enough to twirl the girl into an embrace, and then kissed her back out of sight.

You charmer. You tried so hard to get Kat to go out with you. Did you think this would win her over, or did you really think you were doing her a favour?

I shut off the ignition and switched off the headlights. Even from the driveway with my windows rolled up, I could hear pounding rap music reverberating out of Clancy's trailer. His party was in full swing. I wondered if it was a birthday celebration for someone, or just another excuse to get drunk.

You covered well.... Never came in late, pupils were never dilated. He's one of the best I've ever had in there.

For a good twenty minutes, I could do nothing but sit in the darkness and stare over the steering wheel at the trailer. With the engine off, the cab began to cool down, and condensation began misting the outer edges of the windows. My hands were getting cold, but I was not ready to move just yet. At one point, Clancy's roommate, Marty Collings, a tall, flabby twenty-year-old with a blonde brush-cut, staggered out onto the frosty wraparound deck, wearing only a muscle shirt and boxer shorts, and vomited over the railing, but he did not even notice me before lurching back inside.

You should have just told me, Clancy. You did your job. You were a friend. I wouldn't have fired you for using. I could have helped you. But, you had to go and buy the stuff at work....

Even over the blaring music, I could hear drunken war-whoops, laughter, and the occasional burst of profanity laden rhyme. Freestyle rap contests had become something of a rage amongst the young people of Chetwynd, and most of them were truly painful to listen to.

Clancy Grover.... My friend. My friend who almost killed my friend.

409

I sighed heavily as I bashed my door open and climbed out of the truck, but, once I actually began moving, there was no turning back. I slammed the door shut, and stormed up the creaky wooden steps of the trailer. I never bothered to knock. Clancy never knocked when he burst into my office, and now it was my turn to return the lack of basic courtesy. I just swung the front door wide, and strode in. The building was rank with smoke and the smell of booze, and the music was positively deafening. Clancy and half a dozen friends, some of them no older than fifteen, were gathered around the coffee table in the dimly-lit, cluttered living room. A large red bong was being passed among the guests, while Clancy himself was kissing the pretty redhead in an armchair. I did not know who she was. I did not care.

No one even noticed me until I had crossed to the far side of the room and jerked the plug for the screaming sound system right out of the wall, killing the blaring amplifiers. Silence fell over the room, but only for a brief, heavenly second.

"Hey!" Marty protested. "What gives?"

"Turn it back on!" A short, heavyset blonde girl screamed angrily. Clancy was glaring at me, but I was in no mood to back down.

"Everyone, except Clancy, get out," I ordered loudly, my unflinching stare locked on Clancy's face.

"Whatever!" a large, well-muscled young man with a bleached Mohawk yelled. "Turn the music back on!"

"The music is off," I said. "Get out."

"Who the hell do you think you are?!" Clancy's redhead demanded, twisting around in his lap to glower at me.

"I'm your boyfriend's boss," I replied. "Get out."

"We're not at work, Sid." Clancy sounded more annoyed than angry.

"You get out!" Marty snapped, slamming his beer bottle onto the table.

"You don't get to give the orders tonight, boy," I said coldly. "Get out. *Now.*"

"Who you calling *boy*?!" Marty was livid as he lunged to his feet and began stumbling drunkenly toward me, arms held out from his sides like an Old West gunfighter. "Huh? You wanna call me that again?!"

"Get out of my face and *get out!*" I snarled, not moving a muscle.

"Screw you!"

"Leave, *boy!*" I was feeling fairly reckless by then.

Please take a swing at me. Just try it....

Marty probably would have taken a drunken swipe at me, but Clancy was suddenly in between us, pushing the belligerent man toward the door.

"Out!" he snapped. "Everyone, outside! I'll be out in a minute. Just *go.*"

The others clamoured in protest.

"*Get out!*" Clancy shouted, yanking the screen door wide and shoving Marty Collings through it, tossing a jacket after him. "*Now!*"

The five others made no small fuss about the decision, but they eventually all followed Marty out onto the wraparound, cursing as they donned jackets

411

and boots. Clancy shut the door behind them and rested his forehead against it, eyes closed.

"What do you want, Sid?"

"Thank you," I said mildly. "I needed to talk to you in private."

"You had to kill the party?" he sighed.

"Take a good, long, hard look at your friends, Clancy," I commented. "Do drugs and beer make a good mix?"

"Well, we *were* having a good time," he said sarcastically.

"Until Marty decided to physically assault me for the unthinkable crime of turning off a stereo. Feel the love."

"Marty's mean when he's drunk," Clancy explained. "Turning off his music…. Bad idea."

"Thanks for stepping in." I almost smiled.

"You think I was protecting *you?*" Clancy was disgusted. "I saw your eyes. You were just waiting for an excuse to kill someone. I just saved his life."

"Most likely," I agreed. "His reaction time is extended, and his reflexes are impaired. It's good to know that you have loyalty to some of your friends."

"Sid, if you just came here to insult me…."

"What's your favourite drug?" I asked suddenly.

"What?"

"Drugs, Clancy," I said clearly. "What's your favourite?"

"Sid, what do you want?" he groaned, stepping back into the living room.

412

"Answer the question." My voice was low, but my eyes must have been talking again, because he answered quickly.

"Weed. It's just a good buzz after work. Mushrooms make me try to figure life out too much, but it's better for watching movies on."

"Coke?"

"Not as much, but it's a good high, when I can afford it."

"Do you believe it's killing you?" I asked innocently, folding my arms as I leaned my back against the wall.

Clancy was glaring again.

"I believe in good times, Sid."

"Do you believe in sharing?"

"I don't *sell* the stuff!" he said indignantly.

"Do you ... *share* it?" I asked again, slowly.

"What is your point?!"

"Do you share it?!" I was finished with calmness.

"Of course!" Clancy snapped. "Everyone does! Friends do that, okay? *Friends!*"

"And do you believe in murder?" Clancy's shocked, open-mouthed expression was evidence enough that he had not expected that question, but, by then, he too was losing patience. He shook his head, frustrated, and turned back to the door.

"Get out of my house, Sid!"

His outstretched fingers had almost closed over the doorknob when I seized the back of his jersey collar with both of my hands, and slung him hard across the hallway, lifting him right off the floor. His body was slammed into the opposite wall, the force of impact sending his velvet Elvis crashing to the floor. With one hand still grasping his shirt, and a forearm crushing into his throat, I pinned him fast to the wall, facing me.

"I asked you a question," I wheezed, breathing hard. "Do you believe in murder?"

Clancy struggled vainly against the weight of my brown leather jacket sleeve on his neck. He was several inches taller than me, and firmly muscled, but he was wrestling against pure rage.

"Sid, you get your hands off me now, or I start—" His voice was strained by the lack of air. I flexed the muscles in my right arm, pressing it even harder into his Adam's apple. He was almost choking.

"Drugs are fun, huh?" I seethed, my face only a few inches from his. "Does *this* feel fun? I'll bet almost dying is even *more fun!*"

"Let go of me!"

"She overdosed, Clancy."

"Sid, let go! I can't breathe!"

"Do you hear what I'm saying?" I hissed. "She ODed!"

"Sid!"

"KAT!" I roared, right in his ear.

Clancy froze, his eyes widening.

"You just never could leave well enough alone, Clancy. You couldn't be happy to be a stoner and crackhead. No, *you* have to be a damn friend of Tina, *and* you have to spread it around!" I shook my head furiously, relaxing my forearm just enough to let him inhale a bit of air. "How could you do it, man? To a friend? A girl you tried to date!"

"Sid, what happened to Kat? *What happened?!*" Panic was rising quickly in Clancy's voice.

"*What happened?*" I parroted. "Well, according to the doctor, she ingested a few too many milligrams of very potent crystal methamphetamine. She's still alive, just in case you actually care. Recovery will take awhile."

"Where is she?" Clancy was paler than I had ever seen him before.

"Shut … *up!*" I snapped, pushing hard against his collarbone again. "Where did you get the meth? From who? *Talk!*"

"You think *I* gave it to her?"

The denial was not very convincing, and made me lose my temper completely. I grabbed his head with both hands, and twisted it to the right, forcing him to turn his back to me. Using my left hand to press the left side of his face into the wall, I drove my right fist hard into his kidney.

"*Rrrrrrggghh!*" Clancy screamed through clenched teeth.

"You *did* give it to her! Was it Finn's? He's your dealer, right? Did he set up a meth lab now?"

"Sid, please, where is she?" Clancy pleaded, as a pained tear squeezed from his right eye, down his cheek.

I spun him back around to face me, and then pulled him three feet away from the wall, just so that I could slam him back into it. The impact made him groan, but my forearm against his throat kept him from collapsing.

"She told me she didn't want to say who she got it from, and then she turns around and tells the cops that she found it under a bench!" I shouted. "*Why* would she say that? Why would she protect a dealer? Huh? *She ... wouldn't!*"

"Maybe it's true!" he spat back at me. "Or maybe she doesn't want to admit that she buys. *Will you let go of me?*"

I shoved my free hand flat against the side of his head, grinding his right cheekbone into the drywall. I spoke in a low voice that quavered with fury.

"Even in a moment of pain, even if she was *thinking* about doing drugs, Kat would *not* go straight to a drug dealer! She would come to a friend first, and *you're* the closest friend she has who's connected, who could get the stuff for her. Kat hates drug dealers as much as I do! She would *not* look one in the eye and buy their product! That's why she lied to the cops. Kat would not cover for Devon Finn, or any other dealer, unless she needed to protect *you!* What did you do, anyway? Just hand her the bag and a *cereal bowl?!*"

"Sid, I didn't know!"

"*YES, YOU DID!*" I bellowed, furious spit droplets striking his exposed left eye. "She'd never used before! Don't you get that? And now she's ODed!"

I was now pressing so hard against the side of his face that I could hear the wall creaking under the strain. Clancy grimaced in pain, his eyes squeezed tightly shut, only able to give out short, breathless whimpers.

I put my mouth within an inch of his ear, and spoke in a raspy whisper.

"If she dies, you son of a bitch, you're the killer. Not Devon Finn. *You!* And you ... will answer ... to *me!*"

I let him go so suddenly that his knees buckled and he crashed to the carpet, tears welling in his eyes from the abrupt release of pressure on his head.

"Please, Sid!" he whispered, pushing himself up on shaking palms until he was sitting limply against the wall. "Where is she? I'm still her friend!"

I looked down at him, a cowering, pathetic figure. I could only shake my head in disgust as I strode back into the living room, and heaved the coffee table end over end, shattering every beer bottle and the bong in the process, leaving them to soak into the shag carpet.

Clancy was still crumpled in the hallway when I returned. I hunkered down in front of him, and pushed his chin up with the tip of a forefinger, forcing him to look at me.

"You don't have friends anymore, Clancy," I said simply. "Stay away from her."

Clancy was crying when I left him curled up against the wall. Within the hour, I would come to regret what I had done and said, but as I walked out that door and pushed my way through Clancy's huddled, sullen friends, I felt absolutely nothing except the need for a coffee.

"Hey, you leaving already?"

That was Marty, and he was still looking for a fight. I had just kidney-punched a lifelong friend. It would have been so easy to just spin around and drive a few extended fingers into Marty Collings' windpipe. That would have been the only hit of the fight.

Instead, I turned slowly, and just looked at the drunken mob. Marty stood ahead of them, his bleary eyes burning.

"Yeah," I answered quietly, giving a slow nod. "I'm really tired now. Goodnight."

I got into my truck without saying another word, and drove off into the blackness. It was beginning to snow.

CHAPTER TWENTY-NINE

The snow came down for most of the night. When the sun rose in a clear, blue sky the next morning, the valley town of Chetwynd was buried under six inches of cold, white powder. Life was going on, as it always did. A new season was beginning, and I had to go along to wherever it would take me.

I did not expect Clancy to show up for work that morning, or any day after that, but he managed to surprise me, once again. When I came to the restaurant on Thursday morning, fully anticipating that I would be taking over his prep shift, he was already there, hair combed, tie straight, forest green vest freshly ironed. He was sheeting pizza dough, back to his standard routine, as though nothing had happened the night before. Our eyes met as soon as I entered the kitchen, but neither one of us spoke. We stared at each other for a moment, and then he just nodded at me. I nodded back. I put on my own black vest, tie, and an apron, and we began to work.

There was no hatred left in either one of us. Rather, there was a strange sense of understanding. We did not say a word to each other throughout that entire shift, but we understood perfectly what was happening. Clancy was not going to betray me again. He had given his word when he said that he would complete his last two weeks of work, and he was there to work. And I was going to work with him.

Life and work would never go back to the way they had been. I had let myself get into the same mess that I had warned Clancy and Angel about when they had broken up. I had given in to my wrath, and now I had to live with the consequences. From that time on, Clancy and I would never be more than suspicious, cautious friends, and yet, at an almost subliminal level, we still managed to be friends. We just did not talk to each other for the next two days.

Kat came home from the hospital, weak and nauseous, but still wanted to return to work. I told her that I would fire her if she dared to come back before the wedding. I was lying, and I am certain that she knew it, but she said that she would take one of her vacation weeks early. I did not want her to waste a vacation week on recuperation, but, as much as I wanted to blame Clancy and Finn for everything that had happened, I secretly had to acknowledge that she had done this to herself. Furthermore, I absolutely hated myself for acknowledging that, because I wanted to take some of the blame as well. Kat was truly the best employee that I had, and my oldest friend, and she had almost died. I *needed* to be responsible. I could not let it be her fault. Kat was too strong to make that kind of mistake.

Maybe I was just being irrational. Or, perhaps, I was becoming a good boss, finally.

My friends and I often behaved in ways that were irrational. We would ask questions that we already knew the answer to, questions that had sometimes already been asked and answered. We hated the answer, so we had to hear it, often more than once, before we could really accept it.

I went to Kat's apartment after work on Sunday evening, just because I had to ask "Why?" Kat was reclining on the sofa, wrapped in a heavy green comforter, and still looked exhausted. Her long hair was tangled, and unkempt. I wondered if she had even washed it since her overdose. I poured myself a coffee in her kitchen, coffee that she never drank herself, but always kept for my visits. Then I sat down across the coffee table from her on a wooden kitchen stool, immediately realizing how wrong everything still was. I had not even considered sitting next to her. I had unconsciously put the low table between us, something which we never did, even when playing chess. We always shared the couch, on the same side of the table. Now, the table was between us. When I looked down at the chessboard on it, I saw a fortress with a very high wall.

Betrayal is a common element in most stories, but I did not want it to be a part of mine. Now, Clancy and Kat had both betrayed me, yet they had not done it just to add drama to a plot. They had done it simply by following one of the most basic of human instincts, which was to think only of themselves. That was not always a bad thing, but, for some reason, I refused to think of it that way. I was taking the whole overdose far too personally. Right then, I needed to know why

Kat would do that to me. Looking back, I realize how selfish my own thinking was, mostly as a result of my own fear over her brush with death. The fact was that Kat had done nothing to me. She had done everything to herself.

At first, I thought that Kat was still nervous. She was fitful and twitchy, her teeth lightly gritted. It took me a moment to understand that emotion had nothing to do with her state.

Kat was saying something. I was not listening. My mind was on the chessboard, and we were not even playing.

"What?" I said, feeling slow and stupid.

"I can't eat," she whispered, never moving her teeth. "I can barely keep anything down." She was huddled under the green cover as though she was freezing. The apartment was warm. I took a leisurely swig of coffee, holding the warm ceramic in both hands.

"You're still a bit cranked," I said calmly. "It usually only lasts a few hours, but, with the amount you took.... Well, even on a smaller, smoked dosage, your body would still reject food. Coming down from an overdose, it's worse."

"Coming from a guy with one doobie under his belt, you talk like you know a lot about meth," she growled, probably not meaning to. "Have you been on-line?"

"Most of the night," I admitted, rubbing my tired eyes. "I was curious to know what it was that almost killed you."

"I said never again, Sid," she sighed. "I meant it."

"You could have died," I said quietly.

"I didn't."

"Why?" There was the obvious question. I had to hear Kat say the words herself.

Kat coughed raggedly. "I think I'm getting a cold on top of it. And you know why."

"I have a theory," I pointed out coolly. "Only you and God really know."

"Sid, you live with the same pain as me. I could not take another day of pain, not another minute. And you know what? For a few minutes ... it was gone. I was free."

"And then you almost died. Why did you call me, if you were free?"

Her shake of the head looked more like a short convulsion.

"I don't know. I don't even remember making the call."

"Well," I mused, "I guess some little piece of you still wanted to live."

"I never wanted to die!" she snapped. "I wanted to stop feeling like I already had!"

"Ironic," I remarked, flatly. "How can I ever really believe that?"

"Don't you judge me, Sid!" she said fiercely. "You're in the same hole as me. I turned to drugs. *You* turned to hate. Given the choice, I would take the overdose again in a second before I would accept the kind of hate you have in your life. Clancy was right about you."

"Clancy's the better man, now. Is that what you're saying?"

She closed her eyes, and her shoulders sagged wearily.

"I didn't say that."

423

"But, he did give you the drugs," I said, persistently.

"I asked for them. It was my choice."

"He ... *gave them* ... to you," I repeated, emphatically.

"He didn't put them inside me," she firmly reminded me.

"No. He didn't," I agreed, crossly. "He was just the stork."

"So what? Are you going to fire him?"

"No. I hate firing people."

She looked relieved, closing her eyes and smiling slightly.

"Thank you. I know you're mad at him, but, really, what would the place be like if he was gone? I'd never get hit on again." Most likely as a result of her groggy condition, she seemed to have forgotten that Clancy was quitting. Even so, I smiled, glad that her sense of humour was still alive and well.

"Have you seen him since—" I bit my tongue, not wanting to get into the habit of using her overdose as a historical reference point. "When was the last time you saw him?"

She thought back, still having a hard time focussing her thoughts. "That day after you caught him with the coke. I asked him which drug was good for pain. He told me that Finn had something new, that we probably wouldn't even have to pay."

Promotional free samples....

"And that was it?" I said skeptically. "He was the supply, you were the demand?"

"Pretty much. You're not going to do anything crazy to Clanc, are you? Promise me you won't, Sid. It was my choice. My stupid choice."

I chuckled cruelly. "Sorry. You're a little behind."

"Ah, Sid!" Kat groaned. "What did you do?"

"I talked to him," I replied dryly. "Then I slammed him into the wall a few times, and trashed his living room."

"Sid!"

"It was stupid. But I was mad, and you might have died. Actually, he seemed to be re-examining his life when I left. It was very inspiring to see."

"You beat him up in his own home, and he's still working?" Kat could not believe that.

I shrugged helplessly. I had no real answer for her.

"Like I said, he re-examined his life, I think."

We talked for a while longer, but Kat was still lethargic, and her sentences kept trailing off, or rambling nonsensically. I decided to leave her to rest. I fluffed up the pillow and tucked her in snugly, kissing her forehead before I left.

"You get well soon," I murmured. "Because, when you do, I'm promoting you to assistant manager. Thirteen an hour, instead of twelve, and you'll never have to knock on my office door again. Go to sleep."

She was already dozing off, but she smiled and mouthed the words "Thank you." Right then, her smile was the most beautiful sight that I could remember.

My sister's wedding was less than a week away. Most of my staff was going to be involved with decorating the reception hall in the community recreation centre on the day before the ceremony, so I knew that it would be pointless to even open the shop on Friday. However, the business owner in me could not stomach the thought of closing the restaurant for three days in the same week, even for a wedding. First thing Monday morning, I called Clancy, Boris, and Angel into my office for a staff meeting.

The natural excitement which had been steadily building among my friends had been dampened somewhat in the wake of Kat's accident. All three of my employees were quiet and withdrawn as we crowded into the small room. I downed a whole mug of cold coffee before speaking.

"Sorry to call you all in early," I said. "This is what's happening this week; I'm not losing three days. I'll lose two, not three. We'll still be closed Friday and Saturday, but we're going to stay open on Wednesday. I know, that's desperate, but it's what's happening. Boris, I'm putting you in on prep shift, and Angel will come in at noon to help out. Call me if you get swamped, but, otherwise, I'll be in at three, Clancy at four, and we'll take the evening shift. It'll probably be slow, so we might close early anyway, but … there it is. If you had plans for Wednesday, speak up now."

There was a moment of silence before Angel cautiously inquired, "How's Kat?"

Clancy flinched.

Kat had asked that no one come to visit her, still feeling a lot of shame, I supposed. She privately told me that the stay-away rule did not apply to me, and it had not taken the others long to figure that out.

"She's getting better," I assured them. "She's getting a lot of rest. She'll probably be up in time for the wedding, but we'll have a chair for her at the front of the church. I don't know if she'll be quite ready to stand through the entire ceremony."

"Especially one of Father Makkie's ceremonies," Boris commented. "I love the guy, but his messages are long, and you've heard how slow he talks."

That made Angel giggle, but, after that, no one had much to say. I dismissed them, and Boris and Angel got up to leave. Clancy, however, remained seated across from me, his face looking very hard. When he finally did stand, it was only to shut my office door. Then he turned back to face me, leaning against the door. He wore the expression of a man who needed to talk, but really did not want to. His hands were jammed into his pants pockets.

"Hey," I said dully. "What?"

"Kat came to see me the day after I bought the stuff out back."

I dropped my pen onto the desk, pushed my chair back from it, then bowed my head and leaned forward with a long sigh.

"Sit down," I said.

Clancy's right cheekbone was still bruised from where it had been ground into the drywall. I noticed the red skin when he shook his head.

"No."

"Just sit and talk, man. I'm not going to bash you again. I'm sorry. I just lost my temper."

"I appreciate that."

"What'd she want?"

"I gave her the meth, okay?"

427

I closed my eyes. Again, I already knew the answer to the question I was about to ask.

"Why?"

"Come on, you know why! She said she was missing Roger so much that it killed her. She's been strong for three years, but she wanted the pain to go away, even if just for a few minutes. Heck, anyone could want that, Sid."

"No," I said. "That's why she *wanted* the drugs. I asked you why you *gave them* to her."

"There is no right answer I can give you for that, is there?" he grimaced.

I smirked. "Except that."

"Look, Sid, I'm sorry. That's all I came here to say. I just made the biggest mistake of my life, and I'm admitting it, okay? I almost killed Kat!"

"Clancy, you don't owe this apology to me."

"I know. But I want you to know ... I'm going to make this right."

"You can't," I said bluntly.

I had never before seen his face look so cold as it did when he replied, "Watch me."

"I told you to stay away from her!" I snapped.

"Well, I'll be doing a lot of that, soon," he answered quietly. "I'm not backing out of my last week here, but, after that ... I'm moving."

"Moving," I said slowly. "Where?"

"I've got some cousins in Cranbrook. They said I could stay with them."

"And do what?"

"They've got a construction business. I could work with them for a while. Or, I've got some money saved, and my old scholarships. It's probably time for me to get some college."

"Studying what?"

He grinned. "Business management."

"All the best to you." I managed half a smile.

Clancy finally sat down, and stared at the floor for a long time.

"Sid, you're going to blame me, and I'm willing to take the blame, even if it means taking a few more kidney shots. But deep down, in a grey area that we don't like to think about, we both know … I only did what Kat asked me to do. It's what she wanted."

"She was emotional. You weren't. You knew what was best for her, and you ignored it."

"I know! I know that now!"

"You knew it then."

"Look, Sid, we've gotta work together for one more week. And all I want to know is … how long are you going to hate me?"

I looked up at him, and let out a long, slow breath, rubbing my forehead with my fingertips.

"I don't. All that stuff you told me about hate…. It was all true. I'm still mad, but what can you expect, right? But I don't hate you. I can't."

"Well, that's good," he muttered. "Right now, I hate myself more than you ever could anyway. What kills me the most is that I knew she was using for the first time, and I just assumed that she knew how to."

"Tell me something," I said, leaning back in my chair. "Are you still going to use?"

"Tell me something, first," he responded. "Could you give up coffee overnight?"

429

"Checkmate," I said mildly.

"And some would say that it's worse for you than weed," he commented.

"Do me a favour," I growled. "Don't try to defend drugs right now."

"Sorry." He raised his hands and stood up. "But I'm telling you right now. I'm going to make this right. I promise."

He was turning to the door.

"Clancy?"

"Yeah?"

"How?"

He shrugged, opening the door. "Beats me. I'll figure something out."

I wished that I had his optimism, but, at the same time, I knew that his determination was simply deluding him. What had happened was irreversible, and no amount of confidence was going to change the course of any of our lives. Confidence was the enemy of a rational man. It did not allow for the inevitability of the unforeseen. Still, I was grateful that Clancy would be making the attempt at restitution. His asserted efforts would make it just a little bit easier to start forgiving him. I needed to start forgiving again. It had been far too long since I had even tried. The hate in my life was making me weary.

Something inside me was changing. Perhaps it was because Kat, Clancy, Boris, and Angel had all confronted me about hate within the past two months. I was too much of a realist to believe that this was simply coincidence. They could see me changing, and hating. The rage I felt after my father's death had been buried in my heart for so long, but had now begun to surface, and I had barely even noticed. Now, there was no more escaping it. I had to face my life, and decide what I needed to keep or throw out.

I prayed a lot. I asked God for guidance every day, and never more so than the past week. Lately, I had begun feeling that I was receiving a single word as a reply.

Forgive.

I knew what that meant. It meant letting go of all the anger which had been a savage comfort to me for so many years, a refuge that I had unwisely turned to. I had to quit being so furious with Clancy, and Devon, and Phil Vardega, and Rob Gorman, and even Josh Kelton. He would be the hardest to forgive, but I knew that my compassion was long overdue.

...as we forgive those who trespass against us.

That line of prayer had been constantly in my head ever since I had attacked Clancy. It had run through my mind all night, keeping me from sleep. I knew what was necessary, but was reluctant to actually take that step. I could understand my own hesitation. Forgiveness was not something that was taught much in modern society. Most lessons seemed to revolve around getting even, retaliating, settling scores. Many people scoffed at the idea of forgiving, considering it a sign of weakness in a world desperate to always have the last word. People even took a diabolical delight in holding grudges and tearing others down. It was so much easier to nurse a damaged ego with rage than with empathy, but that was probably the best reason to forgive; It was difficult.

Anything that hard had to be good for the soul. Hating was just too easy.

The most important changes in life often occurred slowly. I am not saying that I suddenly "learned a valuable lesson." There was no big, life-altering revelation. I just slowly became aware of the fact that hate was extremely time-consuming and high maintenance. I remembered how forgiveness used to let me heave a sigh of relief and get on with my life. That was the real reason that my life had stopped when Karl Myers died. The hate had been holding me back.

Finally, late on Tuesday night, after nearly five years of hate, I took a big step. Actually, I took a lot of little ones. I walked alone through the snow across town, until I came to the foot of Mt. Baldy, a small foothill on the northwestern outskirts of town, named for a bald-spot clearing on the west side of the summit. Following the winding hiking trail to the top took me nearly an hour, but I was in no hurry. I had a lot to contemplate.

My father was dead, and drugs and a person who used them were to blame. Nothing would ever change that, but what I did in my heart could change my future. I did not want to forgive Kelton, but knew that my life would never be clean until I did.

Karl Myers used to tell me, "It only takes a pinch of horse manure to spoil the whole batch of biscuits." As I stood at the top of the hill, looking down over the sleeping town, I finally realized that he was probably talking about himself.

I forgave everyone that night. Josh, Clancy, Vardega, Devon, even Kat. I actually said the words aloud, just to make it official.

"Josh Kelton, I forgive you. Clancy Grover, I forgive you. Devon Finn…." I finished by asking God to forgive me. Each word lifted weight from my heart, a weight that I had barely noticed was there until I felt it lifting off. For the first time in years, I did not have pain, either in my stomach, or in my soul. I was free.

It is almost impossible to turn your life around, all in one night. Over the next months, I would have many occasions when I would slip back into a wrathful state, rather than considering forgiveness. However, that night was the beginning of something new for me. It was not the beginning of a new story, but I often wonder if it was the climax of my present one.

I stood up there for an hour or so, looking at the lights of the town, the moon, the stars, the trees, the snow. I did not utter another word until just before I started back down the hill, heading for home.

"I forgive you, too, Mom."

CHAPTER THIRTY

My late night climb was definitely a worthwhile turning point in my life. However, once I started down from the summit with my clean slate, I was struck by a rather obvious fact, which my mental preoccupation had hindered me from noticing before: I was not wearing gloves, and it was bloody cold outside. Also, my lucky cowboy boots were not the best choice for mountaineering.

Suffice to say, I was thoroughly chilled when I finally got back to my house. It was around two in the morning, Cindy was fast asleep, and the house was black. I trudged to my own room, and went straight to bed.

It was then that something very strange happened. I fell asleep.

I could never just fall asleep. I always stared at the ceiling for an hour or two, wrestling with some moral foe, before I ever drifted off, and, even then, I rarely slept soundly. My dreams were often troubling, violent or scary, leaving me miserable in the morning, with coffee being my only hope for consolation.

That night, my head sank into the pillow, and I was gone. It was the deepest, most restful sleep that I have ever had. Even when I dreamed, I dreamed about falling asleep. The Christmas carol describes it best. I slept in heavenly peace.

In that heavenly peace, I snored right through my morning alarm clock, for the first time in history. I only awoke when Angel called from the restaurant at two-thirty in the afternoon, wondering where the window cleaner was. As she put it, "The glass is all yicky-icky, Boss."

By The Slice Steak and Pizza had not been opened on a Wednesday in more than twelve years. We had advertised our special hours, but, as expected, there was still not much business. Almost a foot of snow had accumulated over the past few days, and the people who were not at work or school were staying close to home. The dining room was empty when I came in late at three-thirty, and my faithful employees were sitting around the prep table, bored. At a glance, I could tell that all of the prep work was done, and the whole place was clean. Boris and Angel had been scheduled in for the morning, but Clancy was already there as well. I was willing to bet that he had been in over an hour early. Since Kat's overdose, he had been showing up early for every shift, and hardly even took breaks anymore. No doubt the others were baffled by this, as Kat and I were still the only ones who knew that Thursday was Clancy's last day, and only I knew that he would be moving afterwards. A couple of days earlier, shortly after the staff meeting, Angel had nervously pulled me aside and asked, "Does Clancy have cancer or something?"

435

"No," I had replied. "He has a conscience. Your bow-tie's crooked."

Now that the chaos of the past week was subsiding, I felt guilty about Angel. She had been almost completely neglected by me over the last few days, and I knew that I owed her more of my time. She had just done the unthinkable to help preserve my business, and I had barely spoken to her since. She understood why, of course, and I am certain that she was not feeling annoyed with me, but my negligence was still bothersome. I had never really had a best friend before. That was not the category of friendship which I could afford to disregard. I decided that I would invite her over for coffee that night with Boris and Cindy. I had worked with Angel almost every day that week, but I already missed our talks. I was trying to purge all of the hate from my life. A demonstration of that would be to always let my friends know how special they were to me.

Clancy, Angel, and Boris all looked up tiredly as I entered, buttoning my vest.

"Hey, Sid," they all greeted me, almost in unison.

"Good day," I smiled. "It's been dead?"

"Deader than your disco," Boris said. "I hate to break it to you, but our wages for today might be more than the ring-off total."

I shrugged, knotting my tie. "It might pick up around supper. You can go home now, if you want."

"Thanks," Boris yawned, rising from his stool. "I've got a busy night of pre-marital anxiety to take care of, still. See ya, guys."

"Yo da man." Clancy leaned across the table to give Boris a high-five.

"See you, Boris," Angel called after him, as he headed for the rear exit.

Boris waved over his shoulder as he disappeared into the laundry room. His voice carried into the kitchen as he left the building.

"We still need a good wedding song, Sid. Don't let me down."

"I won't," I called after him, although I had yet to think of a single tune that both he and Cindy had in common, not that I had spent a whole lot of time pondering it. The week had been too full of more pressing concerns.

"Song?" Angel said curiously, propping her cheek on her palm.

"They can't figure out what their definitive melody is," I said. "Pop and classic rock don't have many hybrids."

Angel smiled widely, but it struck me that this was not a smile of amusement over the song predicament. She was smiling at me.

"Everything's done, Sid," Clancy said, stirring the root beer float he was drinking. "Now I know why we take Wednesdays off, of all days."

"Yeah," I said slowly, having a hard time focussing on what he was saying. Angel was still smiling. It was making me nervous.

The take-out phone was a welcome diversion when it rang, likely for the first time that hour. "Got it," I said, snatching the receiver off the hook.

Clancy and Angel must have wondered why I so abruptly froze and fell silent, without even saying, "By The Slice."

"Uh … hello?" the voice on the other end said cautiously, also wondering why he had not heard the self-identifying salutation. Clancy and Angel were both staring at me now, but I still said nothing. I could not speak.

A familiar cold feeling was creeping through my body. The call display read *Devon Finn*.

"Hello?" he repeated.

I blinked.

"Hey, is the pizza place, or what?" he demanded.

"By The Slice," I said slowly, feeling completely chilled in the warm kitchen. "How may I help you?"

"Oh, good, I thought I had the wrong number. I need some pizza delivered, man."

"Certainly, sir." I forced civility into each word. "What kind would you like?"

"Something good. Lots of meat."

"Meatlover?"

"Sure. Two extra larges, bud."

Easy, Myers. This is business. Joke around with him.

"Two extra large Meatlover, you got it," I said, writing the order on the pad. "I guess the party's at your place after work, huh?"

Devon laughed. "Not quite, bud. My woman took off with the kids this morning, says she's moving in with her mom. I've got no one to cook for me! Ha!"

Good girl, Debbie.

"Well, we can help you with that, sir. You'll have a couple days' rations at your door in about thirty minutes."

"Perfect, man. You guys kick."

"208, Spruce Lane, right?"

I could hear Clancy's breath catch in his throat.

"Yeah," Finn chuckled admiringly. "How'd you know?"

"Magic," I said flatly. "Thirty minutes. Bye."

Clancy's eyes were absolutely on fire as I hung up the phone and turned back to the prep table. "Two extra larges," I said quietly, hanging the bill on the overhead rack.

Angel still looked curious, but went to retrieve the pizza crusts from the cooler.

"Devon Finn?" Clancy said coldly.

"He's hungry," I sighed, scratching my hair. "Debbie took the kids and left him with an empty cupboard this morning."

"And you're serving him?"

"You two have a little falling out, Clancy?" I shot back. "I thought you were pretty tight."

"Not anymore," he growled. "It took a near fatality for me to figure out what he was."

"He's hungry," I repeated. "It happens to the best of us."

"*Why are you serving him?!*" Clancy's voice was angry enough to convince Angel to make an exit. She simply set the two sauced dough sheets on the prep table and retreated to the rear exit, muttering something about needing a smoke break. Angel did not smoke.

"Has he given us a valid reason not to?" I replied, washing my hands in the sink.

"How about the coke he sold me, right here?" Clancy was getting red-faced.

I vigorously rubbed my hands with a paper towel, wadded it up, and slammed it angrily into the garbage can. I did not like doing this, either.

"I did not witness the transaction," I said irritably. "He denies all knowledge, and, fool that I am, I told him to call anytime. I'm not going back on my word. Then, I'd be like him. Two Meatlovers."

"He almost killed Kat!"

"We *all* almost killed Kat," I snarled, spreading pepperoni slices over the tomato sauce. "Even Kat. Are you going to make that one, or do I have to do them both?"

"You can fire me, Sid," he stated plainly. "I'm not cooking for him." Angrily, he pulled off his apron and stormed into the back room.

"Go have a smoke with Angel," I said absently, knowing that he would not hear me. "It's about time she got a bad habit."

I guess Angel did not want to listen to Clancy rant about Devon Finn, or else his sullen silence informed her that he wanted to be alone. She returned in time to help finish the pizzas and put them in the oven. After she closed the heavy steel door, she leaned against the wall beside it. Then she was smiling again.

"How are you, Boss?"

I did not answer her. I reached up to the shelf over her head and set the egg timer for fifteen minutes. Angel never could reach that shelf without a chair.

"I'm fine. Kat's a lot better."

"So … why's Clancy so mad?"

I sighed, straightening my tie in the mirror by the telephone, still wanting to look presentable for our nonexistent diners.

"He had a rough week. He and Kat…. They're pretty close."

"He said Devon Finn," she mused. "Who's that?"

"A dealer," I said. "You met him on day one, your first delivery."

"Did he overdose Kat?"

Every fibre of my being wanted to say yes.

"Kat used," I replied, leaning against the wall next to her, and folding my arms. "She overdosed herself. We can't put that on anyone else … or ourselves."

Angel shook her head. "I barely know Kat. I mean, really, I know *Becky* better. I've pretty much kept to myself since I moved here…. You know why. You guys are basically the only friends I've got here. Well, except for the little guy who delivers my newspaper. I think he's got this preteen crush going for me. But Kat…. We've never really hung out, except a few times at your place. There's something between us, all the time."

"Clancy?" I ventured. "I think Kat actually missed his cheesy come-ons while he was with you."

"No. It wasn't Clancy." Angel seemed sure of that. "I think it was you."

"Me?" I had not expected to hear that.

"Who was your best friend, before I came along?" she wanted to know, tilting her head slightly to one side. Out of all of Angel's cute mannerisms, that one had to be both the cutest, and the most annoying.

441

"I didn't really have one."

"But you talked to Kat more than anyone else," she pointed out. I had never told her that, at least not that I could remember, but Angel had a way of either discovering things, or somehow just knowing. "I think Kat's in love with you, in some small way."

"I don't know about that," I admitted. "We both lost family, only a couple of years apart. We needed crying shoulders, even though neither one of us ever actually cried. Heck, we've talked about getting married, but that's all it ever is. Just talk. She even tried to set me up with you, once."

"Interesting...." Angel's quiet smile was starting to bother me. "Have you ever been close to getting married?"

Her curiosity was making me nervous as well, although I could not really figure out why.

"No," I said honestly. "I dated the same girl, on and off, all the way through high school, but it never went anywhere. I haven't even heard from her since she moved."

"What changed?"

I sighed, looking up at the ceiling. "I did. I stopped communicating. Spring.... She couldn't be with a clam like me."

"Was it because of your dad?"

"Sort of. Mostly.... I think we just realized that she was only my girlfriend, not my friend."

"Interesting...." She said it again, and it was just as unnerving the second time. She raised an eyebrow, which made it even worse. "Not many guys learn that distinction. Ever."

"Well, I try to," I said. "That's why I never went out with Karen again. The romance was too conventional. I could predict everything that happened…. How about you? Have you ever been close to wedding bells?"

"Oh yeah, a couple times," she acknowledged. "Heck, I've had three guys propose to me. Actually, it's four, if you count that skinny kid back in grade two. I can't even remember his name."

"Have you ever said yes?" Now I was the one getting curious.

Angel laughed.

"Only to the kid in grade two, Boss. And that engagement lasted until noon recess. I caught him looking at a fifth grade girl, so I force fed him a pine beetle."

"Ow," I cringed. "Thanks for the scary visual."

"It's all protein."

Celebrity engagements…. A dime a dozen. I tried not to laugh at the thought.

"Tell me something." I changed the subject. "Do you ever miss your old life?"

"Some of it," she confessed. "You know, family, home, a few friends who stuck around. I pretty much cut all ties when I left. Jeepers, I feel like a protected witness or something…." She paused, apparently having just come up with that comparison, and rather liking it. "Cool."

"Are you going home for Christmas?" I asked.

"We're closing?" Evidently, no one had told Angel about that.

"A few days for Christmas, three or four, usually."

"Well, in that case, I might go home for a couple days. I miss the farm."

"Do you think your dad's going to be mad? You know, for killing his little venture up here?"

Angel snorted. "Daddy's a bazillionaire, and I'm his little girl. He's probably forgotten the whole thing already. Although, I did get him to promise that Chetwynd would be an official no-fly zone."

"You do realize," I pointed out, "that if the mayor and council ever figure out that we killed one heck of a consumer and tourist attraction … they'll string us up from the Little Prairie Moose statue, and leave us there until our skeletons slide out of the nooses."

"Now, *that* would be a tourist attraction," Angel chuckled. "They could write a play about it. *'Death of a Pizza Man.'*"

"I wouldn't watch it," I shuddered. "Not even if they could get Dustin Hoffman to play me."

Angel was beset with laughter again, but it quickly trailed off, and she looked strangely preoccupied. She hesitated before speaking again.

"Would you come with me?"

"What?"

"Home. For Christmas. Would you come? I want my parents to meet you." I had never before heard a woman say anything that terrifying. I stared at her, blankly.

"No."

"Why not?" She seemed hurt.

"It just seems … inappropriate."

444

Angel looked disgusted now. "I'm not asking for their blessing, Boss. I just thought you and Daddy would have a lot in common."

"Yeah. I have a restaurant, and he has ten thousand. We're only nine thousand, nine hundred and ninety-nine away from being soul-mates."

"One hundred twenty-seven," she corrected me. "Fifteen others still under construction. You're not that far behind him. Just start franchising."

"Thanks, anyway. Boris and Cindy have already got Christmas planned out at his new apartment. I have to be there. It's a combination Christmas, housewarming, and Cindy's birthday party."

"Well ... maybe some other time?"

"Maybe," I agreed.

You are not taking a road-trip with a female employee, Myers.

"Well, I hope so," Angel continued, smiling once more. "You need to take some time off, Boss. It's too much for you to be here, every day. I worry about you, you know?"

Oh good heavens, this girl's in love with you.

I had honestly never thought of that before. The possibility of Angel considering me more than a best friend had just not occurred to me. Even after our impulsive kiss, I had convinced myself that she had just been longing for affection, from anyone. Sure, I had wondered if she was the type of girl that I would want to date. That was just natural male ponderings. I never would have dreamed that she had the same thoughts. Now, I knew better. That smile she had been giving me said it all. It was happy, sly, and teasing. A smile like

445

that could only mean one of two things. Either she was planning to play a truly brutal April Fools Day prank on me, nearly eight months after the fact, or she was in love with me. Even worse, I could not decide which possibility was scarier.

"Boss?"

"Yes!" I said it a lot louder than I had meant to. So much for playing it cool.

"What's wrong?"

"Whattaya mean?" My hands suddenly seemed completely out of place. I did not know what to do with them.

In the pockets? Out of the pockets? Thumbs in the belt? Don't scratch your hair!

Angel looked at me quizzically. "Boss, you're staring at the dish-washer, your eyes are kind of wide, and you're breathing through your mouth. Do you need some water?"

"I need coffee," I croaked, heading for the coffeepot. "I need you to vacuum the dining room."

"I just did it an hour ago!"

"It's still dirty."

I hate to be the one to break this to you, Myers: Your pants are on fire.

Thankfully, it was Boris coffee.

Clancy did not come back into the kitchen until I was already cutting up the pizzas. He was strangely silent at first, with only his eyes speaking a thousand words at once.

"Sorry for storming out," he eventually sighed, taking down a couple of extra large pizza boxes from a shelf, and opening them on the counter next to the round, wooden cutting board. "It's just Devon…. I never would have believed how quickly I could come to hate a friend."

"That's okay," I said empathetically. "We're all under a ton of stress this week. You leaving, and Kat, and the wedding…. It's too much to handle. Have you told anyone?"

He shook his head. "I'll tell them after the wedding. I don't want to wreck it for anyone. You know … Boris and Cindy, they're perfect for each other. Things are going to be a lot better from now on. I just know it." He was sounding so confident again. I wondered where he got his optimism from. He was almost out of a job, and he was planning to leave the only town and friends that he had ever known.

I closed the pizza boxes over the steaming, golden brown cheese topping, and slid them into a canvas oven bag, zipping the flap shut.

"Clancy, I'm sorry," I said, turning to face him as I pulled on my brown leather jacket. "I owe you a major apology."

He could actually grin as he said, "For what?"

"For kidney-punching you … and for the coffee table."

"What about the beer and the bong?" he said wryly.

"I don't give a rat's tail about the beer and bong," I growled, good-naturedly.

Clancy chuckled. "Relax, Sid. It was Marty's coffee table, not mine. I forgive you."

I nodded. "Thank you."

As I turned to leave, Clancy called after me over the whirring of Angel's vacuum cleaner in the next room.

"You know, Sid … I did contemplate hating you for what you did."

"So?" I said, looking back at him. "Why didn't you?"

He shrugged. "Because if the situation had been reversed, I would have done exactly the same thing you did…. I might have saved the beer, though."

I smiled as I left the kitchen. "You're a good man, Clancy."

"You too, Sidney."

Like I had said before, enemies were a lot higher maintenance than friends. Clancy and I could never be as good of friends as we had been, but I held out hope that we might come close. Anything can happen in a life story, especially among friends.

Forgiveness was a wonderful sensation, but that did not mean that I had a positive outlook on life as I got into my blue truck and began the short drive to Devon Finn's apartment. The roads had been ploughed, and the sun was shining in a clear, deep blue sky, but it was quite cold out. I had been hoping that the unseasonably warm weather would hold until after the wedding. Now the cold was very irritating to me, although I am quite certain that my annoyance was more a result of my being just as angry about serving Finn as Clancy had been. I never wanted to see Devon Finn's face again. Although I was trying not to blame him for Kat overdosing, I could definitely blame him for introducing meth to her, and to who knows how many other kids in town.

Unfortunately, in spite of my resolution to purge all hate from my life, I allowed my thoughts to roam back into the darker parts of my heart as I drove. I wanted to hurt Devon Finn, as his products had likely hurt so many others. A dozen violent fantasies had flooded my mind by the time I arrived at the three townhouses of Spruce Lane Apartments on the eastern outskirts of Chetwynd. I knew that I was about to smile politely and make small talk with a man who I wanted to inflict severe bodily harm upon. I had been trying so hard not to hate anyone over the past few days, but the image of Kat in that hospital bed, so pale, kept my rage billowing, just behind the expressionless mask that was my face. Perhaps I would hate the man with every cheerful word that I uttered, but I was going to smile if it killed me. A blonde four-year-old girl was being pushed on the swing set by her babysitter, a dark-haired fifteen-year-old girl with glasses, in the small playground across the gravel driveway from the buildings. Both of them were bundled up in snowsuits, scarfs, toques, and heavy mittens. To this day, I still have no idea why the two of them were outside at all on that cold day. There was no one else in sight as I parked in front of apartment 208 in the middle building. I was mad. I will readily admit that. In my mind, Devon Finn was getting away with murder, and I was about to sell him pizzas, and chat like he was an old friend. My job demanded my civility, no matter what.

They have to love the person that they're talking to....

I had told Karen Malloy that secret of getting annoying customers to come back, and to hopefully be less annoying. Even in an angered state, I was still too much of a good steward to make an exception to that rule. Karl Myers was always patient with customers, and so I would be. That did not keep me from being mad, it just kept me from showing it.

I was cold, and the heater in my truck was taking longer to kick in than it ever had in previous years. It was still blowing cold air when I shut off the ignition, and pocketed the keys. The cold made my anger burn even hotter, and the fact that my stupid door was even stickier than usual did not help my mood at all.

Every life is like a good book, and even a seemingly irrelevant annoyance can play a critical role in the story. It is very possible that rusty door hinges saved my life. I was still fighting with that door when Devon Finn's apartment exploded.

CHAPTER THIRTY-ONE

The movies cannot do justice to an explosion. Sitting in movie theatres, I have seen human beings get shot with rocket-propelled grenades, and burst into a red mist of anatomical fragments. I heard teenage girls scream, and teenage boys whoop and laugh. I have seen rebellious planets blown up by the starships of their dark overlords. The audience had let out a collective "*Whoooaaaa ...!*" as the blue shockwave was launched into space in all directions, devouring tiny, fleeing spacecraft.

The overconfident, nameless bomb-squad officer cuts the blue wire instead of the red one. The hero's car blasts through the intersection under a red light, while the pursuant truckload of thugs is T-boned by a semi-tanker filled with molten sulphur. Hand grenades are thrown into bunkers. Nuclear bombs are dropped on giant reptiles. The coyote pushes the plunger as the roadrunner zooms by, and then walks over to the TNT in absolute befuddlement to determine what went wrong. None of it is real. None of it even comes close. All that I can tell you is that, until you are at ground zero, you will never understand the pure, undiluted horror of the blast.

It was deafening. I never knew that anything could be that loud. The first thing that I remember is clapping my hands over my ears, trying to dull the roar. My eyes instinctively slammed shut, preventing me from seeing much more than a glimpse of a rushing firewall punching through the kitchen window. The front door was blown from its hinges, spinning through the air and straight through the passenger side of my windshield, coming within a foot of decapitating me. The resulting shower of glass drove shards into my right hand, and the right side of my face. I was diving for cover under the dashboard, and, at the time, I did not even know what I was trying to get away from. Then I felt the heat for the first time, and it was then that I became more terrified than I have ever been in my life.

I was huddled on the floor of Sid's Rig for an eternity, an eternity that might have lasted for eight seconds. The blast had faded into an angry roar of consuming flame. Gasping, I had to grab onto the door that was in my passenger seat and pull myself back up to peer over the dashboard, but all that I could see was fire. What was left of Finn's home seemed to be nothing but a ball of flame. Not only had every window and the door been destroyed, but quite a bit of the frames around them had been blown out as well. The front doorframe was now a huge, flaming, cavernous entrance that truly looked like the doorway to hell.

The kid....

I had to get out. This time I only had to give the door one good shoulder slam to pop it open. I almost fell out onto the gravel, not realizing until then how badly my legs were shaking. By then, the entire outer wall of the apartment was also engulfed in the flames, which were quickly spreading to the adjoining units. I was at least ten feet away, and my face was still being scorched.

Someone was screaming from the playground behind me. I spun around to see the small girl cowering under the swing set, eyes closed, covering her ears and screaming. Her crouching babysitter was attempting to shield the child in her arms.

"Are you all right?!" I shouted, running on shaky legs through the snow, toward them. "Is she hurt?"

"What happened?" the babysitter cried out, looking as though she wanted to start screaming as well.

"I don't know, but we've got to get her away from here." Somehow, knowing that others needed my help made me feel calmer. "Come on!" I scooped the child up in my arms and grabbed her frightened guardian by the elbow, rushing both of them over to a large gravel pile at the far end of the playground, which had been dumped there probably a decade earlier. Out of the corners of my eyes, I could see several other people running out from the other Spruce Lane units.

"Everybody get out!" I hollered as loud as my breathless lungs would allow. *"Get out! Fire! Fire!"*

I set the child down behind the gravel pile, where, at the very least, she could not see the blaze. Pulling out my cell phone, I tossed it to the babysitter.

"What's your name?" I asked, a bit snappishly.

"Lois," she replied shakily.

"Lois, 911," I instructed. "Tell them there is a residential fire, 208 Spruce Lane Apartments on Spruce Crescent Road. There was an explosion, and there *is* someone trapped inside. Do you got that? Lois!"

She looked like she was in shock, staring with wide eyes at the flaming building.

"Hey!" I snapped. "I need you to focus, okay? Suck it up! People's lives are on the line here."

She nodded, trying hard to regain her composure.

"Okay," she quavered, punching in the three digit emergency number with a blue, woollen mitten. "208, and someone's inside."

"Residential fire, and explosion, Spruce Crescent Road," I repeated, turning to the little girl, who had stopped screaming, but was now sobbing, hugging the knees of her snowsuit, and rocking her tiny body back and forth.

"Are you okay?" I asked, holding her small shoulders. "Are you hurt? Did you get hurt?"

She managed to shake her head, just once.

"My name's Sidney," I said kindly, trying to keep a quiver out of my own voice, for her sake. "Sidney Myers. What's yours?"

"Tia," she choked out, hiccupping.

"Tia, I need you to listen really close, okay? I know that fire scared you. It scared me, too. It's okay to get scared. But the fire can't get through all this snow, and it can't cross the road. None of that can burn, and neither can all of these little rocks you're sitting on. This little mountain is your safe place, okay?"

She nodded, her movements still short and jerky, but just a little bit more focussed.

"Now, I need you to stay right here with Lois, okay? You'll be fine, but you need to stay with your mountain until the firemen come. You understand?"

"Okay," she whispered.

"You have to promise me," I said firmly.

"I promise."

I held up my left pinky finger.

"Pinky promise?" I forced a grin.

She actually smiled back as she wrapped her whole tiny fist around my finger.

"I already told you which place!" Lois was screeching into the phone. "Spruce Lane Apartments! Spruce Crescent Road! *Welfare Way, you moron!*"

"Good girl," I said to Tia, standing up. "I'll be right back." I began running back toward my truck.

"Where are you going?!" I heard Lois scream after me.

Over a dozen people had rushed outside, and were now gathered around on the road, staring in astonishment at the inferno that was Devon's home. The heat was searing. Someone was shouting about shutting off the gas.

"Fire department's on the way!" I yelled, running up to the crowd. "Who lives in the adjoining apartments?"

"I do!" a burly logger with a walrus moustache called out. "The one on the other side is vacant."

"Is everyone out?" I asked.

"I was home alone," he answered, trying hard not to look shaken. He was cold as well, having rushed out in just a tee-shirt, boxer shorts, and sandals. "Kids and my wife are out shopping."

"We must make sure everyone's out!" an elderly woman with a Russian accent declared. "Someone could be sleeping, still."

"I think the blast would have woken most of them up," the logger replied sarcastically.

"Some people do not wake up for noise," the lady pointed out. "My husband could have slept through volcano in the back yard."

"She's right," I said. "We've gotta pound on every door, make sure the place is empty before something else blows."

"Steve, let's split up!" a thin, teenage boy shouted to his equally skinny younger brother. The two of them dashed off, one angling toward unit 210, the other making a beeline for 206.

"Be careful!" a tall woman in her forties screamed after them.

"Aw, mom!"

"Whose place is that?" demanded a short, bald man, clad only in a bathrobe and slippers.

"That pusher, Devon Finn," the logger said, disgustedly. "I guess justice just caught up with him."

"He'll be in for a shock when he gets home," the short man snorted.

I turned to look at him, my face too tired to bear an expression of any sort.

"He's already home," I said quietly.

His face turned pale, as did many of the others around us. One woman began to cry.

We just stood there and stared at the flames, a strong crowd, united in a time of trouble, and still absolutely helpless. The fire was unquenchable, and had consumed three entire units by then. It was feeding without pause, defying the assembled humanity before it. The fire was so evil, hungry, and invincible. No one dared to oppose it. No one ever dared.

* * *

"DAD!!"

* * *

Even the roof of Finn's apartment was igniting, the tarred shingles providing even more fuel for the flame. I could hear sirens wailing in the distance, but they did not sound like those of a fire truck. They sounded like police cars.

* * *

Cindy's hands were feverishly gripping mine as I awoke. I was in a bed, and the room seemed so white.

"Dad...." I said, my mouth and throat so dry that the word was all but inaudible. "Where's Dad?"

Cindy could not stop weeping. I knew. Right then, I already knew. And, right then, I stopped. I just stopped.

"He's gone," Cindy sobbed. "He's gone, Sid! He's gone."

* * *

"Are you sure he's still in there?" the logger asked me, weakly. "Maybe he smelled the smoke, and got out. Has anyone looked around back?"

"I'll go," the man in the bathrobe said bravely, scurrying toward the corner of the building.

* * *

457

"Mr. Myers?"

I did not recognize the petite Native girl who stood in the doorway of my hospital room.

"Who are you?" I asked rudely.

My father was dead. I should have died saving him. That was all that mattered.

"My name is Pamela Gregson. I was working at the convenience store two nights ago. Do you remember me?"

I blinked.

"No. Who are you?"

"I'm so sorry about your dad. I tried to help. I called the ambulance, but it was too late."

I remembered something that Cindy had mentioned. Or maybe it had been a doctor. I remembered only the words, not the speaker. Someone had said that a girl had pulled me away from the burning gas.

* * *

I knew that Devon Finn was not around back. I knew that he was inside his home, the one place in this world that he considered to be his refuge. With his children and girlfriend gone, it was all that he had left, and it was killing him. The fire always won. It had to win.

* * *

"You did everything that you could, Sid. I say you were a hero." Kat held her hands up, envisioning a headline. "'Sidney the hero....'"

* * *

The short man's voice carried over the flaming rooftop.

"He's not here! I can't see anyone!"

"*DEVON FINN!*" I roared. "HAS ANYBODY SEEN DEVON FINN?!"

* * *

"*Ms. Matthews, I outweighed her by about forty pounds. She dragged me, deadweight, away from a spreading pool of gasoline. She saved me. She was the only hero that night.*"

"*I am inclined to disagree,*" Linda said quietly. "*I spoke with her personally, and she told me everything. I know what you did.*"

"*You know what I tried to do, and failed to do. Three people died, and I lived.*"

"*I do not judge heroism by success or failure,*" she explained patiently. "*A hero is judged by what he strives for, and what he risks to achieve it. The outcome is simply the part that goes into the history books....*"

* * *

Fire had once before killed a man that I hated. Josh Kelton had burned to death, the man who killed my father.

And, yet, I had tried to save him. The fire had defeated me, once.

You can't let it win again, Myers. Not again.

* * *

"*A little flicker of light can shine through a lot of darkness, Boss. But just a little sliver in just the right place can make all that blackness come right back. If you've ever learned a better life lesson than that, I'd love to hear it."*

* * *

I barely noticed my feet moving as I began walking toward the flames. The heat was almost unbearable, but I did not even wince or squint my eyes.

* * *

"DAD!!"

* * *

"Dad," I muttered, almost hypnotized by the blaze.

"Hey, what are you *doing?!*" the logger shouted.

"Get back!" a female voice yelled.

"NO!" I bellowed, beginning to run. "You won't win again!" I charged straight for the fiery chasm that had been a doorway mere minutes before. The flames roared their evil greeting as I bounded up the front steps, three at a time. Even some of the steps were igniting.

"It's too late!" someone else screamed. "Get back!"

"Devon!" I yelled, rushing headlong into the fire. *"DEVON!"*

The room was made of fire. There was no definition of walls, furniture, hallways. All that I could see were insatiable orange tongues, and blinding black smoke, all mixed together into the centre of the sun. The heat was unbelievable, but I was too crazed to stop. I took another step forward, already lost. Even the floor was burning, flames leaping up around my cowboy boots, surrounding me.

"*DEVON!!*"

The strongest hand I have ever felt seized my collar. I was literally jerked off my feet as I was forcibly wrenched back out the front door.

The logger with the walrus moustache was swearing as he threw me into the snowbank next to the road, and rolled over me with his own body, extinguishing the first flames which had begun devouring the legs of my black jeans. My face was seared and turning red, and I doubt that I had been inside more than two or three seconds.

"DEVON!"

"It's too late!" the logger shouted, shaking me by the collar. "Are you *insane?*"

"No! We can't let it win!" I growled, my lungs burning. "*Dad!*"

Sirens were now filling the air. A police car was the first to skid to a stop in a cloud of powdered snow. Two constables jumped out and rushed over to me. One was Maurice Goodman.

"Is he okay?" the Frenchman asked.

"He says Devon Finn is trapped inside," the logger said. "He tried to go in."

"Are you sure he's in there?" the second police officer, a stocky, blonde woman in her thirties asked urgently.

"I'm delivering the pizza he ordered twenty-five minutes ago!" I tried to shout the words, but could only croak.

"Sidney Myers?" Goodman said curiously, recognizing me.

461

"Okay, we need to get everyone back!" the other constable called out. "Ladies and gentlemen, please gather around the swing set in the playground. We need to make room for the fire trucks!"

"We've got to get him out!" I coughed. "He can't see! Too much smoke!"

"Are you injured?" Goodman asked, concerned, bending over me. "We're too close here. Can you move?"

"I'm fine," I moaned, as he and the logger picked me up by the arms and pulled me away from the fiery furnace. "Devon's in there. We gotta help him! Don't let it win!"

"We can't," Goodman said frankly, lowering me onto one of the swings. "The best thing we can do right now is let the fire department do their jobs."

I do not remember many details of the next few minutes, sitting on that child-sized seat, except that my hands were quivering, and I could not make them stop. The police had directed everyone to the playground by the time the wailing fire engine raced down the driveway. Hoses were unrolled, water was blasted into the heart of the flames, and firemen rushed into the smoldering ruins. Ambulances arrived, and Goodman was speaking to one of the paramedics, and pointing at me. The attendant was checking my eyes, and my mouth, and asking me all sorts of questions, not one of which I can remember.

Eventually, the charred remains of Devon Finn were carried out, zipped up in a body bag. Goodman was talking to me, and I was trying to explain what had happened, but kept saying incoherent things, such as,

"I drove into the bomb." The sun had set, and everyone was getting even colder. Some of the people standing around in the snow did not even have coats on, and were stamping their feet and blowing on their hands. Most of them kept looking at me. I could not see Tia or Lois. They still had my phone.

The attendant wanted me to come to the hospital, because my face had been nicked up when my windshield smashed in, and was also turning cherry red. I dumbly agreed, and began walking toward my truck. I was gently guided over to an ambulance. I had a sudden horrifying thought that I would be riding in the same one as Devon.

Of course, the ambulance was empty, but the thought of Devon Finn, the walking, breathing man being reduced to a flame-burned corpse still sent chills through me. If my driver side door had not stuck for those ten short seconds, God only knows where I would have ended up. I could have been knocking on that front door when it blew off.

Devon Finn was dead. I had not heard anyone say that, but I knew. Only one body bag had been brought out, and no one could have escaped that blaze alive. I had barely survived a few seconds in the doorway.

Sidney the hero....

I was stupid, not heroic. All the way to the hospital, I cussed myself out for risking my life on the very verge of my sister's wedding. I hated swear words. I felt that they made me less of a man every time that I resorted to them, but, right then, I was in too much shock to even notice. Just before the ambulance pulled up to the emergency entrance in the hospital parking lot, I

463

overheard the two paramedics talking. I cannot even remember if the speakers were male or female, but I will always remember what they said.

"You think the dealers are choosing sides?"

"Whattaya mean?"

"Devon. He was a pusher. Maybe he was threatening someone."

There was a long silence before the other replied, "You think it was deliberate?"

"He was alone. How often does that happen? Maybe someone knew."

I knew.

And so did Clancy.

CHAPTER THIRTY-TWO

I was treated for minor cuts and burns at the hospital, and the doctor lectured me on how lucky and stupid I was the entire time. I kept nodding and saying, "Yeah, I know," a lot. It helped him to believe that he was getting through to me.

The fact was that the most charismatic of televangelists would have had a hard time getting through to me that night. The catastrophic events did not shock me so much as my own reactions to them. I had driven to Devon Finn's apartment, and I had hated him the whole way. Then I had risked my life to save him, knowing that he must have already been dead. It did not make sense. I seemed destined to never get my life figured out. What penance was I trying to pay?

This time, I had accepted the hospital's offer to make a call, but I did not want to terrify anyone by letting some unknown nurse inform my loved ones that I had just been pulled from a burning building. Before I would even see a doctor, I insisted on borrowing a phone line from the admitting and reception desk. Business was ever my priority, so I called the shop first.

"By The Slice," Angel answered brightly on the second ring.

"Angel, it's me."

"Boss, where are you?" she demanded. "You left two hours ago!"

"I'm in the hospital," I said mildly. "There was a fire. I'm fine."

"*What?!*"

"Fire," I repeated. "Close the shop. Go home. Tell Cindy I'll be home right away, if you can get a hold of her. Thanks."

"Boss, what fire?"

"Devon Finn's apartment burned down. Go home, okay?"

"You were *there?!*"

"No, I was outside. I got a little singed, so they brought me here, just to check me out. I'm fine."

"How did it …?"

"I don't know," I said. "Just close up. I'll see you tomorrow."

"Boss…."

"I'm fine." I hung up.

After an absence of nearly five years, I had now visited the hospital three times in just over a week. I hated hospitals. Yes, I appreciated their value to modern society. I just hated being in them.

My injuries were superficial. After cleaning the cuts and scrapes, the doctor only put two band-aids over the largest cuts, one on my right cheek, and another over my left eyebrow. Then he told me not to put my face near open flame for a few days, and sent me home.

Of course, I had to give another statement to Constable Goodman before I left. That was not a very complex task. As I told the young policeman, Devon had ordered pizza. When I drove up to his apartment, it had blown up. End of story.

"Was he a friend of yours?" Goodman asked, trying to sound consolatory.

"Not really," I replied, pulling my jacket back on. "We went to school together, a couple grades apart, but I was just his pizza guy. Do you have any idea what happened? I mean, apartments don't just decide to blow up."

"I'm sorry," he said, shaking his head. "I know this has been traumatic for you, but this is an ongoing investigation. I really cannot comment. The investigator's findings will be released when they are finished, most likely in a week or two. You're certain you're okay?"

"I'm still shaking," I said honestly. "I can't hold my hands still."

He grinned, putting his notepad away. "Your body is still pumping ninety percent pure adrenaline through your veins, Mr. Myers. You should get some rest."

I wondered if this man was younger than me. He could not have been much older.

"Finn's dead, isn't he?"

Goodman hesitated, apparently unsure of how much information I was entitled to, although he had already referred to Devon in the past tense.

"*Oui*," he answered, slipping into his mother tongue. "He was pronounced before he left the building."

467

"He has family. A wife and two kids. And his mother."

"We're contacting the next of kin," he assured me. "You've had a hard day, Sidney. A hard week. Do you need a ride home?"

"I guess so," I admitted. "My truck is probably evidence or something, right?"

"*Oui.*"

"Ah well, it's a piece of junk, anyway…. When can I get it back?"

"Soon," he promised me, as we walked out to his police cruiser in the dark, chilly parking lot.

"Wow," I said admiringly, sinking into the passenger seat, next to the shotgun. "My first time in a police car, and I get to sit in the front."

Maurice chuckled. "You are one of the fortunate few, Mr. Myers."

"Call me Sidney."

"And how is your friend? Katherine, wasn't it?"

"She's doing fine. She's strong. Always has been."

"She had a lot of heart. I hope she learns to use it more wisely."

As we drove to my home, I could not help but remember how annoyed I had been with this man during our first meeting. Now, I wondered if he might be a new friend. Word travelled fast in that small town, an expression that would have been tired had it not been so darn true. When I got home, every single employee I had was there, even Becky and Mark. They were all crowded around the dining room table, and Cindy rushed over in tears to hug the life out of me, followed closely by Kat. Evidently, Angel had not spread the message of calm reassurance that I had hoped for. Karen and Randall showed up just after I did, and it took a good fifteen minutes to persuade everyone that I was all right, and then another hour to relate the whole story to them. They all had a thousand questions. That is, all of them except Clancy. He never said a single word, and his face was a carved stone.

We all sat and talked late into the night. Randall even ordered in Chinese food for everyone. The conversation was predictable, memories of Devon and speculation as to what had caused his demise being predominant. Even then, Clancy had little to say. I could understand Kat being more quiet than the others, but I could only imagine what was going on inside Clancy Grover. He had lost someone that day, and was still trying to decide if it had been a friend or an enemy. Still, my own thoughts were elsewhere. Angel was not smiling now, but she never stopped staring at me. In the few years that I had owned the pizza shop, I had been given the exact same cautionary words of advice from a dozen other business owners: If you become a friend to your employees, they will take advantage of you. However, not one person had warned me about the possibility of an employee falling in love with me. Bosses are supposed to be too intimidating for that, but I was not an average boss, and Angel was far from being an average employee. We had grown too close, and now I had no idea what to do. I decided to start by going to bed and letting sleep temporarily black out the events of a very unsettling day. I thanked my guests for their support and well-wishing, and excused myself to my room.

I was exhausted, but I could not sleep. Before I even got undressed, I slumped into a chair in front of my dresser and stared at my reflection in the mirror, trying to find any answers to my own questions about that day.

How does an apartment explode? Bomb.... A gas leak.... Electrical fire.... Unstable chemicals....

Then it hit me, an answer so obvious that I was disgusted with myself for not realizing it immediately.

Meth....

Crystal Methamphetamine. It was synthetic. In order to produce it himself, Devon would have had to create an entire laboratory. That meant creating heat, unstable compounds, and fumes. In short, a meth lab could be a ticking time bomb in the hands of an inexperienced person. True, Devon Finn had been a brilliant chemist, but if he had slipped up even once, that might have been all that was needed to make the volcano erupt.

The theory made sense, but, for some reason, the specific trigger of the explosion was a mystery that would not let go of my mind, making sleep an absolute impossibility. Even after I finally crawled under the covers, I could only lie in the dark and stare at the red glow of my digital alarm clock. Something was not making sense.

Finn had sold drugs, reportedly even to young kids. That meant that he fit my definition of an idiot, but was he a careless idiot? He had begun selling weed in junior high, and, as far as I knew, he had never once been raided by the police, or even apprehended with narcotics in his possession. He had to be extremely careful to stay under the police radar, particularly in a town so small. Given his brash attitude, I had always assumed that his eventual apprehension by the law was inevitable, but as I thought back over his years of dope pushing, I realized that he had gotten away with it for almost a decade. Was it possible for someone that thorough and careful to be reckless with something so obviously dangerous as meth lab? I could not believe that.

Every drug dealer had enemies, whether the police, concerned parents, or even other dealers. A lot of people must have hated Devon Finn, but how many were willing to take such extreme, not to mention hazardous, actions?

It was after one in the morning when I realized that the science of deduction was the only way I would find the right answer. To answer the question, I needed to ask a few more.

Who had Devon recently betrayed?

Who knew that he had a new meth lab?

And, finally, if Debbie and the kids had just left that morning, who would have already known that Devon was alone?

Clancy.

The answer made my skin crawl, and I suddenly felt like throwing up. Even under the thick pile of comforters, I felt cold, but now everything was beginning to make sense.

Clancy had been devastated by Kat's overdose. He had blamed himself, but he knew that Finn was responsible as well. For years, Finn had told him how fun and cool drugs were, and had dismissed any questions

471

about the possible dangers. Almost losing a friend to what Finn had promoted as party favours would have been an infuriating betrayal to Clancy. Thus, he was nursing both extreme guilt and an unsubsiding rage.

* * *

"I'm going to make this right.... Watch me."

* * *

Clancy's own words, so impassioned and determined, now made me wonder if his remorse had driven him to do the unthinkable. He had gone outside after Devon called the restaurant, presumably to smoke a cigarette. He had not come back inside until I was taking the pizzas out of the oven, almost twenty minutes later. That was a long time to stand out in the cold.

"His coat," I said aloud, sitting up in bed, shocked. I remembered seeing his coat hanging on the pegboard by the exit to the dining room. He had not taken it with him outside. His cigarettes were always in that coat, as were any hopes of staying warm.

Unless he was in his truck....

Twenty minutes was more than enough time to drive to Devon's home, incapacitate or kill him, and cover it up by igniting some type of fuse in the meth lab. It was bordering on being a perfect crime.

* * *

"Things are going to be a lot better from now on. I just know it."

* * *

He had said that as soon as he came back inside. He had not shivered or complained about the cold, as most would have done. On the contrary, his mood had improved by the time he returned from his break.

I did not want to believe this, but it was making too much sense to be coincidence.

Oh God, please let me be wrong.

I had wanted to kill before. I had wanted to kill Josh Kelton almost every single day since he had killed Karl Myers. He was already dead, but I knew that same rage that Clancy must have felt. And Clancy did not have the inconvenience of his intended victim burning to death before he had his shot at vengeance. I had possessed the motive to kill, but I never had the opportunity. Clancy had plenty of both.

That's why he's moving to Cranbrook, isn't it?

He could have found another job in Chetwynd, whether at the mills, the mines, or even another restaurant. There were plenty of job openings in the town he knew and loved, and he was running away from them.

He's been planning this ever since he heard what happened to Kat. He was just waiting for the right time.

And I had been the one who told him what a right time that evening was. I had told him that Finn was home alone.

I clicked on my bedside lamp, and rolled out of bed, pulling on a black sweatsuit, socks, and gym shoes. Sleeping could not help me now. Only my punching bag could.

The house was empty again as I felt my way through the darkened living room, hoping not to knock anything over, thereby waking Cindy. She had only three nights left with her maiden name, and I did not want to disturb them.

I made it through the house without making a sound, but I could hear something, a dull pounding coming from the garage. As I entered the adjoining porch, I could see that the garage light was shining through the frosted panes of glass in the door. I suddenly wished that I had taken Angel up on her shotgun offer. The pounding was louder as I drew near and eased the door open a crack, peeking into the garage.

Angel was in my garage. That was even more of a shock than a burglar would have been. I recognized her outfit. She was wearing a faded blue, sleeveless shirt, and white sweat pants. Those were Cindy's clothes, used mainly as pajamas.

Angel preferred to use the borrowed garments as workout clothes. She was a furious, sweaty cyclone, alternately pummelling and kick-boxing my punching bag. It was an awing sight, as I realized how agile the girl truly was. In spite of her short stature, some of those kicks could have easily taken my teeth out. I have never seen anyone so blindly focussed on killing a punching bag, with the possible exception of myself. I was not witnessing a simple workout. This was a vent, a release of some very pent-up frustrations. Angel's teeth were clenched savagely, and her eyes were wild, but she was not only enraged. She was crying.

Stunned, I had to watch for a full minute before I stepped into the garage and slowly approached her, not knowing what to expect. By then, she was nearing the point of collapse, wheezing painfully, drenched in sweat. She slumped against her dangling adversary, using one hand to hang onto the bag, while pounding weakly on it with the other, and sobbing.

Her eyes were closed, but I must have made a sound. She stopped punching as one eye opened and looked at me, standing quietly before her. The sweat running through her eyelashes made her blink, but she knew who she was looking at.

"Angel, what are you doing here?"

She was almost hyperventilating, but managed to push herself away from the bag and fall into my arms. I held her under her arms as she gasped for breath, trembling violently. Her tears and sweat were soaking into my sweatshirt as I quickly guided her over to the porch steps, and sat her down beside me.

"It's okay, honey, just breathe," I consoled her, pulling her close. "Just breathe. Deep breaths, okay? You're okay. It's okay, now." I held her quaking body close to mine for several tense minutes, as she fought to get her breathing back under control. She must have been fighting that bag for half an hour to get so breathless.

"Water," she gasped. "Can't ... breathe."

I rushed to the kitchen and filled a glass with water, not too cold, and quickly brought it to her. She took a few deep sips, then grabbed me again. Her breathing was still ragged, but slower.

"You could have died!" she wailed, still shaking. "Why would you want to *do that?!*"

I thought you liked it when the hero died....

"I didn't die," I reminded her. "I'm okay, too. We're both okay, just calm down. And breathe! Are you trying to kill yourself, or what?"

"He was a dope pusher, Boss! You ran into an incinerator to save a *dope pusher*? How could you do that to me?!"

I had wanted to ask Kat that last question so many times after she dangerously experimented with drugs. It was not until that moment that I came to realize what a selfish question it was. I had been faced with a situation when I needed to think only of myself, not in terms of my personal safety, but in terms of my heart. I could not have considered myself a man if I had left Devon Finn to burn. Had I left him, without even making the effort to challenge the flames, I would have written a chapter in my life that I would never want to read, and I already had far too many of those. I had charged into that fire to save myself, even more than I had done so to save Devon. I had known that he must have been dead, but I went in anyway. It was a selfish act that I would never regret.

Now, my actions were being taken personally by Angel, as though a real friend should not risk their own life, or make their own decisions, without consulting a friend first. I believe that was the first time in my life when I really understood why people had to make their own choices. Our choices made us who we were.

"I'm sorry," I said cautiously. "I hate to tell you this, but I wasn't really thinking of you, or anyone else whose life was not in any danger at the time."

"Well, what *were* you thinking?" she sniffled, wiping her eyes with the back of her quivering fingers.

"I wasn't," I said. "I did not have a thought in my head."

Her arms were around my neck now, and she was hugging me as if both of our lives depended on it.

"I couldn't stand losing you, Boss," she whimpered. "Who's going to write my paychecks when you're gone? Huh?"

I gingerly eased back away from her suffocating embrace, taking her small, cold hands in mine.

"Now, as gratifying as it is to know that I'll be missed when I'm gone," I said dryly, "I'm just a little curious. What are you doing here?"

She shrugged miserably. "Me and Cindy were up talking until midnight. She said I could spend the night in the spare room if I wanted, but I couldn't sleep. I kept thinking about you, and all that fire…." She closed her eyes for a long moment, then opened them and stared right into mine.

"Kiss me, Boss."

I cringed. "Angel … the words 'kiss' and 'boss' should never go in the same sentence. Ever."

"Kiss me, *Sidney*." She was inching even closer toward me, sliding one hand up onto my shoulder.

"I can't."

"Why?"

"Because I'm your boss. I have a certain responsibility. Being your friend doesn't change that."

"We're two adults, outside the workplace, on our own time. What are you afraid of?"

Where should I start?

"Well, for one thing…."

"I'm not trying to blackmail a promotion, Boss!" she snapped. "I'm just a woman who wants a kiss. And you need one. That much, I know."

"Angel, this has been a high-stress day for everybody."

"So? What's your point?"

"You're emotional."

"Well, like *duh!*" she scoffed. "What good is a kiss if you're only doing it for the sake of swapping spit? Emotion is not a bad thing, okay?"

"Angel...."

"Just shut up and kiss me, will ya?"

"No."

She raised an eyebrow. "Do you want to?"

Nice going, Myers. You just called her 'honey,' and now you're seriously in the deep stuff.

"It doesn't matter," I said. "It's not happening."

"Boss, if you don't want to kiss me, just come right out and say it. Then I can at least call you a liar to your face. Don't just sit here playing verbal dodge ball with me."

"Verbal dodge ball," I mused. "Did you just come up with that one?"

"I did," she said, with a touch of pride in her voice. "You like it?"

"It's catchy," I nodded, smiling slightly. "You're becoming very linguistic."

"Is that a pasta?"

"No."

"Whatever. I still need a kiss."

"That's my point," I growled. "You *need* a kiss. A man died today, and I got hurt. You all heard that I was

478

in the hospital, and it scared you. Then, you learned that it could have been so much worse, if I could have just opened a car door. I'm alive, but that doesn't completely help you. After all that stress, you need a kiss so that the day will have a happy ending. I'm sorry. Not many people get a happy ending."

"No, that's not it," she murmured, leaning close again, fresh tears glimmering in her eyes like liquid diamonds. "I've known a lot of guys, Boss, and lots of boyfriends. Sometimes, it even got serious. I was considering a proposal before I moved here. He wasn't right for me. None of them were. I could not see them standing by my side for the rest of my life. I just couldn't." One tear ran down from her big, puppy eyes.

"I don't know if you could be at my side, forever. I don't know if you even care about me, except as your friend and your waitress. But this is what I do know. I've kept my Happy List. I've added a new word every morning, all of these months, ever since you told me about your dad. Every morning, there's been one word that I want to add so badly, but I'm afraid to, because I know what it will mean. It's the first happy word that came to me, even before 'puppies....'" She took a long, deep breath through her nose, lips pressed tightly together.

"I wanted to write 'Boss.'" Her voice broke. She had to close her eyes, her lips tight again in an effort to keep the sobs inside.

"What does that mean, Boss?" she whispered, tears now flowing freely again. "Tell me what it means." I could not look into those brown eyes. It was easier to talk to her shoes.

"I know what it means," I said quietly, scuffing the toe of my shoe on the concrete, involuntarily. "But it's not allowed to mean that. It's against the rules."

Angel nodded slowly. Wiping her eyes with the back of her hands, she took a few more deep breaths, composing herself before speaking again.

"I can't keep working with you, Boss. I love you." She stood up and started back up the steps to the porch entrance, but stopped to say, "I'm putting in my two-week notice. I'm moving back to Edmonton."

Then she left me sitting alone on the stairs. Some nights, no matter what you do, sleep is just not going to be an option.

CHAPTER THIRTY-THREE

I was *seriously* not in the mood for a wedding.

Yet, it was Saturday morning, and I was in a church, in a dimly lit back room with Boris, Clancy, and Randall, and we were wearing tuxedos. Obviously, the wedding was not dependent on my mood, which I was trying very hard to conceal with a veneer of joviality. Boris was under enough strain. His face did not have a drop of blood flowing through it, and he kept tugging at his bow-tie.

"Hey, snap out of it!" I said sharply, snapping my fingers twice in his face. "Straighten that tie."

"I'm gonna die, Sid!" he whined, downing a paper cup of water in one long gulp.

"Yes," I said simply. "You are. A lot of people do. Just not today, or I'll kill you. You are going to marry my sister, and it is going to be the best thing you've ever done, career-wise, anyway. I can't fire my brother-in-law. Right?"

"I don't deserve her!" he protested, wringing his hands. I had never actually seen someone wringing their hands before.

"No, you don't," Clancy agreed cruelly. "So get out there and marry her before she figures that out. Where's Mike?"

"I don't know!" Boris panicked. "He's the best man. Why isn't he here yet? Did he miss his flight? Oh, *crap!*"

Randall snorted, adjusting Boris's tie for him. "Dude, you were talking to him three minutes ago. He's in the bathroom." He slapped Boris's hand away from his mouth. "And don't start biting your nails, either. That's gross."

Boris was unravelling fast. I supposed that was as good a sign as any that he was sincerely in love.

The last time I had peeked into the sanctuary of the large, white church in the centre of town, every single pew had been packed with families, and I recognized about one out of every twenty faces. Like I said, Boris was from a Catholic family. I did not know if it was just me, or Baptists in general, but I preferred doing things on a smaller scale. I hated even having ten people working for me at one time. Boris probably had more than that in his immediate family, although he was the only one who had stayed in Chetwynd.

Many people said that there was little incentive for young people to stay in Chetwynd, and plenty of incentive for them to get out. I had my only family, my friends, and steady work in that town, which was more than enough for my simple tastes, and was a lot more than many others of my age had. I had never looked for anything else, but I knew that, for most, something more than a job was needed to keep them in that town. Maybe love was the only reason good enough.

Slice of Heaven

I do not know if love was the reason that Boris and Cindy never moved out of Chetwynd, but it was definitely one of the determining factors. Now, they were about to take the biggest step forward that they ever had in the course of their long relationship, and I was too preoccupied with Clancy and Angel and Kat and Devon Finn to truly appreciate the moment.

As much as I hate to admit this, the photos of my sister's wedding march and ceremony are a bit depressing for me to look at. I had to escort Angel down the aisle in her shimmering navy blue gown, and Grandma Myers and both of Boris's grandmothers caught the moment on 35 mm. Angel looks like she is about to burst into tears, and I look as though I am ready to shoot somebody.

Angel managed to warm up to the wedding better than I did. Whereas I am glowering in every single ceremony photo, Angel is looking calmer by the time Boris, the groomsmen, and bridesmaids are flanking the alter, and she is actually wearing a misty-eyed smile in the shot where Uncle Reggie, in full dress uniform, is walking Cindy down the aisle.

It was, in every way, a perfect wedding. In spite of her bravest efforts, Kat did need to sit through most of the ceremony, but Father Makkie managed to keep himself out of his usual overtime. Cindy was more beautiful than she ever had been, and Boris looked like the most adoring groom alive. The crowd wept, and laughed, and clapped, all at exactly the right time. The wedding was perfect. The only problem was me.

Father Makkie, a tall, bald man who always reminded me of a turtle, asked who was giving "this woman" to be married.

"Myself and her brother," Uncle Reggie replied. A short, heavily muscled man with regulation trimmed brush-cut, my father's only sibling was an imposing figure. In his formal uniform, he was downright intimidating. I did appreciate his mention of me, but my thoughts were still far away from the holy union being formed next to me.

Wow, I need a new prep cook and a new waitress.

Father Makkie asked if anyone could show cause why "this man and this woman" should not be wed. There were no objections, only a congregation of wide smiles. That was a relief. Grandma Morris had been a real point of concern, especially after the debate she and Cindy had once got into over the morality of infant baptism.

Do you really think Kat can handle being assistant manager, Myers? Can you really trust her now? She used once. What if it happens again?

The priest began his obligatory definition-of-marriage speech, carefully outlining the inevitable horrors and hardships that were in store for Boris and Cindy.

If Kat messes up again, you have to let her go. And if Boris and Cindy decide to move on.... Dang, you could need a whole new staple crew.

Father Makkie reached the silver-lining portion of his speech, much to everyone's relief. Some had undoubtedly been wondering if he had been giving the bride and groom one last chance to bail out, before it was too late. The Father was a fine man, but his messages did tend to follow a pattern of a seriously depressing build-up to an inspirational climax.

Angel must absolutely hate you, Myers. Nice going, you insensitive clod.

Boris was repeating his wedding vows, following the priest's lead.

"I, Boris Joseph Morris, take you, Cynthia Adele Myers, to be my lawfully wedded wife. To have and to hold, to love and to cherish, from this day forward, for better or for worse, for richer or for poorer, in sickness and in health. I will love you, comfort you, honour you and keep you, and, forsaking all others, be faithful only to you, for as long as we both shall live, until death do us part."

In two days, Devon Finn's casket will sit just about where Boris and Cindy are standing.

"Cindy, please repeat after me," Father Makkie smiled. Grandma Morris, Grandma Myers, and most of the bridesmaids were weeping gleefully.

"I, Cynthia Adele Myers...."

"I, Cynthia Adele Myers...."

Two children lost their father. A woman lost her son. A girl lost her boyfriend, and most of her possessions.

"... until death do us part."

Myers, you could have died saving a man that you wanted to see suffer. Why would you do that?

Boris was putting a ring on Cindy's finger. I glanced over at Clancy, standing to my right. His eyes were fixed on the happy couple.

Are you capable of murder, Mr. Grover?

"With this ring...."

How'd you do it, Clancy? Knock his head into something, leave a burner turned on?

Cindy took her ring from the bearer, one of Boris's nephews, and slid it onto Boris's hand.

"Please repeat after me, Cindy. With this ring...."

"With this ring...."

Cops aren't stupid, Clancy. They'll figure out that a meth lab was at the heart of the blast, and they'll remember that Kat overdosed on the same stuff a week earlier. Sooner or later, the dots will get connected, and they'll come after you...

"... I thee wed."

"By the powers vested in me...."

... or, they'll come after Kat ...

"... I hereby pronounce you man and wife."

... or me.

"Boris, my dear son," Father Makkie finished softly, "you may kiss your bride."

Boris placed his hands on my sister's elbows and slowly pulled her close to him. Their lips met, and the undertoned murmuring among the assembled guests was replaced with a reverent, awed silence.

That was the longest wedding kiss that I have ever seen. I half-expected them to be blue in the face by the time it was finally finished, but they were still just smiling. Love conquers all, apparently even asphyxia.

"Ladies and gentlemen," Father Makkie announced, raising his arms as if to bless the entire gathering, "it is my greatest pleasure to introduce to you, for the very first time, Boris and Cindy Morris!"

"Oh, *yeah!*" Boris's drunk uncle Rupert Morris roared, leading the standing ovation as the bride and groom rushed down the aisle, hand in hand, grinning widely. The wedding party paired up and followed them to the foyer, first Mike Landley and Kat, then Randall and Louise Park, and finally Clancy and Becky. Angel and I remained at the front, watching them go.

"Are you happy, Boss?" she asked, slowly walking over to me. I was still watching my sister leaving, feeling like I would never see her again.

I managed a smile. "I am happy, Angel. I'm very happy for her."

"Great. Are you walking me out of here, or what?"

"Huh?" I said blankly.

"Boss, no one else can leave until we do."

"Oh," I said, suddenly noticing that most of the guests were looking curiously at us. "Right."

"Well, like *duh!*"

For some reason, that actually made me laugh. Feeling a bit goofy, I turned to Angel with an overly debonaire raised eyebrow, and bowed low, as though asking for the pleasure of her company for the next dance. She laughed, too, and obligingly curtsied.

"Sir," she acknowledged, holding out her hand.

"Ma'am," I replied, taking her arm and leading her to the foyer. She glanced approvingly up at my tuxedo.

"You clean up good, Boss."

"So do you, Miss Bates. Have you told anyone yet?"

"That I love you, or that I'm leaving?" she said boldly.

I grimaced, feeling like I had been punched.

"Leaving."

"Not yet. I'll tell them later. Maybe tomorrow."

The same day Clancy's going to announce his resignation. Jeepers, this Sunday is going to be epic....

"I'll miss you," I whispered to her, as we joined the rest of the party in a line-up by the front doors, waiting to be congratulated by every one of the two hundred plus guests.

Angel did not reply, but grabbed my hand and held it tightly as the first guests approached. I squeezed her hand reassuringly, but she was biting her lip and beginning to tremble.

"Cry," I said soothingly. "Half the people here already are. No one will notice."

She closed her eyes and nodded, a couple of tears escaping down her nose.

Well, Myers, you had her smiling again for fifteen seconds. You are the worst boss on the planet. You need to get a real job, and you need to get a puppy.

At first, I thought that I was being stung by guilt, but eventually began to suspect that Boris had not gotten all of the pins out of my rented shirt.

Naturally, it took us over an hour to get the wedding party out of the church and on the road. Fortunately the day was warm and clear, the snow was melting, and the roads had dried. Winter was inevitable, but it was taking a respectful step back in honour of my sister's special day. The honking horns of the wedding convoy filled the air throughout the town. Having the wedding photos taken at a local studio took another hour, by which time I was positively convinced that my white tux shirt still had a pin in it, somewhere just beyond my reach.

That entire day was an emotional roller-coaster. When I looked at my sister and her new husband, both radiating joy and love, I would instantly be filled with a happiness unlike any other I had ever experienced. Then, I would see Kat or Angel or Clancy standing next to the couple, and my heart would fall into my stomach. Then that pin in my shirt would jab me again, and I would begin wishing that a small rodent would scamper underfoot so that I would have an excuse to kill something.

I will never cease to be amazed by how many different combinations of people and positions are considered to be absolutely essential in the time-honoured tradition of wedding photography.

The bride and groom. The bride and groom, best man, and maid of honour. The couple with his parents. The couple with her parents, or, in our case, Uncle Reggie and Aunt Jessica. The entire wedding party with all the parents. The entire wedding party without the parents. The couple with the flower girl and ring bearer. The bridesmaids. The groomsmen. The bride and groom looking at each other. The bride and groom looking at the camera. Smiling. Not smiling. Sitting. Standing. One sitting and one standing. Laughing. Kissing. The list is endless, and no one in the studio had any coffee. When the photo shoot was finally over, I was ready to munch through a bowl of dry coffee grounds with a spoon.

Ideally, a wedding reception will be held in the banquet room of an upscale hotel. Chetwynd only had motor inns, so the options for a wedding reception were either a convention hall in the recreation centre, or one of the bingo halls. Thankfully, we had booked a convention hall for the evening. I had attended wedding receptions that were not hosted by the recreation centre, and, while not unpleasant experiences, I always expected every guest who stood up for a toast or embarrassing story to shout, "BINGO!"

Boris and Cindy's reception was held in the rather lavish Aspen Plaza Room, which the entire wedding party had spent the previous day decorating before the rehearsal dinner. Tastefully arranged round dining tables were situated around the perimeter of the dimly lit hall, partly encompassing the dance floor. Each table was covered with a baby blue cloth, tiny gold sparkles, and a single pink candle in the centre. Small net bags of candy were set by each place setting as wedding favours. The long, head table was set along one wall, across from the dance floor, and in full view of all the other tables.

We arrived at five o'clock, to the expected enthusiastic adulation of the hundred guests allowed by the fire marshal. The caterers were standing ready by the long serving tables at the far end of the room, and a young, hip-hopping disc-jockey was working at a break neck pace, as he attempted to get the sound system hooked up in time to create a musical dinner atmosphere. As the wedding party led the line to the buffet, I realized how nice it was to have others wait on me for once.

The dinner was excellent, although most of the wedding party was too worked up or stressed out to eat much. The constant tapping of utensils on glasses did not leave the bride and groom with much time to eat more than a few bites anyway, and Boris's family seemed even more voyeuristic than normal. I doubted that Cindy and Boris really minded kissing each other every thirty seconds, but the big brother in me was really starting to wish that I could grab the microphone that Clancy was using for his MC duties, and say, "For Pete's sake, everyone just shut up and let the poor girl eat!"

The program for the evening was basic and traditional, although Boris had ominously warned Clancy that there would be unpleasant consequences if the microphone was opened to the general public.

"But what about the apple juice story?" Clancy had protested. "Your uncle Rupert does such a great job telling that. He's hilarious."

"The *whole world* has already heard the apple juice story!" Boris had snarled. "You let anyone else touch that mike and I will jam it into an orifice that you would never have believed a microphone could fit into!"

Apparently, I was the only person in the world who had no clue what the apple juice story was, but Boris was agitated enough, so I never did ask.

Obviously, I was not expected to kiss someone throughout the course of the meal, but I still did not have much time to eat. Every single guest who approached the table to snap another blinding photo of the bride and groom would also come over to me, seated at the end of the table, to shake my hand and say, "You must be very proud."

"I am," I would reply, wearing an ear-to-ear grin that was only skin deep. I was miserable. That wedding seemed to represent the axle on which my life was already turning one hundred eighty degrees. Everything in my well-established comfort zone was abandoning me. Boris and Cindy were married, and I had no idea what their plans for the future were, but I could not expect them to be delivery driver and waitress forever. Angel, my best friend, was leaving me because I had not fallen in love with her. Kat was seeing a grief counsellor, but was still feeling ill, and I wondered how long it would be until I could fully trust her again, if ever. Finally, Clancy was also leaving, and I believed that he was a murderer.

I did not want my life to change so drastically, and I really did not want the changes to culminate on this supposedly joyful day. Furthermore, I knew that I was going to snap at the next person who approached to inform me of how proud I must have been. I needed cold oxygen. I needed to get outside, away from the lovey-dovey atmosphere that was doing nothing to make me feel better. I was suffocating in it.

Still wearing that forced smile, I excused myself from the table, after Uncle Reggie had toasted the bride and groom, and gave a short, heartfelt speech. As everyone grew nostalgic and misty-eyed again, I slipped out of the hall, and took the two flights of stairs down to the main lobby. Pushing the glass doors open, I stepped out into the twilight hour.

The evening was cooling, but was not yet uncomfortable. With a heavy sigh, I settled onto a bench next to the entrance, and tilted my head back to look up at the first stars, slowly appearing through the filter of streetlights. It was a good time of year, just before the onset of winter. The first blanket of snow made everything look so clean and, in a strange way, revitalized. The first snow was sort of like the first robin in spring. It represented both an end and a beginning. The grass under the snow would die, some wildlife might even starve to death before spring came around, but winter was just the last few chapters of the year to me, and thus held a certain suspense that the rest of the year never could. Winter was the beginning of the end, but I always felt that it would still hold more surprises than the other seasons. It could lead to a climax, or perhaps even a surprise ending. Anything could happen before the book closed, and spring returned.

For as long as I could remember, I had thought of the stories in an individual life to be like a book. I supposed that would be the best way to consider my own life from that point on. Everything was changing, but I had to look at it as the beginning of a new first chapter, not just the closing of the old story. Every life has many stories in it, and I knew that I was just coming to the end of one. Another was bound to start soon after. I did not know what lay ahead in the following days, as I reached my own personal climax, but I decided that I would just face each new challenge, each new chapter, as it came to me. I would survive. Sitting on that chilly metal bench, I knew that all I had to do was live. I had to live my life in such a way as to make it a good book, even if I was the only one who ever read it.

It's life, Sidney Karl Myers. Life is one of those happy things.

Angel had never said a single word to me that was not simplistic or obvious, and yet I believed that she had a better grasp on the intricacies of life than any

493

philosopher, psychologist, or psychiatrist. She knew her own life, and she knew my life as well. Very few people can make a claim like that, which made Angel even more special to me. I did not want to lose her. She was the closest and wisest friend that I had, even with her childlike hope and courage. She was a true soul-mate, and yet the conflict between love and business ethics was driving her away. I wished that I was not Boss. I wished that Karl Myers had never left me the business. I wished that Karl Myers had never left me at all.

Here's an idea, Myers. Just give Boris the restaurant as a wedding present. Go back to being the delivery driver. Life did not have so many complications back then.

I knew that I would never actually do that, but, at the same time, the thought was quite appealing. At first, I thought that would give my life a truly great final chapter, or, at the very least, an epilogue that no one really expected. However, I believed that all of life's stories should be like great works of literature, and for the hero to just give away his troubles was not good enough. It was too obvious, and transparent.

"Hackneyed," I muttered. "It's too cheesy for the protagonist to throw his career away, just for the sake of simplicity. That book would be commercial, cheap Hollywood. No substance."

Quit talking to yourself, Myers. The parking lot may not be as empty as it looks.

I did not like being a boss, and I never would. But I did love my job, somewhere underneath all of the headaches and responsibility and conflict. I truly loved it. For a long time, I had resented the fact that the whole business was mine, but I was slowly beginning to see that I should love the job all the more as a result. I had not just picked up Karl Myers dream. I was making it my own, as he would have wanted me to. Maybe that was my climax, just me figuring out who I was, and who I would be from then on.

My ponderings did not cheer me up, but they did give me enough hope to decide to go back inside and face those I was having issues with. I checked my watch. I had been sitting outside for nearly half an hour, and my friends must have been wondering where I was. Besides that, rental tuxedos were not designed for winter weather, even when it was almost a chinook. I was about to go back inside when a strange voice spoke up from the shadows next to me.

"Do you have a light?"

I looked up, startled, as I had not heard anyone approaching. The speaker was an unfamiliar woman, probably fifty years old, tall, and painfully thin. She had dark brown hair, pulled back too tightly into a bun, and she wore a long black winter jacket over a rather nice red dress. I had not seen her among the guests, but there were too many to remember.

"Sorry, I don't," I said apologetically. "I didn't hear you come out."

"I was just going in," she replied, gesturing over her shoulder at the parking lot she had come from. She seemed hesitant to go into the building. As she stepped closer, staring hard at the glass doors, I could tell that her thin face had once been beautiful, but had been worn and stretched by a hard life.

"I must have that lighter in here, somewhere," she muttered, sitting next to me and digging through her red leather purse. "I really need a smoke. Do you mind?"

"No, go ahead. Doesn't bother me."

"Thank you," she said, relief written all over her tired face. "It's a long bus ride here, and they don't let you smoke. Thought I'd die."

"You just get into town?" I ventured.

"Yeah, just a while ago. Got a cab."

"Just here for the wedding?"

She snorted. "What's left of it. I was supposed to be in this morning, but I got held up in Dawson Creek for a few hours between buses. I didn't know there was a changeover delay." She finally found her pocket lighter, and sparked it into the end of the cigarette between her lips.

"Oh crap," I said empathetically. "Sorry you had to miss it."

"Well, I thought I should be here," she said, smiling a little. "But, man, I hate being late."

"Where are you coming from?"

"Whitecourt." She blew a stream of smoke through her thin lips into the cold air, then took another long drag, and held it in her lungs as she looked out skeptically over the street. "The town hasn't changed much."

I looked over at her, curiously.

"Not very much," I slowly agreed. "It's a small town that'll never get big."

"You're from here?"

"All my life. It's home. Small, drunk, angry, but it's home."

"Same as ever," she nodded.

We sat in silence for a while, and then I asked, "How did you hear about the wedding?"

My tone was blunt and demanding.

She looked surprised. "What?"

I smiled. "You don't have an invitation, do you?"

"I don't know what you're talking about," she said angrily. "I was invited, just like you were."

"No, Carol. You weren't."

Her eyes widened and her lips parted. She was completely astonished. The glowing cigarette fell from her fingers, rolling on the gravelly earth under the bench. I could hear it land in the silence.

"Who are you?" she stammered, her pale face definitely not a result of the wind.

I chuckled humourlessly, looking back up at the stars. They were becoming much more visible, now that the sky had blackened.

"You're not going in there, Mom."

CHAPTER THIRTY-FOUR

People have since asked me how I felt, coming to this moment that I had waited for all of my life. I told them the truth. I had not waited for the moment. As far as I had been concerned, my mother was gone. After I turned ten, I resolved to just stop thinking about her. So, I did.

Every drop of blood seemed to drain from Carol Myers' face. I was actually feeling nothing at all.

"Sidney?" she whispered, her voice trembling. "Is that you?"

"Ironic, isn't it?" I said dryly. "I was, what, three when you left? And you don't recognize *me.* I thought a mother couldn't forget the face of her child."

"Sidney," she pleaded, "I know you're angry, but, please...."

"I'm not angry," I stated plainly. "I've made my peace with what you did. I can't speak for Cindy. You remember her? That little, bald, pink thing you gave birth to a while before you left?"

Carol covered her face with her hand. I can only imagine how she must have felt listening to my words, but I was not thinking about that at the time.

"How are you, Mom?" I inquired mildly. "You're not gonna tell me that you're still with that stoned-out hack you left Dad for, are you?"

She looked at the ground and shook her head, her upper teeth biting into her lower lip.

"Whoever he was...." she said slowly. "He's gone. He's been gone a long time."

"You don't even remember his name, do you?" I said, turning toward her and putting a casual arm over the seat back. "Well, I guess that shouldn't surprise me. You loved his drugs, not him. You left us for those drugs. And you never called, wrote, visited.... Never."

"Your father asked me to leave!" she snapped, hugging herself and rocking slightly, reminding me of a slender willow in a breeze. "Did he ever tell you that?"

"He did," I growled. "He also told me of what a miracle it was that Cindy was not born addicted to crack. He called that an absolute act of God."

"I loved my children!" she cried, trying not to let her tears escape.

"What colour is Cindy's hair?" I asked coldly. "When you left, she didn't have any."

Carol did not answer. I knew that she could not.

"Almost twenty-four years, Mom," I rambled. "Have they been good to you?"

"I'm doing okay," she sighed reluctantly. "I gotta job, running a carwash. I'm doin' good. Sidney, I've missed your whole life. But, when I heard Cindy was getting married.... I couldn't miss this."

"You're going to!" I snarled. "You're not going in there. I'm not going to let you disrupt the happiest day of her life with a surprise visit. You can see her later. I don't care. But not today."

"Sidney, I need to see my daughter! You can't stop me from that."

"Cindy doesn't need you. She hasn't for a long time."

"Maybe *I* need *her!*" Carol shouted.

"Cindy *might* have needed you around five years ago!" I shot back. "You know, at Dad's funeral? When she felt as though she had been robbed of both her parents? Where were you then? Strung-out that week? Huh?"

"Sidney, your father and I had separate lives!"

"And he always told me he'd take you back, if you got clean," I said fiercely. "Did you know that? Of course you did. He told you not to come back until you were off the stuff. Are you?"

"I'm clean, Sidney." She was crying now.

I shook my head. "No. You're not. You keep hugging yourself, and you're rubbing your elbow joints with your thumbs. Your veins are sore. I'm willing to bet that you wear a lot of long sleeves, cover up the redness and needle tracks. You're a junkie, Mom. I love you, but that's what you are."

Carol was not even trying to answer anymore. Her face was buried in her hands, and tears were running between her fingers. I wanted to hug her, but, at the same time, I did not want to touch her.

"Dad loved you, too," I said more softly. "Right til the end. He prayed for you every night. I could hear him. The only time his parent's Irish accent ever came through was when he was talking to God, late at night. Karl Myers never stopped loving you, and you didn't even come to his funeral."

"I'm sorry, son," my mother sobbed. "Forgive me. I'm sorry!"

"I did forgive you," I said. "Actually, only a few nights ago. But, if you go in there…. Don't give me another crime to forgive, Mom. If some part of you really does love your children still, then leave now. I don't care if you want to become part of Cindy's life, it's up to her. You're welcome to try. But, if you do love her … you will not bring chaos into her life on this day."

Carol closed her eyes and fitfully scratched her hair, fighting with herself inside. I started, baffled by the familiarity of her movements. I had never thought about where I had gotten that mannerism from.

I finally slid closer to her and put an arm around her shaking shoulders. She turned toward me, burying her face in my tuxedo, and weeping loudly. I put my mouth close to her ear and whispered.

"I'm begging you, Mom. Please go home now. Prove that you care about her. I know you're so close, it's so hard. If you can just wait one month, then come back. You can be a Christmas present, not a wedding present."

She hated to give in. I could not blame her, but I was not going to back down. I had raised Cindy, I had taught her how to cook, how to do laundry, how to drive, and I had protected her while Dad was away, working at the shop all day. I was not about to hand over the guardian reins. I was protecting Cindy's happiness now.

Carol tried to wipe her eyes clear. "I came such a long way, Sidney…."

"I know. That shows that you do have a mother's heart in there. But today is just the wrong day. Too much is already changing. We have had a couple of really bad weeks leading up to this. Please. Think of her."

"Oh, Sidney," she wept, embracing me. "My strong son…."

"I love you, Mom," I assured her again. "Please just go. I won't even tell her you were here. It'll be too hard on her."

"I love you, son!"

"I love you, too."

We held each other for a long time, and she slowly sat up, blinking away a few lingering tears. She looked up at the stars.

"I need a coffee," she quavered. "But I'll go. I've messed up so much. You're right. I won't screw up her wedding. I haven't earned the right to be here today. She needs my absence, just for a while longer. I'm so sorry!"

"It's okay," I whispered, kissing her forehead. "We're both doing good, and she's married a great man. He knows how to save money."

Carol did not want to leave my embrace, but she forced herself to stand up. I stood as well, and pulled out my wallet. There was two hundred dollars in it, and I handed it all to her.

"Get yourself a hotel room," I instructed. "I recommend the Chetwynd Station Hotel. Stay away from Rocky Valley Inn, it smells like cats have been living there. You can get a bus home tomorrow. Just wait one more month. Please."

"One month," she reluctantly promised. "I'll be a Christmas present for her." She pulled me into one last hug. "Goodbye, Sidney. I love you so much."

"Goodbye, Mom."

She turned away and scurried away across the parking lot. Immediately, I wanted to run after her and plead with her to stay, but I had to be strong, one more time. For her, and for Cindy.

"Blonde," I called after her, pocketing my empty wallet.

Carol turned back, puzzled. She was already crying again. She would probably cry most of the night. Nothing that I said or did could change that.

"What?"

"Cindy has long, blonde hair," I said. "It hangs all the way down her back. She usually wears it in one thick braid, but she wears it loose sometimes, too. She's beautiful, Mom. She looks like you." Then I turned to the doors, and went back inside. I hoped that would make it easier for her to walk away. Furthermore, it was much easier than watching her walk away.

In life, even the shortest chapter can be one of the most crucial. I had just spoken with the woman who had abandoned Cindy and I when we were very young. After twenty-four years, I had spoken to my mother for maybe five minutes, yet my life was forever changed in that time. I realized that I was truly free from my own hate. If I could love Carol Myers, I was ready for the rest of my life.

My hands were shaking, partly because they were cold. I had no idea how I was going to walk back into that hall, and convince everyone that nothing unusual had just happened. However, I did not have any time to worry about that. Just as I rounded the corner to the staircase, the young DJ almost collided with me on his blind flight down them.

"Where have you been?" the thin, spike-haired boy hissed, his dark eyes looking slightly crazed. "We're starting the dance!"

"What are you waiting for?" I said blandly, starting up the stairs with him close on my heels.

"You!"

"What are you talking about?" I said irritably.

"The groom says you got the song. Where is it?"

"What song?"

"*What song?*" This kid was seriously neurotic for someone so young. "The *song* song! First dance song, you know? The one you said you would have?"

"Oh right, that one," I recalled. "Huh … I knew I forgot something. Oh well, we can just … fudge through it, I guess."

"*Fudge through it?!* This is their first dance as man and wife! You *can't* just fudge through the first dance!"

"You've got the whole selection, right?" I asked and answered as we entered the crowded hall. People were mostly sitting around their tables, chatting and finishing their desserts, but there was a definite air of impatience.

"Of course I've got a selection," he snapped. "But we need a song, *now!*"

504

"Chill man," I said calmly. "Get a coffee or something. I'll handle it."

Cindy and Boris were on the outskirts of the polished dance floor, whispering nervously to each other. I wanted so badly to tell her what had just happened, but knew what would happen if I did.

Let it go, Sidney. For today, just let it go.

Cindy spotted me and hurried over, serpentining between the tables, her cream-coloured dress swishing and bustling.

"Sid, where were you?" she asked concernedly.

With Mom.

I smiled tiredly. "I needed some air."

"Do you have the song?"

"It's covered, baby sister," I assured her. I turned to the DJ and gave him the thumbs up. He hopped up onto the sound stage, and spoke into the microphone, his rodent-squeak voice shifting into an Isaac Hayes croon that I never would have believed that he was capable of.

"Yeah baby, ladies and gentlemen. Your eyes should now be on the dance floor. Put your hands together for the first dance of Boris and Cindy Morris, babies. We'll let them do the honorary cuttin' of da rug."

The guests whooped and applauded wildly as a beaming Boris led a blushing Cindy to the centre of the varnished hardwood. They joined hands, and Boris put a hand on her waist. They were staring into each other's eyes, and every other eye in the room was rivetted on them, from my staples at the head table, right down to Boris's drunk Uncle Rupert, who managed to focus his booze-fogged attention onto the couple. Every eye was occupied with the centre of that dance floor.

That is probably why no one noticed me as I sat down at the piano in the darkness of the hall's far corner.

I just plink once in a while. It's therapeutic.

I had never played in front of people before, ever. I did not feel uncomfortable. I just kept my eyes shut, and I pictured the faces of Cindy and Boris and Mom, and I played.

The piano speaks through me. To me, it is a language, and I can speak it more fluently than I can speak English. Whatever message I want to send is sent clearly. As long as my fingers are caressing the ivory keys, the piano is a part of me. Thus, when I set out to play the song that was perfect for Boris and Cindy to share their first dance to, that was precisely what was played.

Time means nothing when the melody is flowing out of my fingers. I can play for hours, until my soul tells me that the song is complete. The song I played for my sister and her husband lasted just over ten minutes, and it was perfect. It *was* Boris and Cindy, in musical form. Their entire lives were both summed up and immortalized in that one song. Happy times, sad times, anger and joy, grief, love, even Boris's inherent weirdness, all of it was deftly celebrated in that one work of musical magic.

I rarely open my eyes when I play. To look at my hands would be allowing my eyes to give them directions. I close my eyes, and, in the darkness, let my hands find truth and perfection. Thus, I did not open my eyes until the last sounds of Boris and Cindy had slowly reverberated into silence.

Absolute silence.

I looked up. The bride and groom were not dancing. They were staring at me. So was every other person in that huge hall, over two hundred stunned eyes boring into me. Most of their mouths were open, but not one sound was heard. I have never, before or since, heard that much silence in a room that crowded.

Okay…. That's unsettling….

I slowly stood up and covered the keys. Then I turned to face Boris and my sister, and I bowed. No one even flinched.

I had to say something. I was in the spotlight, and knew that I was expected to break the silence. No one else would.

"This is a crossroads," I said, only loudly enough for my friends to hear. "Cindy, your life just went in a new direction. It's scary, but it's right. We never know where our lives will be tomorrow, but you will always know where my heart is. It's with you, and Boris. I've never been so proud of you in my entire life. You're always going to be my baby sister, and I love you. Now, you'll have to excuse me. I need to get a coffee." Even then, the click of my boots was the only sound as I left the hall, got into my newly repaired truck, and drove to the restaurant. I never was much of a dancer, anyway.

Thanks, Mom.

CHAPTER THIRTY-FIVE

In all of his years of working for me, I had never known Boris to forget to turn off the coffeepot before closing up, not even once. I had never known him to remember to empty out or wash the pot, either. However, for those like me who did not mind coffee that was three days old and stone cold, Boris's forgetfulness kept the restaurant stocked with a constant supply of what I liked to call "Vintage reserve label."

I knew that I would always regret missing my sister's wedding dance, but I would have regretted staying and having an irrational blowup a lot more. Had Boris and Cindy known some of the things that I knew, if they had known the issues that I was grappling with, who knows what they would have done. For all I know, they might have postponed the wedding. Of course, none of us could have known that Carol Myers would show up. Now, that was just one more thing that I could not let Cindy worry about.

Cindy knew that Kat had overdosed, and that I had been in the vicinity of Devon Finn's home at the time of his death. She did not know the rest of the interplay that I was privy to. In her mind, Finn's death had been a frightening event, but was nothing more than a horrible accident. She knew that Kat was seeing a counsellor and having a speedy recovery. Cindy believed that everything was getting better. How could I tell her the whole truth, especially at this time? She did not know that Clancy and Angel were leaving, she did not know about my fight with Clancy, she did not know that Finn had supplied Kat's drugs, or even that he had a meth lab. I was the only person who knew all of these things. It was too much to deal with alone, but people kept asking me to keep their secrets, or else I kept finding out secrets that I could not share, because I could not prove them to be anything but my own suspicions.

No one else could connect the dots in the way that I had. They all had part of a story, but I had somehow been shown the whole thing. I had to get away from the hall, to leave behind all my friends and their secrets. For a very long time, I sat in my dark restaurant dining room, sipping old coffee at my piano bench, not playing anything, only lightly tracing my fingers over the cool surface of the keys.

You think you know someone, Myers. You think you can predict how far they'll go, what they're capable of. How many murderers throughout history have had mothers and friends who insisted that the charges were just a bunch of crap? Don't delude yourself. You don't even know what you're capable of, let alone another person.

I could have sat in the darkness, in complete silence, for hours more, just pondering what the next days would hold. Thankfully, a short call on my cell phone pulled me out of that miry swamp before I had sunk very far in.

The *Shaft* theme song jingled on my phone, and I pulled it out of my tuxedo jacket. The call was from a pay phone, presumably one of those in the rec. centre lobby. I knew that it was not Cindy. She would know that I had left because I needed to be alone.

"Hello?"

"Boss, where are you? You just left. We're dancing here."

"Hi, Angel. How's the cake?"

"Styrofoam. Where are you?"

"I'm home. Why?"

"Boss, you just played the piano."

"Yes. I did."

"Well … it was good. I mean … *good.* Jeepers Boss, it was unbelievable."

"Thank you. Did you want something?"

"Well, I wanted you to dance with me."

I felt as though I had been slapped with a board.

"Sorry, I just … couldn't stick around. Otherwise, I would have. Honest."

"What's wrong, Boss? Is this about me leaving?"

I hesitated.

"Among other things, yes."

"Did you ever wonder why my favourite TV show is *The Littlest Hobo?*"

With thought patterns as random as hers, I sometimes wondered how Angel managed to keep such good flow in her conversations.

"No," I sighed. "Why?"

510

"The dog is the ultimate hero, Boss. He had zero moral ambiguity. He immediately knew what was right and wrong, and he immediately did what was right. You never once saw him hesitate. Hobo put his own life on the line, even to save the villains, because it was the right thing to do. Not many people do that, Boss. You did, back at that pusher's apartment…. Hobo would be proud of you." That was all she said, and then hung up the phone.

The instant that dial tone sounded in my ear, I was in love with Angel Bates.

I had known her for less than eight months. She was leaving, moving back to Edmonton, because she loved me, too. I was her boss, and she could not have me both ways.

People are supposed to hate their bosses, not fall in love with them! I had never truly loved a woman before. I had dated various girls, some for a long time, some only once. I had not loved a single one of them, because, in the end, none of them were my friends. They were just girlfriends.

Angel was my best friend. Falling in love with her seemed like a logical next step, but that did not make the situation any less terrifying. Angel was the most contradictory person I knew, alternating fluidly between complexity and childish simplicity, in a way that I had never seen before. Nothing was as it seemed with her, and yet she was not in any way dishonest. Even stranger was the fact that I knew she had two million dollars, and I did not even care. I did not want her money. I wanted Angel. Love is a two-way street, and usually it is considered a good thing when the feelings

511

are mutual. However, the story has to end differently when it involves a worker and an employer.

I was almost twenty-seven years old. That was a long time to wait for love, and, now that it had finally arrived, I was obligated to feel guilty about it.

Luck of the Irish, Myers. You find the perfect girl, you both love each other, and you're about to wave goodbye to her. Bates.... Is that English? Who cares? Angel, I love you.

It felt so odd to say those words, even in my head. For a moment, I could not even believe that I had.

I love you.

That time, it was easier. A lot easier.

"I love you," I said aloud, albeit only to empty tables and the darkness. My voice was louder than I had expected.

"And I can never tell you," I added miserably.

But you can go back and dance with her. What good would that do? What would it hurt? She's leaving. You can give her a first and last dance. Show her that you actually care.

You're the worst dancer in this town, Myers. You got kicked out of 'The Bird Dance' in your fourth grade Easter pageant.

I know that! But she would appreciate it, anyway. That's why you love her.

You can't go back there. Everyone's just going to ask how you learned the piano.

Okay, fine, just sit here with your own bloody piano.

I will, thank you.

I could have argued with myself for the rest of the night, but a sudden thought came to me just then, pushing in between my warring moral factions.

Have you ever played her song? Angel's Song?

For a moment, I felt as though I was right back at that May afternoon when I had first hired Angel, sitting in the dark at my piano, sipping from a plastic travel mug filled with Boris's cold coffee of death. It was quite some time before I actually began to play the instrument. The keys were cool to the touch, and made me think of that windy night, as I had held Angel's chilled hand outside of the now abandoned Redmond's Ribs. How could I play Angel as a song? How could even the beauty and magic of music ever capture the fascination and joy that was Angel Bates? Her heart was such a loving puzzle, and I felt that I could never truly play her song unless I had every single piece.

Angel. Laughter. Joy. Grin. Jogging. Nice hair. Littlest Hobo. Rifles. Popcorn. Little Maple. Tire shop. Warm wind. Fear of snakes. Throwing ice water on Gavin. Well, like duh!

Unless the song could deftly encompass all of that, and so much more, it would not be Angel.

Angel's Song took over an hour to play, but each note was utter perfection. All I had to do was picture Angel's smile, hear her booming laugh, and the music just came. I felt as though she was standing right by my side, her small hand on my shoulder. For the first time, I played a song which amazed me even more than the one which I had first played after Karl Myers' funeral. Angel's melody remains the most incredible piece that I have ever played, and I will always regret that she never heard it.

Clancy was the only one who heard it.

I did not hear him come in. I did not even notice that he was there until the song was finished, and I had covered the keys with the black cover. As I stood up and slammed down the last mouthful of cold coffee, I spotted him, seated quietly at table one, on the far side of the dark room. He did not have his tuxedo on. He was wearing casual clothes: blue jeans, a plaid short-sleeved shirt, and a black, winter-lined denim jacket. Aside from the light drumming of his fingertips on the base of an inverted coffee mug, he maintained a respectful silence. I took a deep breath, and gently set my own mug back on the piano.

"Hi, Clancy." My voice was only loud enough for him to hear from across the room.

"I forgot to hand in my key," he said, holding it up for me to see, and then setting it on the white coffee mug.

"Thanks."

"I was just leaving," he said, standing and pushing his chair back up to the table. "I snuck out of the dance. Figured you'd be here."

"I'm here a lot." I almost smiled.

"You never told us you could play." He shook his head, still slightly awed. "No one ever taught you. How'd you do it?"

I shrugged. "I just pressed a key. Then I pressed another one. Music came out."

"Just that simple?"

"For me," I agreed.

"Some people study it all their lives, Sid. Heck, most people have to. What makes you different? Is it more art than science, or what?"

"Not the way that I define it," I replied. "Art and science are pretty much the same thing. Art is just the science that no one can truly teach."

514

"Wow," he snickered. "Deepness."

"I know," I grinned.

"Sid, you had your eyes closed. Did you know that they only danced for about two minutes? Then they realized that you were the one playing, and they just froze. We all did. It was amazing, Boss." I could not believe that he had just called me that.

"Good to know that I have the power of enrapturement," I said dryly. "That'll help my plans for global domination."

"But, Sid, no one knew! No one. Not even your own sister!"

"We all have secrets," I said, my voice lowering. "All of us do. Am I right?"

He stared at me for a moment, but replied, "I suppose so."

I stared right back at him. "Like Devon. He had a lot of secrets. I guess drug dealers have to in order to survive. The whole meth lab…. From what I've heard, not many people even know that he had one."

"We knew." Clancy's voice was cold enough to give me a chill.

"I know. We knew," I sighed, sitting back on the piano bench, propping one elbow on the cover, and leaning my forehead against my fingertips.

"Drug dealers don't have secrets, Sid. They have lies. That's all they have."

"Devon had two kids," I pointed out, a bit harshly.

"And I'm glad they weren't home." Clancy's face was hard as a rock.

"You knew they weren't home," I commented, rubbing my temples. The scar from my car accident had been itching a lot in the past few days.

"And I'm glad," he repeated.

"So am I," I said quietly. "After the blast, as Devon lay there, burning and dying, maybe he was glad, too."

"No." Clancy's head shake was firm and persuaded. "If he had time for final thoughts, which I really doubt, he was thinking about the money he wouldn't get."

I let out a long breath. "I don't like what he did either, Clancy. And, unlike you, I never did. You know I hate drugs. But I don't think anyone should have to die like that."

Clancy spoke very slowly, but spat hateful emphasis into each word.

"He ... sold ... *death!* To kids. And, by buying the stuff from him, I joined him. I was just like him! The difference between us is that I was repentant, when it was almost too late."

"Repentant enough to try to save the other Kat MacDonnell's of the world?" I asked gravely.

Clancy shut his mouth tightly, and gave me a long, expressionless stare.

"He was a bad man, Sid. Sometimes, bad things *do* happen to bad people. Besides, meth labs are sensitive. Drop the wrong beaker, turn on the wrong burner, improper ventilation.... Poof!" He fanned his hands out in front of him, mimicking an explosion.

"Clancy...."

"*Kat almost died because of him, and because of me!* I'm no longer a threat, and neither is he. That is all you should worry about. Kat's safe, so are a lot of other people."

"So, it's justified?" I asked blandly.

"*Death!* He sold it, Sid! To little kids! Teenagers, old people! I once saw him sell cocaine to a fourteen-year-old girl, and he was going to start selling meth! Do you really think he would have put an age limit on that?! Maybe no one died, maybe some did, but what he did was just as bad as giving someone a cash-on-delivery letter bomb! And I bought into it. I have to live the rest of my life knowing that I almost killed a woman I love, a friend who turned to me for help in a time of pain. And my advice to her was to buy death! Could you live with that, Sid? *Could you?*"

He was seething through gritted teeth, his eyes brimming with tears that he was too embarrassed to let fall. I shook my head, still staring at him.

"I can *live*, Clancy. Devon Finn can't."

"I really don't care." Clancy sounded tired, blinking and wiping his eyes with the back of his hand.

"He was only twenty-four," I said. "He may have deserved jail, but his two kids…. They deserved a father."

"He never got another chance to kill his own kids," Clancy muttered. "I can live with that."

We both fell silent, staring at each other from across the dining room. My stare was accusing, his was defiant, both were hard and unflinching. It seemed like an eternity before he closed his eyes, let out a long, whistling sigh, and then slowly crossed the room, pulling out another chair from the table nearest to my

517

bench. He sat in it backwards, his forearms and chin on top of the backrest.

"Sid … when I said I was just leaving, I meant for good. My truck's packed out there, gassed up. This was my last stop. Tell everyone I'm sorry that I missed the dance."

"*What?*" I was shocked. "I thought you weren't going for a couple of weeks yet!"

"I was. I decided I wanted to get out now. For some reason, I suddenly hate this town."

"Clancy, it's almost midnight! Where are you going to go at this time of night?"

"I like the lighter traffic. I'll get through the pass tonight, maybe get some sleep somewhere south of Prince George."

"Clancy…." I was still at a loss for words. "Does anybody else know?"

"No," he said simply. "Just you. I didn't even tell Marty. He's out tonight. I left a note at my place, telling him he can keep whatever I left behind."

"You didn't even say goodbye?"

"Sid, I'm not much of a friend right now, even to the ones who don't know what happened. I didn't want a big send-off. I don't deserve it. But I figured I owed this much to you, to let you know." He looked up at the ceiling for a long time.

"I think I'll take the scenic route down through the Rockies. Banff, Jasper, the icefields…. Have you ever driven through the icefields, Sid?"

I nodded slowly. "Once. When I was a kid, Dad took us down there one weekend, sometime in July. I barely remember it."

"That's no good," Clancy said with half a smile. "You need to drive it in early spring, or late fall, when all the campgrounds are closed, and the weather can turn bad at any second. It's just one endless, empty road. No tourists. No traffic at all. And you can't go with family, or even a girlfriend. You have to drive it alone. A whole day's drive, just you and the purple mountains, and all the snowy peaks. When that sun starts to set, the whole rocky range just glows pink, like you've never seen before. It's unreal."

I smiled at the thought. It was nice.

"I'll have to do that someday," I decided. "I haven't had a vacation in about … sixteen years, or so."

"Have you ever been in love, Sid?" The question was sort of out of the blue, but was somehow not unexpected.

"Yeah," I said introspectively. "Just once."

"With Spring?"

"No," I said. "Never with Spring." Clancy looked at me curiously before replying, "I was only in love once, too."

"Wow. You?"

"We all have our secrets," he grinned. "Four years ago, on my first drive through the Rockies, going to visit my Kelowna cousins, I fell in love."

"With what? A mountain goat?"

Clancy stared up at the ceiling again, as the memory replayed in his mind. "I was almost out of gas when I got out of the icefields, into Lake Louise. I'd been driving about thirteen hours, it was dark, looked like a snowstorm was coming. It never did, it was only dark clouds, but it made the ride kind of scary, wondering if I would be stuck out there all night, just me and the mountains and no gas. I must have been running on fumes by the time I got to Lake Louise. It was a sweet hotel that I stayed at, real fancy, but rustic too, you know? I still have the soap I stole.

"The hotel had like a four-star restaurant built onto the lobby, and Samantha the waitress brought me my steak. She might have been seventeen, but she called me 'Hon,' like all those grandma diner ladies do. I loved her."

"Samantha the waitress …?"

Clancy raised his hands, apologetic.

"I have no idea what her last name was. She never knew mine, either. We started chatting about mountain sheep, and those elk with the radio collars, with the antennas. The restaurant was empty, closing up for the night, and I asked if she wanted to take a walk with me after. She said she did.

"I stood outside in the cold for half an hour while she finished her cleanup, but, as soon as she came out, she took my hand, and it was like the most natural thing in the world. We had met less than two hours before, and she wanted to hold my hand. I've never felt that kind of trust before.

"Lake Louise is like one big hotel and gas bar, but we walked all over that town, talking about our lives, or just saying nothing, just sharing the pure joy of each other's company.

"It wasn't a one night stand, Sid. When we got to her apartment, she gave me one really long kiss on the front steps, and said, 'Don't forget.' Then I hugged her forever, and … I walked away. We knew each other like old friends, and we'd just met. There has not been a single day go by since that I haven't missed her. I date a lot. But they're not her. She was the only girl I've ever loved. And I've never told anyone. But, hey, today's all about change, anyway."

We sat silently for another moment, each lost in our own thoughts, before I spoke up.

"You should look her up. Samantha the waitress. She might still be around, somewhere."

"I think I will," he nodded, smiling. Then he stood up, stretched wearily, and held out his hand.

"It's been good, Sid," he said. "I'm sorry. For everything."

"It's okay, man," I said kindly, shaking his hand. "You're the best. You take care of yourself."

We hugged each other for a long moment, and then he stepped back and nodded knowingly at me.

"Thanks for being my friend, Sid," he whispered. "Take care of Angel. She's worth it."

"I will," I answered, without thinking about what he had just said.

I will?

"Tell everyone I said … goodbye. And that I'm sorry."

"I'll tell them." I nodded solemnly. I still could not believe that he was leaving without saying a word to anyone, except me.

"Goodbye," he said quietly, turning away and crossing to the front desk.

"Clancy," I said in an expressionless voice.

He stopped in front of the lobby door, his head and shoulders hanging heavily, as if he knew what I was going to say. Then he turned and looked back at me. I could not read any emotion in his face, either.

"You remember what you told me about hate, when you put in your notice?" I said. "You never answered the obvious question tonight ... but I never really asked it, either. I will always be your friend, but I hope that I never see you again. Because I am going to go through the rest of my life believing that you killed a man."

I will always remember his last words to me before he walked out that front door, spoken with the very slightest trace of a hard smile.

"A *man*, Sid ...? Is that what you'd call him?"

CHAPTER THIRTY-SIX

Cindy and Boris had to drive an hour to Dawson Creek that night, in order to get a hotel that actually featured a Honeymoon suite and doors that opened into a hallway, rather than a parking lot. I went back to the reception hall after midnight, just in time to watch Cindy toss the bouquet before she and Boris left, but I stayed out of sight in the back. As a final ironic twist, Angel caught the bouquet. She had to elbow check a couple of Boris's sisters and leapfrog over Becky to do it, but she caught it. It was like watching Jackie Chan choreography.

Then, I just went home. I called Cindy's cell phone when I knew that they had to be on the road, and offered my final congratulations and goodnights, along with an apology for skipping the dance. Cindy was too giddy to be mad at me, and she was still awed by my piano debut. I cut her off with a "Goodnight. I love you," before she could start questioning me about my music. I was asleep by one o'clock in the morning.

The two longest weeks of my life were over. Boris and Cindy were married. Clancy was gone, and no one else knew about it. I had seen Clancy's possessions, and knew that he could not have possibly fit even half of them into his short box truck. The remainder was just left where it sat.

Cindy and Boris were not prepared to take a full-length Honeymoon yet. They spent Sunday in Dawson Creek, and then returned home the following morning. It felt so strange to help them move all of Cindy's possessions into Boris's apartment. My house felt bare when we had finished. Cindy told me to consider it "roomier." Angel, Becky, Mark, Kat, and Jason, our newest student recruit, were all scheduled to work with me on Sunday. Kat still tired easily, but was doing much better. Everyone was on the schedule for Monday morning, but not because they all had to work then. It was time for a staff meeting.

I had everyone assemble in the kitchen at ten o'clock in the morning on that cold day. I finished my cup of coffee, and then I told them about Clancy. I told them everything, right from the moment that I had found him with Devon Finn by the rear exit. The only part that I left out was that Clancy had known that Finn was home alone on the day that he died. I did not want them to have to bear the agonizing weight of suspicion that I did.

No one took the news well, not even Kat, who had already known that Clancy was quitting. Angel and Cindy even cried a little. Clancy Grover had been everyone's friend. He was charming, funny, handsome, and kind. He would be missed for a very long time.

"Now, we've got some promotions to deal with," I said. "You guys are always telling me to start taking it easy. Well, I'm starting, and you'd better be able to handle it. Effective immediately, I am promoting Kat to assistant manager, so whatever she says, goes … like it hasn't always been that way. Becky, you're finished high school. I'm offering you a place on my staple crew, filling in Clancy's old job as assistant prep cook. You've proven yourself steady and hard-working, and I'm offering you full-time, ten bucks an hour."

"Okay," she nodded. "Thanks."

That was the longest speech I had heard her give in weeks.

"I know we all miss Clancy," I said. "But, things change. We just follow our own path, try to pick the right one. Thanks for coming in early. Employees of By The Slice Steak and Pizza, please get to work…. Uh, Jason, not so fast. Can I talk to you for a second? My office, please."

The guy was an idiot. As I closed my office door, I could see Kat already heading for the front entrance, holding the 'Help Wanted' sign in one hand. I took comfort in the fact that some things do not change. Work went on, and Angel did not say a word to me.

Devon Finn's funeral was on Monday, as well. I had a hard time not thinking about him throughout the day, a man whom I had barely known, yet one who had died only a few short yards away from me. The blast still replayed frequently in my head, and every time I was sure that I could see Clancy's face in the midst of the flames. Still, I just kept making pizzas, preparing, cooking, and serving. So much had changed, but I felt as though I was ready to carry on, one pizza at a time, two-for-one on Sundays. There were just a couple of things that I felt I still needed to do before my story could end and my book could close.

Boris and Cindy joined me for supper in my big, empty house on Wednesday evening. After the dishes were washed and put away, Boris and I sat at the table, drinking coffee and talking, while Cindy clambered upstairs, to box up a few overlooked belongings.

The night was cool, and light snow was drifting down. Boris and I both had our chairs turned slightly toward the dining room window so that we could watch the white flakes settle onto the window sill.

Boris shook his head, after a long, peaceful minute.

"I still can't believe he's gone. Without saying goodbye, that's just unreal."

I shrugged my shoulders, blowing into my hot mug.

"He couldn't stay forever, Boris. Some people can only handle the service sector for so long."

"Well, I don't see why not. We're like his family here."

"Not many people can be happy to live out their lives in a restaurant," I sighed. "I'm a lifer. You guys all still have choices. It's a big world out there, beyond this little valley."

"This town is Clancy's home, Sid. It's all he's ever known. I know he loves it."

"Well, he left it."

"Maybe he just needs to get away for a while," Boris suggested hopefully. "He and Devon were friends. Maybe he'll just get out for a while, see the sights, find his focus, and then come back."

He won't.

I nodded. "Maybe. I had to let him go, but we left on good terms. I hope he comes back."

But, he won't.

"Are you worried about losing your crew?" Boris inquired, stirring another spoon of sugar into his coffee.

"A little," I admitted. "It's hard to find good help, and I've already lost Spring and Clancy this year."

And Angel.

"Well, relax," Boris commented. "Me and Cindy talked a lot about where our lives are going, and we've decided that we love the full-time employment we've already got. We aren't going anywhere. And you know Kat and Angel will never leave you."

"I don't know what I know anymore," I groaned. "Life just seems like it was easier before. I don't know what changed."

"Most likely ... you," Boris pointed out.

"Who knows...."

"You have changed, Sid," he continued. "I've seen it over the last week or so. There was this ... anger in your face that isn't there anymore. I know you've had a crazy couple of weeks, but you aren't mad. Last month, you would have been."

"I'm just trying not to hate," I sighed. "Call it an experiment."

"Sounds like a good one," he nodded. "I'll have to try that."

"Oh, come on, Boris. You lecture me on hate. You can't tell me that it's even an issue for you."

"Well, it is," he admitted. "When I bit your head off over the whole Phil Vardega thing, I had to force myself to do it. I had to say those words, just to keep myself from admitting that you only did exactly what I wanted to do. I was lecturing myself."

"I don't think there's too many of us in this world who can honestly say that we don't hate anyone," I reminded him. "It's not healthy, but it's human nature. We all have to deal with it."

"Well, that's the weird thing about me. I don't hate people. I hate…. I don't even know how to say this. I hate situations, I guess. Not people."

"Situations?" I did not understand.

Boris shook his head and sighed. "You want the truth, Sid? I know everyone in this town, and I absolutely hate that. Really. I hate it. All there is to know about this town, every dirty detail, I know it. You want to bust some drug dealers? I know just about every one of them by name, face, address, what they order, and how much they tip. I could tell you the names of dozens of kids, twelve to fifteen years old, who buy weed and coke from them. Yeah, I see them knocking on those doors at midnight. They're always laughing, too. It's so fun, so dangerous, everybody's doing it. I hate it all. I mean, I hate finding out which prominent, well-liked men beat up their wives. I hate realizing which sixteen-year-old girls have forty-year-old pusher boyfriends, just to get the free dope. I see it all, Sid. Every week, I see it. Who isn't feeding their kids enough, who leaves their kids home alone when they go to the bar, the kids with bruises that don't look like they came from falling off a bike. It gets to the point where I get mad when I see all of the happy, healthy families, because I don't think they should have anything to be happy about." Boris had to stop talking for a moment, rubbing his eyes with his thumb and forefinger. He leaned back in his chair, and stared vacantly out the window. The snow was beginning to come down in larger flakes.

"Sid ... small towns shouldn't be like this. This is not Mayberry. It should be, though. I would love to have all the stereotypes. People smile and talk on the streets, no one locks the doors at night, everybody knows your name. Well, I do know everyone's name, and I wish I didn't. It's a small, angry, and addicted town. Sometimes ... I have to wonder why I love it so much."

"Stockholm syndrome," I quietly remarked. There was another minute of thoughtful silence before I asked him, "So ... how do you keep going? What's your reason for getting up in the morning?"

Boris shrugged. "God hasn't given up on us yet, so we can't give up on each other. Honestly? I think that all humans are inherently evil. But, I think we can change. You did, I did, Cindy did. Maybe there's hope for the rest of us. People can change."

"Yeah," I said, after thinking that over. "Maybe they can." I stood and downed my whole mug in a few long slurps.

"I'm going for a walk," I told him, setting my mug in the sink. "Just lock up the place before you leave."

"Are you okay?"

"Yeah, I'm fine," I assured him, pulling on my brown leather jacket. "Some nights, you've just gotta walk it out."

"It?" he said curiously.

I nodded. "It."

"So, Sid?" he asked, as I was pulling on my cowboy boots. "What's your reason for getting up in the morning?"

I smiled. "I'll let you know in a day or two. I promise. Take care of my sister."

He gave me a grin and a thumbs-up as I walked out the door into the snow.

The night sky was clearing, and the snowfall had almost stopped. I loved winter nights. They were so peaceful, with an almost unearthly silence. Every house looked warm and secure, the lights glowing more softly than usual upon the snow. Traffic was light or nonexistent, and Christmas lights and decorations were everywhere. The air was crisp and cool, but the harsh cold of winter had not arrived yet. I walked nearly halfway across the town, and only saw two moving vehicles the entire time.

I slowed my brisk pace as I approached my destination, a lonely blue duplex in the Crown Sub-Division. I stopped in front of the door, and took a few deep breaths before ringing the bell. A bit of snow was just beginning to drift down from the sky once more when the creaky brown door was cracked open, letting a sliver of light seep out onto the snow-covered porch.

She was peeking through the crack at me, suspiciously. I could not really blame her. She did not know me.

"Do I know you?" she asked, a bit coldly.

"No," I admitted. "You don't."

"Who are you?" She sounded very tired, also.

"Mrs. Finn …. I'm Sidney Myers."

CHAPTER THIRTY-SEVEN

Amelia Redbird-Finn was a short, petite Cree woman, forty years of age. She wore her black hair in two very long braids, one of the few Native women in Chetwynd who always kept that traditional look. She usually wore a dress, too, and was quiet and conservative. It was always hard to believe that Devon was her son.

Mrs. Finn had worked at the local pharmacy for many years, but was best known for her work as a Native crafts artisan. Her small, rustic duplex was adorned with handcrafted moccasins, beaded leather, and dream-catchers. She also painted, chiefly wildlife and forest scenes, a lot of wolves and mustangs. She had a unique style of deftly reversing the colours of her paint subjects, painting the animals with the colours of the trees and mountains, and vice versa. I never would have believed that a green and rust wolf in a silver forest could have been a beautiful work of art, but Amelia proved it possible. Whether this represented her perspective on the collective unity of the natural world, or was just a well-crafted gimmick, I really had no idea. I had never been inside Amelia Finn's home before, but I had seen her paintings and crafts in businesses and residences all over town. She seated me in a wicker sofa covered with old blue cushions, while she prepared two china mugs of tea, taking the hot water directly from a kettle on her warm wood-burning stove in the living room. I found myself in absolute awe of her coffee table, the glass-overlaid surface of which had been exquisitely painted into a depiction of a soaring blue eagle, against a brown sky with golden clouds. It was the most beautiful work of art that I had ever seen.

I noticed people's mannerisms, a gratuity-ensuring trait that I had picked up during my years as delivery driver. To charm tips out of customers that I only saw for a few seconds at a time, I had to be able to read them quickly. The first thing that I noticed about Amelia Finn was that her knuckles were white. The cup of tea that she offered me was being gripped very firmly, whitening her knuckles, and even causing the veins in her wrist to puff out slightly. She was trying very hard to keep me from knowing that her hands were shaking. I hated tea, but I smiled my thanks, and took a long, grateful sip. Amelia settled into a rocking chair across from me, holding her own mug with both hands. She was blinking. That could have been nerves, or she could have been trying not to cry.

"You were with my son when he died?" She said it more like a statement than a question.

"I was there," I replied.

"Did he speak to you?" She was looking at her mug, rather than my face.

I shook my head, bobbing my tea bag up and down. "I'm sorry. He was dead. I could do nothing."

"Why are you here?"

I was surprised by how little expression was in her voice. She just sounded weary.

"I don't know," was my honest response. "Your son was not my friend. I hated what he did."

"You're an honest man," she said. "Did you hate him?"

I nodded. "At one time, yes." I set my mug on the coffee table, vaguely wondering if I should request a coaster. "But, as of late, I have been trying very hard not to hate anyone. I believe that it was poisoning my life."

"Loving your neighbour," she mused. "Does that work?"

"It's very hard," I admitted.

"Most good things are," she said. "Do you have children?"

"No, ma'am. I'm not even married."

"Hmmm. Not many people in this town consider that a prerequisite. My son never did."

"How are his kids?"

"They are sad, Sidney Myers. They are very sad. Much more so than their mother, I imagine…. Or their grandmother."

I froze, with my mug almost touching my lips. I could not believe that she had actually said that.

"I know what my son was," she explained simply. "He chose to invest his great mind into the construction of a drug trade. Others likely would have died if he had not. Greed and selfishness are my family's legacy from now on. My son is my dishonour."

"It wasn't your fault," I said slowly. "He made his own choices."

"I'm his mother," she snapped. "I had a duty to raise him better. Tell me, are parents nothing but blind fools? We tell our children not to play with guns, and then we give them water pistols so they can play 'Bang, you're dead,' in the backyard. Is that failure, or just a cruel irony?"

"I suppose it could be either," I said carefully. "It all depends on how your child turns out, and maybe there's no way to predict that. In any case, you didn't give Devon a model meth lab to play with in the back yard."

"No," she sighed. "I did worse. I gave him a father who introduced him to pot at age three. And I did nothing. I watched them get high together. I didn't do anything."

"You were scared of him," I said, rather stupidly as all that I knew about her husband was from rumours. "No one can blame you for that."

"I can," she answered. "Are you sure you don't know why you came here?"

I looked at my own reflection in the tea for a long time before I could reply.

"I think I came here to tell a mother how sorry I am that I didn't save her son," I muttered, eyes closed. "I'm sorry."

"Do not be," she said. "It was a chemical explosion. I doubt even a fully equipped firefighter could have gotten to him in time. You tried, and I owe you thanks for that."

"You don't understand," I sighed, turning away to stare through the living room window into the blackness outside. "This is the second time that I have been unable to save someone from the fire. Four people have died flaming deaths around me, and I couldn't do a thing about it. The last time, I was so filled with hate that it never even occurred to me to pay respects to the families. If anything, I thought they owed me something…. I just can't live like that anymore. I had to come here."

"I do not miss my son," Amelia said flatly, but her voice grew progressively shakier as she continued. "But, I thank you. You tried to save him. Had you succeeded, perhaps he would have changed. Perhaps he did need another chance…. Regardless, you are a good man who risked his life to save a bad one. Not many would do that. I do not think I would."

I still could not believe what I kept inferring.

"Did you hate your own child?" I asked cautiously, feeling queasy in my stomach.

A tear ran down Amelia's face, and her voice trembled even more.

"Yes," she quavered. "God forgive me, I hated him for who he became. People come here now, giving me flowers, and my heart is just glad that it's all over. God, forgive me!" Tears were now flowing freely.

"I understand," I said quietly. I could think of nothing else to say that would even sound remotely appropriate.

"Do you?" she wailed. "He was my son, and I…. He was my son!"

I did not try to respond to that. Instead, I found that my gaze was suddenly fixed on her right hand, as she wiped her eyes with the back of it. She was no longer squeezing a mug, but the veins on her hand and wrist were still white and puffy, while the skin surrounding them was red.

Her hand was blistered.

"Have you ever lost family?" she finally sniffled.

In spite of the tea, my mouth was dry. Very dry.

"My father, in a car crash," I said, barely able to focus my thoughts. I was still looking at her hand. "My grandfather, before I was born. Maybe more on my mother's side, but I don't know … who else … maybe…." My voice trailed off, as did my entire train of thought. I could not think of one more word to say.

Her hand is blistered….

Never blinking, I took a long sip of tea. It did not help my cotton-mouth.

"Did you … hurt your hand, Mrs. Finn?" My voice almost shook, but I managed to steady it.

She flinched. It was an almost imperceptible movement, but I saw it.

"I punched a hole in my bathroom mirror when the police told me about Devon," she said, very calmly.

"I thought you said you were relieved."

Her lips pressed together tightly for a moment. "Yes … but I was quite emotional, even so."

"You punched a mirror?"

"It hurt my hand."

"Your hand is blistered," I pointed out.

She was looking at her tea mug again. "I punched the mirror," she repeated. "It hurt my hand."

"Did you burn your hand?" I asked, very slowly.

She sipped her tea. I quietly stood up and set mine on the coffee table. There was a very long silence. "You must have hated him very much," I said, looking her in the eye.

"I did," she agreed coolly. "More tea?"

"I think I should go," I said quietly. "Thank you, Mrs. Finn. I am sorry that I couldn't do more. And I am sorry for your loss."

She smiled grimly through her tears.

"Thank you for your efforts, Sidney Myers. I hope, someday, you will save someone from the flames. Someone worthy."

"Perhaps," I said, uncertainly.

Amelia Finn stood and folded her arms. Her smile was growing stronger.

"There is justice and there are rewards in this life," she stated determinedly. "Good people will be rewarded, and bad people will be punished. My husband beat me, and tried to hurt my son. He is dead. My son tried to hurt many people. Now, he is dead. There is justice, Sidney. Sometimes, it just needs to be sought, diligently, for a very long time."

My mouth was open but no words were coming out. I had to leave, get out of that house.

"I am glad that you are a good man, Sidney Myers," she said, her misty eyes narrowing, her smile hard. "Good things should happen to you, I trust."

I could barely make my lips and tongue coordinate.

"Thank you for the tea, Mrs. Finn," I managed to say, backing out of the room.

"The Finns are gone," she said. "From now on, I will be known as Amelia Redbird again."

I nodded, unable to look away from her, even as I pulled on my boots in the porch.

"It's a beautiful name, ma'am. Goodnight." I had to back out the door. I could not turn my back on her until the door closed in front of my face.

You did not punch a mirror, Amelia Redbird.

I turned to walk away, but the sidewalk ahead of me suddenly seemed to be swaying back and forth. I started running through the snow.

The next thing that I remember was being doubled over behind some nearby shrubs, throwing up. My mouth burned with the taste of bile and tea, my eyes were watering, and I had to slowly take a few deep breaths. Looking quickly around me, embarrassed, I hoped that no one had seen me, but the only movement that I saw was falling snowflakes. I gripped my kneecaps tightly, trying to keep my legs from shaking.

No way. It's impossible.

I raked my sleeve across my mouth, and spit several times, trying to clear the foul taste from my mouth. It was several moments before I could stand up straight, and, even then, the blood was pounding in my head. I needed coffee.

Her own son.... No. That just doesn't happen.

I had been absolutely convinced that my friend Clancy Grover was responsible for the death of Devon Finn. However, since my only visit to Amelia Redbird, I no longer know what to believe. All I know is that punching a mirror would have cut and stabbed her skin. It would not have caused blisters.

538

CHAPTER THIRTY-EIGHT

The snow fell all night long. By morning, there was another foot of it, all over the valley town. It was Thursday, the beginning of a new work week in my world. A snow day was Boris's moment of glory, as people moped about the accumulation, stayed close to home, and ordered in pizza deliveries. It was going to be a very busy day at By The Slice Steak and Pizza. I knew that before I even left my big, empty house that morning. I woke up early, ate some toast and eggs, then showered and dressed for work. I stood in front of my bathroom mirror as I carefully knotted my black tie, and buttoned the black vest. Maybe Angel was right. Maybe my uniform needed more "ambience." My cowboy boots were sitting on the shoe rack in the porch, freshly polished and glossy. After a very troubling visit to Amelia Redbird, I had sat up in the living room for half of the night, just thinking and polishing my boots. I had also made an important decision.

My truck was running in the garage as I bundled up in a heavy, blue, winter coat and leather gloves, and locked the front door. Sid's Rig had a new windshield, but, aside from that, had survived with only a few paint scratches. I could live with paint scratches. I had come to understand just how much imperfection I could live with. My truck was old, and I loved it, sticky doors and all.

Snowplows were flying down every street and back road in town, trying to help the citizens get to work, while pushing huge snowbanks into their driveways at the same time. Life was good.

It was nine o'clock in the morning, the sun had not yet risen, I had gotten three hours of sleep, and I did not even care. I was in the good mood that often follows a big decision. I had plenty of time to shovel my driveway and still be at work by ten, but I did not. I got into my toasty truck, and backed through the heavy mat of snow over my driveway, easing the rig into the partially plowed street. Even if the sun had been up, I would not have known it. The snow was still falling thickly from a sky white with clouds. Visibility was poor, and the roads were a bit slick. I still did not care.

Angel's home was only a few blocks away, but I still almost went into the ditch once, when I tried to navigate the right turn at a stop sign. I was overdue for my annual snow-tire changeover.

I'll bet Angel would do great in a tire shop....

December had arrived, and winter had officially started, in spite of the calendar's insistence that it was still autumn for more than two weeks. Christmas was already in the air, and I knew that it was going to be my best one yet. It just had to be. My good mood would not allow anything else.

Only after I parked in Angel's driveway did I begin to have second thoughts. I had made my decision, and I would carry it out, but I was suddenly hindered by nagging doubts.

Is this the right thing to do, Myers?

There was one way to find out. I karate-chopped my door open and stepped out into the snow. I almost slipped on the ice, fiendishly concealed under the white blanket of powder. I regained my footing and my determination, and I carefully made my way up to the front door.

Sorry you had to miss this, Dad. I think you would have been proud of me. I was always proud of you.

In front of the door, I froze. I just could not bring myself to reach out and touch that doorbell. I had to wait. I had to breathe.

The snow was coming down even harder now, and the flakes were big and wet. I probably stood in that storm for the better part of thirty seconds before I finally rang that glowing red doorbell. Or maybe I stood there for an hour. The only thing that I really remember about that eternal hesitation was that my hair was snow-matted and, thus, not perfect. I liked my hair to be perfect.

Oh well.

Angel did not burst out laughing when she opened the door and saw her snow-coated Boss standing on her doorstep. I was actually a bit disappointed. Any outburst of mirth would at least have broken the ice that my tongue suddenly seemed to be made of. Angel was just grinning. Widely. Affectionately.

Her hair was not perfect either. It was tied up in a ponytail under an old blue and white rag, with only a couple wisps of her springy brown bangs hanging down her forehead, partially covering her puppy eyes. Her brown plaid shirt was a couple of sizes too large, tail untucked, sleeves rolled up to her elbows. It was the first time I had ever seen her wearing blue jeans, and they were grungy and paint stained, with both of the knees worn right out. Try as I might, I have no memory of what her footwear was. She might have been barefoot. I do not remember. My best guess was that I had interrupted either a house cleaning or painting project. She was an absolute mess, and I have never seen a woman look so beautiful. I did not see a beautiful face. I did not see a beautiful body. At that moment, all I could see was the beautiful heart that was Angel Bates. She was my best friend. She was my reason for getting up in the morning.

Angel had only worked for me a few months, and she was quitting in one week. During those past months, I had endured some of the most painful moments of my life, and, yet, I will always remember Angel's ROE as my own slice of heaven. Angel Bates had made them all worthwhile.

"Boss," she said, looking like she wanted to laugh. "Sidney."

"You're fired," I said dryly. "Will you marry me?"

She really did laugh then, but she also opened the door wider. I figured that was a good sign.

EPILOGUE

After an investigation by the local fire department and an RCMP arson unit, the death of Devon Finn was ruled to be the result of an accidental chemical explosion. I was never questioned about the event after my initial witness statement, and I do not believe that Clancy was ever questioned about it. Two months later, Amelia Redbird moved to Burnaby, British Columbia, to care for her ailing father. A collection of her artwork was published a year later.

Randall Harrigan and Karen Malloy still operate the Randall's Ring gym. Both have married, and Randall and his wife, Bess Nolan, are expecting their second child.

Boris and Cindy Morris still work at By The Slice, and recently moved into a new, larger apartment. Boris has yet to spend any of his tips, and the balance in his gratuity account would probably make me sick if I ever dared to ask him what it was. Also, despite the fact that they both refused to know the results of the ultrasound, Boris is sure that it is a boy.

After fully recovering from her overdose, Kat MacDonnell took her second vacation week, which included a cruise with her sister-in-law, Evelyn MacDonnell. Kat has told me that her time on ship allowed her to realize that Roger MacDonnell was the only love of her life, and that her memories of him are sufficient to keep her happy. She says that she will never marry again. I do not know if I believe her, but am relieved that she is better dealing with the pain of her loss. Although the rift between us took time to close, she remains one of my closest friends, my most valued employee, and I have yet to win a single game of chess. Kat has also spoken to various school groups about her overdose, as part of drug-awareness programs.

Clancy Grover is gone. I never saw him again, after I watched the front door of my restaurant swing shut behind him. He never called, never sent a forwarding address, never even sent a single letter or Christmas card. Although I have no real reason to think otherwise, I have no definitive evidence that the man is still alive. I have not tried to find out.

Carol Myers was invited to, and attended, the wedding of myself and Angel Bates.

That is my story. Or, I should say, that is one of them. The record of employment of Angel Bates at By The Slice Steak and Pizza was a definite story of its own, but it was not my only one. Every life has many stories, and I hope that you will remember that when you next encounter a stranger, and are tempted to dismiss them as irrelevant. We can all learn from each other's stories.

A new story has just begun for me. I wish I could say that the new first chapters will be easier than the last, but, unfortunately, I cannot really believe that. To be frank, I believe that the pain and remorse of my past have only begun. My next years will be a constant struggle to find solace under the weight of overshadowing guilt. My hope is that having the woman I love by my side will make the search easier to conclude.

Almost a year after Angel and I were married, I had another dream about the night that my father died, one much different from any before it. It was my surprise ending, a crucial missing puzzle piece that made so many aspects of my life come into context.

* * *

Blackness was all around me. I stood alone on a dark street, looking up at the red and white of a stop sign. I was dressed in black. My suit and mock neck sweater were black, as were my glossy leather shoes. I did not know why I was dressed like that, or even where I was. I did not move, not because I could not, but rather because I knew that I was not supposed to. Something deep and dark inside of me knew that I was not permitted to interfere with whatever would follow. Only my eyes were allowed to move, scanning the dark for any familiarity.

Thunder rumbled overhead, and a drop of rain struck my face. Almost like an echo in the back of my mind, I heard a familiar voice. There was no sound, but I still heard it.

"I think we're gonna get wet."

Ice.

All I could feel was ice. I felt as though I had been sculpted from it. The rain which was now slapping my face burned like fire, but my blood was frozen.

I knew where I was. The 48th Street intersection. I could not see the lights from any of the buildings around me, but I knew exactly where I was. My nice clothes were being pelted with heavy rain drops, soaking in and clinging to my skin. My matted hair was dripping down my forehead, but I could not move a hand to wipe the rain from my eyes. I was not allowed to.

I had relived this scene a thousand times before, but never like this. I was supposed to be in the passenger seat in that old Chevy Blazer. Not here, not like this. This was the first time that I had been so detached from the memories, so removed. I was an outsider in my own memory.

Then I saw the headlights. My headlights. Dad's Blazer. It was ploughing slowly through the blinding downpour in my direction. I knew what was happening, what had to happen. I heard a roaring engine growing rapidly louder over my shoulder, but there was no second set of headlights to cast a shadow ahead of me. I could not bear to watch what followed. I closed my eyes, wishing that I could cover my ears as well.

By the time the sound of the smashing vehicles was replaced with dead silence, and I had opened my eyes again, it was all over. The wrecked vehicles were crushed together like pop cans, almost as though the two were one. Alicia Mann was nowhere to be seen, but I could see Josh Kelton's red ball cap slumped against the steering wheel of his once beautiful truck. Flame licked at the wreckage, but I could not even tell which truck it was coming from. And I could hear a voice. It was my own. I could not speak, but I could hear myself talking.

"I'm getting you out! Come on, talk to me!"

Sidney Myers crawled from the debris before me, dragging the crushed, bloody form that was once Karl Myers, in a vain search for safety. I was desperate to save him. I pleaded with God to let me rush to my father's side, but, at the same time, I knew that it was too late. Karl Myers was obviously dead. I knew that, but the Sidney Myers who fell to his knees beside the body did not know. I wished that I could tell him.

"DAD!!"

That should have been the end. My scream was the last thing I ever remembered, the part where I always woke up.

I did not wake up. I continued watching Sidney as he clung to his father's bloody shirt like a frightened child, weeping and shouting, "No! No!"

At that moment, I saw something which horrified me, and horrifies me to this day. Josh Kelton moved his head, just barely lolling it off to one side, and moaned. He was not unconscious.

Somehow, Sidney heard the moan, and slowly looked up at the crumpled F-250. I recognized the look on his face. It was expressionless, like a stone. I knew with certainty that he was feeling the same chill that I was. The difference was that I felt afraid, and I knew that he only felt ice.

Blood flowed down Sidney's right cheek from the gash on his temple, a rose-coloured patch flowering on the white collar as hot red liquid soaked into his shirt. He was standing up and limping toward Kelton's open window.

Kelton had groggily raised his head, and was trying to look around, although he, too, was disoriented and woozy. A trickle of blood from his left nostril dripped into his open mouth.

Sidney could barely stand. He had to grab onto the base of the window frame to keep himself from collapsing. The loss of blood was making him light-headed.

547

"Are you okay?" he asked Kelton in a low, strained voice, his breath coming in short, ragged gasps.

Josh Kelton actually laughed. I could not believe it. He was laughing.

"I'm good, I think," he replied, his voice slurring. "The airbag didn't even work." He turned to stare at Alicia's shoe, which was all that was visible of the girl, as it protruded from the shattered canopy window of the Blazer.

"You had your seatbelt on," Sidney managed to whisper, squinting and blinking, trying to keep his disoriented eyes focussed. "Can you move?"

"I'm good, dude," Josh said, smiling. Recognition slowly dawned on him. "Sidney?"

Sidney could not reply. He had doubled over with his hands on his knees, trying not to black out. His legs were getting shaky, and the flames were getting larger around him.

"Dude, you gotta move your truck," Kelton said slowly, also having a hard time thinking straight. "I can't get mine out of here if you don't." He honked his horn to emphasize the urgency.

Sidney managed to straighten up, but was still getting rapidly dizzier. He tried to look at Josh, and almost fell down again. He caught himself on the side view mirror, wrenching it loose as he pulled himself up one more time. He was about to pass out any second.

"Hey, Sid!" Kelton sounded impatient, tugging at his jammed seatbelt.

Sidney did not try to open the door. In a lightning fast move, his hands shot through the window and seized Josh Kelton's head and hair. I could only watch as he slammed the boy's face into the steering wheel, just as a surge of flame ignited the gas tank.

548

* * *

"*No!*" I yelled, jolting awake. It was the only awakening that I can remember where I was literally sweating and cold, my heart beating madly.

No! That cannot have happened!

"Boss?" Angel gasped, startled awake. Even as my wife and business partner, she still called me that. "What's wrong?"

I never tried to save him?

"Sid, talk to me!" Angel sat up beside me in her favourite blue and white teddy-bear print pajamas, and wrapped her arms around my shoulder. I turned to embrace her tightly, my eyes clamped shut and my whole body shaking.

"A bad dream," I whispered, near tears. "Just a bad dream."

Angel was clearly relieved as she rested her chin on top of my head, which I had buried into her shirt.

"It's okay," she murmured, rocking me like a baby. "It's okay now."

He might have lived....

"What was it?" she asked, after we had held each other for a long time.

Pamela Gregson was fifty yards away, and it was still raining. What if she just thought you were trying to help?

I sighed and gingerly lay back on my pillow. My mouth was so dry. I reached up to pull Angel down close to my side. She kissed me softly, and stared into my eyes. I could not help breaking her gaze and staring at the ceiling.

"I dreamed that I killed someone," I said slowly. I needed water.

They're based in the deepest of truths....

Boris had told me that about dreams, and Boris was a pizza guy. He knew everything.

What do you think, Myers? Amnesia ... or repression?

Angel's tired puppy eyes slid shut, and her cheek sank onto my chest. She slid her right hand up my tee-shirt to touch my chin.

❋ ❋ ❋

"*Then why do you still hurt so much, Boss? The pain that I see in your eyes.... It's guilt. Why do you blame yourself?*"

"*I don't know, Angel. I have to. Ever since it happened, I've just known that some part of that night had to be my fault. I had a part in it, like I had guided Kelton into our truck. It had to be me.*"

"*Kelton killed himself, Boss. He killed everyone who died that night.*"

"*So ... why can I never accept that?*"

She sighed helplessly. "*Survivor's guilt.*"

"*Have you ever had that kind of guilt, Angel?*"

"*No.*"

"*We aren't always responsible for the things that happen to us. We can get hurt, but knowing that we were the ones wronged helps us to get through. We can hide from that. What we can never hide from is ourselves. The possibility of our own crimes cannot stay behind us forever. Our wrongs will find us, sooner or later, and that is where the true torment is. That is the pain that can stay with you all your life.*"

❋ ❋ ❋

"It's okay, Boss," Angel said sleepily. "It was just a dream." I knew that she would sleep long before I did that night.

Sidney the hero....

I read my Bible every day. I try to live my life by the wisdom found in those sacred writings, and yet I now realize that I may have waited until it was too late to learn so simple a lesson as forgiveness.

An old saying tells us to be careful of what we wish for. I had spent five hateful years secretly hoping for a seemingly impossible revenge. Now, I must spend the rest of my life wondering if my wish was granted, and the possibility haunts me. A new book has opened in my life.

A real life is a good book. And, in real life, not many people get a happily ever after, and even fewer get a happy ending. Well, I am not at the end yet. Not yet. Maybe I just need to find my old Happy List, again. Angel still has hers.

It's life, Sidney Karl Myers. Life is one of those happy things.

"Yeah," I said quietly, stroking Angel's thick, reddish-brown hair in the silence of that dark room. "Just a dream...."

ABOUT THE AUTHOR

Lane Bristow began writing short stories as soon as he learned to write in the first grade, and has never lost his love for the written word. Growing up on a remote ranch in the northern foothills of British Columbia, Canada, Lane passed the time and entertained friends and family with his humourous short stories about life on the ranch. After graduating high school, Lane enrolled in the Long Ridge Writers Group Correspondence Course for Freelance Writers, and spent the next year being rejected by every major magazine he could submit to, from Outdoor Life to Rolling Stone. Persistence eventually paid off, and two of his short stories appeared in Farm&Ranch Living, and Small Farmers Journal.

Working at a pizza shop in the evenings to pay the bills inspired Lane's first novel, Slice of Heaven. Believe it or not, the part about the snake living in the pizza delivery vehicle is true.

Lane is currently attempting to publish a collection of his cowboy stories, while working on his second novel.

Printed in the United States
95982LV00001B/4-15/A